"You want to give the Bosses the blockchain hack?" the Indian woman asks.

None of them like that idea.

"You started a *war*. It's the only thing that might, and I emphasize *might*, bring them to the table to stop."

Caesar shakes his head and the others look dubious.

"Seven minutes, twelve seconds," Puo adds.

# The Cleaners' War

Published 2022 by New Rochester Publishing, LLC.

Cover designed by Ravven (www.ravven.com)

ISBN-13  978-1-941557-43-3
ISBN-10  1-941557-43-0

# THE CLEANERS' WAR

## SUNKEN CITY CAPERS BOOK 5

by
Jeffrey A. Ballard

NEW ROCHESTER
PUSBLISHING

# What You Need to Know

Since a five-year gap exists between the publication of book 4 and book 5, this section gives a broad overview of the relevant pieces of the previous books and stories. If you have just finished books 1 through 4 and are launching right into book 5, feel free to skip this section. No new information is revealed.

## The Events of Underwater Restorations, Novelette

Isa, Puo, and Winn are underwater reclamation specialists—a special breed of thieves that steal artifacts from the sunken cities. When they can't unload their most recent heist to Charlie, their long-time fence, it becomes apparent that Paranoid Pete, the holder of their current debt, betrayed them to the Feds as a hedge to make sure he got paid. Either Isa would unload the heist and pay Pete, or the authorities would arrest Isa and pay him an informant's reward.

Isa and Puo break into Pete's office to steal his ledger and are able to prove he is embezzling from the local Atlanta Boss, who is revealed to be Isa's father. They free Winn from the authorities' clutches, and with the Boss's finder's fee for whistleblowing, they have enough money for the first time ever for one of them to go legit. They offer it to Winn who turns it down to stay with the team. They now need to set up shop in a new city since they burned all their assets in Atlanta when the authorities were hunting them.

## The Events of The Skim Job, Short Story

Isa, Puo, and Winn pull a game on Ham, a member of the local Cleaners Guild—the group responsible for getting into, and more importantly, out of locations with smart house technology. They set up Ham to think they are stealing a rare book from a lake house in upstate New York, when in actuality, they are stealing Ham's copy of the Cleaners' code. The code is highly sought after and tightly controlled by the guild.

## The Events of The Solid State Shuffle, Book 1

Isa, Puo, and Winn have set up shop in the Seattle Isles. They used the finder's fee they collected in Atlanta to put a down payment on three modified Citizen chips from a Citizen Maker, and the next payment is due. Isa and Puo have never had Citizen chips before and already they can't go back.

They steal a hard drive they think is loaded with digital currency but soon learn it contains sensitive files of the local area Boss, James Colvin. Colvin approaches Isa to track down the thieves. He thinks the thieves are someone close to him and that he can trust her because her father, the Atlanta Boss, vouched for her. This sets off a cat and mouse game as Isa tries to figure out what the files mean and how to dump the drive without it being tied to them.

They soon learn the files are how Colvin launders money to his sisters, whom he doesn't publicly acknowledge in order to keep them safe. They also learn that Christina, the head of Colvin's security detail, is actually the Cleaners' Seattle Isles Guild Master. In an altercation, Isa inadvertently steals Christina's squeegee—the custom hardware all Cleaners carry their code on.

Isa, Puo, and Winn then uncover a plot involving Christina and several others to overthrow Colvin--framing them was the first part of the plan. Through Puo's fast fingers and Isa's quick thinking, they escape and Colvin murders Christina and the other conspirators to end the coup. Winn, an ex-surgeon, is appalled. He was told all they did was steal artifacts; they didn't hurt anyone.

Isa wakes up to find Winn has left and is not coming back. She does not take it well. Colvin then offers her a job to protect his sisters in the event an emergency causes them to become exposed. Isa accepts, feeling the work is redemptive and that Winn would've approved.

## The Events of the Elgin Deceptions, Book 2

After setting up protocols to keep Colvin's sisters safe, Isa and Puo head to Europe to help clear Isa's head—she has not been taking Winn's departure well. They successfully pull one job to make one payment to the Citizen Maker, but already need to line up another one for the next payment.

Her increasingly reckless behavior sees them take on their biggest job yet, hitting one of the most protected underwater sites in the world, the British Museum. The job comes with a new third, Liáng, a muscled distraction tied to the Chang'ans, a dangerous Chinese international gang.

During the job, Isa continues to struggle with Winn's leaving, seeing him in the corner of her eyes and even experiencing her first panic attack brought on by Winn's abandonment and the deepening situation they find themselves in. While preparing for the job, Isa also has a chance encounter with Ham, who is on the run and scared. He alludes to larger things in play, but Isa and Puo don't know what he means.

They pull off the British Museum heist and uncover that Liáng is actually a Chinese government pawn. After putting a fix in place with the Chinese government and getting paid, Isa makes the decision to find and confront Winn to get closure and clear her head.

## The Events of Leverage, Book 3

Isa and Puo head to Vancouver, Canada to confront Winn, but Isa gets cold feet and instead starts to plan a job as a distraction. The tour boat they're riding to scout the job's location suddenly explodes. Isa and Puo are the only survivors, and after another attempt on Puo's life at the hospital, it becomes clear that the bomb was meant for them.

On the local news, Winn sees Puo, after suffering a heart attack from the explosion, being airlifted to the hospital. Winn rushes to help, and the confrontation Isa had been avoiding is now thrust into her face. Even worse, she needs Winn to take care of Puo while they figure out who is trying to kill them and why.

They soon learn the Cleaners are blackmailing Nix, the Vancouver Boss who also acts as an informant to the authorities. The

Cleaners, knowing Nix is an informant, threaten to expose her unless she kills Isa and Puo, but Isa has no idea why the Cleaners want them dead. If they can remove the Cleaners' leverage on Nix, Nix will agree to leave them alone.

They break into the Royal Canadian Mounted Police headquarters and destroy the evidence that Nix is an informant. With the evidence destroyed, Nix keeps her word and leaves them alone.

As Isa contemplates their next move--they still need to track down why Ham was running scared in the UK and figure out why the Cleaners are after them--she receives a panicked call from Colvin. The Cleaners have launched an all-out war against the Bosses. Colvin barely escaped, while her father has gone missing.

## The Events of The Brummie Con, Book 4

Isa, Puo, and Winn rush back to her father's estate outside of Atlanta. Several Bosses are dead, others are fighting, and some have rolled over to swear fealty to the Cleaners. Only Isa's father is missing.

Isa and the group barely escape a Cleaners' trap and are forced to go underground. Isa then visits Charlie, their long-time fence and surrogate mother, who trained them, and determines this must have been why Ham fled to the UK to hide.

Isa, Puo, and Winn return to the UK to track down Ham. As they search, the Cleaners become impatient and publish an image of her father's beaten and bloodied face along with a forty-eight hour timer. They can't track down Ham and get back to the States in that time frame.

Isa makes the agonizing decision to stay and locate Ham to better understand what's going on. She convinces herself the timer is a bluff--if they killed her father, they would lose their leverage. The decision consumes her and she experiences another panic attack on Christmas morning.

They locate Ham and intercept him while he's being arrested. They learn from Ham that the Cleaners are organized in a shadow organization called the National Syndicate. They know Isa stole their code from Ham, who stole it from Caesar, a National Syndicate member and Ham's Guild Master. Isa denies this and learns the National Syndicate members keep tabs on each other through a private blockchain on their squeegees, and that Ham thinks this private blockchain recorded the theft.

Isa reasons this is why the Cleaners tried to kill them in Vancouver. Christina, the Seattle Isles' Guild Master, had to be a National Syndicate member, and the plot to overthrow Colvin was part of a larger scheme. Isa thinks Christina's squeegee, which Isa stole during the events of *The Solid State Shuffle*, must contain proof of conspiracy on this private blockchain. This is why the National Syndicate wanted to kill them--to cover their tracks. They weren't ready to move against the Bosses. When they failed to kill Isa, they accelerated their plans and launched their war anyway.

As Ham reveals details about the private blockchain, Puo realizes he knows how to bypass the blockchain and that's what all this is about. Puo thinks the Cleaners switched from trying to kill them in Vancouver to capturing them when they learned he could bypass the blockchain—a supposedly impossible and history-altering hack.

Book 4 ends with Isa witnessing her father's execution on a live feed while she is arrested by the British authorities. As her life falls apart, a new live feed pops up with a seven-day timer overlaid on Charlie's beaten and bloodied face.

And now, *The Cleaners' War*, Sunken City Capers Book 5.

# Chapter One

"ALL RISE FOR District Judge Blackwell," a spindly man in a black flowing stole I think is supposed to be a robe announces.

I don't have time for this shit, but I keep the thought from my face.

It's the morning after they arrested us and now there're six days and two hours until the Cleaners blow a hole through Charlie's head like they did to my father. All because she took a chance on us as kids.

I bury the rage and panic threatening to erupt. Instead, I put on the confused face of a scared, wrongly arrested woman. Which isn't hard—I am confused. No one in here is wearing one of those white-haired curly wigs. Or robes.

District Judge Blackwell is a squat, middle-aged man with thinning brown hair. He wears a dark navy three-piece suit with a skinny red tie, and his stiff white collar looks too tight, choking him off, creating rosy cheeks under a black beard.

In fact, the whole court is dressed in business clothes, except for the spindly man with the stole/robe thing.

Honestly, I'm disappointed. If they're going to fuck me over, the least they can do is get properly dressed up.

I'm forced to stand off to the side behind a glass balustrade in striped yellow-and-green coveralls. My hands are bound in front of me and leashed to the balustrade in the specially made slot for that purpose.

The coveralls are not a flattering look, and I'm given to understand—based on the handy-dandy pamphlet I received on intake—it's not normal for a prisoner to be forced to wear one prior to a trial and sentencing.

I'm a "category A" prisoner. The highest risk of prisoner with the fewest rights.

Judge Blackwell makes his way up to a raised bench overlooking the court, sets down his tablet, and sits. He calls the court to order, upon which everyone else goes back to sitting or doing whatever it is they're supposed to be doing.

The courtroom is empty except for the judge, the prosecutor, and my duty solicitor. And Stole Man, the only one of the lot decent enough to attempt to dress the part.

I'm still standing—no seat for me, anyway. I think of sitting on the floor out of spite, but have to continually remind myself to stay in character.

Puo and I put protocols in place in case we were ever arrested, but it's the Cleaners' countdown that makes this shit show an absolute blaster can of diarrhea.

Don't get me wrong, getting arrested in any situation is a nightmare scenario. The first thing they did was take our images, fingerprint us, and take a cheek swab for DNA. Puo and I have lived off-grid for years before and we can do it again—better that hell than one behind bars. But first we have to escape and absolutely zero of our protocols took into account a one-week timer.

We're fucked.

It takes time to work through any court system anyway. Which is why we're here according to the duty solicitor assigned to me. It's a perfunctory Magistrate's Court hearing, a box they have to check before my case gets passed up to the Crown Court.

The real question to get settled today is whether I'm to be allowed bail. This is the whole point of my confused, innocent act. They denied me bail last night and denied access to legal advice and a state department representative.

Apparently, they're rather upset with me.

Judge Blackwell clicks on his tablet and then turns to me. "Would the defendant please identify themself to the court?"

I take a visible deep breath and then say, "Vikki Gilbert."

This answer causes a flurry of activity in the courtroom. After they picked me up, I didn't say anything other than they had the wrong person and I wanted legal representation. Representation they are legally allowed to deny me for thirty-six hours, although it's rare to do so.

Judge Blackwell looks between his tablet and me. "The arrest warrant identifies you as Isa Schmidt."

"No, that's not right—"

A sharp-nosed, pencil of a woman prosecutor who looks like a hawk eying a scurrying squirrel cuts me off. She's more sharply dressed than those around her and looks meaner, a whole lot meaner.

"Sir," she says, "the defendant is an accomplished thief and con woman with many aliases. We have detailed several of them in her file."

Judge Blackwell looks down at his tablet and starts nodding.

"I'm Vikki Gilbert," I rush. "I'm from Aberdeen, South Dakota. I don't even know why I've been arrested. Check my identity with the American State Department and let them know I've been arrested. They wouldn't even let me talk to them," I add in a slightly hysterical note.

Judge Blackwell looks up sharply at this. "She has been denied access to a consular officer?"

Hawk Lady doesn't miss a beat. "The defendant is a category A prisoner and can be denied legal access for thirty-six hours. The Crown exercised this right given the extreme nature of Ms. Schmidt's crimes."

Hawk Lady keeps her bird-like focus on the Judge. "She has been accused of infiltrating the British Museum and theft of its artifacts, assaulting police officers, kidnapping a person of interest from police custody, and a host of digital crimes too long to list. The Crown seeks to remand the prisoner to a higher security facility before granting access to legal representation."

I grip the balustrade and pretend to hold myself up. "This ... this is wrong—"

Hawk Lady talks over me, "As I stated earlier, she is an accomplished con woman. It is entirely conceivable that she has a number of aliases set up for just this purpose that are not on that list. I would like to note she was arrested with a modified CitID that identified her as Kristina Peters."

"I had to—" I stop and collect myself. "I had to lie. My real name is Vikki Gilbert. Vancouver," I stutter. "The tour boat explosion. I was on it. Look in the news. They reported me dead to protect me. They switched my CitID. Someone wants me dead. Look in the news, there's a picture of me and everything."

Judge Blackwell leans back.

It's an audacious claim to make. Easily checked and absolutely damning if false.

"Is this true?" Judge Blackwell asks.

"This is new information to come before the Crown," Hawk Lady says. "Information that could've been verified had she made this claim earlier."

"It's only new information, sir," my duty solicitor finally breaks in, "because she was denied legal representation. She didn't have an opportunity to understand her rights and make any claims." He's a young Indian man—younger than me. Youth isn't what you typically want in these situations, but he's picking up the lead here well enough.

"We explained her rights and gave her several opportunities to make statements," Hawk Lady says, leaning forward.

Judge Blackwell turns back to me. "Why did you not bring this up before?"

"Sir," I say, visibly choosing my words through strained emotion. "Someone tried to kill me in Vancouver and the Canadian government reported me dead to protect me. I then came here to hide and I was suddenly arrested and denied legal representation. I don't know if it's a mistake, or if the new CitID the Canadian government gave me had a past. I don't know what's going on!"

"Sir," my duty solicitor says, "we request the defendant be granted bail while questions of her identity are resolved. The potential for the miscarriage of justice is too high."

Well, hey, hey, hey. That's *exactly* the point. Once on bail, I can work on getting Puo and Winn out and then getting the hell outta of here.

The Vancouver cover story should be enough to muddy the waters to provide cover for a few hours, but once the two governments officially connect and copulate, the gig will be up.

"Do you have hard proof of identity?" Judge Blackwell asks Hawk Lady. "Birth certificate? Driver licenses? Passport?"

Like hell they do, I would never have those things in my original name.

Hawk Lady really doesn't like that question.

She didn't expect me to make this easy, did she?

"No," she bites off.

My duty solicitor is all over it. "Given the serious nature of these crimes, the Crown's willingness to deny the defendant customary legal representation, their severe treatment of the defendant, this question of identity must be resolved before moving forward."

"The Crown agrees that these are serious matters," Hawk Lady says, still not liking the turn this perfunctory hearing had taken. "We request the defendant be remanded into custody while further investigations are made into this matter. It should not take more than twenty-four hours to resolve whether this claim has any merit."

This almost makes me smile. If that's the next bar to clear, then the waters should be sufficiently muddied enough for that.

My duty solicitor starts to speak again when Hawk Lady speaks again, the corners of her mouth quirking up, a bird playing with its prey. "Before the question of bail is resolved, sir, I would like to submit to the court bodycam footage of the defendant kidnapping a person of interest from police custody."

"The defendant's identity has not yet been resolved," my duty solicitor says. "My learned friend cannot claim at this juncture that the person in this video is indeed the defendant before us today."

Hawk Lady stands pat.

Eventually, Judge Blackwell says, "The Crown may submit the video for consideration."

A large float screen rises up to the right of the Judge and the lights dim.

The video is taken from shoulder height and shows the bearer of the video escorting Ham out into the rain to a waiting dark-gray sedan hovercar. Two uniformed officers approach. One is clearly a woman and the other a tall, muscular man. Other than that, nothing can be discerned. Right where their faces should've been are a scramble of pixels—the digi-scrambler really was the perfect gift for me.

The thought suddenly makes me ache so bad for Winn it's a whole new dimension to this disaster.

The camera escorting Ham breaks off and heads to the two pixelated officers. He asks the two officers what they're "doon'" and then chaos ensues with Ham struggling and the camera man sprayed in the face and falling to the ground.

The video stops there. The lights come back up. For a second nobody speaks.

My duty solicitor finally breaks the silence with, "That video is inconclusive. It does not show the defendant or indeed anyone who allegedly committed these crimes."

Idiot. He had been doing passably well up until this point. This is clearly a set up and he just obliged to butter Hawk Lady's toast for her.

Hawk Lady says, "The perpetrators wore digi-scramblers. Two of which were found on the defendants at the time of their arrest."

"Circumstantial," my duty solicitor argues. "There's no way to link one specific digi-scrambler to a scrambled video."

"No, there's not," Hawk Lady agrees. "That is indeed the whole point of the things. With the court's permission, I would like to call the owner of the bodycam footage to testify, Inspector Shane O'Sullivan."

*Oh, hell.* This can't be good.

The spindly man in the drooping stole steps out for a minute and comes back with a short man and round face. He's wearing business casual and comes to stand in what I can only assume is the witness box. He keeps his gaze on the judge.

They verify his identity and then ask him to go over what happened. The whole time he's speaking, he never mentions me or refers to me, only referring to the person that attacked him as "the assailant." He continues not looking at me.

It's a shrewd move. There's nothing there for the duty solicitor to work with. Nothing to contest or argue with.

They're going to deny me bail—I can feel it.

I *need* to get out on bail. It's the only way Charlie has even the smallest chance.

My heart pounds, bashing itself against my ribcage.

Finally, at the end of Inspector O'Sullivan's testimony, Judge Blackwell asks the Inspector the question Hawk Lady had teed up so nicely for him, "Does the defendant here today match the description of the assailant that assaulted you?"

The short Inspector looks over and studies me with his small brown eyes. "Aye."

I swoon and hold onto the balustrade. "What's happening?" I say breathlessly. "This can't be happening."

Hawk Lady continues, "I have here four sworn affidavits, two by An Garda Síochána inspectors and two by British Secret Service agents who were there that day, that the defendant matches the description of the assailant they witnessed assault Inspector O'Sullivan with their own eyes."

Judge Blackwell takes a minute to scan some documents on his tablet.

My pulse beats against my neck. I look at the cuffs, assess how sturdy the balustrade is.

*Can I make a break for it? How far would I even get?*

Judge Blackwell looks up and says with a finality I can do nothing to stop, "The defendant is hereby remanded into the Crown's custody and a new hearing will be set within twenty-four hours to resolve the question of identity."

# Chapter Two

*F*<small>UCK.</small>
My heart thunders like it's going to burst right from my chest. I can't catch my breath.

I want to sit down. I want to run away to someplace where none of this shit is happening.

I want to throw up.

*Oh, God, not now. Not again.*

My peripheral vision blurs away. I look around.

Twitchy. So twitchy.

"Keep it moving," the guard behind me says. It's not aggressive, like he can see the panic attack forming, but it's not soothing kumbaya either. He's got a job to do, and it's going to get done one way or another.

They shuffle me along from the courtroom to the prison hovtransport, my hands still bound in front of me and connected to my ankle cuffs. My legs feel funny as they move, like my thighs aren't taking orders from my brain anymore.

I try the anchoring technique I read about after those dumbass breathing exercises didn't do shit during the panic attack on Christmas morning a few days ago.

Five sights, four touches, three sounds, two smells, one taste.

Five sights: the shiny black-and-white speckled marble floor they're shuffling me along. The ceiling lights above washing out sections of the floor. Beige, marbled walls rising above to moulding that hides inset lights illuminating a plastered ceiling with a square-mould pattern. Sun beams cutting through the empty private holding cell they're ushering me past. Two guards in dark navy and black tactical gear standing at the end of the hallway.

The police hovtransport is open at the end of the hallway, leading to a shiny metal interior dead end.

The jackknives in my stomach unfurl.

*No good.* That last thought is no good.

Touches. Focus on touches.

Cold air billows in around the police hovtransport. The yellow-and-green coveralls are rough on my skin, like stiff canvas. My socks are soaked in cold sweat. The silver handcuffs are loose and weigh my hands down from the chain binding them to my waist and ankles. I couldn't even stretch if I wanted to, or run. I'm trussed up like an animal.

No escape. No way to break free.

The jackknives take a layer off my stomach.

Sounds. I need to find three sounds.

For fucks sake, the first thing I hear is my pulse pounding against my ears. Not helpful. My feet scuffle on the polished metal floor. The guards communicate on their radios up ahead. The shuffling *clink* of my chains. The *clinking* sound I'll probably hear for the rest of my life.

*Oh, God.* This anchoring bullshit was a terrible idea. I skip over smell and go straight to taste: bile.

I think I'd throw up if I wasn't terrified of what the dancing jackknives would do. There's nothing in there to come up anyway.

I pinch the webbing between my thumb and forefinger, another grounding tactic. I pinch so hard I know it's supposed to hurt but I can't feel a thing.

I don't even expect it to help at this point. But anything—I'll try anything. I can't lose it now. Not here. Not in front of these people.

My nose whistles as I wheeze. That silver box at the end of the hallway shuffles closer no matter what I do.

Running steps echo in the hallway behind me. The guards in front of me perk up. The guards behind me turn around.

It's a buff, middle-aged Hispanic woman in black flats and a business skirt suit running toward me. Her dark brown eyes look as if they know me. "Isa Schmidt?" she calls out.

"Stop where you are!" one of the guards calls out.

One of my guards goes to intercept her while the other guard grabs my upper arm and begins pushing me toward the silver coffin. The two guards near the police hovtransport have their rifles in the crooks of their arms.

"Isa Schmidt?" she calls out again.

"No, I'm Vikki Gilbert," I manage to say over my shoulder. I have to continue to play the part of confused and innocent Vikki Gilbert. It's the only card left to me and once it's burned, it's gone.

"Wait!" she calls out.

The guard keeps pushing me forward.

There's some commotion and frantic whispers. I can't turn around with the guard's grip on me.

I'm only a few shuffled steps away from the silver coffin of the hovtransport when the flats slapping against the marble start again. "Wait!" she calls again.

This time, the guard that intercepted her calls out, "It's a U.S. Consul! Hold the prisoner!"

Relief hits like a wave. *Oh, thank God.*

I'm allowed to turn around and watch as the consul approaches. She carries a pamphlet and a container of something else in her other hand.

"Please," I say as she gets closer, "you have to help me. Please!" I wish the desperation was an act.

I want to ask about Puo, about Winn. I want to tell them to save Charlie, but all of that would give me away.

"You have to get me out of here." My gaze latches onto her eyes like the lifeline they are.

The older consular woman shakes her head no. Her eyes are soft, pitying. Her shoulders droop. "We can't do that. I'm so sorry."

She holds her pamphlet out. "Please, take this. This will cover what we can do and can't do. Make sure you read it."

I take the pamphlet mechanically, while I desperately search my mind for someone, anyone I can have them alert that may be able to get word to people who can help me.

There's no one. Only one name even remotely floats to the surface: Kathy, our neighbor in the Seattle Isles. But she wouldn't know what to do, and it'd be wrong on so many levels to drag her into this swirling toilet bowl.

There's no one. Outside of Puo and Winn who are already locked up. No one.

I'm all alone.

"I'm Consular Officer Vázquez," the woman says in an understanding voice. "Is there anyone you want me to contact?"

I blink away tears at the question and shake my head no.

She gives me the awkward look a stranger gives another person in obvious distress with no way to help.

She then hands me the container she carries. "These are vitamins. They're the only thing I'm legally allowed to give you besides the pamphlet."

My hearts roars back into place at the thought this is good-bye. "Please," I say, "you can't leave me. I'm ... I'm Vikki Gilbert. This is all a mistake."

"We'll get it worked out as soon as we can," she says, and nods to the guards. The guard, still holding my upper arm, pushes me into the silver coffin and down on the bench.

The woman stands in the hallway and watches them fasten me to the seat, the pamphlet and vitamins still in my wooden hands.

"Make sure to read the pamphlet—!" she calls out as the steel doors clang shut, cutting me off in my silver coffin.

\*\*\*

I sit in the back of the hovtransport, chained to the seat as it climbs into the sky. I'm numb, like my body maxed out on bio-chemicals and now my nervous system is shot.

Alone. All alone.

The thought suddenly infuriates me. No, not the thought. The fear—the fear from before. The way I tried to glob onto the consul, begged her for help. My cheeks burn. It's what Vikki Gilbert would've done, but that hadn't been acting.

I've been alone before. I can be alone again—at least until I can get to Puo and Winn.

One of the two guards in the front cabin gives an update to his superior over the radio. "The prisoner is secure and hasn't moved," his voice drifts through the small air vent between the spaces.

Apparently, I'm so dangerous they need to give regular up-dates every time I shift in my seat to fart.

It's only then I realize my hand is cramped from squeezing the small vitamin container the consul gave me.

I loosen my grip and lift it up to look at the two round gummy vitamins, one red and one green.

Vitamins. God, what dumbass lawyer fought for that? That's the only thing they're allowed to bring prisoners? We can't get you out, or provide food, or legal advice, or medical care, but we absolutely have to make sure you don't have a vitamin D deficiency—that shit is serious.

I snort and turn over the pamphlet in my hand, something thin and gossamer flutters inside.

I set the vitamins down and open the pamphlet. There's a thin piece of tissue paper with a note scrawled across it.

*Do not eat the vitamins. Smash them together and toss away from you toward the front cabin. Destroy this note first.*

I read it again and glance toward the front cabin—the officers give no indication they know something's up.

Did Puo escape? Winn?

I don't need to be told twice. It doesn't matter who's helping me at this point. First, I have to get out of here, then I can work on who that is and why.

I crumble the paper up and swallow it. It goes down like a slimy spitball—*gross*. I take the vitamins out and smash them together, mix them up and throw them toward the front cabin.

The wadded-up mixture sits there.

And sits there.

No explosion. No nothing.

Was I set up—?

It's the last thought I have before I black out.

# Chapter Three

A WARENESS SNAPS back into place like a switch.

"Welcome back, Vikki Gilbert." Consul Vázquez sits in a gray upholstery armchair set ninety degrees to the gray upholstered couch I've been laid out on.

"Who are you?" I ask. There's no grogginess with whatever they drugged me with.

She considers before answering, "A potential ally."

I sit up. I'm still in the yellow-and-green striped coveralls, but the hand and ankle cuffs are nowhere to be seen.

The living room I find myself in is light and airy, mostly whites with a vaulted ceiling and exposed wooden beams. There's an unlit brick fireplace painted white at the end of the room and another matching gray couch like the one I'm on across from me. A dining space behind me opens into a kitchen.

"Where are we?" I ask.

Again, she takes her time before answering, "I'm not the one to tell you that."

I look more closely at her. She's well-muscled. Her warm brown skin is stretched with middle age. Her wide cheekbones give her no-nonsense face a short oval shape, and she's wearing the same business clothes as before.

Her knee-length skirt is loose and she's wearing a white short-sleeved blouse under her unbuttoned suit jacket. Her dark brown hair is short and combed back. Her black flats look good for running in—or kicking ass in.

"Shall I call you Goon Number One?" I ask.

Her eyes narrow in annoyance and she turns slightly to keep an eye on me and says over a comm-link I can't see, "Our guest is awake. ETA on arrival?" There's a brief pause before she says, "Understood."

She turns back to me. "The rest of the party will be here in a few minutes. All your questions will be answered then."

I get up to pace. Who's in this party? What do they want with me? What about Puo and Winn?

Unfortunately, the house I find myself in doesn't know anything either. It's a generic house, a rental or safe house of some kind. No pictures of people who live here, none of the everyday detritus that accumulates in a home.

It's gray outside. The rolling landscape is white with snow, broken up by trees and hedges every so often. We're most likely still in England somewhere.

The air is cold and the house smells empty, like we only just arrived.

I consider asking if there's a change of clothes but decide she'd only blow me off again. It'd accomplish nothing except to telegraph how twitchy I am. I also discard the idea of wandering through the house or sitting down to stare at her to make her uncomfortable.

I've been told I can be difficult sometimes, and I'm not sure yet if these people are friends. They definitely want something from me—but they did break me free, so I'll be nice for now.

A generic forest-green hovercar sedan catches my eye flying toward the house—it's the first hovercar I've seen that low in this area.

Ms. Vázquez—she certainly is not with the U.S. Consulate—stands and goes into the back of the house leaving me alone.

The hovercar lands and doors slam shut. A deep Samoan voice filters through the windows, "I've had a heart attack once already—"

I run the shortest distance to the front door and yank it open. "Mika!"

"Vikki!" he shouts back—doesn't miss a beat, my Puo.

I sprint over and grip him in a hug that I never want to let go. He's lost more weight. He used to be a solid three hundred pounds.

He wraps me up with strong meaty arms. His black ponytail cascades down his back, brushing up against my arms.

"Good to see ya, kid," he murmurs.

"You too. And it was a coronary heart spasm."

"Heart attack," he maintains.

Winn comes around the corner of the hovercar, his crystal blue eyes drinking me in. He's content to watch me hug Puo, but I break off and run to hug him.

He smells like I remember him, the warm woody scent of his cologne. His muscled arms lift me up and I melt a little into him—it's hard not to.

Earlier this morning I thought I was never going to see these two again. Or at least, not for a very long time.

I want to run my hands through Winn's curly dark hair, cup his square white southern face and kiss him long and deep—but I'm mindful of the other person with them. A black woman who's my age ushers us toward the door and looks around.

All three of us are together.

Then I remember: Charlie. My elation slashes away.

The jackknives stir. We need to rescue Charlie.

I drop down from Winn's embrace.

"We need to get inside." The woman eyes all three of us in our yellow-and-green striped coveralls, glancing overhead.

A sentiment I couldn't agree with more.

\*\*\*

Ms. Vázquez waits in the white living room with two others: an older Asian male and a young white woman who looks a few years younger than me—I'm twenty-seven.

The driver from outside moves off to the side and Ms. Vázquez moves to join her, leaving the two newcomers to face us.

The older Asian male is about five feet nine—my height—with short, nearly buzzed salt-and-pepper hair. He has a wide chin and small forehead, with a calculating weight to his dark eyes. He wears a white checkered button-down shirt with black slacks, both neatly pressed—a stark contrast to the young woman standing next to him in a maroon university hoody and tight jeans.

"Please." He gestures holding a black leather folder to the square upholstered couch across from him.

I sit down with Winn and Puo next to me.

The odd couple sit on the couch opposite us and the other two break up to patrol around.

If it wasn't clear before, that seals it in my mind: the man sitting across from me is in charge and the other two are some type of hired help.

"I am Ken Chao and this is Lucy Bennett." He indicates the young woman next to him.

28

She nods in greeting, long dark blond hair spilling over her thin face.

"Time is of the essence," he says, "so I am going to put all our cards on the table and hope you will do the same. We have a common enemy: the National Syndicate."

A chill runs through me at the name. They're the ones responsible for my father's death. They're the ones holding Charlie.

I nod to show him I understand.

He continues, "Two weeks ago when the Syndicate moved against the Bosses they took the opportunity to purge certain pockets of troublemakers within their own ranks. They made it look like a retaliatory strike from the Bosses."

The young woman next to him, Lucy, sniffles.

"You two are Cleaners," I say. The pronouncement changes the tenor of the room. Winn and Puo sit up. Winn sizes them up and Puo is looking for the exits.

"Yes," the Mr. Chao says, no attempt to disseminate or lie. "We are all that's left of the Greensboro Guild. We—" He indicates himself and Lucy. "—were out on a last-minute job when they struck. We are not a large guild, so it was easy to get everyone at once. When we returned everyone was dead—gunned down. Our Guild Master had a note clutched in her hand."

He unzips his black leather folder and carefully takes out a single sheet of paper held in a plastic sheath. He lays it on the white coffee table between us.

The paper is ripped and stained with dried blood. Scrawled hastily down the paper are three lines: *National Syndicate. Private Blockchain. Find Reginold Hamilton.*

I look between Puo and Winn. Reginold Hamilton is the full name of Ham—the repellent shit-stain Cleaner we recently kid-

29

napped in front of the cops and let loose somewhere in the train tunnels below the Irish Sea.

"We have been able to decipher two of those lines, but not the middle one," Mr. Chao says. "We had been watching Reginold Hamilton—"

"Ham," I say. "He goes by Ham." I can't stand to hear that ass's full name. Makes him sound almost human.

"We had been watching Ham, collecting information before making contact, when you made a rather remarkable entrance—"

"And now he is gone again," Lucy breaks in.

"And you two were the last ones to have seen him," Mr. Chao finishes.

Ham. Are you fucking kidding me? This all comes back to Ham? God, if I knew how much trouble that little man-ferret would be, I would've never picked him as the one to steal the Cleaner's code from.

"Unless, of course," Mr. Chao says, "you know what that second line means."

I do know what that second line means. The National Syndicate uses a private blockchain hidden in the root of their squeegees to keep tabs on one another. If you had access to it, you could conceivably work out everyone involved and what they did. Unfortunately, we were arrested right after we figured that out and Christina's squeegee was confiscated. Puo has mirrored that code elsewhere, but we don't currently have access to that either.

Rather than explain this to him, I ask, "Everything on the table, right?"

He nods. "Yes."

I flick my gaze to the older Hispanic woman who had posed as Ms. Vázquez standing by a window at the end of the room. "Who are they?"

"Mercenaries," he says.

The woman turns toward us and then walks over.

"We had worked together several years ago," he continues. "They are independent contractors and are being paid a large amount of money to protect us."

"Blood money," Lucy mutters.

Mr. Chao glances over but doesn't correct her.

The older merc shrugs. "Blood comes out in the wash like everything else. We'll protect you as long your money's good—which given the capital spent to bring these three in, will only last another eight days."

Mr. Chao mimes a smile. "Yes, of course. You have performed admirably so far. We have every confidence in you."

Lucy fails to hide a knee-jerk snort.

"How many of you are there?" I ask the merc.

She hesitates a half second, the debate clearly playing through her mind on whether this all-on-the-table business applies to her. "Two," she answers.

"And you set up all of this in less than twenty-four hours?" I gesture to the house around me. We were arrested yesterday morning. Even for us, that's quick.

She glances at Mr. Chao who nods that, yes, this all-on-the-table does extend to them. She answers, "This is where we planned on bringing Reginold, so we already had this set up. As for your arrest, the best chance to break you free was when they would be moving you, and the preliminary hearing before the Magistrates' Court represented that best chance."

I study her openly while she explains. I've done my fair share of hastily cobbled-together stupid shit so I have a refined nose for such things. "And the vitamins?" Something like that takes time to prepare or procure.

She glances over and nods at the younger black female who had wandered closer for the discussion. The younger merc heads away farther into the house and comes back carrying two palm-sized plastic containers. She sets them down on the table in front of us. One is filled with green vitamins, the other red.

The older merc says, "We've found having a stock of useful supplies continues to pay dividends."

I can appreciate that, but the sheer absurdity of the situation we find ourselves in makes me suspicious. This is balanced against the fact that we are now free, and if the Cleaners across from me were secretly working with the National Syndicate, they could either have already killed us, or turned us over to force us to reveal how Puo bypassed the blockchain. Neither of which has occurred.

I turn back to Mr. Chao. "What exactly do you want from us?"

"We need to understand that middle line and how it fits in with the rest of the note. Do you know what the middle line means?" he asks. "The reference to a private blockchain?"

"Wait," Puo cuts me off as I open mouth to respond. "The cops have logged our CitIDs and done deep scans on them. We will need new ones to be able to move at all and our images scrubbed from their databases."

Mr. Chao stares at Puo. "We can swap out new identifications easily enough, but we don't have time for new hardware or to remove your images from their database. The best we can provide is digi-scramblers."

Puo actually appears mollified a bit at this, though no one else would recognize it except me. "They'll still be able to detect us if they do deep scans—"

"Or if you enter areas that prohibit digi-scramblers," Mr. Chao says. "It is however, the best we can do in the circumstances."

Puo nods, but then says, "Then we want your word after the circumstances change and this is dealt with, you will remove our images from their databases and procure new hardware for our CitIDs."

"Springing you from prison, wasn't enough?" Lucy asks.

"No," I say, tracking with Puo. There's a chance here, however slim, that we may be able to slip back into anonymity if we ever get out of this. Any chance for that, no matter how small, is worth taking.

To Lucy I say, "You sprung us from jail because you had no other choice. You did not do it for our sakes. If leaving us in jail would've suited your purposes, you would've left us there. Now you need our cooperation, and we need to be able to move around when this is over."

"You are fugitives—" Lucy tries to lean on us.

I sit forward and smile. "So are you. What is the first thing you think we'll say if we're back in custody?"

The older merc shares a look with the younger one.

Mr. Chao looks between us agitated.

Lucy starts to respond when Mr. Chao puts a hand on Lucy's arm. "Would you excuse us for a second?" he says to me. He stands and leaves with Lucy in tow.

The two hired mercs stay where they are so Winn, Puo, and I pass the time in a strained silence. I want to talk to them about what happened, how they were busted free, what their impressions of the situation are. A conversation I'm not sure when we'll get to have—certainly not as long as we're in this house.

Mr. Chao and Lucy come back. Lucy has her arms crossed and Mr. Chao carries a squeegee, the brick-like device all Cleaners possess that carries their code.

"We agree to procure new hardware for your CitIDs once this is concluded," Mr. Chao says. "And we provisionally agree to help with the removal of your images from the British Government databases. However, we cannot, in good faith, guarantee your images will be scrubbed. Such a task is high risk and may prove impossible."

I consider the offer as the two sit down again. New CitID hardware with new identities for free is a pretty big carrot. But even without new CitIDs, getting us back in the States—which is where we need to go—along with digi-scramblers will allow us some freedom of movement.

Puo is surreptitiously signing me to take it.

Instead of agreeing to the deal right away, I ask, "What is your ultimate goal here? Let's say we know what that middle line means, then what?"

Mr. Chao takes a deep breath and studies the floor. "I don't know." He looks up at me. "I don't know what the long-term plan is. We have to understand the note in its entirety before forming a long-term plan. Here is what I do know." He shifts forward on the seat. "The National Syndicate wants us dead. Why? I don't know. I can only assume that if, and when, they learn we're alive they will come after us to finish the job. I have eight days—" He glances at the older merc. "—to find answers to these questions. After that it becomes much harder and considerably more dangerous. I also know the National Syndicate is hunting you. Six days left on the timer they broadcast all through the Manchester station."

The jackknives come alive at the mention of Charlie's timer.

"We are both being hunted on a compressed timeline. Our goals are aligned: stay alive and figure out what's going on."

I consider his words. Our goals are not really aligned, they only happen to be traveling in the same direction for the moment. We need to rescue Charlie—a goal these two will care nothing about. Not only do we need to get Charlie, we will then need to deal with the National Syndicate once and for all, otherwise they'll keep coming after people close to us.

There's something else hidden in Mr. Chao's tone, his furtive glances, and the words he's not saying. He wants a potential long-term alliance—someone to have their back when their money runs out with the mercenaries. Having two Cleaners on our side could prove invaluable to getting Charlie out.

"We know what the second line means," I say. I extend my hand out over the table. "New identifications, new CitID hardware when this over, and a provisional agreement to help erase our images from the British databases."

Mr. Chao glances at Lucy and leans forward to shake my hand.

I could've negotiated harder, forcing them to help us recover Charlie, but I'm going to make sure to steer this ship in that direction anyway.

I half turn to Puo. "Explain it to them." Computers, hacking, blockchain—those are Puo's areas of expertise.

Puo sits up straight, holds his arms out, grabs one forearm and then other and bobs his head, mimicking a genie. "Yessa mistress, of course mistress, right away mistress."

*Freaking Puo.*

I can't be too frustrated though—it's Puo's way of signaling he agrees with the way things have gone. It's when he's not being a smart ass that I know something's up.

Puo explains about Christina's squeegee, the private blockchain, and how it could lead to the National Syndicate, leaving off, of course, his ability to bypass it.

Mr. Chao and Lucy share concerned looks as they mull over this new information.

"Do you still have Christina's squeegee?" Lucy asks.

"No," I answer. "Not unless you busted our possessions out as well." We had Christina's squeegee on us when we were arrested. All the equipment we had in England was possessed. I feel a sudden pang at the loss of my digi-scrambler. And then a worse pang for losing Winn's caduceus digi-scrambler—I had been close to giving it back. They're easy enough to replace, but mine had been a gift from Winn for no other reason than that he loved me and thought I would like it. I had gotten him the caduceus pendant in return. There's a history there now lost, sitting forgotten in some evidence box. The only silver lining is that we left the anti-gravity suits back in the States after using them in Atlanta. The authorities getting their hands on those would've made the arrest a thorough wall-smearing shit show.

Mr. Chao looks at the older merc, who shakes her head no. "It's one thing to spring prisoners on the move, it's another to break into a government facility."

*We've done it*, I think but don't say, remembering our time in Vancouver. Instead, with a heavy sigh, I say, "There's another way."

# Chapter Four

I CAN'T BELIEVE how the universe keeps forcing Ham back into our lives. With all our equipment impounded by the authorities, the only squeegee left with access to the private blockchain is the squeegee I left Ham back in the tunnels—all our squeegees have it since the original copy was the one we stole from Ham who stole it from Caesar, a National Syndicate member and Ham's Guild Master.

That leaves us with no choice but to scoop Ham back up.

Fortunately, the mercenaries aren't the only ones who think ahead and prepare. The squeegee we left Ham also has one of Puo's trackers in it—even if Ham did find the tracker, he wouldn't be able to remove it until he had access to more serious equipment and he *needs* that squeegee, tracker or not, to be able to disappear.

Which is how I find myself cramped in a wooden crate on a cargo transport headed to Paris, France. It's clever, I'll give the mercs that. They're posing as AirCargo employees while the rest of us are shuttered into these wooden boxes—no scanning of CitIDs necessary.

The wood smells of freshly cut pine, and I have to continually work on my breathing to steady the jackknives. I never was good at sitting still.

Five days and nineteen hours left.

Charlie. We have to get Charlie.

No matter what happens when we find Ham, I have to make sure Mr. Chao's and Lucy's goals align with rescuing Charlie and putting a stake through the National Syndicate's heart—somehow.

More than anything I want to talk to Puo and Winn alone, but that will have to wait. They gave us a change of clothes and burned our prison coveralls, but knowing how well Puo can hide trackers and witnessing how well the mercs like to be prepared, I don't trust the clothes they gave us.

I breathe slowly through my nose and shift in the crate. The wood is hard on my ass.

I have a two-pronged problem: where are they holding Charlie? And how to manipulate the Cleaners and Mercs into helping me rescue her?

It's the first part of that problem that's the key. Any game run on the Cleaner/Mercs will be an outflow of that solution.

The National Syndicate wants us dead—that's what the tour boat explosion was about in Vancouver and why they accelerated their plans and moved on all the Bosses when they failed.

Puo thinks they're after us because he figured out a way to bypass the blockchain, a potentially history-altering hack when it comes to digital currency. But I'm not so sure now that I've had time to think about it. The tour boat explosion doesn't make sense if they wanted the blockchain hack. Why kill us before they knew how we did it? It would be the kind of information they would want to control.

The ploy with my father, and now Charlie, is to flush us into the open. To force *us* to come to *them*. It could be because they want to force Puo to reveal how he did it, but it feels more like them cauterizing loose ends, flushing us into the open to cut us down.

They started rabidly pursuing us after we took Christina's squeegee and Colvin killed her. Her squeegee contains proof of conspiracy, but that was rendered moot after the National Syndicate revealed themselves and moved openly against the Bosses.

So then why continue to pursue us? Is there something else on her squeegee they don't want us to find? What am I missing?

Questions I can't easily answer since Christina's squeegee is now in the authorities' hands. We're not getting it back anytime soon.

I keep coming back to Charlie's timer. They want to flush me out, but there's no information to go on in that timer. Am I supposed to simply stroll into a Cleaner's Den and announce myself?

If I wanted to flush someone out, I would funnel them directly where I wanted them to be. I wouldn't let them dictate the terms.

The National Syndicate wouldn't leave this to chance.

I stir in the crate—I'm sure I just hit on something. We stole one of their National Syndicate squeegees, slipped the noose more than once in Vancouver, and escaped in Atlanta. If they're going to flush us out, they will want to flush us to an exact location of their choosing.

But how do we know where to go?

We never did get a chance to study Charlie's video after we were arrested. There has to be something more there.

# Chapter Five

H AM REALLY IS a clever bastard. If it weren't for Puo's tracker, we'd still be in Paris waiting for Ham to never show up,
nibbling at the false digital breadcrumbs he's throwing off.

Long afternoon twilight shadows spill out of the narrow,
cobblestoned lane I'm waiting in, out onto Quai Romain Rol-
land, the main thoroughfare along the Saône River in Lyon,
France. Small snow speckles cling to the street corners, gray
from the passing traffic. Cold wind bites across my exposed face.

I lean up against a stone building, keeping an eye on Pont
Alphonse Juin, the main bridge over the Saône and then the
Rhône rivers—the fastest route on foot between the hovbus sta-
tion and Part-Dieu, Lyon's main train station.

"He's coming out on the Quai soon," Puo says in my comm-link.

"Roger," I reply.

The mercs took a bit of convincing to let us run the operation
to bring Ham in. We argued since Ham knew us he was more likely to cooperate, but in the end it was the fact they'd still be waiting
in Paris without Puo's tracker that finally convinced them.

Ham is an accomplished Cleaner. He knows how to launder
identities, except now he has the same problem we have: the au-

thorities made us. If he's going to jump borders, he needs to do it in a way that doesn't invite extra scrutiny—he may claim the image they captured of him back in New Dublin is different than the one tied to his CitID, but that's not something he's going to bank his freedom on.

So, when Mr. Chao and Lucy found a last minute transfer request for a Vice President of Operations of Swiftus Air from Paris to Malta that roughly matched Ham's description they figured that was our guy.

Except Puo's tracker kept zigzagging southeasterly from Paris—a hovbus.

So now I'm waiting in the cold to get eyes on Ham. The cold stone seeps into my back past my mustard yellow ski jacket. Don't get me wrong, it's a nice coat for what Nova could get on short notice, but it doesn't fit quite right.

"He's on the Quai," Puo says. "Came out north of you. Heading south to the bridge."

I peek around the corner and catch sight of his small rotund figure. His bald head shines in the setting sun and his thin black coat doesn't look warm enough for the near-freezing temperatures.

"I got eyes on him," I say. "Moving to trail."

I pull the fur-lined hood up and slip on black sunglasses against the setting sun.

Ham is in a hurry. He looks around occasionally, but not nearly enough. He keeps his head down, his hands in his pockets, and his short stubby legs moving. White puffs of breath rise off of him like a struggling smokestack.

Once he's on the bridge, I cross to the opposite side.

The bridge itself is plain, no statues or typical European architectural accoutrements. The town itself is pretty. A large cathedral sits behind me on a hill and to the north is a pretty collection of red-roofed buildings.

Foot and hovercar traffic are busy in rush hour. I draw level to Ham across the street as we near the end of the bridge. We head straight into a narrow street leading to the next bridge over the Rhône.

I cross the street and sidle up to him, slipping my arm in his. "Hiya, Ham!" I smile sweetly at him.

He blanches. His arm stiffens.

"Did ya miss—oof!"

I double over, cradling my stomach. *That bastard punched me!*

He runs full tilt down the street and jerks down the first side street.

*Ugh! Why isn't anything ever easy?*

"Est-ce que ça va?" a concerned older man rushes over to me.

I don't speak French, but his intent is clear. I nod and wave him away. "He's just playing hard to get is all." I jog after Ham.

Luckily, no one follows or appears to be calling the authorities or, aside from one old man, appears to give a shit a rat-shaped man punched a gorgeous woman in public.

I turn the corner to see Nova, the older merc holding up a fake badge and Ham looking like a rabbit caught between a wolf and a bear.

The younger merc is at the other end of the street.

I walk up still cradling my stomach and put a hand on Ham's shoulder. "Ham, Ham, Ham—that is no way to greet a lady. I see you've met Inspector Contreras."

The older merc is posing as Interpol officer Nova Contreras.

"I knew you'd be the death of me," Ham mutters, looking much too pale. It really wouldn't be helpful if he passed out.

"Relax," I say. "They're not with the An Garda Síochána. They're after bigger fish."

That flushes him out of his stupor and his dark beady eyes snap to me. "You're working with them," he hisses.

I shrug. "Well, like you Ham, we didn't have a choice. It was either work with Interpol for a partial pardon and reduced sentence or work through the British court system for a prison cell."

"You escaped this morning," he argues.

"Staged."

He looks between me and Nova.

"We are giving you the same choice, Reginold Hamilton," Nova says. "Work with us or plead your case before the local magistrates. The choice is yours, but this is the only time this choice will be given."

She turns around and leaves him there. I hurry to follow, looking back at him like he's an idiot for standing there.

This is the part of the con the mercs liked the least. It's the convincer, the moment the mark could walk away, but *chooses* to follow along. It's that choice that is critical. It has to be his own idea—everyone trusts themselves.

We get near the end of the street. Nova is silent, but tight. She doesn't think Ham will follow—*oh ye of little faith*.

Sure enough, I hear Ham's hurried footsteps coming. He falls in behind us. "I want it in writing with a lawyer to look it over."

Nova stops and turns to look at me. "Good Lord, I thought you said he was competent?"

"He is," I insist. "In things we need him to be. Not so much in common sense, or talking and stuff."

"I—" Ham starts again.

Nova snaps to him. "You saw what went down this morning, right?"

Ham glances at me and nods.

Nova continues, "Then what the fuck makes you think this is an above-board, official act? Here is the deal I gave your friends that I'll give you. You help us, and when *we* deem we're done, you're free to scurry off to whatever hole it is you can hide in and we'll leave you alone."

"They're not my friends and that's what I was already doing," Ham says through clenched teeth at the same time I say, "You said you'd erase our images."

"And yet, here we are," Nova says to Ham. "Despite your obvious breadcrumbs leading to Malta." To me she says, "I said we'd alter your images so they wouldn't return a hit, not erase."

"They can help us get over borders," I say to Ham. "This is as good as it's going to get." When Nova walks away, I mouth to Ham as I follow after her, "I have a fix."

Ham vacillates for several seconds before running to catch up again.

When he reaches us, he asks, "So what is it you need my help for?"

***

Ham looks at the squeegee we left him—one of the squeegees we recovered from the marina back in the Seattle Isles—laid out on the motel table shoved up against the wall like a wax apple he had bitten into. The forest-green brick is connected to Mr. Chao's tablet, but it's Puo driving the displays.

We're all crowded into a small motel room on the western edge of Lyon's fifth arrondissement except for Winn, who is out running errands for me. The dated room smells musty and looks like a prime candidate for one of those black-light investigative vids—I remain standing.

The curtains are drawn and space is tight with seven of us in there. No one is foolish enough to sit on the bed.

Information jumps down on one large float screen as Puo pages through it. He stops and sticks his forefinger right through the screen and growls. "Stupid float screens."

"Well," Mr. Chao asks.

Puo looks to me first and I nod for him to go ahead.

"Here's the blockchain from Christina's squeegee that I mirrored and copied onto this squeegee back in Seattle." He points to a string of gibberish on the screen, his finger wavering without something solid to rest against. "It's all a series of SHA-1024 hashes. We need to know who the hashes belong to in order to understand it."

Ham stands off to the side and gives Puo a funny look Puo can't see.

"We should be able to figure out Christina's hash ..." He points to the floating screen. His hand wavers not finding what he's looking for. "What?" he mutters to himself. "They're all different."

Ham rolls his eyes. "The blockchain's encrypted." Then under his breath for everyone to hear he adds, "Amateur."

Puo swivels to face Ham. "No. This doesn't look encrypted."

"Yes. It is." Ham crosses his arms in a smug expression no one could miss. "It's *made* to look like it's not encrypted. Keeps the peasants from—" He waves his hand around airily. "—hurting themselves. I know, because—" He shudders involuntarily. "—Caesar let it slip when I was ... working for him."

Puo flushes, but rather than argue with Ham he locks eyes with me. There's a lot in that look, communicated in seconds over decades of knowing each other. He hates being wrong in front of outsiders and is worried he might have missed something else. But more immediately, he's thinking this encryption might be the same one encrypting the data embedded in Charlie's video metadata.

I had him comb Charlie's video for breadcrumbs from the National Syndicate the second we were free from the AirCargo shipping crates. There was an encrypted data package in the metadata.

"Can you decrypt it?" I ask, hoping the marina squeegee might hold some clues. He couldn't decrypt the video's secrets.

Puo shakes his head slowly. Stops. Then shakes no, again. "Not without the private key." His face is still flushed—he always did have a hard time with making mistakes.

Ham, standing behind Puo, fidgets like he wants to kick Puo out and drive the displays.

"Ham?" I prompt.

He hesitates, exhaling out his piggish nose. Then, as if it were being dragged out him, he says, "This doesn't make sense. It never made sense to me that they would encrypt the blockchain. The whole point of the private blockchain is to keep tabs on each other. They would have a way to decrypt it to make sense of it. Otherwise, it defeats the point."

I raise my eyebrows—that was well reasoned. It never was Ham's abilities I objected to, just his general dickishness.

Puo shakes his head. "I've looked," he says, but not as confidently as before. "There's nothing on here that could even remotely be used that way."

Ham glances around furtively, particularly at the other two Cleaners. Eventually he swipes his nose and says, "Take a break. Go for a walk."

"What?" Puo asks, still rooting around in the squeegee.

"Take a break. Go take a walk, clear your head. Let the grownups work."

And there's his dickishness.

Puo stops what he's doing, turns in his chair, and asks in a low voice, all uncertainty from before vanishing. "What did you just say?"

Ham repeats himself like talking to a deaf old man. "Let. The. Grown. Ups. Work." He even makes a shooing gesture with his hands.

*Ohh, bad move, Hammy boy. Very bad move.* Puo may be embarrassed about missing the encryption earlier, he may even have his confidence shaken, but he would never, *ever*, show that to an outsider.

Puo gets out of his chair and towers over Ham. Puo is a six-foot three-hundred-pound Samoan man, and Ham has the presence of mind to take an unexpected, unsteady step back.

"Puo!" I say to call him off.

"You can't honestly be suggesting I go take a walk!" he roars, never taking his eyes from Ham.

"Of course not! Just don't do anything stupid." Puo doesn't have a violent bone in his body—he's a big softie. But, like Lenny in *Of Mice and Men*, sometimes I don't think he understands how big he really is and the kind of damage he can do.

Ham starts to speak.

"Oh, shut it!" I snap at Ham. I could tell from his narrow little eyes it wasn't going to be anything helpful.

I turn to Nova, but it's really for Mr. Chao's ears. "You brought us together to hunt down the National Syndicate—" That's not exactly why they brought us together, but it's not too early to plant that seed. "—trying to protect some secret sauce at this point is stupid and counterproductive."

It's Mr. Chao that answers, "I agree." To Ham he says, "Ham, tell them."

Ham stares at Mr. Chao who appears unruffled from Ham's imperious gaze. "What guild are you from?"

"Greensboro," Mr. Chao answers.

"Elsie Buchanan?" Ham tests, asking who the Guild Master is.

"No, Angela Jimenez," Mr. Chao answers.

"Not that it matters," Lucy breaks in, "since they're all dead. So, Ken Chao, actually."

Ham doesn't look surprised at the news they were all dead— he already knew.

"Ham," I prod him to answer the unanswered question.

"Yokels," he mutters under his breath again for everyone to hear and turns to Puo towering over him. Ham takes another unconscious half-step back. "Most Cleaners keep cold storage on their equipment. It's an open secret in the community."

Puo whips around to stare at the marina squeegee, then he shakes his head no. "I've looked through the guts of several squeegees more than once. It's not—"

"It's not meant to be found," Ham snaps derisively. "We'll have to open—"

A knock at the door cuts off Ham's and Puo's arguing. "It's Fred," Winn calls. Fred is the new identity Mr. Chao and Lucy swapped out on his CitID.

The room breathes a collective sigh of relief and I go to open the faded eggshell white door.

Winn enters carrying several bags of clothes.

"Where were you?" Nova asks, eyeing the bags with obvious agitation.

"Shopping," Winn says.

She starts to ask more questions, but Winn takes his cue from me and ignores her. There's no profit to be had in an argument right now.

He spreads the bags out on the bed and I start to go through them. The clothes Nova and company provided us were from a second-hand store and mine don't fit right.

"What'd I miss here?" he says, after wading through the tension in the room.

"Puo and Ham were arguing about who has the bigger hard drive," I say.

Winn cocks an eyebrow.

Puo snorts. "Weak, Isa. Dick jokes? I expect better from you."

"Yeah, well," I say airily, while pulling out a caramel-colored oversized knit sweater and a pair of light-blue jeans. "It's been a rough couple of days."

"You did good," I say to Winn, holding up a long fur-lined dark-blue parka jacket. Then for Puo's ears I say to Winn, "Ham was instructing Puo on how squeegees actually work."

"Party foul," Puo hisses at me as I grab the bag of girl's underwear and head to the bathroom to change. "I know how squeegee's work!" he whines after me.

"You shut it!" Puo snaps at Ham, who said something I didn't catch as I closed the door.

By the time I return in all new clothes, Ham and Puo have the marina squeegee open and are trading barbs with one another.

"I told you I looked it over," Puo snipes.

"It has to be there." Ham leans over the squeegee. He then asks Mr. Chao, "Do you have any tools?"

Mr. Chao nods to Nova who nods to the younger merc who then ducks out of the room at the same time Winn goes to change.

The younger merc returns with a small gym-sized black duffel bag, and soon Ham and Puo continue to trade barbs while leaning over the squeegee wearing headband magnifiers and holding thin pointy hooked tweezers.

Winn comes to stand next to me in a pair of dark chinos, a light gray sweater over a white buttoned shirt, and the same pine-colored ski jacket Nova and company had supplied. They had given all three of us the same model ski jacket. Puo's is a different shade of green, moss colored, while mine was a mustard yellow before I had Winn upgrade me to something that fit better.

"Didn't get yourself a new coat?" I ask him.

"It's a nice coat." He pats at it. "A little big."

It is a little big on him, but the new clothes fit his frame well, and I'm tempted to linger on the view when Ham's voice cuts across the room.

"You put a tracker in my squeegee." He stands up straight and turns to look at me at the back of the group.

"No," I explain as if to a child, "*our* squeegee, that we let you borrow, happened to have a tracker in it."

He looks at me with dark malevolent eyes, but before he can respond Puo says, "Found it."

Ham whips back around and grudgingly says that's probably it. They both debate how to do whatever it is they're about to do, and they lean in with their tweezers.

"Bored?" Winn asks.

"Yeah," I state the obvious.

"Yeah, this really doesn't have your panache, does it?"

I wish we could be alone, go take a walk. We have new digi-scramblers—mine's a cheap white-gold circle pendant—I feel the pang of loss all over again for my pearl necklace and Winn's caduceus pendant. But we need to be here. As soon the squeegee divulges its secrets, we need to be able to move.

I look at all the others in the room in turn. Thinking of the situation we find ourselves in. Yesterday, my father was murdered in front of the world and I was arrested. This morning, I was arraigned in front of a British Magistrate's judge. Two and a half weeks ago Puo had a coronary heart spasm after Nix tried to kill us on an exploding sightseeing tour. A month ago, Liáng tried to double-cross us into government servitude. And five months ago, we were framed by the Cleaners to trick Colvin into eliminating us as part of a larger plot we're still trying to untangle.

*Five days, seventeen hours.*

My pulse races out to find the edges of panic. The jackknives awaken and eviscerate any appetite I might have had.

"Is this the track you tried to warn me about?" I whisper, surprising myself at the thought. My heart beats against my ears.

It was the morning after we lifted the solid-state drive from a sunken branch of Pacific View Bank. We had no idea the shit we were about to land ourselves in, but for a brief period, we were back on easy street. Sunlight filtered in through the blinds of our Queen Anne Victorian bedroom. We were hung over. I couldn't understand why Winn couldn't simply enjoy the moment. Instead, he dumped his existentialist angst on me, about our future, about what path we were on. He couldn't understand why I didn't see a problem.

Winn glances over at me from the corner of his eyes and nods slowly. He whispers, "Yeah. But no matter what happens, we're in it together."

He means it. I can see it in his face—his luminous blue eyes hold no lie, no designs of a sappy line.

It's a cruelty to have missed each other by a few months, that it took me this long to have finally understood what he was talking about that morning.

Puo and Ham stop fidgeting with the squeegee. They both make for the seat, but Ham backs away after a glare from Puo.

Ham starts backseat driving and Puo starts huffing while banging on the desk using the light-projected keyboard. Eventually they both quiet as they study the float screen.

"Balls," Puo mutters and slumps back in the chair.

Ham rests his hands on his head, airing out his wet pit stains for us to admire.

"What?" I ask.

"There's no private key here," Puo says.

I look at him like he's trying to make a smoothie with his feet.

"What?" he asks cautiously.

"Of course there's no private key on there," I practically explode. "That's one of the squeegees we lifted from the marina. Not a National Syndicate one." I thought they were checking it to see if it had any cold storage that held anything useful—not that they actually expected it to have a National Syndicate private key.

Understanding blooms on Puo's face. "Oh, right."

"Yes. Right."

We all stare at each other for a beat. Even Ham looks chagrined—could be the room's lighting though.

"Well," I say, "is there anything on there we *can* use?"

Puo and Ham go back to working, while I'm left shaking my head.

Five days, seventeen hours, and these two are making smoothies with their feet.

The two of them thump on the light-projected keyboard for several minutes. Eventually, both shake their heads. Puo turns to me. "This is likely a dead end. We'll keep looking. But we need an alternative plan."

"So, we need another squeegee?" I say, having already thought ahead.

Ham says, "From one of the National Syndicate masterminds. Do you happen to have another one of those lying around?" he asks with a smirk.

"We did," I say, thinking of Christina's squeegee now in British custody.

Puo nods. "Yeah, we need another squeegee."

I rub my temples and then start thinking out loud. "Christina's squeegee is in British custody—"

"Does it happen to have a tracker in it?" Ham asks with another self-satisfied smirk.

"Yes. Fat lot of good it will do us."

No one objects to that—not even Ham. Everyone knows it'd be way too stupid to go back to the UK right now. Even if it weren't, we don't have the time to case the job and pull it off. It'd have to be a smash and grab like Vancouver, but we have zero intel over here.

"I have Christina's squeegee mirrored back home," Puo says.

Ham snorts and shakes his head no. "It's the cold storage we need, mirroring won't copy hardware. Or don't you know that?"

"We're brainstorming!" Puo growls back. "Or don't you know how that works? Being brainless and all."

Ham starts to respond when I cut across, a parent separating two fighting children. "Ham! Puo! Stop! Ham, come stand over here." I point next to me.

To my surprise he actually does it, while Puo sticks his tongue out at Ham's back.

To Mr. Chao, I ask, "Do you have Jimenez's squeegee?" Their Guild Master may have something on her squeegee we could use.

"No," he says. "We don't know what happened to it."

Ham, Puo, and I all look thoughtful at that.

"But Angela wasn't even part of the National Syndicate," Lucy says, appearing frustrated at this suggestion.

I shrug. It's always easier to see if a door is unlocked first before trying to pick it. Her comment shakes something loose in my brain.

To Ham I say, "Do you know any of the other National Syndicate members?"

"No." Ham suddenly looks like a pig caught in the slaughter line.

"Haaammm," I say like I'm coaxing a timid dog out from hiding. "Who do you know?"

"You're nuts." He shakes his head. "Better to steal back Christina's squeegee."

That's the heart of the problem: Five days, seventeen hours.

Either we go back to into the lion's den in the UK or we steal a squeegee off a National Syndicate member.

But which is fastest?

There's only one way to know. "Ham," I say. "Spill it."

# Chapter Six

**P**UO SQUEEZES MY shoulder. I wake quickly and sit up in the ivory leather seat of the private transport we chartered.

The cabin lights are dimmed. A steady thrum of air rushes over the hull. Everyone else is asleep.

I reach out and squeeze Winn's thigh next to me. *Mmmm, muscly.*

Winn sleepily opens his eyes, sees Puo and me, and nods once.

I get up and follow Puo in his moss-colored ski jacket back to where he has a computer set up. Winn stays put to keep an eye out.

It's past midnight and everyone else is either curled up in their seat or slumped over unceremoniously sleeping. Only Aliyah, the younger merc is awake standing near the front of the cabin with arms crossed—I think the mercs are keeping a watch schedule.

Aliyah is my age, taller than me, but a few inches shorter than Winn (who is six feet) with a good balance of muscle. She has a crisp, curly Afro Mohawk with sharp lines that look like she goes every week to the barbershop. There's intelligence in her russet-brown eyes as she watches Puo and I head to the back. She stays where she is.

Once Ham spilled what he knew, which wasn't much, there wasn't any choice. Izaak Mitchell is the Boston area Guild Master and a National Syndicate bona fide member. But that's all Ham knew. Not where, or how, to find him.

The most Ham could give was a description: African-American male, mid-forties, average height and weight. He couldn't give us anything more specific. We can try to use that description and Ham's memory to reconstruct a facial rendering when we get to Boston and Puo is tapped back into his own systems and the facial rendering software we have.

But even with a semi-accurate rendering, there's no way Izaak as a Guild Master will be easy to track down—we already did a cursory search. Some Cleaners like the notoriety of celebrity, but they don't last long for obvious reasons. No Cleaner who likes the limelight ever rises high enough to be a Guild Master.

No. If we're going to find Izaak in the time frame we need, we're going to have to call in favors. Favors it would be better for the mercs and Cleaners not to know about.

This is only half the reason we chartered a private hovtransport. One, I'm not going to spend a six-hour flight back to the States stuffed in a cargo box. Two, we need to use this time to figure out how to get Izaak's squeegee and start to set things up. Because between running a game on Izaak and hitting the British police, Izaak is both more likely to succeed *and* gets us physically closer to where they're holding Charlie—which has to be in the States somewhere.

I sit down in a small booth, facing the plane's tail. Puo sits down across from me, two float screens between us.

"Here." Puo slides a comm-link over the table to me, his moss-colored ski jacket rustling across the table.

"You didn't want a new jacket either?" I ask, thinking of Winn and reaching out for the comm-link.

He shrugs. "It is a nice coat. A little tight though." He glances between me and Aliyah at the front of the plane.

I slip the comm-link in my ear. "You have the encryption worked out?" It's the only reason Aliyah hasn't crashed the party—they're sure with two Cleaners on board they can monitor any signals originating from the hovtransport.

"Sí." Puo nods with a hint of a grin. "Ellos no compreden."

I raise an eyebrow at him.

"¿Qué?" he asks. "Nosotros vivimos ... ahora." He trails off, his face screwed up in thought. Puo's been trying to learn Spanish on and off for years. It appears he's trying again.

He shakes his head, clearing out the cobwebs of thought. "We can live anywhere now," he whispers to explain the latest round of Spanish. He shrugs to make his point.

That's true. We're debt free. No need to work. We can go anywhere. Assuming we make it out of this alive, of course.

It's a strange feeling to finally have everything we've been working for. And ass-backwards, too. Like the universe was watching us fumble our way around in life and finally took pity on us and handed us everything we've ever wanted. Then smacked us upside the head when we were too slow to realize it.

It hasn't really sunk in yet.

Even earlier when Mr. Chao and Lucy dragged their feet on chartering the private hovtransport, concerned about how it impacted their ability to pay the mercs, I hesitated. We could've easily covered the cost, but I haggled to cover only half.

*What are we going to do when all this over?*

The thought sprints down and coils around my adrenaline

gland like a boa constrictor, squeezing until ever last drop of adrenaline surges through my body.

*Oh, God. What the fuck is wrong with me?*

"Hey." Puo nudges me under the table. "You okay?"

"No." I look around wildly. This booth is too small. I can't breathe.

There's nowhere to go.

*Fuck.* I can't believe this. First, we never have enough money, and now that we do, my body is falling apart.

"Hey." Puo moves the float screens out of the way and reaches out to take my hands.

I pull away but his large hands engulf mine. Their weight is surprising, comforting, gentle.

"It's going to be okay," he whispers in a calm voice. "Your body can handle this. It's your sympathetic nervous system responding to a threat. You've gotten through it before, you'll get through it again. Breathe in through your nose, out through your mouth."

I nod and start breathing, letting Puo's calm voice keep me in the present. He walks me through a grounding exercise, squeezing my hands for one of the touches.

Eventually, the roar of impending death subsides to a trickle of idle death threats.

I pull away from Puo, my hands shaking in the aftermath.

Puo stares at me, unsure what to say.

"Been reading up on this crap?" I ask, finding my voice again. *God, I hate this.*

"Yeah." Puo studies me for a minute and apparently decides I'm okay because he follows up with, "That might be the first time you've ever listened to me."

"It would've been better in Spanish."

"Por supuesto."

I don't know what that means, so instead I say, "Ready?" I nod to the float screens and the call we need to make. I want to get this over with.

"We can wait a bit, it's only four thirty in the afternoon there."

"No. I'm ready."

Puo brings the float screens back in front of him. He types on the light-projected keyboard and then nods to me through the screens.

The comm-link rings two, three, four times.

"Who is this?" Colvin asks aggressively.

"Sapphire Sanders," I answer quickly. We're calling from an unlisted number.

It's quiet on the other end, a heavy silence filled with mental calculation. I'm sure he's seen the news of our arrest and escape and he's trying to figure out if we flipped on him.

"An aggrieved third party with a common enemy sprung the gate," I say.

He's silent at this, but he hasn't hung up. From my experience with Colvin, this isn't a good sign. It means he's calculated the risk the authorities might be on the call is acceptable enough to hear what we have to say, and if that's the case, the situation with the Cleaners can't be good.

"Sebastian has secured the line."

Still silence. So I play my ace card—well, my only card really.

"I know who's responsible—" I let that sink in before adding, "—and I intend to make them pay."

Colvin breathes heavily and then finally speaks. "What do you need?"

# Chapter Seven

G OD, I LOVE BEING in the water. I may not know what's going to happen after all of this, when we don't have to work anymore, but I do know I'm going to keep diving.

It's peaceful in the water. Quiet. The ocean gently cups you into weightlessness. Gravity has no pull down here. It's all so effortless, so free.

It's twenty-four hours after our hovtransport back to the States, but there was nothing for it. That's how long it took to set things up.

"Izaak's taking off now," Ham says over the comm-link.

"Roger," I say at the same time Winn says, "I'm tracking him."

"How are the squiddies looking, Chameleon?" I ask Puo. If the autonomous eyes and ears of the Federal Government get even a sniff of what were about to do the whole operation is wasted.

"They're mostly to the northeast helping with the recovery efforts," he answers petulantly. He doesn't see why he can't do both, keep an eye on Izaak and the squiddies. But it was better to give Ham a simple job to do, rather than have Ham unoccupied—who knows what that oily snake would get up to.

"There are a couple to the east of you," Puo continues, "but they're far enough away not to be a problem—as long as you don't linger."

"Won't be a problem," I say.

"I still don't see how Muscles is going to pull this off," Nova says, holding onto the ocean-encrusted windowsill next to me.

We're both in scuba drysuits with built-in heaters (best invention ever) in an abandoned, three-story brick building in Watertown, west of old Boston and halfway between the Lexington Isles and Waban Island.

It's dark eighty feet below the ocean at midnight. We have our helmet lights off, our wet sacks of goodies tight to our backs, and our nightvision turned to max—which is currently useless.

The windows are all shattered, and this floor of the brick three-story building appears to have been some kind of arts studio when the mega-quake hit—we cased the building with our helmet lights on when we first arrived. I imagine it must have been nice in the summer with the large windows open and a breeze, but now it was silent, stale, the ocean slowly reclaiming it. Uneven ocean crud coats every surface. Little marine plants cling to the outside straining for sunlight. Inside the building is mostly a haven for small schooling fish and some bottom-dwelling crustaceans.

The rough sea crashes overhead.

"Won't be a problem," I say to Nova about Winn's part. I shift around the wet sack to a more comfortable position—the DPV, diver propulsion vehicle, was knuckling into my spine. Then to change the subject I ask, "How's it fit?"

Technically, she's in Winn's scuba drysuit, but he's in an anti-gravity suit getting ready to pay Izaak a visit. I need her focusing on the suit she's in, and not the one Winn's in.

She's been poking at how Winn is going to pay Izaak a visit ever since Winn took off alone to gather supplies from our Seattle Isles home—after we briefed Winn on some of the, uh, surprises Puo and I had left for him at our Queen Anne home when he wasn't in our good graces. Ever since then, she's been all up in our business: how do we know this or how do we know that?

This whole plan has been like that, me coming up with everything and everyone else poking at the edges. There was a lot of consternation in the beginning since I wasn't willing to tell them certain things (like Colvin putting me in touch with the Boston Boss) or how we were going to maneuver Izaak to where we wanted him (use of the anti-gravity suits). It was only when Puo asked me straight up in front of everyone what we still needed them for did they get the message and switched from fighting me so much to asking nonstop questions.

"It's loose," Nova says. "I feel like I'm sliding around in someone else's skin. And you've already asked me that. Why won't you tell me—"

"ETA to position?" Winn asks. He's up in the skylanes, preparing to intercept Izaak.

"Four minutes," Ham says.

"Three minutes and fifty seconds," Puo corrects. "Call exact times. This is a precision op. Noob."

"Ten seconds doesn't matter," Ham snipes back. "It's less than five percent of the total time, and I'll get more specific as we get closer."

"It does too matter!"

*Grrr.* "Shut it! Both of you. You're like ex-lovers—"

Puo growls disgust and for once Ham agrees with him.

"Is he headed in the right direction?" I ask Ham.

That's where the Boston Boss, Valerie Quezada, comes in. Turns out, Quezada has an informant in the Massachusetts State Police (probably more than one). But this specific one knows of an informant for Izaak in the same department. Quezada's informant planted tantalizing information with Izaak's informant, and now Izaak and this informant have a meeting set up on Waban Island. So now we know when and where Izaak will be moving.

"Yeah," Ham says. "Straight line as predicted from Lexington to Waban."

"Good." I listen to the waves crash overhead as we wait.

Several minutes later, Ham says, "One minute."

"One minute, aye," Winn says. "I'm in position."

My heart rate increases and I freeze at the sensation.

*Is this another panic attack? Is it going to happen again? Here? Now?* My heart rate suddenly thunders at the thought.

Adrenaline crashes into my system.

*No. No it's not,* I tell myself. Normal rush on a job. My heart rate stays elevated but it's there, the panic, lurking on the periphery.

"Thirty seconds," Ham calls out.

"Squiddies?" I ask for a final check.

"All to the northeast," Puo says. "The ones to the east are still too far to be of any concern."

I nod and gather what little moisture I have in my mouth to swallow, waiting for the show to begin.

"Ten seconds," Ham says.

"I got 'em," Winn says.

Ham counts down, "Five, four, three, two, one."

"Mark!" Winn says at the same time Puo mutters, "Noob."

I can hear Winn's big southern grin. He loves dropping in the anti-gravity suits.

I tap Nova next to me and pull myself out of the building. A blue targeted bullseye appears above me where Izaak's hovercar needs to hit for the next phase.

"Painting the target!" Winn calls out.

A red "x" marker, where Izaak's hovercar is projected to land in the blue bullseye blooms above me as I swim forward. The depth counter off to my left levels off at fifty feet.

"Ten seconds to contact!" Winn calls out.

I reach the target area center and keep my eyes glued to where the red "x" intersects the blue bullseye.

Winn grunts as he lands on Izaak's hovercar. "Gentlemen."

I imagine him tipping his head to them as he slams the magnetic disrupter down.

There's no sound as it scrambles the hovercar's insides.

"Didn't work!" Winn calls out.

*Fuck!* It appears the Cleaners learned from the same exact stunt we pulled in Vancouver.

"Move to explosives!" I yell. We knew this could be a possibility, but it throws everything off.

The red "x" shifts off the target area center.

*Damn it, damn it, damn it.* I start to get out my DPV from my wet sack of goodies. Even though the squiddies are to the northeast, DPV's are loud—better to have used them only when we planned.

"Negative," Winn says, followed quickly by, "I mean, roger, but not quite. Well, you'll see!"

"What?" I stop retrieving my DPV. Winn doesn't respond.

"Blowing out the windshield," Winn says eventually.

"What!" I call out along with everyone on the line, but I already know where he's going—old school hijacking.

"This only works if we hit the target area," Winn says. He would know, he was the one who did the hypothermia calculations. "Only one way to make sure that happens now. I'm free. Detonating."

There's a distant pop over the line.

"Reengaging," Winn says. He must have pushed off to detonate the explosive.

The red "x" has completely moved off the target area.

I turn on my helmet lights to two percent power and with the nightvision turned on it's enough to paint Nova in blue pixels. She's in the process of getting her own DPV out.

"Wait," I say to Nova.

Winn grunts over the line followed by more grunts and struggles as he enters the cabin to commandeer the hovercar.

I bite my tongue to keep from asking what's happening and strain to hear if there's gunfire.

The red "x" swings back over the target area.

"Commandeered!" Winn yells. "Coming in hot! Three total passengers not counting me!"

"Roger!" I say, gauging where the hovercar is going to hit.

The red "x" narrows into a smaller tighter "x."

Winn grunts again. "Argh! Get off me!"

A timer pops up on my HUD. Eleven seconds.

That's not right.

There's more distant popping over the line.

"Drogues deployed," Winn calls out.

The timer jumps to thirty-four seconds. The "x" widens, but still over the target area.

"Get out of there," I say.

"Negative."

I am going to kill that man—assuming we live through this.

"I'm bringing her all the way in. Our passengers are not very cooperative." He punctuates this statement, with what I'm sure is an elbow to a Cleaner's face.

"We need them conscious!" I remind him.

"Roger that," he says.

"We only have enough rebreathers for three," Nova says, frustration bleeding through.

"Muscles can handle himself," I say.

"How—?"

"Don't worry about it."

The projected "x" creeps smaller. Nova and I swim to stay in the center. Three is going to be challenging since there's only two of us.

Twelve seconds.

"I have Izaak," I say to Nova, "you take the other two. I'm support if you need it."

Nova repeats it back to me and ends with, "Roger."

Three seconds. Two. One.

Nothing.

I'm about to make a helpful observation to Ham and Puo when the hovercar slams into the ocean surface and starts sinking.

"Let's go!" I'm all amped up and can't help yelling.

The hovercar's headlights cut down through water and illuminate the ocean around us. Unfortunately, they don't illuminate the part we need to see most—inside the cabin.

We both turn on our helmet lights to their max as we swim up to meet the sinking hovercar.

"I'm free," Winn says through gritted teeth—he must be falling back up into the skylane for Puo to pick up.

I register relief he's free, but keep focused on getting to the hovercar as fast as we can to make sure none of the worms inside wiggle free.

"All three are here," I call out as I sprint forward and grab the top of the blown-out windshield.

Nova is right behind me and manages to grab my left calf. She shimmies down next to me.

The depth readout ticks down from twenty feet as we sink.

I dip my head in. All three have their heads in an air pocket along the back windshield. They're yelling about how to escape.

Can't have that.

I consider my options. Every second we wait the deeper we go and the easier this will be. On the other hand, we're in forty-degree-Fahrenheit water. They really don't have long, less than four minutes tops before they lose dexterity to swim themselves and fifteen to twenty minutes before they lose consciousness.

They're quite lucky we're here, to be honest—I'll make sure to remind them later.

I grab Izaak's leg and pull him under the water. He tries to fight me—yeesh, ya know, you try and help someone and all they do is fight you. But the cold sucks away his strength quickly enough.

I get him outside the hovercar, clip a weight belt around him, and grab his jacket before he sinks out of sight. I shove a rebreather into his mouth linked to my tank—no mask.

Nova moves into the cabin right behind me.

Izaak bucks and twists, but clings to that rebreather.

"I've baited my worm," I say. "How are you with the other two?"

"They're weighted and baited," she says.

I don't have time to feel any relief at this. It's good news—we need all three to disappear, everything falls apart if one of them escapes. Now it's a race between authorities showing up and hypothermia setting in.

As if on cue, Puo says, "Squiddie to the east is headed in your direction. ETA four minutes. Authorities have dispatched a rapid response team. ETA six minutes."

*Four minutes?* "I thought you said they were far enough away not to be a problem," I say through gritted teeth as I prep my DPV and string a rope around it.

Puo's quiet on the other end for a quick second. "Yeah, how did they respond so fast?"

"Not helpful!" I loop the rope around Izaak's waist with a carabiner. He's gone worryingly still. He's still breathing though, if rapidly.

"You should be all right, though," Puo says, but I know him too well, he's trying to sound confident and failing.

I start my DPV. "Status?" I ask Nova.

"Stringing number two, ready to go ... in a few ... seconds. Done." Her DPV starts up.

"Let's go." I turn on the DPV headlights and motor down into the depths.

I optimize our path to our destination to change depth as gradually as possible to give time for our worms to equalize the pressure. Our worms aren't fighting at all, which is the sensible position to take. It's near freezing cold, you have no idea how deep you are, or even which direction is up. Like or not, your best chance of survival is to accept the rebreather and do what you're told. After all, if we wanted them dead, why shove a rebreather in their mouths?

The lights can't be helped, as much as I hate them. It feels like lighting a fire in the middle of the night for your enemies. Fortunately, light doesn't travel far enough in water to be too worried about it—as long as the squiddies stay far enough away.

There's nothing to see at forty feet deep except particulates floating through the water. The depth readout and a three-minute, ten-second timer floats off to my lower left and a green triangle marker floats in front and below me.

The timer is Winn's rough estimate for when hypothermia will begin to take hold in earnest based on his medical training. At that point, things get more complicated and we'll have less than ten minutes until they lose consciousness.

The empty space of particulates starts to resolve into the dark square tops of buildings. HVAC and chimney shadows break up the flat roofs. Black ditches of pooling darkness mark the roads' and alleys' locations.

Sixty feet deep.

A hulking shadow looms ahead over the buildings, like the buildings were tinker toys cast aside in a child's playroom. The green triangle marker snaps to a part of the imposing shadow— the *H.F. Odense*, a two hundred thousand tonnage cargo ship out of Denmark that happened to be docked at the Port of Boston when the mega-quake hit. They didn't make it and now it lay smashed on its side in the remnants of Watertown.

"Almost there," I say. "Squiddies?"

"The two to the east are making a beeline for the crash site," Puo says. "Two minutes and fifty seconds out."

I grit my teeth. We still need to leave here after dealing with our shivering worms.

The outline of the *H.F. Odense* stern takes shape, the multistoried bridge blooming up from the deck, lying on its side. The ship is too long for my nightvision to resolve in its entirety, but the green triangle marker hovers over an open hatch.

According to its manifest, the *Odense* was loading up auto and aircraft parts when the mega-quake swept it inland and ultimately sank it. I couldn't tell you how much of the ship still held the spare parts, but what I can tell you is that the ship possesses some rather strategic air pockets.

In what feels a lifetime ago, before fleeing to the west coast, before Winn, before the anti-gravity suits, Puo and I had cased the Boston Sea for sites like this. We had considered hitting the Harvard Museum of Natural History, and holing up in an air pocket was part of the escape plan. We never did go through with the job—we couldn't find an air pocket close enough to the museum to work.

But the air pockets on the *H.F. Odense* will act quite nicely as a holding cell while the rest of the world thinks Izaak and his goons are dead, drowned as part of a war with the Bosses. Quite nicely indeed. It's a lie Quezada will help propagate by taking credit for bringing down Izaak's hovercar.

Two minutes.

Numbness is probably settling into our worms now and exhaustion/unconsciousness will be around the corner.

I stop outside the hatch and take the rope off the DPV to guide Izaak in.

The interior is all gray and seafoam-green metal. Pipes run along the ceiling, steep metal staircases slice up and down decks. Sickly yellowish silt drapes over every surface. Porthole doors open into the interior darkness.

I pull Izaak close, grabbing him by the chest and guiding him through the porthole door into the interior. The HUD lays out a path to take with green triangles snapped to the floor, which is really the wall since the ship is on its side.

The path is complicated. Up two decks, cross into the interior, down a hallway past four doors, down a deck, back along a longer hallway and then up three decks and then some twists and turns and up one last deck.

The green triangles are superfluous—I always was good at memorization, a requisite skill for cons and games. Even if I didn't have the route memorized, evidence of our previous passings marks the route. A handprint in the silt here, a broad brush of silt blown away there. It wouldn't be hard to follow if you weren't in a rush.

The stairways present the most problems. They're a tight fit and they slow us down further than I planned. With our worms already close to hypothermia, the last thing we need is a head wound.

The hypothermia timer for when they lose their dexterity runs out when we're three-quarters of the way there. There's nothing for it though, only to keep going and hope the timer is off a bit in its estimates.

A new timer takes its place: nine minutes and thirty seconds until unconsciousness—but we're so close to our destination at this point I'm not worried about it.

Nova manages behind me without complaint and we arrive at our destination: the officer's quarters with the timer at eight minutes and forty seconds.

As soon as Izaak broaches the water he comes to life, ripping out the rebreather and frantically looking around. White gobs of breath escape into the warmed room, already lit for his arrival.

I slip further underwater.

Izaak does the only sensible thing a person can do, the only option we left him—he fumbles out of the near-freezing water onto the pea-green metal decking wall at the start of the officer quarters.

I help Nova with the other two and they soon scramble out of the water like nearly frozen fish.

We wait for a minute below the water, letting our worms thaw a little and take stock of their surroundings. I check my wet bag for the square block of Izaak's squeegee and smile to myself at the brick's solid feel. I wonder how long it will take him to discover the fake I swapped it with.

Once I hear movement and their muffled voices, I increase my buoyancy enough to rise above the water from the shoulders up.

All three lock onto me. It'd be more threatening if they weren't shivering uncontrollably.

I take my helmet off, as careful as I can not to spill any water down my suit—that shit is cold.

"Hello, Izaak Mitchell," I say, "nice to meet you."

"Y— Yo— Y— Yooouuu," he finally manages to get out between shivers. His dark African American skin is pallid.

"I'm not sure we've ever been formally introduced. I'd shake your hand, but you look cold and my hands are kinda hot and sweaty, to be honest."

"Yoo— Y— Yooouu've killed ... killed us."

"Nope! There's a plum little survival package behind you: blankets, chemical heaters, food, dry clothes. Rather thoughtful if you ask me." When they don't say thank you, I continue, "You should be able to scavenge mattresses from the officer quarters up ahead and find tools in the small galley nearby to open the canned food and water." Aside from the whole ship being on its side, we left them pretty well off—except for a serious medical emergency or gash to the head of course.

I really should be a patron saint of something.

Izaak mumbles, "Car— Ca— Carlos. Ga— Go!"

A thick Hispanic man in his mid-thirties with a shaved head and chubby cheeks stumbles deeper into officer country for the survival package.

"Ah— Ah— Oxygen," he finally gets out.

"Ahh," I say with a smile. "Near as we can calculate for three adult men in this space you have four days and four hours." The exact time left on Charlie's counter.

He glares at me.

"Unless you want to cut the bullshit and tell me where she is."

He doesn't answer.

I didn't expect him too. All the rats that feared for their lives—like Ham—had already jumped ship before they launched a war with the Bosses. I can't risk wasting time trying to make Izaak talk. He knows how long he needs to hold out for.

Of course, I don't have a clue how long the oxygen will last in this makeshift prison. Once Winn's calculations showed it was well past when we needed it to last, we didn't pay it any mind.

Now to make sure they don't get clever.

"And since I'm feeling benevolent, I thought I would let you know I saw a rather suspicious hard drive in your hovercar I'm sure the authorities will find. And, although I'm no expert, it looks like the kind of drive filled with stolen bank accounts, transfer records, compromised emails from the Governor, that kind of thing. So I hope the hovercar wasn't registered in your name." I'm sure it wasn't, but if it was, all the better. "Anyway, ya know how it is. I'm sure they'll link any survivors rescued down here to that hovercar and hard drive. So, I wouldn't tap Morse code on the metal walls, or make much of a ruckus for them to find you."

I stop to pretend to think a second. "Rotten luck, really. Sorry about that."

Carlos stumbles back with a shiny, silver thermal blanket which Izaak immediately wraps himself in. "How— How long?"

It's impossible to shrug bobbing in the water like a buoy. "I don't know," I say. "You have three options. Sit tight and wait for my return. Hope your friends barter for your lives and send someone to get you. Or bang away and call the authorities down on you."

Izaak's stares daggers at me while shivering in his blanket.

It's not hard to guess what he'll do, at least in the short term. He'll wait it out while Charlie's timer runs out, then he'll reassess.

I start to put my helmet back on to make our escape.

Izaak lets out a parting shot through shivers that slips in under my helmet before I lock it into place.

"Tick tock."

# Chapter Eight

GOOD HIDEOUTS ARE hard to find. They need to combine accessibility and anonymity, which are in constant tension with each other.

Which is why I'm super annoyed we had to burn a hideout in Marlborough, Massachusetts that we cased for the nonexistent Harvard Museum job. A good hideout the mercs, Cleaners, and Ham now know about.

I should charge them rent. Or a finder's fee—definitely a finder's fee.

Money discussions are turning themselves into their own little game we have to dance around. The Cleaners want to penny-pinch, but Ham thinks Nova is Interpol and backing everything. So all those discussions need to happen without Ham around.

All eight of us are back in the hideout, a furnished three-bedroom apartment above *The Slot*, a bar and gaming establishment in the middle of *The Triangle*—a mixed-use development of restaurants, bars, apartments, condos, businesses, and office space.

If that sounds like a mouthful, it's because it is and that's the point. It's Yuppie Disney Land. There are adults moving about at all hours of the day here. Puo hacked into the Triangle's rental agency's database of available apartments, found one we needed, grabbed the smart lock's punch code, and marked it as occupied and up to date on rent.

Hell, we did them a favor. No one wants to live above a noisy bar, even if the sound-proofing is everything it's advertised to be. By deleting this apartment from their database, we bumped up their ratio of apartments-rented-to-available—always a good metric for a rental company.

"Well?" Nova walks out from the master bedroom after taking a shower. The back collar of her emerald-green long-sleeved shirt is damp from her short brown hair.

It's almost two in the morning, but everyone is still amped up from the job we just pulled, and we're dead in the water until Izaak's squeegee is decoded.

Four days, two hours.

"Nothing yet," Winn answers, sitting next to me on a barstool at the kitchen counter overlooking the festivities in front of us.

Puo has taken over the dining area to the right of Winn and I, ensconcing himself, his computers, and his old-school monitors that Winn fetched for him on the table. He doesn't bother turning around from Izaak's squeegee to acknowledge us mere mortals.

Not to be outdone, the Cleaners have taken over the living room in front of us. Their area is much less impressive with organized cabling, exact-matching dual float screens per setup. It all looks very prim and proper—I much prefer Puo's slapdash style.

All three Cleaners stand around Izaak's squeegee near Puo. They're all wearing headband magnifiers with tweezers and bendy flashlights in hands, hunched over.

"What's the name for a group of toads again?" I ask Winn, watching them work.

"A knot."

"That won't do." I bring up a tablet Puo set up for me and start searching. "A prickle of Cleaners?"

Winn considers it. "Close, but not quite right."

Nova comes over. "What are you two doing?"

"What's the name for a group of Cleaners?" I ask, keeping my knee-jerk annoyance to myself. She's been all up in our business recently, but this time I think it's actually an innocent question.

"A clump of Cleaners?" she guesses.

I grin.

"Closer," Winn says.

"The Cleaners' Clomp?" I say smiling. "I kinda like that for a theme song."

"We can hear you, you know," Ham says in a small aggravated voice, not turning around.

Puo stands up from leaning over and kneads his back. "Herd," he says, continuing to focus on the squeegee in front of him. "It's a herd of Cleaners."

Only Mr. Chao doesn't react. Ham tightens and Lucy straightens up. "We are *not* a herd—" Lucy says.

"Found it," Puo cuts her off before she gets started.

They all lean down closer.

"It's on the underside of the RAM."

Mr. Chao locates it and shares a look with Lucy. Ham shifts between them to get a better look.

"How long have you been sitting on that?" Ham asks.

Puo shrugs. "I would've found it faster, now that I know what I'm looking for. But all the herd trampling was distracting."

"We are not a herd!" Lucy swirls around.

Puo wisely ignores her and sits down at his computer.

All three of them come to stand behind him. Lucy is tight, arms crossed, huffing and puffing, ready for a fight—can't take a little banter, that one. Some people can't—that's actually good information to have.

Winn and I stay put. There's not anything we could glean from scrolling gobbledygook anyway.

Several seconds pass with Puo banging away and then there's a flurry of activity.

The Cleaners lean in closer. Puo types faster. There're mutters of "Try this." Slamming a finger on the screen. Puo trying to restrain his annoyance and failing. Ham looks like he wants to kick everyone out and start driving himself.

Finally, Puo rests his forehead on the table.

My heart sinks. "What?"

"It's only one half of a key," Puo says.

"It's a dodecagon cipher with a two-part entry," Ham corrects.

"Or," Puo says, "it's one half of a key." He turns to face me and talks before Ham can correct him again. "The private key to the encryption is encoded in a twelve-part cipher. This squeegee has one part of the cipher, but you need at least one other one to be able to unlock the cipher."

It all clicks into place. "It's another measure of control," I say. "They can't look at the blockchain unless they look at it together." This also probably means there's twelve National Syndicate members.

Puo and Ham nod.

Puo says, "Any two parts combined will unlock the cipher."

*We need another squeegee. Fuck!*

My heartbeat thunders against my ears. My face flushes.

*Four days, two hours.*

Winn's voice breaks through my pounding heartbeat. "Christina's squeegee ...."

It's the lifeline I need, a problem I can solve. I latch onto it. Then a new thought hits me.

"That's why." I stiffen at the thought.

"Why what?" Winn asks.

Puo looks up at me, concern flitting across his face.

My mind and heart race so fast I don't have time to be annoyed that I spoke without realizing it.

They knew we had Christina's squeegee and they suspected we had Caesar's squeegee—which we stole from Ham who stole it from Caesar. Ham told us that on the train between New Dublin and Paris. They must have thought we had Caesar's cipher as well. But how?

"Ham," I say controlling my rising anger—if he already knew all this and didn't tell us .... "Did you steal Caesar's cipher?"

"What? No." Ham straightens up, his tight beady eyes looking between me and Puo's screens.

They're assuming we have Caesar's cipher, that's why they encrypted the breadcrumbs they left in Charlie's video. They thought we'd be able to decrypt it and follow it to wherever they wanted us to follow it to.

It's devious.

This two-part entry business also explains why they came after us full throttle once we had Christina's squeegee. It was only then that we posed a real threat to their machinations.

I stand up. "Ham—"

He backs up. "No. I never had it. I knew about it—not this dodecagon cipher business—but that it was encrypted and the key was likely in cold storage. But I never found it. I swear it."

His word is meaningless. He lies as easily as he breathes. But his reactions tell a more honest story. Ham may be competent in the digital arts, but not in misdirection and persuasion. He's easy to read, and the story fits in with the other pieces I know. Still, the National Syndicate must think we have it somehow. Or more likely, now that I'm thinking about it, they have to *assume* we have it. The cost of thinking otherwise and being wrong is too high.

I stare at Ham a second longer before sitting back down, and saying to Winn, "They knew we had Christina's squeegee. This key business is why they freaked out and came after us so hard." I keep the bit about Caesar's code and Charlie's video to myself—Ham still doesn't know we stole his code and I'm not sure what's hidden in Charlie's video yet.

Puo knows me well enough to know I'm not telling the whole truth but he doesn't press it.

Nova then asks the question I'm dreading, "What do we do?"

Christina's squeegee is mentioned again but I shut that down. "No. Too dangerous, too long to prep, too far away. There's not enough time."

"What other squeegee is there?" Ham asks. When nobody answers he continues, "We need to read the blockchain to know what the National Syndicate is up to. To read the blockchain we need a second cipher. To get a second cipher we need another National Syndicate squeegee."

The room is silent. The logic itself is flawless. Ham's face on the other hand, is royally pissing me off.

He doesn't give a shit. Charlie's timer means nothing to him. He has nothing to lose if the timer expires.

"If there's not enough time," he continues, "then we need to start prepping to recover Christina's squeegee."

"No," I bite off the word.

Another silence settles into the room. Mr. Chao and Lucy exchange looks. Puo and Winn look to me. The mercs watch us all like mildly observing animals at the zoo.

Ham looks around for help. For him, there is only one move. It doesn't matter if that move will result in people dead. What are those people to him, so long as it's not him? It's all there on his face, even if he's not stupid enough to say it.

When he doesn't find any allies, he sputters, "No? What do you mean, no?" Still, no one speaks. He continues, "Listen, sweetheart, sometimes hard decisions need to be made—"

Never mind—he was stupid enough to say it.

Puo moves before I do—all six foot, three hundred pounds of him.

He isn't quick. He doesn't rush Ham. He stands up slowly, deliberately and faces Ham. Puo towers over him, looms as he approaches, a gathering storm rushing into the center of power.

Puo owns the room. Even the people in the bar below us are probably holding their breath.

Ham backs up slowly, looking around wildly.

No one comes to his defense.

Puo backs Ham up to the back of a couch where he can't get away and Puo gets within a few inches of his face, looking down.

"Don't ever," he says with quiet intensity, "*ever*, suggest leaving Charlie to die. Don't *ever* equate her life—" he chokes up a bit. "—with a 'hard decision to be made.' We—*I*—will burn the entire system to the ground before we let her die."

"And if we're willing to do that—" I come stand next to Puo. Winn is right behind me. "—imagine what we will do to you."

Puo nods. "Are we clear?"

Ham looks between us, leaning back over the couch. He gulps. Sweats beads on his temples.

He nods.

Puo shakes his head. "Say it."

"We're clear," he croaks out.

"And don't ever refer to Isa as 'sweetheart' again," Puo adds for good measure. "Unless you really, *really*, want to get on our bad side."

He nods again.

Puo backs off.

Charlie took a chance on two street orphans and taught us a craft to get us off the street. She's the closest thing we have to a mother. But I wouldn't know, the woman that gave birth to me and left me when I was six would never be described as a mother. I'm given to understand that mothers engender strong positive feelings from their children. That woman who birthed me certainly doesn't qualify, but Charlie does. We could no more abandon Charlie than a young child could abandon a beloved parent.

Puo returns to his seat. The rest of us remain where we are.

A new, thin silence settles over us.

Ham's face pales. He's breathing heavy, but his dark, beady eyes look as malevolent as ever.

I shake my head at the absurdity of the random connections that have led me here.

Mr. Chao delicately breaks the gossamer silence with, "What are our options?"

No one answers. They all look to me.

Even Ham, except he can't keep the contempt from his face, whereas the others are genuinely hoping for an answer.

I hate that prick. If I had known stealing his code would've led us to crossing paths this much, I would've never done it. It wasn't even his code. He stole it from—

There's the answer, lying right in front of me the whole time.

To the group, I say, "There's another National Syndicate member we know of."

"Who?" Ham asks, not able to help himself.

Puo and I look at each other in understanding. He nods.

It's the only play left.

We both look at Ham.

Ham looks between us. Understanding dawns on his face and his eyes grow round. "No." He shakes his head. "No. There's no way. They'll see me coming a mile away."

I nod. "I'm counting on it."

# Chapter Nine

Ham, of course, did not immediately acquiesce to my brilliant scheming and it was late before we were all on the same page. In the end, Nova shoved her imaginary Interpol authority down Ham's throat to get him to shut up and help pack.

We arrived on the outskirts of Albany, New York an hour ago. The morning sky begins to lighten outside my window.

We're holed up in an abandoned hospital in a deserted part of an outskirt town. As far as hideouts go, it's a decent option on short notice. Lucky even. Abandoned buildings are good short-term solutions, but finding one with beds in it is harder. Usually, it's some kind of abandoned factory which leaves you scrounging for mattresses or sleeping on a hard floor. Even luckier that the building is empty as far as we can tell—no squatters, which isn't surprising given it's in the middle of a suburban wasteland. Squatters depend on a certain population level to be able to live off their dregs—something I'm too intimately aware of.

I'm pacing back and forth between dirty, fogged windows in a run-down patient room. Dust and debris crunch underfoot. Yellowing cracked paint peels off the upper half of the walls. The lower half is a grubby teal-colored tile with rain streaks running to the ground. The room smells of decay and moldy disinfectant under the cold winter air.

It's better than being outside, at least.

I'm in that weird space of exhaustion ready to waylay me the second I close my eyes, but my mind won't shut off. I can't bring myself to lie down.

Three days, twenty-two hours.

There's too much to do and nothing to do *right now*. It's a terrible combination. The right thing to do is get some sleep, but while my body is willing, my mind isn't.

Puo and Mr. Chao are already sleeping. Nova, Aliyah, and Lucy are all off with useful things to do: line up supplies for the night ahead, procure food, basic necessities, et cetera.

Not me though. A lot of hurry up and wait. But then, when it's finally my turn—*bam*, shit moves fast. I like that part. The waiting part, not so much. In fact, the waiting is getting harder and harder.

It's the jackknives that screw me. They're always there now, lurking in the background, waiting to unfurl and scrape a layer off the inside of my stomach, sending my heart into overdrive. I can't shut my brain off anymore; it always latches onto something. Currently, it's that we've never before relied so much on others. Can't eat either. No appetite—everything turns to ash in my mouth.

I don't like it.

There's a light knock on my door.

It's Winn. He stands there in the same dark chinos as before and an eggshell-colored half-zip sweater with the collar up. He's watching me, concern in his eyes. "Can I come in?"

I nod.

He closes the door behind him. The rusty hinges screech in the silence and he comes to stand across from me. "Can't sleep?"

"No," I say quietly, then add, "Exhaustion will come at some point."

He doesn't state the obvious—it would be a whole lot better to sleep now so that exhaustion doesn't hit at an inopportune time. He just studies me, like he's trying to decide something.

"What?" I ask. My pulse quickens at the sudden thought that he wants to talk about us now. I—I just don't have the bandwidth for that right now.

He comes to his decision, takes out a little brown circular pill, and holds it out to me. "This will help. It'll calm your mind, help you sleep."

I look into his blue eyes. He's worried, torn.

"What's the pill?"

Winn takes a deep breath. "I'm not going to tell you. You're going to have to trust me."

"What?" My eyebrows rise at that.

"These are serious meds. Habit forming—"

"You think I'll turn into a junky?"

"I think it's better to mitigate that risk as much as possible."

"I'm not a junky, nor do I have an addictive—"

"You're an adrenaline junky, but that's beside the point. These can form a physical dependence scary fast. You're having acute panic attacks brought on by external stressors. Completely understandable under the circumstances. We need to get through this period and then your body is going to need some time to reset. It's a balancing act now and a delicate one. Treat the symptoms to get through the rough period, but don't form a dependence, with withdrawal later at best and addiction at worst. It's better if I control the meds to remove temptation and if you don't know the name so you can't procure it yourself."

"So, you're my drug dealer?" It wouldn't be hard to learn the med's name, but I leave that unsaid.

"Yeah." His hand is still out.

I've never been interested in drugs. I've seen firsthand what can come of that life. Puo and I even keep each other's alcohol in check. When you live on the streets, you see the bottom of the barrel, how a person loses everything and, even more horrifying, how they lose all sense of control and self-destiny—they lose all hope.

I study the little brown pill in Winn's hand. What will it do? Will I like it too much? Will it work at all? Will I finally be able to sleep through the night?

Three days, twenty-two hours.

We still have to get Caesar's squeegee, decode the private blockchain, use it to follow it to Charlie. Then we need to put a fix in place with the National Syndicate to make sure they leave us alone forever.

Three days, twenty-two hours. I take an unsteady breath. My heart claws against my ribcage. My face flushes. *Oh, God.*

The jackknives dance.

I pop the pill in my mouth with an unsteady hand. I have my own personal doctor to monitor me, after all, or so I tell myself.

"Now what? How long does it take to work?" I cross my arms to stop my hands from shaking. It's there, on the periphery, lurking—a full blown panic attack.

"Fifteen, twenty minutes. I could give you some BS about having to stay here and monitor you for medical reasons, but the truth is, I'd like to stay just because I want to be near you. Is that okay?"

I nod, not entirely listening. I don't want to be alone. I inhale and exhale through my nose, feel it deep within my chest. Push the darkness back.

"When did you get it?" I ask about the pill.

"When we were in Lyon, while I was out getting clothes."

"You don't speak French, or have a license in France." The thought pulls me out of my head, gives me a problem to solve.

"There are other ways to get things. Something I learned when I was working for Paranoid Pete."

Press-ganged more like it. It's how we met. He was patching up thugs for Paranoid Pete and I saw him on a trip to Pete's. At first, I was only interested in a fling, and then we needed a third for a job. Now, we're here.

The memory pushes the darkness back even further. Look at us. We have a history. I never would've thought it possible at the time. It's nice to have him close.

"How'd you know I'd need it?" I ask.

"I'm a doctor," he says, puffing up.

"Puo told you?"

"Puo told me."

*Freaking Puo.*

"But I noticed something was up Christmas morning and asked him. I've never known you to wake before dawn. Or bake."

Yeah, mornings have sucked lately. My favorite time has turned into the worst. They start way too early since I can't sleep and then there's nothing to do but stew, wait, and try not to let the thoughts spiral out of control.

I shrug. "Turns out I like baking. It's predictable." I let out a large, unexpected yawn.

Winn checks his tablet. "You should lie down."

I look at the dilapidated hospital bed, a thin striped single mattress. No sheets. No pillows. Questionable stains.

I've slept on worse.

Winn hands me a thin blanket scrounged from somewhere, and I go over to the bed to lie down in my clothes—it's too cold and gross for anything else.

"Come on," I say, "you have to keep an eye on me, right?"

Winn looks at the single mattress, obviously figuring out how it's going to work.

"You have to keep me warm," I say.

We climb in together, fully clothed, and spread the blanket over us. Winn puts his arm around me and I snuggle my back into him.

He's warm. His woody scent is familiar, comforting.

We lie there together, not saying anything, enjoying each other's presence.

I feel the meds the second they hit my bloodstream. It's like someone used a dimmer switch on a harsh, bright white light in my mind to a warm soft yellow pleasant glow.

*Whoa*, is all I can think. It's the first time in weeks I have had some space in my head.

I snuggle closer to Winn, breath in his scent. Exhaustion overtakes me.

# Chapter Ten

THE BOAT ENGINES' steady thrum eases to a low whine as the motor yacht slows its approach.

It's nearing midnight of the same day we bivouacked in the abandoned hospital. Another half day wasted, simply waiting for the sun to set.

*Three days, five hours.*

Time keeps slipping away.

The jackknives stir, but I breathe and keep my focus grounded in my body.

"Do we—?" Ham starts to whisper.

I hit him on the leg to shut him up—probably harder than I should've, but it's nice to have a temporary outlet for the jackknives. Not that the noise matters with the party continuing to rage above us, but it's the principle of the thing.

We're lying next to each other, hidden below decks in a crawlspace used to access the motor shaft. It was the best way to get us both into the festivities—the locally famous underground Albany boat races. I could've passed for a party girl. Ham—not so much.

The boat races are the post-ocean-rearranging-itself equivalent of the street races of yore. Late night secret locations. Tricked out boats. Partying. Gambling.

And wherever there's gambling, there's a Boss to be found. Except this Boss, Hazel Phelan, is under the National Syndicate's thumb.

That's what this boat race is tonight, a show of a return to normalcy. The first since the Cleaners made their move. *See everyone? Everything's back to normal. No need to worry about that little coup.*

It's a pretty smart play. The more that people are making money and their lives continue pretty much unchanged, the less they'll care about what's going on at the top.

The boat races were always the most public intersection of the Cleaners' and Bosses' worlds, which is what makes it such a smart play. The Boss provided physical security, a clearing house for gambling, and a public stamp of approval for the winner, while the Cleaners provided digital security and cleaning the authorities' surveillance feeds of the race and party boats. If the races are back on, it means those two worlds are back in alignment—or at least, that's what it's meant to signal.

The smell of motor grease and salt water isn't enough to overcome Ham's stress sweat in the small space. Wafts of wet cheese assault my olfactory sense, but not enough for me to become habituated.

The engines pick up again for a few minutes before the boat slows for a final time and the engines cut. The loud splash can only be the anchor.

We've arrived.

"The race hasn't started yet," Puo whispers in my ear through a comm-link hidden from Ham. There's an undercurrent of uncertainty to Puo's statement.

This is the crux of our problem: when to start our shenanigans.

Caesar personally oversees the cleaning of the boat races which has to be done on site. This means Caesar will be here somewhere—the real debate is *when*.

Ham insists Caesar leaves it to lackeys and only makes a causal appearance to check on the work—he likes the parties more.

But Ham doesn't really know. According to Ham, he was never junior enough to be ordered around like that, but more likely Caesar didn't trust the oily snake.

"There're four race boats I can see," Winn whispers on the comm-link. "They don't seem to be forming up yet."

Winn is our eyes and ears. He's on the New Scotland Finger with a pair of auto-binoculars watching the starting point near where Stingerlands Bypass sinks into the sea. Cleaners can't clean good old-fashioned eyeballs—which tells me the authorities must already know about the races and Phelan has a fix in place. The Cleaners are really here for plausible deniability and to make sure no images end up in the news feeds for the public and politicians to get all riled up about.

Puo, with our own copy of the Cleaners' code, probably could've bypassed their efforts to keep an eye on things digitally, but we don't want to take a chance on revealing ourselves. They'll be looking for snoopers, particularly news crews.

All we know at this point in time is the race has yet to begin, party boats are gathering, and the Cleaners are already cleaning the feed. Now, whether it's Caesar doing the cleaning or lackeys, we don't know.

It's a pretty safe bet Caesar is either already on site or will be shortly.

I tap Ham again. "Start."

"You sure about this?" he asks.

"A little late to be backing out now."

"And you have a way out?"

"We're going to stroll right off. Trust me."

"Both of us?" he demands.

"Yes, both—"

"And I don't trust you," he rushes over me.

*I don't trust you either,* I think.

Ham continues, "Or do I need to remind you of our past history. Stealing. Kidnapping. Drugging. Snitching—"

"Snitching!" I hiss and look over at him in the dark. "You would probably be dead if it weren't for us. Your kidnapping prevented you from being arrested, where the Cleaners would've finished the job. Your drugging made sure no one would find you—"

"Until you led Interpol straight to me."

"With an agreement they'll alter our images and leave us alone when we're done."

"When they say we're done." When I don't respond right away, he says more quietly, "There's something not right about those Interpol agents. Or the Greensboro crew," he says that last statement more to himself.

I look over at him out of habit but can't see anything in the dark. *Is he getting wise to the game we're pulling on him?*

He mutters to himself, "Yokels," but doesn't expand.

I'm about to ask him to explain what he means, when Winn breaks in, "They're lining up."

*Damn it.* "Ham," I whisper. "Start."

The urgency in my voice must snap Ham out of his reverie, since the blue-light glow of the squeegee—the same one we gave him in the tunnels under the Irish Sea, the one from the marina with the tracker in it—illuminates his round perspiring face as he works the controls.

Now the question is, how long will it take them to find us?

# Chapter Eleven

NOT LONG AT all, apparently.

Less than five minutes later the cover to our hidey hole is ripped off and two angry guys point guns at us.

Ham shouts, "Don't shoot! Parley! I want to parley!" at the same time they're shouting, "Hands! Let me see your hands!"

I oblige and hold my hands out in front of me.

"Ham," I say, out of the corner of my mouth, "Shut. Up."

These two are definitely not Cleaners. They have the build of enforcers and, more distinctly, they're carrying guns. It's not that Cleaners can't be muscly or carry guns, but it's rare. So to have two of them on the same boat as us is near impossible.

The Cleaners must have called ahead.

"Get out," the one closest to me says, motioning with his gun.

I hate guns. And I really hate having them pointed at me.

I do what he says.

Music rumbles down from the party still going on upstairs. The two enforcers are in suits, no ties. One is a bald, olive-skinned man, while the other is a white frat boy on roids.

Ham gets out next.

The four of us are alone in the small maintenance tunnel.

Ham starts to speak again, but I shut him up.

"Stay where you are," Baldy says while getting out his tablet.

Roids keeps his gun trained on us.

Baldy's tablet gives the telltale *beep-beep-beep* of a video call followed quickly by someone picking up.

Ham winces at the sound of the other voice.

"We found two stowaways," Baldy says to the tablet.

"Let me see them," the tablet says.

Baldy flips the tablet around and there's Caesar's Hispanic face with puffy cheeks and dark brown eyes staring back at us.

*Shit. We need to meet him in person.*

Before I can think of how to make that happen, Ham starts blubbering, "Caesar! I can explain—!"

"Kill them," Caesar orders upon recognizing Ham.

"Wait!" Ham and I shout.

Roids looks to Baldy who shakes his head no and Roids doesn't pull the trigger.

"Kill them!" Caesar screams, flecks of spit flying.

Baldy flips the screen around. "With all due respect ... sir, we don't take kill orders from you." Baldy's voice and words may be respectful, but his eyes certainly aren't.

I'd burst out laughing if Roids didn't have a gun trained on me.

A turf war. A turf war is going to save my ass.

Phelan may be under the National Syndicate's thumb, but they're still trying to sort out the boundaries and exert independence.

There's a stony silence, and I don't need to see Caesar's face to know the look he's giving Baldy. "Very well," Caesar says, pronouncing each word as if, if he weren't careful, they'd fly out and attack Baldy right there. "I will have Phelan contact you with the order and clarify the chain of command."

"Yes, sir," Baldy says as if Caesar had just asked him if he thought the local team would win the game tonight.

I open my mouth to catch Caesar before he connects with Phelan, but Ham beats me again. "Parley!" he shouts. "Parley! I want to parley!"

I roll my eyes and resist the urge to hit the goober, but to my surprise, Caesar commands Baldy to turn the tablet around.

*Whatever works.*

It's a short-lived thought as Caesar lays into Ham. "Parley? What the fuck do you mean *parley*—?"

"I have something to offer—"

"This isn't a movie, jackass! Parley—" He rolls his eyes. "—I told you what would happen if I ever saw you again."

I try again to get a word in edgewise, but Ham bowls over me. "I know where the rest of her team is!"

"You son of a bitch!" I deck him.

He goes down like the little bitch he is.

Roids and Baldy scream to stop.

I jump on Ham and pummel him. "You asshole! You called them here on purpose!"

"Get off me!" he shouts through his arms over his head.

Roids's gun pushes against the back of my head. "Stop."

The jackknives unleash at full force and time slows down. Adrenaline primes every muscle in my body to fight. My thoughts stretch out into branching possibilities.

I see all the possible end games, and it's in that moment with a gun pressed into my skull I know we've succeeded. They haven't killed us. Caesar is quiet, contemplating. They've bought in.

That's the first time the jackknives have ever been *helpful.* They can be helpful. That realization is empowering.

The best play is to comply, so that's what I do. I stand slowly, keeping my hands up, but never taking my disgusted eyes from Ham.

"Where are they?" Caesar asks Ham once the commotion is over.

Ham picks himself up and feels his face for blood.

"Where?" Caesar presses.

Ham furtively looks between the goons and the tablet. He then gives a small nervous headshake no.

Caesar raises his eyebrows, readies another fusillade.

Ham speaks before the storm, "Parley in person."

"There's no fucking parley! Stop saying that! This is not a negotiation—!"

"Yes, it is," Ham says in small voice. Caesar is too stunned to respond and Ham says more forcefully, "I have what you need. You also want me dead. There's nothing to stop you from killing me once I give you what you need. I want to negotiate in person, in front of the court."

Caesar leans back at the mention of "court."

That's the key. Court is the fancy way of saying in public, in front of all the other Cleaners. If Caesar publicly agrees not to kill Ham in exchange for the location of Puo and Winn, then killing Ham becomes a whole lot harder. Not impossible, but there are steep, intangible costs to breaking your word that way.

Caesar doesn't respond for several breaths. He just stares at Ham, weighing him, studying. If he were a cartoon villain, he'd be twirling his mustache.

"Fine," Caesar bites off. "I'll send a boat for you. The other two will standby to kill the thief."

"No—" Ham says.

I look at Ham in surprise at the same time Caesar says, "She's too dangerous to be left alive."

"You'll need her to flush out the other two. They'll want proof she's alive."

"I thought you knew where they were."

"I do—it's complicated. I'm not saying don't kill her. I'm saying don't kill her *yet*."

Roids still has his gun trained on me, but I take the opportunity to start to kick Ham in the balls when a gunshot explodes in the narrow hallway.

I drop and whirl toward Roids. My heart hammers. My ears ring. I can't feel anything.

Roids yells something. My ears don't understand it, but my eyes recognize the words past the gun in his hand. "Don't move!"

No blood. No pain. Ham is still standing, looking as stunned as I am.

A warning shot.

"Don't move," Roids says thickly.

"Please move," Caesar taunts. I can hear the smile on his face.

I, again, comply. It's harder not to move this time. There's too much adrenaline. The jackknives are fully awake with nowhere to go.

"Fine," Caesar says after we all continue to stare at each other. "Bring them both. Search them first."

I keep the smile off my face.

\*\*\*

Any urge to keep smiling was wiped away as the small boat carrying Ham and I skipped over the winter waves toward a large, fully enclosed trimaran yacht.

The thing looks like it's out of an old Bond movie. The center hull resembles a speed boat on growth hormones with two smaller, stabilizing hulls flanking it. Two angled vertical stabilizers rise from the back. It reminds me of a pit bull—all muscle and built for one thing. In this case: speed.

If things went south during a boat race, no authorities would ever catch this thing—at least not on the water.

The thing kept growing as we neared. I was afraid the back would simply open up and swallow us, boat and all, as we approached. But it wasn't that big and we were soon escorted on, the icy wind slicing through my thin gray buttoned sweater, and shuffled inside.

The Cleaners sent their own people and now four of them escort us *down* into the boat.

*Down? What the hell?*

But down we go. Two in front of Ham and I and the other two bringing up the rear. The main hull extends below the water line farther than I would've expected. A hydrofoil?

But no. The truth becomes apparent when we come to a ladder: a submarine. This freaking thing has a submarine attached to its underside.

I want to turn to Ham and ask him if he knew about this, but that would ruin the act that successfully landed us here.

The ladder is cold metal with a clear gap where the hatch to the submarine would close. The thin metal bars dig into my palms. All I can think is: *this is going to suck.*

The ladder lets down in the middle of a narrow hallway. More Cleaners wait on both sides of the ladder to escort us. At least, I assume they're Cleaners. They all have a build that could go either way.

The air is surprisingly warm and there's a weird smell almost like diesel.

Ham and I are ushered down the narrow hallway toward the front of the submarine.

I trip Ham in front of me.

I'm grabbed and thrown up against a wall before I can enjoy my handiwork. I push back against the Cleaner-brute, but not that hard—I don't actually want to escape. If that were the case, I would've done it before going down the ladder.

"What the fuck?" Ham groans on the ground. He picks himself up and stares daggers at me, red in the face more from embarrassment than anything.

Cleaner-brute shoves me in front of him. Ham trails behind still nursing his injuries.

It's a short walk. The hallway ends at a small stairway leading down into an expansive room. Well, expansive for a submarine.

It's the size of a typical living room, maybe a little bigger, with ten-to-twelve-foot ceilings. The walls are a thick glass, which show nothing in the dark. It's nothing like the museum military sub we used for delivering Colvin's tribute five months ago.

Five months ago. *Has it really only been five months?*

The jackknives swim in a different direction.

I flush. Prickles ripple down my neck.

*Not now.* I breathe deep into my chest.

*Three days, five hours.*

Fuck. Not a helpful thought. Where's that empowering bullshit of the jackknives being helpful from earlier? Maybe it'd help if they fire another gun?

Caesar is holding court at the front of the room, sitting in a tan leather Eames lounge chair. He's wearing gray slacks and a maroon buttoned shirt with a sheen to it. He sits forward at our arrival and moves some float screens in front of him to the side.

The teakwood covered area holds eight others. Five of them stand around Caesar, the other three crowd around a loveseat to the side tapping on several float screens. I catch a visual on one of them as we walk by of the room we're in—they're scanning us.

They all turn to stare as we enter.

I keep my pupils focused on Caesar, but in reality, I'm drinking in everything in my periphery.

It's not hard to read. This is a custom, luxury setup. If the teakwood and exorbitant space didn't give it away, the windows do. Windows on a freaking submarine—only a rich idiot would insist on that. This thing must not be made to go to any real depth.

Real submarines are jam-packed full of stuff; two people can't pass easily in a hallway. They try to fit as much gear and stuff as they possibly can into every nook and cranny to survive at depth and complete their mission.

But if the mission is providing a bunch of fluffy dick unicorns a route to safety, then you don't need to be submerged long, or need a lot of gear to run away. You do need a chic set up to pamper the underwear sniffers though.

Come to think of it, I wonder if this sub is even operational or just a cool clubhouse for Caesar to show off in.

They march us up to Caesar and his coterie framed by a dark window behind them.

One of our escorts, a Middle Eastern male with a wispy beard and a solid build steps forward and hands Caesar a cloth bag. "Two squeegees, one tablet, and one comm-link."

"Two squeegees?" Caesar nods an acknowledgment to the group that scanned us and then rifles through the bags.

"Yes. The woman had one on her as well."

Normally, I'd be offended at the use of "woman" here, but considering they could've gone with a lot of other terms, it's downright cordial.

Caesar brings out both squeegees. His eyes narrow on the one that had been hidden on me. He boots it up and starts flipping through it.

"What is this?" he asks with an easy amusement.

Ham opens his mouth to answer, but I take the opportunity to reach out and flick him in the throat.

Ham swats me away.

I push him to create a scuffle.

Wispy Beard separates us.

"I'll tell you what this is," Caesar says to his coterie once our scuffle is sorted out. "It's a poor imitation is what it is." He then reaches around in the chair and brings out his squeegee. They're the exact same block shape, and should have close to the exact same software. Puo transferred the mirrored software we stole from Ham (who stole it from Caesar), as well as the latest private blockchain updates from Izaak's squeegee, onto the other marina squeegee Winn retrieved from our Seattle Isles home as a decoy squeegee. The only problem is Caesar's is an olive-green color, while the extra marina squeegee is a forest green.

"You think I wouldn't notice?" he asks.

I make sure to keep my shoulders square on him and smile. "I needed to make sure they brought me right to you."

His amusement evaporates and flicks his glance over to the group's scrolling float screens before looking back at me.

We lock eyes.

"You are going to tell me where Charlie is," I say, "and release her. Now."

"Or what?" he asks heavily.

"Or, Izaak Mitchell never joins another one of your circle jerks again."

Caesar's lip twitches. His coterie exchange glances. He's pissed. They're worried.

Caesar gives me a knowing look. "You're not a killer."

He's right. I'm not. We're not. But they don't know that. They may think they know. But they don't.

"You shot—" my voice breaks as rage swells to the surface. "—you *shot* my father on camera." *Jesus*. It all comes back. His brown eyes staring at the camera. His ... his execution.

I can't breathe all over again. Sweat breaks across my skin. I'm hot. My pulse drowns out any sound. *Oh, God.*

It's these fuckers. This fucker in front of me. He's one of the ones who did this.

Wispy Beard grabs my arm to hold me back. "Don't tell me what I'm capable of anymore." Hot rage spills out of me. "*You* opened Pandora's box, not me! So if you want to bet Izaak's life on old data when everybody played by the rules, then be my guest. But you gotta ask yourself, dickwad, how are your National Syndicate friends going to feel about you leaving one of their own to die?"

He gives a sharp look at Ham at the mention of the National Syndicate.

Caesar regards me for a hot second and then nods to Wispy Beard who pulls out a gun and presses it to my temple.

"Not going to do it yourself?" I taunt. Caesar doesn't carry a gun. None of the upper-level Cleaners do. It's beneath them to get their hands dirty. A crude show of power. That's what lackeys are for.

"*You* are going to tell *me* where Izaak is. Now," he says with a small smirk.

I stare at him in silence, letting him dig himself deeper.

He gestures at me carelessly and says, "There's nothing to say you weren't killed *before* you gave me this information. So, either I kill you now, like I originally wanted to, or you tell me where Izaak is."

I nod at the hangers-on. "You're so sure every one of them is loyal?"

"Yes," he answers with no hesitation. "Except for that one." He indicates Ham with a nod. "He'll be dealt with."

Wispy Beard pushes the gun harder against my temple when I let the silence hang, hoping Caesar keeps digging himself deeper.

"I'm not going to ask again," Caesar says.

"First," I say, "get that poor excuse of a penis substitute away from me." The gun doesn't move. "Second," I say in my best announcer voice, "smile, you're on Candid Camera!"

Caesar's forehead scrunches up in confusion.

No one appreciates the classics anymore.

"You're on camera," I explain, all the fun sucked out of the reveal. I point to the camera embedded in my top sweater button. "Say hello to all your National Syndicate friends."

Caesar rocks back and looks over to study his float screens. He then looks between the screens and the other Cleaners. They all shake their heads at him.

"You have a camera on your shirt that's recording us, livestreaming?" Caesar asks.

"Yes."

"That little button, right there?"

"Yes."

"I ... see."

The other Cleaners snicker.

"And perhaps," he mocks, "the button above it is a boom microphone?"

The snickering spills over into stifled laughter.

When I don't answer, he continues, "Tell me, do you hear your own theme music everywhere you go?"

I think of the German techno music over the North Sea last month—maybe I do have my own theme music. Doesn't everybody? "You're—" I start when Caesar cuts me off.

"Listen, I'm sure your secret video is very powerful—" More snickers. "—very powerful, but here in the real world we searched you—" He drops the fake replica of his squeegee into the cloth bag of our electronics. "—and there are no signals leaving this boat we are not aware of. There are no signals coming off of *you*. So—"

I open my mouth to set this triple nipple straight when he interrupts me again.

"Ugh!" I yell over him. "Puo, introduce yourself to these piss guzzlers!"

There's a brief pause where nothing happens before the Cleaners break into a beehive of chittering and activity on their float screens.

Mutters of, "That's not possible," and "How?" are sprinkled in among the mix of looking between me and their float screens.

I have no idea how Puo announced himself. But he definitely has their attention now.

Caesar sits there, mouth ajar, still holding the cloth bag of our electronics forgotten in his hand.

That fake replica squeegee is pulling triple duty tonight. It was kind of Caesar to power it on without even being asked so it could pick up the low powered signal from my camera I activated in the scuffle with Ham. The Cleaners wouldn't question signals originating from Caesar himself, now would they? It is his own software, after all.

"Here is how this is going to work," I say. "You are going to release Charlie. Once Charlie is safe to my satisfaction, I will tell you where Izaak is."

Caesar is quiet for several seconds. His dark eyes dissect me, dissect the situation.

"No," he says.

"No?" I stare at him.

"No." He shakes his head. "One, I don't believe you. Two, I can't simply order your friend's release—that's a group vote."

"Puo—" I start to say when Caesar waves me quiet.

"Oh, I believe your friend is in our system somehow. Not that you're livestreaming." He sets the cloth bag down beside him and waves over for his tablet. He points the tablet at me once he has it. "No concerned calls from my friends."

I smile, thinking quickly, recalling what we've said to this point. "I never said we were livestreaming. I said we were recording. More powerful a negotiating position, you see," I lie my ass off. Livestreaming or carrying through on my threats would require us to know who the other members actually are—which we don't.

Caesar shakes his head and snorts to himself. "No."

"And you want to take that risk?" I ask. "You have an opportunity to save your circle-jerking friend, but you'd rather leave him to die?"

Ham raises his hand tentatively like he's uncertain of an answer in class.

"Yes, Ham," Caesar calls on him.

"I know where Izaak is."

The guy holding the gun to my head holsters it quickly and restrains me from launching myself at that asshole.

"You gravy-faced corpse fucker! Shut the fuck—" I'm wrestled to the ground and something is shoved over my mouth. I continue to scream into the gag.

My head is smashed up against the teak deck, turned toward a smiling Caesar. He rises and comes to stand before Ham.

Ham says, "I want assurances in front of the other National Syndicate members that I will not be touched, that I'll will be left alone. I want it put to a vote. Pardoned for providing this information." Ham studiously keeps from looking at me.

That puss-filled meat bag took long enough. I was wondering when he would get around to selling us out, although I actually liked the way things were going. We may have actually gotten Charlie's location.

The betrayal on the first party boat that brought us here was planned. This—this is pure back-stabbing opportunistic Ham. We knew it'd be coming—it's not our first time working with the moldy ass cheese.

Caesar nods to himself. "We can do that." He snaps his fingers for his tablet, left back on his throne. He comes over to me and squats down. "So, this was your big plan. Extortion?"

I stare razor blades at him.

"She said you would just let us go," Ham supplies, his voice more confident. "Stroll right off."

Revulsion is too mild a word for Ham. He's loyal to no one, flips whenever it's convenient.

Caesar's eyebrows rise. "Stroll right off? Well, that's not an option anymore, now is it? So, how are you going to get away now?"

I muffle a response through the gag.

He looks at me in amusement and then starts to get his fellow mouth-breathing wall-lickers on group chat. He does not order them to take the gag out. Which is a damn shame, because I had an amazing return.

*So, how are you going to get away now?*

*I'm a good swimmer.* It would've been perfect, scared the shit out of them. Oh, well.

Several hundred-pound rocks slam through the trimaran yacht and down into the sub underbelly before Caesar can get anyone on group chat.

# Chapter Twelve

OLD TRICKS ARE the best tricks. Well, more like old tricks we know will work are better than trying to think up new shit.

The point is: sink Caesar's boat. Dropping rocks is a whole lot easier to pull off than something cleverer or done from under the water.

*Boom! Boom!* The sub shutters violently. Metal wrenches and screeches throughout the cabin.

*Boom!* Another one slams right on top of us. The windows crack. Thin waterspouts launch into the cabin.

Cold water starts trickling in from the stairway behind.

This is the part that's going to suck.

Wispy Beard tumbles off of me in the commotion. I spit the gag out. "Break the windows if you want to live!"

Ham looks around in wide-eyed terror. "What have you done?"

Caesar yells at the same time, "Kill her!"

I'm a half second ahead of everyone and kick Wispy Beard in the face.

Ham runs with the stampede toward the narrow hallway— poor choice.

Wispy Beard's head snaps back and I'm up and running toward Caesar's throne, which is thankfully, not bolted to the deck. I barely pick it up—that shit is heavy—and throw it at the window.

It bounces off and clatters to the floor.

*Um, shit.*

I rifle through the cloth bag of confiscated electronics Caesar left on the floor by his throne and slip in my comm-link.

"Chameleon, you read me?" There's no need for code names on this one, but old habits die hard.

"Yeah, I got ya— Wait, why do I have you?"

"The stones did half their job. We're sinking, but— Fuck!"

Wispy Beard has turned around, gun out and pointed at me as he too tries to push his way out.

I dive behind the overturned throne.

*Crack! Crack! Crack!*

Two bullets whiz past and *ping* against metal. The throne jumps from the third shot.

"Don't fire blindly!" Caesar screams as he pushes his coterie out of the way to the exit.

"Was that gunshots?" Puo asks in alarm.

"Yes, that was gunshots! We're in a sub attached to the bottom of the yacht. It's sinking! No easy way out!"

Puo's silent for a panicked second. "What are you going to do?"

"What am I going to do! Did you just ask me what the fuck am I going to do?"

"Yeah—"

"I'm calling you for help! That's what I'm doing!" I peek around the corner. At least Wispy Beard has stopped shooting and appears to be hurrying out, glancing back every so often.

"That's not good."

"Arrgh!" I scream in supreme frustration. "Ideas, Chameleon! I need ideas!" Stupid sub, complicating an otherwise brilliant scheme.

"How deep is it here?" I ask.

Puo bangs on his keyboard. "Sixty feet. You thinking of waiting it out? Dicey. Squiddies are swarming in the area from all the commotion."

"I know it's fucking dicey! I don't have any other options."

"Are you in an air pocket?"

"Yes." Relief floods me now that Puo has got his ass in gear and is thinking. "But water is leaking in through the hallway and through several small cracks in the windows."

"Windows? Break one of them and swim out."

"I already tried! I wasn't strong enough!"

"Try again. Right on the crack as hard as you can," he explains as if I were learning to tie my shoes.

"Are you serious with this!"

"Yeah. In fact, why haven't you already done this?"

I'd pull my hair out if I wasn't cowering behind a tipped-over chair. "They were shooting at me!"

There's a beat on the comm-link when we both realize it.

"Get the gun!" Puo shouts.

"Duh!"

I glance back around. Wispy Beard is at the back of the rapidly diminishing crowd. He keeps looking over his shoulder, but it's clear from his pale face his priority is escaping.

The small stream of water pouring down the hallway turns into a rapid river feeding the ankle-deep pool sloshing around the cabin bottom.

I peek around the chair.

No time like the present. I rifle through the discarded bag with our electronics and fish out Ham's squeegee, and then run toward the back of Wispy Beard with the bag.

He hears me and whirls, bringing his gun up but not before I throw the squeegee brick and hit him in the face.

*Crack!* The bullet pings off the metal ceiling and Ham's squeegee falls into the rising icy water.

"Careful!" I yell in my best deep-throated Caesar impression.

It'd actually kill two birds with one stone if he shot a window, but I rather he didn't while I'm between the bullet and window.

He recovers quickly.

I'm four paces away and kick a bunch of near-freezing water to blind him.

He raises his hands to protect his face and I drop kick him.

I twist and catch myself on my hands and knees—*Holy God, it's freezing!* I land near Ham's thrown squeegee and scoop it back up into the cloth bag.

He flies back into the last two people trying to get out, slamming them up against the door frame. They both take one look back at me charging Wispy Beard and scuffle with each other to get out the door.

Icy water pours over Wispy Beard. His mouth opens in a permanent "o." He raises his gun, shivering, but the icy water costs him—he's too slow.

I kick the inside of his wrist and the gun plops down into the water.

The sub gives a horrible *screech* and the rapid river turns into a torrent.

Icy water drenches me and now I have to fight the same hypothermia-avoiding reflexes as he did. It's impossible to catch my breath.

Wispy Beard's dark eyes are terrified.

The stream of water entering the large room is too strong and too cold to fight our way out.

Instead of going for the gun, I stutter over the roar, "I ... I can save ... save us both!"

He looks at me. There's none of the killer in there from before, none of the us-versus-them. Only pure consideration, *can this beautiful, amazing chick, do what she says she can?* "How?"

"The gun! Quickly!"

He hesitates.

"We're both dead in five minutes anyway! Hurry!"

That snaps him out of any doubt and he fishes the gun out from under the water.

The icy water is up to my thighs. Each new inch brings stabbing pain, while another inch below goes numb.

"Now what?" he asks, holding the gun.

"Give it to me!"

Again, he hesitates. We both may be dead in five minutes, but I will very likely be dead in fifteen if we escape and he holds onto that gun.

I look at him like, *What do you want to do here?*

He hands the gun over.

I take a couple steps away and turn it on the largest window across from me and fire.

Nothing happens.

Wispy Beard moves toward me. *That asshole!* He put the safety on to flush out what I was going to do, or to protect himself, or some other dumbass reason.

I swing the drenched bag of electronics at him with one hand while flipping the safety off and firing as many times as I can with the other. The window shatters on the second shot but I keep firing anyway—less bullets to kill me with later.

Wispy Beard smashes into me as the water surges in. I throw the gun away and fight the urge to gasp for air as we tumble under the water. I keep a tight grasp on the cloth bag holding the two squeegees.

The submarine gives a violent jolt downward followed by distant crowd screams.

I easily fight off Wispy Beard—a combination of experience and freezing water.

I come up gasping for air, steady my breath as best I can, thread the cloth bag's drawstring around my shoulders like a backpack, take a deep breath and plunge back under, swimming like mad for the shattered window.

Wispy Beard doesn't need to be told twice. He follows behind either for self-preservation or to try and kill me. We'll sort that out later.

The icy water strips away my warmth and ability to swim.

My legs pump like mad, or at least, that's what my brain tells them to do.

I peek to see how deep I am and if I'm going in the right direction.

*Ow. Ow. Ow. Not fun.*

Twinkling lights and the whine of emergency vehicles hover twenty feet above me.

Thank God they're here—Puo should've called them the minute the drones launched with the stones to drop. He knows I hate being cold.

I swim mostly up, but also try and put distance between me and the sinking yacht.

The yacht and submarine groan and wrench.

My head breaks the surface to a cacophony of noise. Emergency rescuers shouting instructions from vehicles hovering overhead throwing life jackets. People are being airlifted. The rest in the water are yelling for help through shuddering breaths.

The trimaran yacht doesn't look so mean sinking below the water.

Caesar is one of the first ones being airlifted—I bet he doesn't even wonder why that is, simply assumes that's his due. He probably won't even notice the young African American tech with a sharp Afro Mohawk working on him.

I swim away from the group.

Something breaks the surface behind me. Wispy Beard looks at me and then the cluster of emergency vehicles. He only hesitates a second before swimming toward the emergency vehicles.

I need a life jacket soon. My legs are numb, and my arms are almost numb too.

A hovervan flying low over the water zooms toward me from a different direction.

It pulls up a foot over the water and Winn opens the back doors. He pulls me into the back of the hovervan. "Holy crap, you're freezing!"

"No … shit," I chatter.

# Chapter Thirteen

WINN HAD A WARM, dry change of clothes waiting for me, and a heated blanket. My fingers were numb so he had to help me change—there is no modesty when freezing to death.

And, it wasn't weird. It's only now that I'm properly warm, getting dressed in a steamy motel bathroom, that I'm able to appreciate that. I don't know if it was the specter of freezing to death, the fact that he's a doctor, or that something has normalized between us, but it wasn't weird.

We're in a motel on the northern edge of Albany—the abandoned hospital didn't have hot water which we knew we were going to need. Not that we told Ham that—he's in an adjacent, connected motel room warming up.

I don't why we bothered fishing him out—I mean, I know why. But still, I hate that prick. I'd much rather be rid of him, but he's flat-out too dangerous to be left alone. He'll either try to sell us out for himself, or the National Syndicate will scoop him up and make him talk.

He's already tried to sell us out—the second time, the for-real time when we were in front of Caesar. I mean, I knew he was going to do it, counted on it. But still—a prick. The galling fact is that the best play is to put him on a tighter leash without him knowing, which means welcoming him back without too-serious repercussions—too tight a leash and he'll chafe and look to slip the collar.

I come out into the motel room. The room's cold dry air is an affront after the steamy bathroom.

"There she is!" Puo calls out, sitting in an old speckled-blue upholstered wingback chair. "Hungry?"

I catch myself before giving him a weird look. It's after midnight and he already knows I burned my mouth scarfing down hot soup on the way back. He's staring at me, like he wants to say something else.

Winn stands nearby, arms crossed. Mr. Chao and Lucy sit in armless desk chairs with their backs to the front door facing the bathroom in the back. One of the chairs is pulled in from the connecting room where Nova and Aliyah are keeping the leash on Ham, who's in the other bathroom heating up. They'll have some words for him when he emerges—they insisted the words coming from them rather than me would be best, given "my history" with him.

I shrug. "You?" I ask Puo, giving him some runway for him to talk about what he really wants to talk about.

"Mmmm, pie," he says to himself, eyes closed, savoring the word and putting on a show for everyone else in the room. He opens his eyes and looks at me. "You remember going to Promontory Pies? I miss that place. Good memories. We should all go out for some pie."

I remember Promontory Pies back in the Seattle Isles—it's not exactly what I would call "good memories." We regrouped there after following Hayes to Chavez and Valle, and Puo debriefed us on what he found on Colvin's solid-state drive. It takes me a second to connect it to the current circumstances.

It's the debrief. Puo is drawing my attention to the place we debriefed. It's the only time we were ever physically there.

"Can we all go out for pie?" he asks me.

The reference finally clicks. He knows something. If he really wanted to go for pie, he would've asked Winn first or recruited others, or even more likely, simply announced he was going and left, expecting others to follow. The only reason to ask me first is if that isn't really the question.

What he's really asking is, can he reveal what he knows in front of everyone, or should he keep quiet. Whatever he found, it's time sensitive or he would keep quiet and wait to fill me in later.

"No," I say. If Puo isn't willing to say it outright, then I don't trust everyone else enough to make that call without knowing it ahead of time. "Did Aliyah make the lift?"

Puo pouts and points to the olive-green brick squeegee on the table. It was so helpful of Caesar to show us the exact shade of his squeegee earlier.

"Does he suspect anything?" Aliyah should've swapped Caesar's squeegee with a dummy.

"Not that we can tell," Puo says.

"Good." I glance back at Aliyah in the other room, who's unaware we're talking about her. *Nice lift.*

Something else passes over Puo's face: frustration. He wants to include everyone, reveal everything in the open.

Hard to make that call without knowing what the information is. We may be currently allied with them, but that doesn't mean I trust them. They are Cleaners, after all. And I really, *really* don't trust Ham.

"Did you find the cold storage?" I ask.

"Nope!" Puo says, like I asked him if he would unload the dishwasher. The big ol' grin on his round Samoan face is giving me emotional whiplash from the frustration in his eyes. He's doing this to needle me.

"Then why are you so chipper?"

"Let me tell you a story."

*Oh, Lord.* Puo's stories are ... unique. Maybe I should've included everyone.

Winn hides a ghost of a smile. Mr. Chao and Lucy look curiously at Puo.

"Come—" Puo gestures expansively to everyone to gather close, a Mister Rogers's smile plastered on his face. "Come my little ones. Come, sit at my feet and learn."

Winn, fighting a grin, sits down cross-legged in front of Puo, looking up at him like a child, back straight and eager.

Puo looks at me expectantly—I swear there's frustration layered deep down in his dark eyes. Only someone who knows him exceptionally well would see it.

"I am not sitting on the floor," I say.

Mr. Chao and Lucy stay seated in their chairs, bewildered.

Puo ignores them and makes an exaggerated sad face at me. "It's okay little one, you can stay there, where you feel safe. Knowledge does not discriminate between the standing and sitting. But you should know, you can trust us, all of us. This is a safe place—"

"Puo!"

Puo holds his mock-sad face a beat longer while looking at me. Then asks, "Now, who knows what a cheetah is?"

Winn shoots his hand up. His whole body strains upward.

"Anyone?" Puo asks.

"Oh, oh!" Winn agonizes.

Puo draws it out and then finally calls on Winn. "Yes?"

Winn explains about cheetahs in a know-it-all voice.

*What is happening?*

"And are cheetahs native to the United States?" Puo asks his prized student.

"No," Mr. Chao answers before Winn could.

Puo looks absolutely delighted.

Lucy looks as confused as I do annoyed, that Puo's managing to pull them under.

"That's right!" Puo smiles widely. "That is why the cautionary tale of the Oak House Cheetah is so extraordinary, and so important."

My interest perks up at "Oak House."

"Now," Puo says, "Oak House was a private high school outside of Hattiesburg, Mississippi whose mascot was a cheetah, and it was school tradition to have a live cheetah as part of the animal husbandry program that they could trot out at sporting events and rallies."

I can't help but shake my head.

"True story." Puo raises his hand as if swearing on a Bible at my reaction.

Winn nods sycophantically without looking around.

"This went on for decades," Puo continues, "until vegan mania swept through the youngest generation. Vegetables were in, animals were out! Including their animal husbandry program—"

"Let me guess," I say. "They released all the animals at once and the cheetah slaughtered all the other animals and cross-bred with a pig."

"Don't be ridiculous." Puo sniffs. "They trained the cheetah to be vegan."

I give Puo a dirty look, pretty sure he just stole one of my ideas from his Ronny the Rhinoceros story.

"No—" Lucy shakes her head. "—that's not possible. Cheetahs are carnivores. They can't break down plants."

Puo ignores me and holds his finger up. "I said they trained the cheetah to be vegan, I didn't say they succeeded. The cheetah wouldn't eat and became very weak. This alarmed the head of the now-banished husbandry program and he recommended the cheetah needed a pacemaker to get its heart rate back up. The cheetah is the fastest land animal after all, so it should have a fast heart rate."

I start to shake my head no at this lunacy, but Puo raises his hand subtly to stop me and I keep my mouth shut. The sound of Ham's shower fills in the brief pause.

"The kids, of course, would not hear of it. Surgery on a cheetah? Ridiculous. They took the cheetah to the local marina to go tubing instead."

"Tubing?" I can't help myself.

"Yes. Tubing. Very exciting group activity you see—help get the ticker back up." Puo taps his chest.

"Should've taken it sky diving," I say.

"Stop being ridiculous. It would've torn the kids apart all cooped up in the plane like that."

"Nonsense, send the cheetah up alone. Hell, it could've probably flown the plane if they smeared the controls with chicken blood."

Puo rolls his eyes—but I swear the frustration that bleeds through is probably more because he didn't think of it himself then his underlying frustration at freezing out everybody else. Hell, he'll probably steal that idea too. "Well, that's not what they did. They took it tubing. And at first, it looked like a success—despite the white sheen to the cheetah's face. But it didn't last."

"Heart attack?" Winn asks.

"Alligator ate it."

I snort and stifle laughter—best not to encourage him.

Mr. Chao and Lucy are a combination of shocked and confused which only makes me want to laugh more.

"What was the point of that?" Lucy asks.

"Oh, c'mon!" I throw my head back. "You're playing right into him."

"The point is," Puo says, ignoring me, "that when you ignore expert advice—" He points to himself. "—bad things happen."

"And what expert advice would that be?" Mr. Chao asks.

I can only shake my head at these two letting Puo lead them around by the nose.

Ham's shower cuts off, ushering in a silence that Puo lets build.

Finally, with everyone captivated he says, "We can't power on Caesar's squeegee."

Mr. Chao and Lucy exchange looks.

In that brief second Puo flicks his gaze to me and I understand my role here.

I look between them and Puo before asking, "Whadda ya mean we can't power it on? After everything we just went through," I say my voice growing heated. "It's useless?"

"Not useless," Puo says. "We just can't use it—yet." He holds up his hand when I open my mouth to ask what that means. "There's a homing beacon on startup. We can't power it on without it phoning home."

"How do you know this?" Mr. Chao's voice never wavers from calm interest.

"I was in their system on the yacht. Since we were tunneling Isa's video out, I was keeping a close eye on all the yacht's signals. That's how they knew the decoy squeegee was a fake—no homing beacon at startup. I saw the alert go out, then I looked at the pingback log."

"Disable the emitter," Lucy says.

"Can't. The emitter is integrated into the boot up sequence. No emitter, no boot up. With the right equipment, maybe. But the best option is a dead room."

"And we're just supposed to take your word for it?" Lucy asks.

"Remember the cheetah." Puo looks down his nose at her. "But you can check the squeegee yourself and figure out a way around it. Me, I'm going to look for a dead room."

Winn shoots his hand up. "Can I help?"

Puo nods and then looks at me.

"I'm going to bed," I say. Puo and I share a look that communicates over the decades we've known each other: *Message received, see you in a bit.*

# Chapter Fourteen

"Y OU ALREADY FOUND the cold storage, didn't you?" I ask Puo as I climb into the front seat of the hovercar.

"Yup." Puo sits in the back, laptop open and banging away with one hand and pointing some sensor at me with the other. He doesn't bother looking up.

"And there's no homing beacon on startup, is there?" It effectively freezes them out of doing anything while we're gone.

"Nope," he answers, still not bothering to look up.

Winn pulls the hovercar up into the early morning, still several hours before sunrise.

It's just the three of us—the three musketeers back together again.

"Did you stopgap the ride?" I ask the cabin in general.

"Yes," Winn answers. "We swapped out the old hovercar with a new one from a hotel."

Good. Any presents the mercs might have planted on the old hovercar will also be left behind. "Did you harden our comms from outsiders?" Puo's been able to get a rough location from that in the past.

"Yeah, and I scanned us as well," Puo says, still not looking up. "Thoroughly."

I nod.

I slipped off to the meeting point at a nearby marina an hour after I was supposed to be asleep—the tubing reference clued me in. We had done something similar on a job in Hattiesburg, where we had to meet back up at a marina.

It's odd they let Winn and Puo simply take off alone to find a dead room, even if I wasn't with them. It suggests they have another means to track us.

"Do you have Caesar's squeegee?" I ask.

Puo lifts up and waves Caesar's squeegee. "Yeah—I swapped the casing with one of the marina squeegees. So long as they don't power it up, they won't know the difference."

Why did they let us go so easily?

Not that it matters.

Charlie. We know where Charlie is. That's what the Oak House business was about. Her auction house was on Oak Street in Atlanta. The pacemaker meant whatever needs to happen, needs to happen fast. So, whether they can track us or not, we need to *move*.

"Where we headed?" I ask, suppressing a flash of anxiety.

"Aberdeen, South Dakota," Puo says, his voice dry.

"Bullshit." I turn around to look at him.

His dark eyes flick up from his blue-light screens and hold my gaze. There's no bluff there, no joking, no sense of irony. Only deadly seriousness.

Aberdeen, South Dakota is the town tied to my CitID. Well, my old CitID, the one tied to Vikki Gilbert. The identity tied to the bomb blast in Vancouver when the Cleaners leaned on Deona Nix to try and kill us.

That can't be a coincidence. My thoughts race a thousand miles an hour. "What's the pacemaker?"

"They're going to move her soon. I saw the chatter when I burrowed in from the decoy squeegee and followed the digital thread to Aberdeen."

"Move her where?"

"Some place called the Citadel. Other than that, I don't know."

"You don't know?" I ask reflexively, my mind still off and racing. It would probably be easiest to grab her when she's on the move. Even easier if we knew their route. "It's not on their private blockchain?"

"I haven't decoded it yet."

"What? Then how'd you know to go to Aberdeen?"

"Do you not listen?" Puo snaps. "I said I found the cold storage, not decoded it. I was in Caesar's system on the yacht through the decoy squeegee. I copied a whole bunch of info including their chat logs. That's how I know about Aberdeen."

"You need to decode the blockchain," I huff. "We need to know what's on there. If we know where the Citadel is we could intercept them en route. What are you doing now?"

"I'm pulling the building permits to a farmhouse outside of Aberdeen to get the layout to try and minimize the insane risk we're about to take! There's only one of me. I can't do everything. It would've been nice—" He cuts himself off and shakes his head.

I study his face, suspecting I knew what that was about when Winn cuts in, "Why are they even moving her?"

That is a good question.

"The Tit Twister—" Puo looks up to see if I know the name.

I shake my head no, although I can hazard a guess.

Puo continues, "—is meeting them at the Citadel. There was

a lot of back and forth, but apparently the Tit Twister refuses to travel to South Dakota to work."

*Shit.* "They're going to torture her." My father's beaten and bruised face floats to mind. The jackknives awaken and take a layer off the inside of my stomach. I flush.

Puo nods solemnly, still working frantically.

*Three days, one hour.* We're taking too long. They wanted to lure us out to Aberdeen, but when we didn't get their message in time, they're moving her to a more secure location and upping the ante.

"It gets worse," Puo says.

I focus on suppressing the jackknives rather than responding.

Puo continues, "Has it even occurred to you why they chose Aberdeen?"

I shake my head no. I had assumed they were taunting me.

"They've planned for us. There's a reason they choose a spot nowhere near water, in a farmhouse nowhere near skylanes. They know how we operate. After your stunt in Vancouver, they'd be daft not to know about the anti-gravity suits. Which, by the way, cuts off trying to intercept Charlie en route. The chatter made clear they were not going to make that mistake again. Izaak's hovercar probably had the same precautions."

"How are they moving her?" I ask.

"I don't know."

"When are they moving her?" Winn asks.

Puo throws his hands up. "I don't know! I don't know how they're moving her! I don't know when they're moving her! I don't know what to expect at the farmhouse! I don't know!" Sweat drips down his temples.

I reach back and grab his hot sweaty hand. "It's okay—"

He looks up at me with wild eyes.

"We'll figure it out. Like always." Somehow comforting Puo quiets my own jackknives.

His chest continues to rise and fall, and suddenly I'm worried about him having another heart attack.

We stare at each other for several breaths. Finally, his breathing evens out and he nods once and exhales out his nose.

"How long until we get there?" I ask, glancing at the clock: two forty-seven a.m.

"Four and half hours," Winn answers.

My heart sinks down into my toes. More waiting. The sun will be coming up when we arrive, even with the time change. We can't outrun the dawn.

***

Puo was right. They planned for us coming.

There's no other way to describe the desolate farmhouse, isolated from any form of covert approach. Any hovercar would be seen for miles before it got close. There's no water anywhere near the house for us to use to sneak in, no city sewer system, and the land for half a mile around is clear cut.

The sun is coming up, early morning twilight. Something about that really bothers me. We've pulled games and entries in daylight before, but damn. Having it dark would've been a whole lot better.

Any freefall we'd do stands a good chance of being spotted in daylight. The human eye is scary good at picking out movement—survival depends on it.

Winn and I are inside the tree line half a mile away, studying the farmhouse through auto-binoculars, while Puo is back at the hovercar a mile away from us on the comm-link and pulling whatever he can on his computers to be helpful.

The simple two-story house is a faded white with a first-story wrap-around porch in the colonial style. There's not a lot to see, aside from two hovercars parked out front and a week's worth of unopened packages piled up near the front door. A light dusting of snow covers the hovercars and ground. In fact, the snow all around the whole house is unmarred.

We can't even tell if there's anyone in the house. No one's stepped out, and all the windows have the curtains drawn. The only clue the house is occupied are the icicles on the eaves of the roof in isolated spots from poor insulation with the heat running.

"I can't see anything," I growl while still studying the house. "Phoenix, can you see anything?"

I don't know why I let Puo pick our call signs this time—lack of imagination I suppose. It's getting a bit ridiculous how often we have to change them. Honestly, it'd make way more sense to pick generic names like Nancy or Matt or something, but apparently that's too hard a substitution for our brains to make in a crisis. Or so Puo says.

Puo answers, "I can see they're monitoring the digital systems, to do anything more would be to announce our presence—I'm sure they're on alert for it."

I mean, our whole shtick is cons, assuming other identities as if it were natural. Too hard in a crisis. Ridiculous.

"Computer," I say, renaming Puo to something generic that'll be easy for him to remember, "Can you really see them monitoring or are you guessing?"

"It's Phoenix! And remember the cheetah."

"I am not calling you Cheetah."

"No. I— Ugh! I can't tell for certain without them knowing someone's looking into them. Trust me on this." Then he adds more petulantly, "And it's Phoenix."

"Computer, silence."

It's a loaded silence on the comm-link and I can perfectly picture Puo's annoyed face, which causes me to smile.

"Harpy—" Puo says after several heartbeats, trying to re-name me from Pixie.

"Do not speak that way to your empress. You may refer to me as Empress only."

Winn tries to break in.

"Quiet, Consort. I do not permit my men to speak unless spoken to."

"Centaur, can you talk some sense into her?" Puo asks.

Winn stays silent, but gives me a what-are-you-doing look.

I smile benevolently and pat him on the head.

When it becomes clear Winn isn't going to say anything, Puo tries again, "Centaur—"

"Silence, Computer. Consort knows his place—"

"It's Phoenix! And don't pull me into your weird sex games."

I blush. That's not what we're doing now. *Is it?* Although the Empress and her consort do bring some ideas to mind. "Well," I say, "way to go and make it weird."

Puo says, "Weird flew way past when Tony the Tiger was late on rent a couple months back."

I burst out laughing. That was ... memorable. "You heard that?"

"The neighbors heard that. It was not *grrreeeaat!*"

I can hear Puo grinning.

"Can we *please* focus!" Winn turns a shade of red I've never seen him. I grin ear to ear as I ready myself to pile on, but Winn plows over me. "What are we going to do about this?" He gestures to the farmhouse. "We can't see anything. We don't even know if Charlie's in there or, if she is, where she is. We don't know how many Cleaners are in there—"

That wipes the smile off my face.

We need to know where Charlie is located. Puo pulled the layout from the building permits, but we're completely blind to how the people are distributed within the house.

"Easy, Tiger," Puo says, and snot flies out of my nose as I try to stifle my laughter.

Puo snorts over the line.

Winn turns a deeper shade of red and shakes his head. He stares daggers at me and mouths, "Never again."

We all take a minute or two to collect ourselves. *Shit—I needed that.*

I go back to studying the house and the pile of delivery boxes out front. Other than that, there really isn't much to see.

"I hate to ruffle your stripes—" Puo says.

"Aw, c'mon!" Winn snaps.

"—but even if we knew where Charlie is, we couldn't get close to the house without them seeing us."

"What equipment do we have?" I ask.

"The anti-gravity suits, some tracker chips, a couple disrupters, a microwave scanner, snuffers, boosters, three beacons, a couple stunners, a laser cutter, the drone, and two auto-binoculars, of course."

That's a decent haul. I give Winn an appreciative look for collecting all that from our Seattle Isles hideout two nights ago after we first got back to the States, and for keeping it hidden.

He just glares at me, still a shade of beet red.

"When are they going to move her?" I ask Puo.

"Before noon is all the messages indicated. So anytime in the next five hours."

"It's going to have to be a smash and grab," I say.

"Yeah," Puo says like I just commented on the weather, "but where are you going to smash, and how are you going to grab?"

*We need to be able to see inside the house*, I think but don't say as Winn says, "The anti-grav suits are out. They'll see us coming and there's no quick way into the house from above."

"The beacons are out," Puo says.

Beacons are digital-scramblers on steroids. They're small drones that fire infrared light at cameras among other things. They're out of style with Puo and me these days for the exact reason we can't use them here: they're too overt—surveillance systems are designed to detect them and alert their masters. We need to minimize the time between when the Cleaners become aware something is happening and our arrival.

"And you can't smash a hole in the roof without knowing where Charlie is," Puo adds, familiar with my thinking. Or maybe it's my lack of imagination considering how often we've been using that. But he's right, at least with the boat we knew where people *couldn't* be and aimed the stones there. That's not possible here.

"It has to be a low altitude drop," I say. "It'll kill two birds with one stone. They won't see us coming from above and we can enter in at an angle through a window."

"Ooookkaayy," Puo drawls. "We still have the same problems. They'll see the hovercar coming and we still don't know where Charlie is."

"We have Caesar's squeegee, right?" I ask.

"Yeah."

I look back through the auto-binoculars at the pile of unopened packages. "I have an idea."

# Chapter Fifteen

"T HIS IS A terrible idea," Puo says, which, makes me feel better. Puo is never on board with my more brilliant schemes.

This *is* a terrible idea, although I would never admit it to Puo. But it's the only one we have and the clock is ticking.

It's near nine in the morning and the sun is up, fighting through a hazy gray mix of clouds. Puo drives us toward the farmhouse while Winn and I are in the back of the hovercar with anti-gravity suits and helmets on.

"Any chatter about our arrival?" I ask over the comm-link in my helmet.

Puo glances down at the laptop on the front seat next to him. "Nothing out of the ordinary. Which doesn't mean jack-poo. I have no idea what ordinary is here, or how they would react to an unannounced visit from Caesar."

"Don't be too confident, kemosabe," I say.

Puo used Caesar's newly acquired squeegee and some deepfake software to inform the Cleaners he was coming to question Charlie before they moved her to the Citadel and the Tit Twister got hold of her. The message came directly from Caesar's squeegee, which they don't know we have. So, they should push the

"I believe" button without being suspicious enough to scrub the video for deepfakes—so now we have a perfectly plausible excuse to fly a hovercar in low and close.

"Winn should be flying," Puo complains, "leaving me to deal with all this." He makes circular gestures over the laptop.

"We've been over this," I say, "we need both of us in the house to quickly cover more ground."

Puo growls under his breath.

I almost ask him to elaborate, but decide having a fight with Puo right now isn't worth it.

This *is* stupid. We don't know where Charlie is. We don't know how many Cleaners are in the house. We don't know when the Tit Twister is arriving, or how many Cleaners are showing up to make the transfer. Once we announce ourselves, we're going to have only minutes to get in and get Charlie out.

The white faded farmhouse comes into view.

We're committed now—they can see us coming, and we're about to make it very clear we are not Caesar.

"The microwave scanner?" I ask.

"Delivered." Puo avoids looking at me. "Other than that?" He shrugs.

"It's set up to forward its data directly to us?"

"Yeah." Puo looks at me this time. He's pissed. "Assuming it works."

The microwave scanner is the second part of our plan. We packaged it up to make it look like a standard drone delivery and dropped it off on the pile of unopened packages out front. That's the key with a microwave scanner, it has to be close to map out a space—that, and it has to send the data to Puo's computers for post-processing, which he then needs to forward to our helmets.

Which is one source of Puo's ire. The scanner can't be broadcasting data before we're close enough to take the Cleaners by surprise—they'll be on the lookout for suspicious signals. So the scanner is on standby mode, awaiting a signal from Puo to wake up and start scanning and transmitting data.

Which gives Puo a very narrow window to do any troubleshooting.

This is all on top of Puo having to take out those two parked hovercars in the driveway after he drops us off—which is the real reason for Puo's ire. He hates fieldwork.

But there's nothing for it. We don't have enough bodies, enough time, or enough assets. This is the hand we were dealt, and now it's time to play it.

Puo slows the hovercar as the farmhouse nears.

"Set your mark," I say to Winn, while setting my own marker on the first-floor living room window with my retina controls.

"Mark set," Winn says.

"Approach the west side first for Winn," I tell Puo, "then circle around back for me. Stay twenty-to-thirty feet high and the same distance away from the house, we need to come in at an angle."

"Understood." Puo continues to avoid looking at me.

I consider him as the farmhouse gets close enough to see the individual slats of the house siding.

"Get ready to wake the scanner," I order.

"Scanner ready to be awakened," Puo repeats woodenly.

We fly over the driveway and approach the house's west side. Still no sight of anyone inside.

Winn positions himself to be ready to fling the door open with one hand, while holding a stunner in the other—there's no telling what we'll encounter in there.

"Pipe in music," I order, having just thought of it.

"Are you serious?" Puo snaps.

"Yes!" I snap back. "We need to know if we're jammed!" Mostly I want to make sure any delay in receiving the microwave layout doesn't become distracting. "What's with you—?"

"Take the wheel!"

"I—"

"I can't do everything, Isa! We're seconds away from dropping Winn, and you want me DJing on a laptop—"

I lean forward calmly, scoot his laptop closer, type in the basic command on a new tab and hit enter.

A string piece with long drawn-out notes pipes in.

I stare at him. His chest heaves. Sweat slides down his temples. There's a wild look in his eyes. The farmhouse looms.

"Puo, I don't know what that was all about, but table it. I admit this is stupid, but it's what we got—"

Puo opens his mouth to argue, but I continue on. "—We'll deal with it later."

"If there is a later," he mutters.

"Ten seconds out," Winn announces, as if Puo and I weren't arguing.

"Ten seconds out," Puo repeats, and angles the hovercar to the house's west side.

I shift over to Puo's original tab on the laptop. The command "ping micro_scanner -c 1" is queued up. "Is this to awaken the microwave scanner?" I ask.

Puo glances over and nods.

"Awakening the microwave scanner," I say and hit the button. The Cleaners are about three seconds away from knowing we're not Caesar anyway.

Gobbledygook streams down the laptop.

Puo glances over. "It's connected—" Puo starts to say as Winn throws open the door and jumps out, stunner in hand.

The door slams shut behind him, but not before cold air rushes in.

A heartbeat of silence stretches forever before the general mayhem of Winn crashing through the garage window comes over the comm-link. It abruptly cuts off with a *thump* and an "Oww!"

"Consort! You okay?" I press my helmet up against the hovercar window to try and see back toward the garage window as the hovercar banks around the house to come in for my entry.

There's a low groan on the comm-link and what sounds like Winn punching a box. "These people are hoarders! This garage is full of ... crap!"

"Can you get to the breaker box?"

"Yeah— Yeah, I see it."

"Make sure to pull the circuit breakers all the way out," Puo says, "but don't touch the metal bus at the back."

"Roger," Winn acknowledges. "No sign of company."

Puo glances down at his laptop as the hovercar comes around to the east side.

I grab my stunner and shift over to be ready to open the hovercar door for my own entry. Four seconds to entry.

"The bridge to the scanner is set up," Puo says. "Data is being pushed to your helmets now."

I throw the door open and launch myself out.

I'm forty feet up hurtling toward the first-floor bay window.

The anti-gravity routine kicks in immediately, tugging me upward around the armpits and crotch.

Right before I slam into the bay window, a three-dimensional rendering overlays the house with colored stick figures spread throughout the house, including one right on the bay window's other side.

I don't have time to register where any others are as I curl into a ball and slam through the window, glass shards shattering around me.

I slam into a rectangular wooden table, flipping it up like a lever, before that too crashes and slams back down. The table and I skid across the floor. I manage to keep hold of my stunner.

"Ow!" I knew it was going to hurt, but I wasn't anticipating a table on the other side to break my fall.

The interior is lived in with prairie style decorations and mostly clean—*must have shoved everything in the garage.*

I bounce up and take stock.

The table I slammed into from the breakfast nook area has flown halfway out of the room. The wooden chairs left behind look lost and confused. The kitchen to my right has a pile of crusty breakfast dishes next to the sink and unopened mail on the counter. Pictures of different generations and dogs dot the walls.

An unconscious male Cleaner is splayed out on the floor—a victim of a rogue table—gotta be careful around those things.

A red stick figure from the microwave scanner overlays the body. *Cool.*

There's a figure, a mix of red and blue, toward the garage—Winn—and another two down in the basement. One looks tied to a chair with their hands bound behind them—Charlie.

"Abuela located," I rush over the low classical music. "Moving to basement to retrieve. Consort, join me when finished."

As if on cue, the lights go off in the kitchen—Winn's pulling the breakers.

"Wait for Consort!" Puo shouts at me. "Something's—"

"Negative." I run toward the particle-wood door leading down to the basement from the kitchen. "They heard our entry. Surprise is lost."

Puo realizes it's pointless to argue and shuts up. The music changes to a fluty wind piece and the tempo picks up.

The other stick figure in the basement looks to be hiding in front of Charlie, off to the right. I ready the stunner and ease the door open.

Rickety stairs lead down into a pool of shadows. I can't see beyond the stairs—no windows down there. Whoever's there is going to hear me every step of the way down those things.

Good thing I don't need the stairs. I ease onto the first step and close the surprisingly heavy door behind me, sealing the basement off in darkness. My nightvision kicks on and I quickly set the retina controls on the anti-gravity suit and leap down, landing on a cold stained and cracked cement floor in a crouched position.

Charlie sits in a chair twenty feet in front of me outlined in blue pixels, hands bound behind her and a pillow case over her head. A single unlit bulb hangs over her on a cord. What is it with basements and creepy lighting? At least the power's been cut.

The basement is a wide-open space segmented with random dusty boxes piled up to chest level in different collections. Metal shelves are shoved up against the walls, covered in smaller box-es and glass jars of stuff.

The Cleaner in the basement crouches behind a wall of one of those dusty box collections. The stick figure's core is red, while the limbs and head are blue, so I'm pretty sure they're crouched. They haven't moved.

I angle off into the box maze, hoping to circle around on the hidden Cleaner. The stunner in my hand is thick like a spray paint can, but heavier. We dialed down the power to incapacitate a human instead of a squiddie, which is what it was originally designed for.

I step lightly through the paths created by the boxes. There's definitely some weird organization to this chaos.

The crouching Cleaner still hasn't moved.

Why haven't they moved? They must have heard me land, or at the very least seen the light from opening and closing the door. They sure as hell heard me crashing through the bay window.

The music is loud, filling in the silence of the basement. It was already hard to hear anything in these helmets. Now it's impossible.

"Cut off the music," I whisper. "Consort, where are you?"

I risk a glance off in the direction of the garage. The red-and-blue stick figure looks to still be in the garage.

The crouching Cleaner is around the next corner and still hasn't moved.

The music hasn't shut off, but rather than chastise Puo, I ready the stunner, and peek around the corner.

The crouching Cleaner is in fact, crouching, facing away from me and toward Charlie. It's a guy. His hands are on the ground and one of them looks to be holding zip ties, but other than that, no weapons.

The music finally cuts off.

I move around the corner and jam the stunner into his side.

He bucks and spasms and then flops to the ground in a *flump!* Those *were* zip ties in his hands.

Charlie hears the commotion and starts shifting in her seat and mumble-yelling through a gag.

"Moving to collect Abuela." I run toward Charlie. "Restart the music, and where are you on taking out those hovercars?"

Puo doesn't answer as I run toward Charlie.

I rip the pillow case off. "It's me, your star pupil!" I have no idea if she can hear me or not through my helmet. Her face is covered in blue pixels from the nightvision—she looks odd that way.

I start to move around to the back to unbind her, when she suddenly reaches around and grabs me.

I barely register a cord trailing from one of her hands before jolting electricity shoots through me.

My muscles tighten uncontrollably. The nightvision winks out. The power in the suit cuts off.

The ground rushes up to greet me. The single light bulb flares to life.

The last thought I have before blacking out is, *That's not Charlie.*

# Chapter Sixteen

I JERK ON the ground and lay still when the juice cuts off.

*Holy Gods, that hurts.* Every muscle in my body feels like it was clenched for hours and only now released. There're muscles I didn't even know I had.

My suit is fried. No power. Completely dead.

The basement, on the other hand, has a number of lights that all suddenly work. The space is actually well lit, like a construction zone or something.

The woman in the chair is African American and large like Charlie, but definitely not Charlie. She stands up and kicks the stunner out of my hand.

*Ow!* I play dead though and don't react. I don't know what they hit me with, but it was no idle trinket. Being unconscious would not be a surprising result—I probably would be if it wasn't for the anti-gravity suit taking the brunt of it.

Impostor Charlie gets up, gives me another kick, and then heads behind me toward their downed colleague.

There's something funny about that chair in front of me. It's fixed to the floor, with cords running up from the cement through drilled holes.

This was planned.

I mean, obviously, in retrospect, this was a trap. And not a half-assed trap or one thrown together at the last minute. This was a well-thought-out trap that took time to prep. *How long have they been here? Where are the people that lived here?*

Impostor Charlie shuffles back toward me. I wait until she's towering over me and spring forward on the ground and grab the same cord she shoved against me. I jump up, whip around, and shove it against it against her chest.

*How do you like that?*

She glances down at the cord which is definitely *not* jolting electricity into her. She shoves my helmet up and away and then sucker punches me in the stomach.

*Ooof!*

I back up, cradling my stomach. She is definitely not Charlie, so I don't feel bad at all rushing her.

She takes a step back into a defensive posture.

*Ha!* I launch myself in a flying tackle and we tumble together and slam into the cement floor.

She didn't expect me to square off against her fairly, did she? That jack-assery might work in stories and movies, but in a real fight, the only thing that matters is who is standing at the end.

Zip ties spill out across the floor from her.

I knee her in the crotch as we tumble and grab her tit and twist.

"Ow! What is wrong with you!" she yells at me.

"Call me the Tit Twister!" I yell in a sudden burst of inspiration. We come to a sliding stop and I end up on top of her.

I need to end this quickly—I have no idea of Winn's and Puo's status.

She scrambles to get a purchase on me, but the sleekness of the anti-gravity suit makes it hard to get a grip.

I start punching down, more to distract her and give me time than to do any damage.

I shove a finger up her nose as I grab a zip tie with my other hand—again, not meant to hurt, just annoy and distract.

She growls in frustration, ignores my finger in her nostril, and uses the flat of her hands pressed against my abdomen to bench press me off her and toss me over her head.

I use the momentum to cartwheel onto my feet—*thanks!*

The stunner lays on the ground in the crook of a box island ten feet away. I dash for it as Impostor Charlie pushes herself up.

I grab the stunner, whirl around, and run at her. She tries to protect herself, but that's the nice thing about the stunner—I only have to make contact, doesn't matter where. In this case, I slam it against the underside of her upper arm as she tries to shield herself.

Unlike their floor contraption that took out my anti-gravity suit, the stunner still has some juice. Impostor Charlie goes stiff, clenches her teeth and topples over. I keep the stunner in contact all the way to the ground.

"Timber!" I yell.

*Whump!* She crashes down hard. If the stunner didn't hurt, that fall certainly did. Not that I care, mind you—God only knows what they had planned for me.

She's unconscious, but still breathing.

I disengage the stunner, gather some zip ties, and have her trussed up like a prized show dog in less than two minutes. I give her unconscious friend near the stairs the same treatment.

I unhook my helmet with a *hiss.* The cold, stale air invades my helmet as I take it off. I drop the fried, useless helmet.

The basement smells mostly like decaying cardboard with mildew and stale cleaner undertones. I take in the space. Whoever lived here before was a magpie, but a strangely organized one.

The furnace kicking on jump-starts my heart, and brings to attention what was lacking before—a soundscape. Nothing moving around upstairs.

I need to get to Puo and Winn.

I run up the stairs and pull on the door. *Locked!*

*Damn it.* I didn't hear it lock behind me.

No matter. I grab the railing for balance, lean back and kick the door over the locking mechanism. *Wham!*

The door doesn't budge.

*Wham! Wham! Wham!*

*Shit.* I run back downstairs and look for something to break open the door with.

There's nothing along the walls like a broom, or preferably an axe, that would indicate a collection of tools to pick through. I rifle through the nearest box island—old paint supplies, mostly drop cloths. Under that are books. Next box over, baby bottles? Never mind on the magpie being organized.

The next nearest box island holds random bric-a-brac, framed photos, a tangle of electronic cords. *Bingo!* The bottom-most box holds a random twenty-pound metal dumbbell.

I grab it and run back to the door, knocking over a stack of boxes on the way. I set my helmet down and heave the dumbbell as hard as I can and jam the end of it right where I had kicked the door.

*Bam!* The door doesn't budge—doesn't even bounce in the frame.

The vibrations sting my palm and travel up my arm.

*What the hell?* I closed the door to come down here. There's no way it should be that solid. The door's flat wood surface is cool to the touch. It feels like an interior door should, not too solid, not too thick. It feels like a solid kick should do it.

*So, what gives?*

I run my hands along the seams. *Nothing.*

There're still no sounds coming from within the house. *Where's Winn?*

I take the dumbbell and start swinging it like an axe against the door. If I can't bust it open outright, I'll tear a hole through it and reach around to unlock it.

*Bam! Bam! Bam! Thunk!*

*What the hell?*

My initial strikes yield the expected results, splintering and dented wood. The last strike hits something solid—well more solid than the wood.

*Thunk! Thunk! Thunk!*

I dig away the splintered wood.

Metal. There's metal underneath the wood.

What. The. Hell.

I quickly gouge out other parts of the door—all metal underneath.

*Oh, God.*

My heart thunders in my chest, waking the jackknives.

This whole house is a trap. Not just the electric shock they hit me with. They planned for everything.

*Where's Winn? Puo?*

I'm about to call out to Winn, when I hear Puo's indistinct muffled yelling from the side of the basement.

I rush down to the source of the noise. Puo's muffled yelling brings me right to the basement's edge. Behind the faded-green metal shelving unit is a covered-up window. All the shelving units strategically cover the windows.

I topple the shelving unit into the nearest box island, glass jars shattering on the cement floor. I rip off the thick black cloth covering the window and wince at the bright, clouded-over daylight and white snow.

Puo stands between the two hovercars in the driveway hemmed in by two Cleaners. He has snow crumpled on his back, likely from lying on the driveway to apply the magnetic disrupter to the undercarriage since we're assuming the hoods are shielded like Izaak's hovercar was. He's brandishing a stunner at both of the Cleaners and yelling for them to stay back. The snowdrift up against the window prevents me from seeing much else.

I use the dumbbell to smash the window. *Clang!* The stupid thing bounces off.

*No freaking way.* I try again. Same result.

Molecular reinforced windows. How long have they been planning this? Were the windows activated once I broke through, or were they always reinforced to hold me in?

The commotion calls the attention of a third, previously unseen, nearby Cleaner who crunches over. It's a younger Indian woman, around my age, with a wide face and a single braided ponytail of dark hair that contrasts with her white teeth. I can attest to her teeth's whiteness, because this snow demon is malevolently grinning at me. Laughing.

"Fuck you!" I smash the dumbbell against the window again.

She jumps, but then that grin slides right back into place.

"Don't you dare touch him!" I try again with the dumbbell to no avail. *Fuck!* What am I going to do? They can't get their hands on Puo. They just can't. He hates being in the field.

*They're not the only ones with a hostage.* The thought hits me out of nowhere, but before I can turn to drag Impostor Charlie over here, Indian Cleaner starts piling snow up in front of the window to white out my view.

*No!*

I glance around quickly, there's only one other window with a view of driveway. I rush over, throw the metal shelving down with a large crash, and rip off the thick black cloth.

The jackknives spring to life, reach up with razor-blade fingers and slice my heart, puncture my lungs. A snowbank covers the window, whether from the Cleaner or nature, it doesn't matter. The effect is the same, I can't see anything. There's nothing I can do.

*Oh, God.*

I can hear Puo's muffled yelling, but I can't help him.

I look around the basement for something, anything. But there's nothing.

There's a scuffle, the sound of something smashing into the hovercar.

More indistinct yelling. It's hard to hear over my thundering heart.

Seconds peel away in bursts.

I step back and hurl the dumbbell as hard as I can against the window. It bounces off.

*Damn it!*

I rush back to where I found the dumbbell, looking for something heavier. Nothing. Just one random dumbbell, a sad leftover of failed fitness dreams.

I rifle through the rest of the boxes, no care given to the mess or noise I'm making. I need to find something, anything to help get me out of here.

I glance up at the wooden slat ceiling. If I can break through that, I can climb out of this tomb. Is there a drill in here somewhere? Surely, they didn't run metal all the way through the floor.

Steps creak from above. I freeze.

There are people upstairs. At least two. Walking toward the door down to the basement.

I grab a short, broken wooden handle from something—no idea what—and my fried helmet, the two closest things at hand and tiptoe quickly over and up the stairs. I squeeze to be out of view when the door opens, gripping my wooden handle and helmet, readying to shove them straight into whoever is on the other side of the door.

The steps approach and stop on the other side. There's soft whispering. Then nothing.

My heart beats in my chest. One. Two. Three.

Still nothing.

I don't dare move. This might be my only shot. I suddenly worry maybe they have their own microwave tech and can see me standing here. But then why are they waiting and not forcing me back?

Sudden deep *thunks* sound in the door—the metal bars sliding back.

I ready my wooden handle and helmet.

The door handle turns and a crack appears in the door.

I explode through the door with my shoulder.

The door slams against one smallish man who goes flying. Another taller woman—a Cleaner—is standing off to the side—the one that opened the door. I jam the end of the broom handle at her torso as I tumble out.

The Cleaner grabs the broom handle and shoves it to the side and uses the momentum to pull me off balance deeper into the kitchen.

I whirl around. "You!"

Nova Contreras stands there eyeing me warily.

I risk a glance at the man on the floor picking himself up. Ken Chao.

"Bastards!"

# Chapter Seventeen

I THROW MY helmet at Nova, then run and grab the dirty dishes next to the sink, chuck them at her, and start to sprint from the kitchen.

Nova is a trained fighter holding the high ground. Fighting her one-on-one is a bad idea, particularly with Mr. Chao lurking in the background.

Speaking of which. I kick Mr. Chao's arm out from pulling himself up—anything more risks throwing me off balance.

His cheek *smacks* against the linoleum.

Nova swats away the airborne dishes with a clatter. "Wait! Ugh!"

"We're on your side!" Mr. Chao shouts.

*Like hell you are.* I round the corner and make for the broken bay window. Once I'm outside I can swing around to get Puo and then figure out what happened to Winn.

"Isa, stop!" Puo shouts from behind me, deeper in the house.

That brings me up short. I whirl around to see Puo, Winn, and Aliyah strolling toward me like arriving back from a matinee.

"What the hell?"

Winn is still in his anti-gravity suit, helmet included. Aliyah's cheeks are flushed from the cold or fighting, I can't tell. Her shoulders are set and she's continuing to look around as they walk into the house—well, she's more stalking than walking.

But it's Puo face that arrests my attention. His face is a pale, chalky complexion I've only seen once before: when he had a heart attack. Melting clumps of snow stick to his long dark pony tail spilling over his shoulder.

*He didn't have another heart attack, did he?*

"They're on our side," Puo says. "They saved us."

Winn mumbles something and gestures at himself, clearly meaning, *What about me?*

Puo waves him down.

I turn to study Mr. Chao and Nova. Mr. Chao stands there cradling his shoulder where it smashed into the ground. Nova flicks scrambled eggs off her thin, shiny teal down jacket, giving me dirty looks, but not saying anything.

Winn takes his helmet off with a *ka-tish*. "He's right," Winn says. "They're here to help. They helped me rescue Puo."

Aliyah's eyebrows go up at that.

I don't believe it. "Where's the rest of 'em?" *More specifically, where's Ham, that dirty backstabber?*

Nova and Mr. Chao share a look before Mr. Chao answers, "Lucy is keeping an eye on Ham in the hovercar." When I don't look convinced Lucy could do such a thing, he adds, "Ms. Contreras handcuffed him to the hovercar."

That I believe. But something still doesn't add up. Given how elaborate this booby-trapped house is, how do we know this isn't part of a longer con? "How'd you follow us here?" I ask.

Before anyone can answer, Nova says, "Why'd you steal Caesar's squeegee and take off without telling us?"

Of course they would check the squeegee themselves—Puo even invited them to do it.

A silence settles over the group, thickening quickly into a staring contest.

"This isn't the place for this," Puo says. "We need to leave before more Cleaners show up."

Nova starts to speak, but I talk over her. "He's right. This whole house is a trap designed to catch us. The basement has molecular-realigning windows, a hidden steel door, and … something that fried my suit."

Puo rocks back at that.

"We can't stay here," I continue. "We'll debrief elsewhere."

"Where?" Mr. Chao asks.

"We'll figure it out on the way." I start to move toward Puo and Winn.

"Aliyah," Nova commands, "you ride with them. Isa, you ride with us."

"No," Puo growls. "You three—" Puo motions to Nova, Mr. Chao, and Aliyah. "—follow the three of us in your hovercar."

Nova makes a discrete hand signal to Aliyah to stay with us, but Puo isn't having it.

"Follow behind us in that hovercar. And so help me Neptune—" He glares at Aliyah. "—if you try and come with us, good luck getting in the hovercar." Puo crosses his arms and towers over her. Even with his pale complexion he gives off the I'm-two-hundred-pounds-heavier-than-you and you-can't-do-jack-shit-about-it vibe.

Aliyah looks like she wants to give it a shot, but at the last second glances over at Nova who waves her down. The really interesting exchange was Mr. Chao subtly signaling Nova to drop it.

"Then give us Caesar's squeegee," Nova demands.

I don't even bother to respond to that stupidity as I move toward Puo and Winn.

"Your helmet," Puo says.

The helmet rests on the kitchen floor from where I threw it at Nova. "It's fried," I say feeling contrarian and revved up from Nova's and Mr. Chao's sudden appearance.

Puo rolls his eyes. "It's not fried."

"It doesn't work—"

"Get it anyway, it won't be hard to fix. Definitely easier to fix than to fabricate." The helmets are part of the anti-gravity suit's specialized tech, so Puo's insistence makes sense.

"We'll get it," Mr. Chao pipes up, cutting off Nova wanting to argue about Caesar's squeegee. "This will alleviate Nova's concern. You won't leave your helmet behind, will you? We'll return it to you when we meet up."

"She was just about to leave it," Nova says.

"But he wasn't," Mr. Chao says succinctly.

The exchange sends a chill through my chest. I wasn't really going to leave it behind—I was just blowing off steam with Puo. But now I'm suddenly reluctant to leave the helmet behind in their hands.

Puo and I share a look, and I can read the question plain on his face: *Is it really fried?*

*Yes, it's really fried.*

"Fine," Puo says to Mr. Chao. "You get the helmet, while we get our hovercar. Be ready to roll. We'll swing by the house so you can follow us."

"Understood," Mr. Chao says.

"Just don't let the basement door close on you," I add helpfully as Puo, Winn, and I book it out of there.

***

The frosty walk to the hovercar has nothing to do with the freezing temperatures outside. Puo charges ahead without looking back.

I know that set of his shoulders. I know too well how much he hates being in the field and I know how fucked up the last twenty minutes were.

I'm in for an earful—and maybe not undeserved at that. *Maybe*.

I can't tell from the back of his head what Winn thinks, walking in front of me.

We trudge through the snow to our hovercar parked behind the other two hovercars in the driveway. The Cleaners that had Puo surrounded lay splayed out in the snow, like they fell over ready to make snow angels and then forgot to move.

Winn drops down to the nearest one and checks for vitals. Of course, he can't feel jack shit through the anti-gravity suit gloves and soon motions for me to do it.

I kneel down next to the young Indian woman Cleaner. "She's alive." Other than that, I can't tell how Aliyah put the three down on the ground cold.

Winn looks back to the house.

I roll my eyes, but was already thinking the same thing. We can't leave the ankle biters out here in the snow and low temperatures to freeze. Sometimes I hate being the good guys—they definitely would've left us.

Once Puo realized why we've stopped, he switches from sulking to helping. Well, he at least helps; his sulking face hasn't changed. Either way, I'm going to hear about it once we're alone in the car.

With Puo's help, it doesn't take long to move the first two Cleaners inside.

Mr. Chao and company watch us bring the first two in with arched eyebrows, but then Nova comes out wordlessly to help with the last one while instructing Aliyah to search the house for the original occupants. God only knows what the Cleaners did with them. We bind the knocked out Cleaners' hands and feet behind them and Puo will notify their friends to come pick them up once we're far enough away.

Once that's taken care of, we head back out to our hovercar. The tension grows between Puo and me every step of the way until I'm not sure I'll be able to get the hovercar door open, it's gotten so thick.

I'm tempted to make Winn sit up front with Puo driving so I can hide in the back, but I suck it up and put on my big girl pants and head to the front seat.

"Winn," Puo says, "you drive." Puo climbs into the back seat. *Booger.*

I get in the front passenger seat and shut the door behind me. Winn gets in and glances over at me, the unspoken question about the building tension with Puo left unsaid.

Once everyone settles, I expect Puo's tongue lashing to commence—I already have my ripostes ready. But Puo keeps his mouth shut as the hovercar climbs up into the air. He doesn't even look at me as he reaches forward and grabs Winn's helmet off the seat.

I turn around, ready to pull the band-aid off and get it over with.

"I'm sorry," Puo says, cutting me off and staring down at his laptop as he connects Winn's helmet to the laptop.

It's so unexpected my mouth hangs open for a beat before I process what he said and respond eloquently with, "What?"

"I'm sorry." Puo's shoulders slump as he looks up at me. There's a deep sadness in his face and something else I can't place. "We never should've come here."

"It's not your fault—"

"No. It's not. At least, not what happened once we got here. But we should have *never* come in the first place. Things felt off from the very beginning—"

"You voiced your concerns. I didn't give you much of a choice." *Wait, what am I arguing here?*

"That's the problem. I gave *you* a choice, when I never should've given you one. I should've announced what I found in front of everyone."

My breath escapes me. "What?" Puo has never talked to me like this. We've argued, fought, screamed at each other, but never has he had such regret, such distance, such *disappointment* in his voice.

"We can't keep doing these things on our own."

It takes me a second to connect the dots. "You trust them?"

"No. But their interests are aligned with ours for now."

"But Charlie—!"

"Yes, Charlie! She would've been the first one to say how stupid it was to go off by ourselves. What did she always say?"

"Stop looking at your ass girlie?"

Puo rolls his eyes. "Never leave tools behind—"

"Or money on the table," I finish for him. It was one of her mantras.

"We rushed into a job and left assets on the table."

"You think they would've helped?"

"I don't know. But they're not without their own resources."

"You're the one that mentioned Charlie and the pacemaker."

"That's why it's my fault. I knew better. I *knew* better. We should've questioned Ham about the Citadel. Figured that out." Puo rubs his eyes with his palms. "I never should've put the situation in code in that brilliant story."

That's the first glimmer of the old Puo in there. I let it slide, hoping more of him will come through. "You didn't know if they would've helped and we didn't have time to argue about it with them."

Puo doesn't respond, instead he focuses down on his laptop and starts typing sporadically.

"Where should I set us down?" Winn asks.

Mr. Chao and everyone else are following behind us a couple car lengths behind. Which is ridiculously close when it comes to hover-cars, particular since we're the only ones out here. *Paranoid much?*

"Take us east outside of Aberdeen, then find a country road in the middle of nowhere and set us down there," I say.

Winn banks the hovercar to the east and sits up to look down for a spot.

"What happened back there?" I ask the cabin in general.

When Puo declines to answer, Winn speaks up. "I came through the window into the garage and crashed into a pile of paint cans. The only reason I'm not covered in paint is they must be at last thirty years old, dry as bedrock. The whole garage was full of stuff that hadn't been touched in decades. I found the break-er box, flipped the breakers and ripped them out as planned—"

"There," Puo cuts in, staring at his computer.

Both Winn and I look at each other in confusion.

Puo flips his laptop around for me to look at. It's a video feed from Winn's helmet showing the garage's interior. Winn wasn't kidding—the place resembles the basement with the piles of random stuff. The walls are wooden slats with no insulation.

Puo stares at me—his frustrated, sulking face back in place.

"What am I looking at?" I finally ask.

Puo leans forward to look down at the screen and then taps the side, pointing to some wires. "That."

I look again. "I don't know what that is."

"Exactly," Puo snaps. This is more the attitude I was expect-ing from him. "Those are two-gauge wires. Notice how they pass right through without connecting to anything?"

The wires Puo's pointing to are thick black wires entering the breaker box from the upper left and thread right through to the upper right. All the other wires are thinner and come in from the upper left and split off to connect directly into the breaker box somewhere, including another pair of black wires that aren't as thick as the ones that pass through.

"These—" Puo points to the other pair of black wires. "—are twelve-gauge wires. The North American standard for homes. Notice how they're smaller?"

"There was another power source into the house," I say, putting it together. "One with way more power than normal."

"Not just another power source, but one wired directly in without any breaker. One with enough power to trip the breakers in the anti-gravity suit. You're lucky they turned the blasted thing off and didn't just keep zapping you," Puo finishes with an I-told-you-so tone.

Except he didn't tell us so. He never even mentioned it as a possibility. How were we supposed to know? Or even better, how would this have changed anything based on what we knew at the time?

As if reading my thoughts, Puo says, "If I hadn't been disabling hovercars, I could've caught this."

"How?" Puo's shaken—I get it. But he's lying to himself to think things would've come out differently if we had had more people and he was safely tucked away running support.

"I would've had Winn send me an image and I would've recognized it instantly. And that, coupled with the dead spot, would've been enough to cut tail and run."

"And then what? Winn and I were already in the house—Wait. What dead spot?"

"The dead spot the microwave scanner couldn't penetrate at

the back of the house. The one I told you about after you refused to wait for Winn."

I shake my head no. "You never said that."

"I most certainly did."

I look to Winn who also shakes his head. "I never heard it either."

We're all silent for a beat. "The music?" I ask. "Mine never stopped."

"Mine either," Winn said.

"Neptune's balls," Puo swears and goes even paler. He flops back in his seat, flips the laptop around to face him and rips Winn's helmet from the laptop. "They selectively jammed us."

"They broke our encryption?" I ask. That isn't supposed to be possible. Jam it yes. Break it open entirely, no.

Puo's nodding to himself, looking like he's about to throw up. "It's worse than that. They either had to have someone off site to do this, or they got to our equipment."

"Fuck." I instinctively look around outside—there's nothing of note. "Keep going," I say to Winn, who was starting to set us down out on a country road. "Get us outside the state."

Puo sets his laptop on the floor and folds down half the back seat to the trunk. He glances back there and tries reaching in, comes out empty-handed and then looks at me. "I need my tools to look in Winn's helmet."

I know what he wants and instead of snarking about being a human fishing pole, I slip back there and get out what he needs. Look at me being an adult.

To the other two, I recap everything that happened to me, from busting through the window to getting zapped and trapped in the basement.

"What happened after you pulled the breakers?" I ask

Winn. I turn in the seat to look toward Winn and keep Puo in my peripheral vision.

Puo slips on a loupe-magnifier headband and retrieves a fine, spindly pair of tweezers, but I can tell from the cock of his head that he's listening intently.

"I ran to join you. I heard you crash through the window while I was pulling the breakers. I heard Puo's admonishment to wait for me, but not your reply. Since the music was still going, I assumed you were ignoring him—"

Puo snorts without looking up from Winn's helmet.

"When I got to the door it was locked. I couldn't get through."

"Did it have the metal bars through the middle?" I ask.

"No, I don't think so. But I didn't really have time to check. I was ransacking the garage to find something to pry the door open, when I heard the Cleaners taunting Puo."

Puo stiffens briefly while working in Winn's helmet.

I do some quick mental math—I must not have been zapped-out for long.

"I snuck back out the window to help Puo, but by that time, Aliyah had already brought one down and was advancing on the other."

"How she'd bring them down?" I ask, curious about their methods.

"Stun gun, from what I could tell."

"I never saw it," Puo answers slowly. He's focused on Winn's helmet, but based on the way the way he draws the answer out, it makes me think he's onto something in Winn's helmet.

"Where'd she come from?" I ask. Nova and company still trail behind us. I expected her to get antsy the longer we haven't pulled down to debrief, but they appear content to follow us for now.

"I don't know," Winn answers about where Aliyah appeared from. "By the time I got out there she was already in position."

Puo's tongue sticks out as he stares into Winn's helmet and picks at something.

When Puo doesn't answer, I ask him, "Puo, did you see where Aliyah came from?"

Puo shakes his head no, but remains focused on the helmet. He suddenly exhales and leans back, his eyes disturbed. His tongue slips back in his mouth like a perturbed gecko.

On the end of his long, slender tweezers, he pulls out a black chip the size of a small tick.

A heavy pall settles over the cabin, punctuated by Puo announcing, "We were bugged."

# Chapter Eighteen

*F*UUUCCCKKK!
      All I can picture is Ham's fat, smug face installing this bug and chortling to himself how much cleverer he is and the delight he'll feel when he sells us out.

Except Puo has me nearly convinced it couldn't have been Ham. The bugs would've had to have been installed after Winn picked the anti-gravity suits up from our Seattle digs, but before our operation on Caesar—we split town too quickly after that. That's less than one and a half days. Plenty of time in my book.

But Puo argues if Ham was going to screw us over, the Caesar op would've been the optimal time. In fact, he *did* try to screw us over.

*So maybe he planted it sometime before the op and kept it as a backup plan?*

Puo doesn't think so. The bug, according to Puo, is a basic commercial-off-the-shelf variety used for tracking and comms listening, and not even that great for comms listening. Puo insists Ham would've used something more sophisticated, so I'm trying to keep an open mind, but it's hard to shake the mental images of that smug, piggy face gloating, even if he is handcuffed following behind us.

"Set her down over there," I say to Winn, pointing to a lonely country road in southern Minnesota.

We need to get a look at my helmet that I stupidly left behind to start to be able to try and piece together who is bugging us and *why*. Which means talking with Nova and company sooner rather than later.

The cabin silence had weighed on us all over the past hour as Puo searched his comms equipment and didn't find any similar bugs. We only started talking again once Puo assured us the bug he pulled doesn't work without being plugged into the helmet—which brings its own set of problems: namely, will they know we found it since we removed it?

Puo thinks so.

Which—shit. We lost all the advantage of having found it and it forces our hand into investigating quickly. Or making sure not to use the anti-gravity suits on any future ops, which, given Puo's bitching about leaving assets on the table, seems like a bad idea.

The jackknives stir at the thoughts of all that's pressing on me. It's not a sharp, sinking-its-claws in feeling, but a slow scrape, a taunt, a promise of things to come. I break out into a cold sweat.

Nova and company follows our hovercar descending slowly down to the blacktop road cutting through flat, snowy white fields. Most of this area is divided flat farmland, with only the barest hint of rolling hills to the landscape.

Once we come to a stop, I say before opening the door, "Let me do the talking."

Puo and Winn share a look.

"What?" I ask.

"You always do the talking," Winn says.

"Always," Puo adds.

"Do you know why she wouldn't do the talking?" Winn asks Puo.

"No," Puo answers with a small headshake. "Do you know why she wouldn't do the talking?"

"No."

"Guys," I cut them off. "It's just something you say."

"Huh," Puo says. "She's continuing to state the obvious."

"That's not a good sign," Winn says.

"She did get zapped pretty hard. Maybe she shouldn't be the one to talk."

"Guys!"

"Now she's repeating herself," Winn says. "I think you're right, Puo. I'll do the talking."

"Okay," Puo says. "Make sure to get the helmet, but without seeming too interested in it. I'll watch to see if there's any hesitancy on their part. Isa, you stand there and try not to repeat yourself."

"Argggh!" I pull my hair.

"That's better, but still not as articulate as we need." To Winn Puo asks, "Ready?"

"Break," Winn says.

They open the doors, letting in gushes of cold Minnesota air.

I scream inside my head and then hurry up to follow them.

Nova, Aliyah, and Mr. Chao get out of their hovercar and walk toward us. Lucy and Ham's silhouettes are visible through the windshield.

"How did you follow us?" I ask. Winn and Puo can irritate me all they want, but in the end they defer to me.

Hot steamy breath rises out of all our mouths and wisps away in the biting wind. The sun stays hidden behind a gray blanket of clouds.

"Why'd you steal Caesar's squeegee and take off without telling us?" Nova asks.

And we're right back to where we left off. Except now we're in the freezing cold and my patience for this shit has plunged past zero.

Freezing wind cuts right through the fur-lined dark-blue parka I'm wearing, making me gasp and huddle my arms closer. I really don't have time for this.

"We had a questionable lead and time was of the essence. There wasn't time to debate it. We went for it."

Nova huddles her own arms close. "What was the lead?"

"How'd you follow us?"

We stare at each other again. This time I'm not going to give. I already went, now it's her turn.

"We bugged Caesar's squeegee," Mr. Chao says, breaking the blockade.

More like they bugged our anti-gravity suits.

Puo doesn't believe it either.

"What I want to know," Nova says, ignoring Mr. Chao and not letting us get a word in edgewise, "is what you would've done if you managed to find and rescue your friend after barreling in there like that." She stares at me like I was planning to abandon them or stab them in the back.

Which, honestly, only confuses me. "Why do you care? Your money runs out in three days anyway and you'll split then, right?"

"We are currently hired to protect Mr. Chao and Ms. Bennett. I need to assess all possible threats, like a former ally turning on them in exchange for amnesty."

Which sounds perfectly plausible, except I saw her hand stiffen for a split second. Is she planning on staying beyond the money? Is she involved with Mr. Chao outside of a professional relationship? Involved with Lucy?

Puo and Winn scowl. Backstabbing isn't our style.

"We would've stashed Charlie away and then returned," I say this more to Mr. Chao than to Nova, since he's the one who would ultimately care. "You promised new CitID hardware and to scrub our images from the British Government databases, remember?"

Prior to Puo's ability to digitally conjure quants, new CitID hardware would've been well worth the price of our services. It took us several jobs to pay off our first modified CitIDs. Now we could buy legit ones with a flutter of Puo's fingers.

"New CitID hardware," Mr. Chao says, "and a *provisional* agreement to remove your images from the British Government databases. I remember."

"We're not going anywhere," I say. "We also both still need to permanently deal with the National Syndicate."

"Then why did you split without telling anyone?" Nova asks, a dog that won't let go of a bone.

Puo turns and gives me a look that says, "That's a great question."

*Freaking Puo.*

"I told you," I explain again. "There wasn't time to waste to debate it."

"It took five hours to fly out here," Puo says. "We couldn't have discussed it then?"

"Puo!" I whirl on him. *What the fuck!* Argue all you want, point out how stupid I am. But do it in private. Never in front of people we don't trust. Now they could sense a rift and try to exploit it.

Puo holds my gaze, but gives away his discomfort when he labors to swallow.

"No," I snap. "We couldn't discuss it then. I didn't know where we were going when we slipped away. And once we were under way, calling back would've only slowed us down. We couldn't wait for them to catch up. Speed. Remember?"

Nova opens her mouth to irritate me further, but I bowl over her, "And if you're so good at following us and altruistic, why did it take you so long to intervene?"

"We rescued you as soon as we could—"

"Bullshit." I jab an accusatory finger at her. "You saw our entrance into the house. You hung back and waited. Don't fucking lie!" I stamp over her as she opens her lying mouth again. "How else would you know we 'barreled in there like that'?"

The more I think about it, the more it fits and the more it pisses me off. They sat back and watched us enter a trap, instead of warning us. *Why didn't we see them?*

Nova is visibly agitated. Mr. Chao and Aliyah look worried.

"We rescued you as soon as we could," Nova strains to say more slowly. "It was an unknown situation—the house had a hundred-and-fifteen-amp input line—"

"How do you know that?" Puo asks, while giving me a suppressed look of rage that this could've all been avoided by slowing down and including them.

"I pulled the most recent renovation invoices from two weeks ago," Mr. Chao answers.

Puo's already shaking his head no. "I pulled the permits—including from local utilities. There wasn't anything—"

"They kept the input line off any official forms, but contractors still want to get paid," Mr. Chao says.

Puo's still shaking his head. "I want to see it."

Mr. Chao nods, while I say to Nova, "And you still didn't warn us?"

"We couldn't warn you without exposing ourselves," Nova picks up her bullshit right where she left off. "Rushing in could've incapacitated both of us. Once we saw the power surge, we moved."

I shake my head at Nova. "Liar." She could've approached us before we entered the house.

I dart forward unexpectedly before anyone has time to say anything, and all three shift a foot back and anchor themselves expecting an attack. I blow past them toward their hovercar, and by the time they figure out what I'm doing I'm already too far ahead.

"Wait!" Nova shouts.

I rip the back door open. Ham has his hands bound behind him in the backseat, while Lucy sits up front. I grab my burned-out helmet, slam the door before they can say anything, and stalk back. I throw it at Puo who catches it with a smack against his hands and a surprised look.

"Let's go," I order Puo.

"Wait," Nova says again.

"No," I say over my shoulder, stomping to the car in the snow. "No fucking waiting. You waited enough back there. And you—" I whirl on Puo. "—these are the people you wanted to bring along? Lot of fucking help they would've been waiting around to see if it's safe."

Puo slides the helmet opening to point up and wisely keeps his mouth shut as he follows after me.

Nova starts to speak again—I whirl around. "We may have left without notifying you, but *you* hung us out to dry." I jab a finger at her, taking an involuntary step forward. "So we are not going to fucking wait, or have one of you backstabbers ride home with us—"

None of the three like the term "backstabber," but from Aliyah's face, she really doesn't like it.

"—You're going to follow us back with your tail between your legs and think about what backstabbing assholes you are. Then you're going to apologize when we get back, or sit facing the corner until you do."

Nova looks ready to murder me right there, and Aliyah actually looked chagrined until that sit-in-the-corner comment. *Oh, well.* We got what we came for.

I stomp toward the hovercar, Winn and Puo in tow. Much to my surprise, Nova watches us go in silence.

\*\*\*

"It would've gone differently if we looped them in from the beginning," Puo says as our hovercar climbs back up into the sky.

"Maybe," I concede. "Probably. But that's not what happened. More immediately, we needed to get the hell out of there before one of them tried to worm their way into our hovercar or get the helmet back."

Puo's eyebrows climb as he looks down at the helmet in his lap.

"There was a fine jewelry toolkit open and spread out across the backseat," I tell Puo. "A riffler and a small pliers were missing from the kit—my guess is a bent nose based on the placement in the kit." *Or Ham palmed it*—which wouldn't surprise me.

Puo exhales out his nose and reaches for his own tools, looping the loupe-magnifier headband back on. He sets to work and then says without looking up at me in the front seat. "I'm sorry—about back there," he clarifies when I shift in my seat to look at him. "Well, half sorry," he amends.

"Half sorry?"

"About suggesting we should've called them on the way to the house. I wanted to piss you off—"

"Arrgh!" I pull my hair again. It's remarkable I'm not bald yet working with these two.

Puo shrugs. "You work better that way."

"I hate when you do that."

"Well, it seems to have worked." Puo nods down at the helmet he's working on, flipping his headband light on. "But that comment was ..." He stops and looks up, searching for the right words, shining the light in my face. "Too close to airing dirty laundry in public."

"Yeah—"

"But," he cuts me off, "it's still true. So, half sorry."

*Freaking, Puo.*

I study him as he works. The tools look like fragile playthings in his hands, but he's so delicate with them, precise.

"You really think we should've looped them in from the beginning?"

He nods, still focused on dissecting my burned-out helmet. "Yeah."

"You?" I ask Winn, who's driving the hovercar.

Winn looks over at me with his bright blue eyes and then looks away before nodding. "Yeah."

*Damn.* "Even before everything went to hell?"

"I agree with Puo, we left assets on the table sprinting into an unknown situation. They saw things we didn't and with more bodies we would've planned differently." Winn holds his hand up to hold me off. "But even if everything went well and Charlie was there and we got her out. Then what?" He glances over at me and answers his own question. "We'd have to hide her—"

"Charlie can hide herself," I say.

Winn gives me a look that says, "Then how'd she get captured?"

"She knows they're coming this time," I say.

"She knew they were coming before we went back to England," Puo says quietly.

I open my mouth to argue Charlie can take care of herself when Winn talks over me, "Regardless, we still need them to take care of the National Syndicate and to scrub our images from the British Government's databases. At the very least, we can't do that last one on our own. Who knows how they might have interpreted our disappearance and reappearance."

"I am not going to let some backstabbers' hypothetical opinions dictate our actions—"

"It's not that one factor," Winn says, "but the sum of all of it."

"And I can't keep doing all the things," Puo says, with some bite. "We need more people. Look at the Izaak and Caesar jobs. Neither of those would've been able to have been pulled off that quickly without the others. If they had been ... if ... they had been ...."

Puo's shoulders deflate, his hands still inside the helmet. The headband light shines down over his loupes. "Balls."

"You find the bug?" I turn to look at him.

"No. I found where the bug was. The burn marks around where it was and the clean pin indicate it was removed after you were fried. That's how they followed us here."

*I knew it.*

Puo looks resigned, like he knew it too but hoped their lie about bugging Caesar's squeegee was true.

"Maybe they saw the power line to the house," I say in vindication, "and things we didn't, because they already knew they were there."

# Chapter Nineteen

THIS COMPLICATES everything.

When did they plant the bug? Was it planted before the Izaak op? Nova was way too interested in Winn's role during that job—was that why? Or did they plant it after, once they knew we had some secret equipment and they went looking for it?

This is the problem when working with Cleaners. They're a bunch of backstabbing prima donnas and, unfortunately, skilled in the digital arts.

Fortunately, it doesn't make any sense that they're working with the National Syndicate. They could have turned us over at any point with a phone call. It's likely some good ol' fashioned eavesdropping, but how do we make sure? We still need to rescue Charlie and put a fix in place with the National Syndicate.

The jackknives flutter to life as we enter the punch code and walk back into the three-bedroom apartment above *The Slot* in Marlborough, Massachusetts. Just enough to let me know they're there. Just enough to remind me that, when everything's pressing down, when everything's on the line, they can shred me to pieces and bring me to my knees.

*Fuck.*

We needed a place that had power and internet access that would hide our usage of both, and this apartment fit the bill. We already had access and had gone through the work of securing it.

The only downside is the extra travel time to get here. More time lost.

*Bad thought.*

Everything suddenly feels immediate, demanding my attention. Right fucking now. Never mind we have two-and-a-half days to get Charlie and figure out this bug situation. We've done more on less time before.

Everything needs to be done *right* fucking *now*. And I have no idea where to start.

*Oh, God.*

The jackknives were just fucking with me before, an opening act's sick joke. They unfurl in force.

I stumble as we move past the entrance hallway deeper into the apartment. Lucy is in the middle of the living room setting up their computers. Ham helps bundle cables, his hands free from the handcuffs. The dining room table is clear, waiting for Puo's set up.

*Fuck.* I clutch my stomach in pain.

Puo hurriedly hangs up his moss-colored ski jacket in the hallway behind me and grabs my arm. "C'mon, we need to talk." He pulls me down the closest hallway to a bedroom.

Puo closes the bedroom door behind me. "Breathe. Focus on—"

"Don't tell me to fucking breathe." *God, I hate this.* My heart feels like it's going to break a rib. I *need* to run away, like it's the only overriding imperative that matters. I have nowhere to go, but that doesn't matter.

I can't stop pacing around the small bedroom.

"Anchor yourself," Puo tries to sound confident and fails. He's scared. He has no idea what happened, what set me off.

That's the worst fucking part. There's no rhyme or reason to this shit. A stray thought kick-started this. *How am I supposed to control that?*

Anchor myself. God, that seems so stupid. That's the problem—I'm too into my own body, my own experience.

"Tell me five things you can see—" Puo says.

Winn enters the bedroom. His worried face says it all. He saw the panic attack happening, Puo intervening. Which means everyone else saw it too.

My heart rate doubles.

"Five things," Puo repeats.

Winn walks up to Puo and rests his hand on Puo's arm. "Go set up your computers, decode the blockchain. I'll help Isa." Puo makes to argue, but Winn talks over him. "They know something's up. Go. Tell them—- Tell them we're having alone time."

"Alone time?" Puo asks.

"Sex—"

"Winn!" I stare at him disbelief.

"It's a lie," Winn says. "Puo can make it out like you two have been arguing about us getting back together, with Puo against it and you deciding to go for it and Puo's trying to talk you out of it—"

"Ushering her into a bedroom for a talking-to was a poor choice then," Puo says.

"Yeah," Winn says, "play that up. Just go. Before they send someone down to eavesdrop."

Puo looks helplessly at me.

"I got this," Winn says, much more confidently than Puo. "Doctor, remember?"

Puo looks between us again and then nods. He takes a deep breath, slips on a frustrated face and leaves, even slamming the door behind him.

Winn turns his focus to me. "Do you know what diaphragmatic breathing is?"

I nod.

"Start. And Puo was right, start with telling me five things you can see." When I look at him like he's an idiot, he says, "The practice anchors you outside your body in the present. You need to get out of your head."

*Can't argue with that.*

I continue to pace. "I see a geometric art piece above the bed. A white bed spread. White wooden nightstands, painted to look distressed. Looks cheap, maybe particle board—"

"Three more," Winn says.

"Green throw pillows. A steel wall sconce. A painted-over nail pop in the ceiling."

"Now four things you can feel."

My heart continues to thunder as I turn around. Winn fishes around in his pockets and comes out with a brown opaque pill bottle.

He looks up at me distracted as he opens the bottle. "Four things."

I stare at him and at the little round brown pills that tumble out into his hand.

When I don't respond with anything I can feel, he looks at me properly.

"I thought those were habit forming." I took one a little over twenty-four hours ago.

Winn's nods. "Like I said, a balancing act. Treat the symptoms in the rough period, then reset when things calm down. You're in a rough period." He puts all the pills but one back in the bottle with hollow clinks.

"No shit." Still, I hesitate. I swear my heart is going rip out of my chest. Cold sweat drips down the underside of my arms. "What happens if things never calm down?"

Winn's quiet for a second and then says, "Then we'll get through it together. It's your choice. Even though it doesn't feel like it, the anxiety attack will eventually pass—"

I nearly throw something at him. Being told this will pass is like being told the bone sticking out your arm squirting blood will eventually heal.

"—this—" He holds out his hand with the little brown pill in it. "—will take the edge off."

I stare at that little pill, consumed with what path I may be headed down by taking it. It suddenly becomes another weight amidst all the other things needing to be dealt with right *fucking* now. *God, I can't breathe. I can't live like this.*

I walk forward and pick up the pill, my hand shaking. "We're in this together, right?

He nods.

"I'm trusting you."

He looks deep into my eyes. "I'm not going anywhere. Not ever again."

I pop the pill.

\*\*\*

Winn insisted on continuing the anchoring exercise and diaphragmatic breathing while the pill took the edge off. But that edge? Still there, like a sheathed blade pressed against my heart, exerting pressure, but not slicing in. The pill may have helped round it off, but it did not remove it completely. Not like the first time I took it. There's no way I could fall asleep now.

It took us a full forty-five minutes before I was ready to leave that little bedroom and rejoin the wider group. There is work to do in decoding the blockchain and coming up with a plan of action, but somehow in those forty-five minutes that bedroom became my safe place. Never mind that we were supposed to pretend we were having sex and the length of time we were gone played right into that. Even with that, I couldn't bring myself to fake noises and bed thumping and whatnot.

I've been doing cons, playing various roles, for as long as I can remember and now suddenly pretending to just have had sex with a person I've had plenty of sex with before in front of a group of people I'm familiar with seems the peak challenge of my life.

I mean, even if they sense something's off, we can just say I have a stomach bug. *In fact, why didn't we say that? Instead, we went with sex?*

I roll my eyes as I come out of the bedroom. Freaking men. It's the first place their minds go. I study the back of Winn's head in front of me—it's clear what he's been thinking about. If I hadn't been so addled, I would've seen the obvious choice and put a stop to this farce.

Lucy and Mr. Chao sit at their dual float screens in the living room, and Puo has taken over the dining room table again with his old-school monitors and cabling running everywhere. Nova and Aliyah are on the barstools Winn and I occupied last time. Sandwich and snack stuff are spread out on the kitchen counter. The smell of potato chips and deli turkey nearly makes me gag. Apparently, a fun side effect of panic attacks is that your mouth tastes like ash with zero appetite.

Everybody looks over at us as we walk in. Puo even scowls— staying in character.

"Any progress?" I ask the room in general as Winn goes to look over the food layout.

"You look terrible," Nova observes.

"That's a terrible apology, Backstabber. Try again."

"My apologies, Deserter," she says without missing a beat. "You look terrible."

Puo periscopes up from behind his computer screens. "You do look terrible."

"No afterglow," Ham observes with a smarmy smile.

"What?" I ask, a cross between confused and pissed—the pissed part, at least, is real.

"They know," Puo says.

"You told them!"

"What was I supposed to say?"

"Lie! Tell them we were secretly plotting against them."

"I thought we were supposed to be building trust. They should know about this colossal stupidity."

*Building trust my ass—where'd that bug come from then?*

"You were back there a long time." Ham smirks. "Took a while to get started?"

I pick up a metal geode knickknack off the closest side table and chuck it at him. There're several things that run through my mind at the prick's comment, but then, since this sex farce was Winn's idea, I say uncertainly, "It's been a while. We've been under a lot of pressure. Winn's older now. And we weren't able to finish." I shake my head. "It's completely normal—"

"Hey!" Winn shouts.

Puo snorts.

"Yuck it up, Viagra man—" Winn says.

"Hey!" Puo turns red.

Puo's reaction is so good, I wonder if there's some truth to it.

Winn continues over top of Puo, "—I'll remember this when you need a refill."

Ham cackles with delight.

All three of us zero in on Ham, but Winn snaps first, "You won't be laughing anymore when I slip you a little surprise at dinner, you'll be king of the limpies for life."

Ham's face wilts and he looks around the room as if to verify Winn wouldn't do any such thing. No one reassures him.

There's a beat where the room freezes.

Puo and Winn's faces are red. Puo avoids looking anyone in the eye while Winn stares down Ham. Nova and Aliyah sit back in their chairs watching things develop. Lucy looks like someone smeared poop under her nose—which I'm starting to think is her default face. And Mr. Chao looks embarrassed, staring intently at his float screen.

Eventually, I say, "Now that's over, can someone please tell me what we've found so far?"

Mr. Chao answers quickly, as if he's eager to put an end to the stream of dick jokes, "Nothing yet. We found the cold storage on Caesar's squeegee and its private key—"

"Now that we have the real squeegee and know the homing beacon was fake," Lucy mutters.

Mr. Chao continues, ignoring Lucy, "—We are now decoding the blockchain with Caesar's and Izaak's private keys."

Puo cocks a superior eyebrow through the crack between his monitors. "I've decoded most of the way through November." When everyone turns to look at him, and he has the audience he wants, he adds with a shrug, "Audit logs—I write out progress as it churns rather than wait for it to be done all at once."

I wonder how long he's been waiting to reveal that one—I guarantee you he saw their mistake and didn't correct it. Part of that is pride, but part of that pure pragmatism. He can crow all he wants about teaming up and "using all assets on the table," but this little slight reveals how he really feels. He doesn't trust them anymore than I do. By reading the blockchain first, we can act on that information before they learn of it or hide it if we need to.

"So what have you found?" I ask.

"It all started the night at the marina, when you stole Christina's squeegee." Puo squints at his monitor. "August fourth, in the wee hours of the morning."

"We already knew that," I say. We figured that out on the train between New Dublin and Paris.

"No, we suspected that. *Now* we know it. There was a whole bunch of chatter once Christina was free from the marina between the other members—"

"The other members—" I cut in, getting ahead of myself, "—do you know who they are? Where they are? Do you know where Charlie is?" *Is she in this Citadel? Does it say where or what this Citadel is?*

Puo's shakes his head no to knowing where Charlie is. "It isn't done decoding to that point yet. It's still in November."

I deflate a little and take a deep breath. Patience.

"But," Puo says more cheerily, "we do know who they are and where they operate."

"Good." My heart swells with righteous indignation. No matter what happens, I am going to burn each one of those fuckers to the ground.

"What was their chatter from the marina about?" I ask, bringing it back to what Puo was trying to tell me before I cut him off.

"The extra squeegee we had at the marina. It really spooked them—they wanted to know where we got it. And given what we know about the dodecagon cypher now, you can see why they kinda freaked when we disappeared with Christina's squeegee."

"Wait," Ham says, studying the ground as if trying hard to remember something, "that was in August? What was that date again?"

"August fourth," Puo answers.

"What day of the week?" Ham asks. "Was that a Thursday?"

Puo clicks on his keyboard for second and then says, "Yeah."

Ham's eyes go wide and he rocks back on his heels.

"Whadda ya know Hammy boy?" I ask.

"That's when it started."

"What started?" Puo asks.

"Caesar—" Ham's eyes are distant, reliving a memory. "—he started poking at me, probing around everything I did, who I worked with after the Waylon Lo job."

"After they knew you stole his code," I clarify.

Ham nods.

Mr. Chao and Lucy perk up. They hadn't known that little fact. And none of them know Puo can hack the blockchain— that's supposed to be impossible.

"And then you split town," Puo says about Ham, reading from his screen.

"Yes," Ham says breathlessly. "That's in there?"

"They let you go," Puo says. "They wanted to see if you would lead them to us."

Ham pales and gives small headshakes as he thinks it over. "They knew you stole Caesar's code from me."

"No," I say. "They knew we worked together and we were in possession of Christina's squeegee. They probably figured you were after another National-Syndicate-level squeegee and wanted to make sure we weren't working together." We've never confirmed to him that we stole his code. That little nugget would reveal what Puo can do with the blockchain.

Ham starts to argue when Mr. Chao cuts in to ask Puo, "Can you please send us what you have?"

Puo glances at me and I nod. A couple of taps later, Mr. Chao and Lucy are each reading on their own screens.

Ham won't let it go. "You must have stolen it. How else did you have another squeegee at the marina?"

I'm about to argue when Lucy, reading their decoded part of the blockchain, unexpectedly comes to my rescue. "They sent a team to the marina to find out the answer to that very question."

"When?" I ask.

"A couple days after we split town." Puo rests his finger against the monitor.

I mull that over. "We left town two, maybe three weeks after all that. What took them so long?" We spent those weeks setting Colvin's sisters up in case of an emergency—come to think of it, I'm curious if those protocols were activated in the wake of the Cleaners moving and if they're all right. But after that was done, I was restless and Puo thought it was a good idea to do a job to get my mind off of Winn so we headed over to Europe leading to the now infamous British Museum heist.

There's a silence as Puo, Mr. Chao, and Lucy scan the block-chain for clues.

Ham, still pallid, comes to stand next to Mr. Chao and read over his shoulder. "Wait, back up."

Mr. Chao does as requested.

Ham mutters to himself. "Back up more." It's clear Ham wants to kick Mr. Chao out and drive, but Mr. Chao doesn't give up his seat, instead scrolling back as requested.

"There—" Ham points at the float screen. "—They were scared."

Mr. Chao and Lucy lean forward.

"Where?" Puo asks.

"August tenth around ten a.m.," Mr. Chao answers. "It calls for a meeting in person, and then nothing until the nineteenth."

Puo runs his finger down the monitor and then stops.

August tenth. There's something about that date that sticks in my mind.

It's sticking in Puo's mind too—I can tell by how rapidly his eyes scan the monitor. He looks up at me. "That's when Colvin announced Christina's betrayal and execution." That was the Wednesday after her murder, four days later. "Up until then, no one knew where she was. All their messages before that are asking for updates that never came."

"They were scared," I confirm. "With Christina's squeegee loose, they didn't trust their own blockchain."

"Then why did they wait so long to send a team out to investigate?" Mr. Chao asks.

Puo answers, "The message on the tenth wasn't for a meeting in person, it called for a 'sit down.'"

That fits.

A sit down is a very specific type of meeting between the higher-ups. Colvin had just whacked one of their leaders, and announced it publicly with evidence for just cause. A sit down made sense between Colvin and the Cleaners to make sure a wider war didn't break out. Of course, that's what the Cleaners were planning all along, but they weren't ready to move yet and that type of meeting would be expected.

Puo explains this all to the group while I mull it over.

It would take time to set up a meeting like that, especially after what precipitated it. With Christina's squeegee missing, the Cleaners would be extra-cautious.

"That's what the gap was about until the nineteenth," I say, filling in more of the pieces of that gap. "They were worried about a trap. They didn't know if we knew about their grand plans and had told Colvin. They didn't know if we could read the blockchain—"

"Because you stole Caesar's code off me," Ham starts his nonsense again.

"No," I say again, "That's what they feared, not reality."

"Then where did you get that squeegee?" Ham asks.

Rather than answer, Puo says to me, "So they stopped communicating that way until they were confident Colvin didn't know about their plans."

"And once they determined Colvin didn't know, they needed to track down Christina's squeegee so they sent a team to investigate the marina," I say, trying to order the events in my head.

"You're the hirudineas they reference," Lucy says.

"The what?" I ask.

"In the blockchain," Lucy says, "it says the marina and yacht—" She says that last word as a question and looks at Puo and I.

"Valle's yacht," I supply. "Where Christina was killed."

"—were too clean. They were going to track down the hirudineas and visit the den."

The den is a reference to the local Cleaners headquarters, but hirudineas could be anything.

Puo cuts in, "She's right. There's more references later that makes sense it's us."

"What are hirudineas?" I ask.

Aliyah answers, "Leeches." She stops there as if it's the most obvious thing in the world. We all stare at her. She even manages to leave the phrase "probably deserved" unsaid and hanging in the air.

"How do you know that?" And we are not leeches.

"It's Latin. I went to school." Aliyah tilts her chin up. "Didn't you?"

"No. I didn't." There was a time in my life I was pretty bitter about that. Until I saw the life most "educated" people end up leading on leaving school. Puo and I avoided that conveyor belt of life pumping people through school and into a soulless job to spend their days wondering where they took a wrong turn. No, missing out on that experience no longer pisses me off. Her chin-tilting attitude, though, that's another matter.

Puo, knowing how I was likely to respond, cuts in again, "Early- to mid-December has been decoded. 'December third: The hirudineas have slithered over the border.' They were watching our Queen Anne home." There's no point in trying to hide our home from Nova and company—the address is right there in the freaking blockchain, but I still have a knee-jerk response to Puo announcing it so blithely.

That's when we headed over to Vancouver. We didn't stay long after returning from England.

Lucy and Mr. Chao scroll down to the end.

"Can you send us the updated file?" Mr. Chao asks Puo.

Puo answers with button clicks and keyboard clacks.

*Damn it.* They had our house under surveillance. It makes perfect sense. Christina knew its location—they swapped out the solid-state drive when we were at our neighbor's Kathy's party. But I thought Colvin cauterized that threat.

*What else have I missed?* I frantically think over all the times we've gone back to the house since Christina's death. That dulled jackknife's edge pressed into my heart bares its blade. Slices right through the medication.

*Fuck.* Blood pounds in my ears. Down my neck. *Fuck, fuck, fuck.*

I can't leave. There's nowhere to go. They'll all know.

*I can't leave. I can't leave. I can't leave.*

Puo's looking at me. He knows. They know. They all know. *Shit. What do I do?*

"Come look at this," Puo says to me.

The weight of the room swivels toward me. The moment builds into something I can't hide or ignore. Every millisecond of delay exposes my weakness. I walk over to Puo, too aware of my own body, feeling like a gangly newborn giraffe. I breathe through my nose, try and regulate my breath.

"Not you!" Puo barks, looking past me at Ham, who was starting to follow.

I duck around the kitchen table and Puo scoots over on the bench. Once I sit down, he pushes two monitors together to form a fortress, cutting off line of sight to the rest of the room.

I sit on my shaking hands. *Damn it, I don't need this right now.*

"Look at this." Puo points to the audit log of the decoded blockchain to the term "etching."

The term goes all the way back in the audit log to right after the National Syndicate team visited the Seattle Den, and the term peppers the next several messages.

"What?" Ham asks about what Puo is showing me.

I hide behind the monitors, breathing. Trying to get my shit together. My face flushes. Cold sweat breaks over me. I can feel Ham wanting to come over, feel the room peering over at us.

Puo sticks his head up above the monitors. "The term 'etching,' what is it?"

I can't see Ham's face or body language, but I can see Puo's. Whatever Ham just did, it pisses Puo off.

After two beats pass where Ham should've responded Puo tries again, "If you don't know what it is ...."

Once more there's a beat where the room holds its collective breath. Still no answer.

"Ham," Mr. Chao finally cuts in, "you are clearly more experienced in these matters. Please explain it to them."

That snaps me out of my downward spiral. That's the second time Mr. Chao has deferred to Ham, and this last one was downright obsequious. Very un-Cleaner like.

I lift my head up to stare at Ham. My heart still thunders in my chest, but I have a handle on my breathing.

Ham looks between Lucy and Mr. Chao, the latter of whom stares right back. Ham sniffs and then indicates he wants Mr. Chao's seat who, surprisingly, gets up. Ham starts, "An etching is a deep system capture. It's capturing the information at the lowest levels, enabling a trawl-through later to see if a Cleaner has been in the system. The best Cleaner code can remove the software fingerprints, but not the hardware traces. We're talking at the magnetic bit level, where code has run and stopped, leaving hard edges in the magnetic signature. Only National Syndicate–level tech can pass that type of scan. It's why I was after it."

Puo leans back a hair and suppresses a smile—he must have an idea of how to do it. It must be costing him a supreme level of effort not to throw that back in Ham's face.

Puo and I look back at the messages referencing the etching.

"Christina had taken an etching of the marina," I say to Puo.

"She was trying to figure out where we got our squeegee," Puo says.

"She never finished it though." Ham drives the displays now, reading the log. "Those scans are slow, meticulous. It could take days to do a deep scan of a whole system. The National Syndicate team went to collect the etching to finish the scan." Ham trails off scanning the blockchain.

I see it before he does—*shit*.

"I knew it," Ham says, self-satisfaction dripping from every word. He stares at me over his monitors.

My mind kicks into overdrive. My heart is still thundering in my chest, but now it's a secondary problem. If I can't stop the bullet aimed for my head, a heart attack is the least of my problems.

"What?" Lucy asks, scanning her own copy of the blockchain.

"The deep scan didn't turn up anything," Ham explains. "'August twenty-ninth, three fifteen p.m.: No residuals in etching. A second is loose.' They knew you stole Caesar's code!"

"No they didn't!" I snap. "They thought we did—"

"Then why was the etching clean?" Ham asks.

"We never plugged in." My mind comes into sharp focus at dealing with this prick. "We had it on us but never had the chance to plug in before they confronted us." That's not even remotely true. Winn plugged in at the marina and I plugged into Valle's yacht, but there's nothing in the blockchain to indicate the Cleaners saw us plug in.

"Then why did they go to Waylon Lo's house?" Ham asks. When he sees my confusion he says, "'August thirtieth, seven eighteen a.m.: Sending a team to Upstate Neverland.'"

Waylon Lo was a collector of children's toys and nostalgia. We worked with Ham last July to steal a very valuable copy of *Where the Wild Things Are* from his Keuka Lake house. The 'Upstate Neverland' description fits.

"That could mean anything," I say.

I ignore Ham and go back to reading the blockchain. It's the entry right after the twenty-ninth that captivates my attention: *Tighten the noose and kick them off a ledge.*

That's when they made the decision to kill us. When they thought we had two National Syndicate squeegees and they couldn't risk their plans leaking out. But Puo and I were already in Europe. No one knew where we were.

I skim ahead to when we came back to the States before heading to Vancouver. It's all starting to make sense.

There. I jam a finger against Puo's old-school monitor and Puo looks at it and nods. The day we came back, the Cleaners had our Queen Ann Island home under surveillance and followed us to Vancouver. That's when they leaned on Nix to do their dirty work while I farted around, too scared to confront Winn. They needed us dead, but, because of my father, they couldn't risk it being tied back to them—they were still trying to remain hidden.

Ham continues to blather on about stealing his code but I'm focused on reading the blockchain as Puo's code continues to update the file.

There's grabbing Winn and questioning him. They saw Kathy visit our home and travel to Canada but lost her at the border, when the Cleaner following her got detained (serves them right). And there's my high-altitude, late-night rescue of Winn. *Shit*.

There's a note about my anti-gravity suit on December eleventh. They don't identify it as that but mention that we have some unknown tech that lets us drop out of the sky—at least there's no reference to falling *up*. They even connect the suits to being the source of our likely entry into underwater reclamation jobs.

Movement through the crack between the monitors catches my attention. Mr. Chao leans down at Lucy's screen and shares a look with her. His gaze subtly flicks to Nova who watches them as well.

I highlight the section referencing the anti-gravity suits and delete it with Puo watching.

Puo undoes my change and opens up a text editor: **Already sent it.**

Puo starts typing faster seeing me agitated: **They're independently decrypting the blockchain. It'll only serve to highlight that we deleted it when they do a diff between the files.**

Ham really starts blathering now. He's stood back up and is shouting, commanding the whole room's attention. "December twelfth, nine eighteen p.m.! They knew! They proved it!"

"What the fuck are you talking about?" I shout back, straightening up in my chair to take in the room. My dislike of this prick is overtaking the I'm-about-to-die feeling hijacking my nervous system.

"They took an etching of Waylon Lo's systems and completed a deep analysis on it. They only detected anything the last time I plugged in, when they detected the presence of a shadow program—"

That was the whole point of the Skim Job, to force Ham to plug in that last time in a panic and not have time to put all the proper protocols in place.

"No they didn't." Puo scans the blockchain finding where Ham indicated. "It says there was something weird and that it may be a shadow program."

"December twelfth nine eighteen p.m.! 'Analysis concludes likely point of theft.' It's also the only job I ever pulled with Caesar's code. It's the only time it could've been stolen."

"*Likely stolen,*" Puo emphasizes. "They didn't know if it was stolen or not."

"And think about what you're saying," I pile on. "You're saying we stole Caesar's code without it registering on the blockchain. That's impossible—"

"That's it!" Ham's jaw goes slack. "You can do it, can't you?" he asks breathlessly, looking at Puo in wonder.

Puo looks distinctly uncomfortable with the way Ham stares at him and doesn't respond.

"That's what all this is about," Ham continues in the same breathless way. I can see him putting it all together. "I've been wondering why they went from trying to kill you to luring you into a trap in Aberdeen. Why kidnap your father, and then this Charlie? To lure you out into the open. The only reason to keep you alive is if you know something they want to know." He rocks back. "It's Puo they're after. They want you—" He points at me. "—to get to Puo. It all fits."

It does all fit. I consider deflecting, but there's no credibility left there to exploit. The room has turned against us. I can see it in the way everyone is staring at Puo. The story fits all the facts too neatly. Any alternative story at this point faces an uphill climb and would only succeed with irrefutable proof, given we have every incentive to lie here.

I stand up, even managing not to shake. All eyes swivel to me. "This does not change anything—"

"This changes everything!" Ham says.

"No, it doesn't. We still need to save Charlie. We still need to deal with the National Syndicate."

"They're never going to leave you alone about this." Avarice suddenly blooms in Ham's eyes.

"Is it true," Mr. Chao asks, "you stole a copy of their code without it being encoded on their blockchain?"

Puo looks at me and then nods once.

The room breaks into mutters and glances at each other. Ham's blatant look of avarice deepens.

"Yes!" I say over everyone and start lying my ass off to make sure Winn and I don't get stabbed in our sleep and Puo kidnapped. "Puo, and only Puo, knows how to bypass the block-chain. And he's sure as hell not going to tell anyone. If anything happens to any one of us, we have a failsafe set up to push that information out into the public domain to make it worthless." If everyone knows the blockchain can be bypassed, the whole technology and financial world it underpins becomes worth-less—the information is only valuable if it remains secret.

"Who cares?" Ham says. "They'll be looking for that. The scrubbers will be on it faster than if our own code got out."

"Scrubbers?" I ask. Puo peers at him in sudden interest.

Ham looks like he just zippered his ball sack. "It doesn't matter—"

This is why their code never makes it out into the open. They have these scrubbers out looking for it, trawling the open web. *Why hasn't Puo seen these scrubbers?*

"Ham—" I want to know more about these scrubbers.

"It doesn't matter! You can bypass the blockchain. Do you know what that means? Don't deny it. It all fits."

I can't believe it's come to this. All our secrets laid bare, right there in this stupid blockchain. We've fought for so long to keep the anti-gravity suits secret and didn't even have the secret of the blockchain for more than a week. *And* we didn't get anything in exchange for it. *Fuck!*

That last thought fires off a starter pistol in my mind. Greed, and the desire to reduce the amount of shit I have to do, takes off running in a new direction. I turn to Mr. Chao. "And since we're laying it all out there—we found the bugs in our helmets. What the fuck?"

Mr. Chao pinches the bridge of his nose and looks at Nova. "Yes. About that. We thought it prudent to be able to keep track of everyone—"

"I insisted," Nova says, sitting up straighter. "And I was right to do so. You disappeared with Caesar's squeegee and without those chips we wouldn't have known where you went."

Ham looks between us. His whole countenance and demeanor read like this is new information to him—but he also keeps flicking his gaze to Puo.

"In fact," Nova continues, "you should be thanking us. Otherwise, you'd still be there—"

"Unlikely," Puo breaks in. "Those chips are HPD 7500s—"

Ham looks sharply at Mr. Chao and Lucy at that information.

Puo continues, "—That's how the Aberdeen Cleaners selectively blocked us. Those chips have a widely publicized kleptographic backdoor the Cleaners used to break our encryption. We never would've fallen into that trap if we knew we were being selectively jammed. You screwed us."

*Son of a bitch!* It appears Puo's been busy while I've been losing my shit in the bedroom.

Nova and Aliyah look suspicious, while Mr. Chao and Lucy share a look.

"Any other chips we should know about?" Puo asks.

Mr. Chao says, "A few. We'll have them removed."

Nova scowls.

Puo shakes his head. "I want access to your tracking programs. All of them. It's the only way I'm going to trust they're removed."

"No," Lucy says.

Puo's raises his eyebrows and then clicks on his keyboard.

"Hey!" Lucy yells.

"Oh, I'm sorry," Puo says. "Did you want access to the decoded blockchain?"

Mr. Chao raises both his hands to settle the room. To Lucy he says, "Give him access." To everyone else he says, "The tracking chips were a bad idea from the beginning and they're a bad idea now. I should've never agreed to it."

Ham looks both confused and agitated and it takes me a second to figure out why. He's still operating under the assumption Nova and Aliyah are Interpol, they're the ones supposed to be calling the shots.

To Nova I say, "No more tracking chips. Agreed?"

She doesn't look happy, but nods.

Ham can't contain it anymore. "Who cares about sharing the private blockchain? He can *bypass* the blockchain. Use *that* as leverage to barter for our freedom," Ham says to me, looking over at Nova.

"No," I say. When Ham looks like he's about to argue, I talk over him. "We still need to work together. We need to get Charlie. We still need to deal with the National Syndicate." And from the murderous look in Ham's eyes, we're going to have to put him on an even shorter leash. I can't have that prig breaking off right now to spill our secrets to Caesar in exchange for his life.

To distract Ham and everyone else from this whole bypassing the blockchain business, I ask Ham, "What do you know about the Citadel?"

Lucy and Mr. Chao share a confused look. But Ham darts a look at the private blockchain, and looks suddenly suspicious. There are mentions of the Citadel in the private blockchain but not anything specific.

"Ham, what do you know?"

Ham looks like a little ferret caught in a trap. "How do you bypass the blockchain?"

"Are you kidding me?" I bite back, ready to go over and stomp little ferret man, but Nova's already moving. He doesn't see her coming.

"No," he says in the same way I shut him down earlier on trying to blackmail the imaginary Interpol. He's completely focused on me and not Nova. "I have information you want. You have information I want—"

Nova jerks his hand behind his back and slams him face first in the floor. "I'm sorry, did you think this was a negotiation?"

Ham sputters into the wood floor.

Nova whispers something into his ear and Ham blanches. She releases him, stands up, and backs off, smiling.

Ham picks up himself up slowly, looks at Nova who motions for him to continue.

Ham flicks his gaze around the room, weighing his options for several breaths, before settling back on Nova and eventually answering, "The Citadel is a headquarters of sorts—"

"Of sorts?" Lucy asks distractedly, working on her computer.

"Yeah, of sorts. It's less of a place and more of a concept. It's used to denote the physical meeting place of the National Syndicate members, but it moves around to various locations. Wherever the members are meeting, that's the Citadel. They take turns hosting."

It's another measure of control, a way to dilute power.

Puo explains to the room about finding references to it in the lower-level Cleaners chatter when he was burrowed in from the decoy squeegee during the Caesar Op. Puo went back and combed through those messages on the drive back from Aberdeen to see if they were plants to lead us to Aberdeen. They were. Near as he can figure they were dropped there once they knew he was in their system, a crime of opportunity from a quick-fingered Cleaner. He was more impressed by how fast they were able to do it than by the quality of the messages. But there were other things Puo found that weren't plants that made him think the Citadel was a real place.

"Did their messages reference a location?" Mr. Chao asks.

A location was never mentioned in the few blockchain entries referencing the Citadel.

Lucy stops what she's doing to look over at Puo.

"No," Puo says. "I was capturing their most recent messages and the planted messages they left. I didn't have access to any real history—I would need direct access to their central hub to break that free." The central hub is a clearing house for a guild's message traffic and activities. Each guild maintains its own.

"Do you know where the Citadel is?" I ask Ham, already knowing the answer.

"No, that's the whole point. A way to reference a location without revealing an actual location. You need someone to tell you."

"Why aren't the locations in the blockchain?" Puo asks.

Ham shrugs. "Either it's something everybody already knows or something they only communicate by word of mouth."

I throw up my hands in exasperation. "The fact remains this Citadel is our best guess on where they're holding Charlie and we have no leads on finding where it is."

"That's not necessarily true," Lucy says tentatively.

The room all turns to her in silence.

"Can you explain that?" I ask when she appears oblivious to everyone hanging on her words.

She looks at Puo. "You said you needed direct access to their central hub to read their history. If you had access, could you get the Citadel location?"

Puo thinks it over. "There's no way of knowing if that information is in the central hub. It could be absent like it is in the blockchain."

"It'd still be a gold mine of information," I say. "There may be something in there we could use. Do you know where their central hub is?" If nothing else I can burn it to the ground.

Mr. Chao looks at Lucy in confusion.

She nods. "I think so. Look at this," she says this last statement to Mr. Chao pointing at her screen. "It's all the same cities." Mr. Chao looks at the screen and then at Lucy, surprise on his face. "This has to be why," she says to him.

Mr. Chao leans back and rubs his chin.

"Why what?" I ask. "What cities?"

"All the National Syndicate members," she answers, "they're Guild Masters in cities Angela was quietly sending members of our guild to."

Angela Jimenez was the head of their local Cleaners guild until she was killed. "What was she sending them for?" I ask.

Lucy and Mr. Chao shake their heads, lost in thought. Eventually Mr. Chao says, "Based on this new information, what we knew then, who she sent, and how she tried to keep it quiet, I think she knew about the National Syndicate and was targeting each Guild's central hub to spy on them."

"That's why they wiped us out," Lucy whispers.

"How does this tell us where the central hub is?" I ask.

Lucy shakes her head, throwing off painful memories. "It doesn't. Not exactly. But the teams she was sending out were definitely for something highly specialized like the central hub."

"*Cities* are not a small enough unit of measure for us to start searching." Hope leeches out of me like a three-week old balloon, slow and stale.

"Francis was part of the team to Old New York City." Lucy then hastily adds, seeing the room's confusion, "he was part of the Blue Diamonds crew."

That name I do know. Blue Diamonds is an underwater reclamation crew. There's not a lot of us underwater reclamationists around; most who attempt it get arrested on their first time out. Blue Diamonds is small-time. They never dare anything exceptional, but they're consistent and they stay out of jail.

If they brought an underwater reclamation specialist with them on that particular job that means whatever they were doing was underwater. But it's Old New York City, the entire place is a watery graveyard of crumbling skyscrapers.

"That still doesn't narrow it down," I say. "An underwater city is still not a small enough unit of measure for us to start searching."

Ham once more looks suspicious and steals fearful glances at Nova, who notices.

"Reginold?" Nova asks Ham. "What is it?"

"Strobilus," he blurts out. "That's all I know. I heard Caesar refer once to it as 'strobilus.' I never could figure out what it meant."

"Pine cone," Aliyah announces. "What?" she asks when we're all looking at her. "It's Latin."

What is it with this girl and Latin? How do you still know Latin years after school and becoming an enforcer in a mercenary squad?

"I know it means pine cone!" Ham defends himself. "Any simpleton can look that up—"

Puo already has a browser up and is searching variations on Old New York City and Pine Cone. Hits are coming up, but the first one is a gut punch pulling me from the conversation in the room: 70 Pine Street, an old-school Art Deco skyscraper. It's one of the last few still standing in the financial district and it's certainly big enough to hide something like this—Caesar's submarine below his trimaran yacht takes on a new meaning.

"Work to verify it," I tell Puo quietly.

He nods.

Ham may have known it meant Pine Cone, but he didn't know about Old New York City or it being underwater. I try not to run out ahead of the facts, but it all fits together neatly.

I cut off the bickering in the room with, "We have a lead."

# Chapter Twenty

P UO VERIFIED IT in a very Puo-like kind of way—he found a science survey, monitoring ocean plant life, showing organic buildup near a couple of storm drains two hundred feet down at street level. Puo then claimed the storm drains were the outlet of the central hub's cooling system warming up the water there.

This was not enough for me to launch a major operation on a compressed timeline. That extra buildup wasn't even the point of the science survey or the ensuing academic publications. With minimal grumbling Puo went back and found enough other scattered crumbs of invoices from underwater repair crews, questionable flyover-filed flight paths, and images of one very specific trimaran yacht buried in a refueling station's logs cross-referenced to a tourist pass for the area—the official tourist pass, unsurprisingly, was conspicuously missing the standard identification image of the vessel.

"Are you sure about this?" I ask Puo about being left back in the apartment to run support with Ham and Aliyah during the upcoming op. There was nowhere else to stick Ham. The rest of us have to be out in the field. So that's Aliyah's sole job—keep Ham on a short leash and from backstabbing us.

Puo cocks an eyebrow but continues flipping through a float screen. He eventually says over the din of the indoor ice skating rink, "No. That lime-green hat makes you look like a walking booger. Clashes horribly with your coat."

It's nine in the evening and Puo, Winn, and I are relatively alone sitting up on the mezzanine level at a black wooden high-table overlooking the packed ice rink and the parking lot outside. Thrumming club music fills in the steady background of people arriving, skating, shout-talking, and falling, causing us to have to lean in to be able to talk. The ice rink is more popular than the popup bar set up at the far end.

New Englanders are weird.

"No," I say, taking off the hat—I *like* this hat. It's warm. And it does not clash with my dark-blue parka. "I mean—"

"I know what you mean. But seriously, that hat is atrocious. Stands out like a radioactive frog in an empty parking lot. Do you even understand what we're doing here?"

"Puo!"

"It's the best of bad options," Puo sighs, addressing my real question, then corrects himself. "It's our only option."

"It's not our only option," I say. I don't trust that oily snake Ham and came up with quite a few options where he ended up far away from Puo. When Puo doesn't respond I continue to prod, "You trust him?"

"Of course not," Puo says. "But look, it can't be done any other way." He starts talking faster when I start to object. "It's the only option where things might actually work—"

I stick my tongue out at him.

"—where the plan doesn't depend on some crazy-ass stunt with only a hope and a prayer of succeeding."

"Those stunts have more than a hope and a prayer of succeeding. In fact, all of my previous 'stunts'—" I use air quotes around that word. "—*have* worked—"

Winn snorts and then tries to cover it up as a cough.

"We all have to act as a team," Puo says, ignoring me, although his eyes definitely want to argue. "All of us."

"My plan had us acting as a team." I'm already regretting taking my hat off. My ears pinken. Every breath brings in the cold scent of artificial ice and wet rubber mat floors.

"No," Puo says. "Your plan had us acting as a team—" Puo motions around the table to the three of us. "—and getting everyone else out of the way."

"Would've worked," I mutter.

Puo shakes his head, continuing to work on the float screens.

"I don't trust them," I say. "You sure you got all their tracker chips?"

"Yeah. They're pretty basic chips, so they were easy to find once I knew what I was looking for. You've got to let your trust issues go," he says, and holds up his hand to stop me. The motion accidentally closes one of his float screens and he scowls. "I'm not saying trust them completely." He opens the screen back up. "But really, we would've done the same thing—"

I stick my tongue out at him again.

"—*and* you're going to need to trust them down there, and they're going to need to trust you. You can't let the distrust displace the need to work as a team."

"Well, that's mature of you. And what do you think?" I ask Winn, trying to enlist him.

"I think you're not going to like what I think." Then he goes on anyway, "Working as a team is the only way out of this. They know this too. It's why they even let all three of us go off alone. It's a show of trust."

I roll my eyes and exaggeratingly pat my fur-lined dark-blue parka jacket—it had one of those tracker chips hidden in the lining.

"They removed them all," Winn says. "Puo verified it."

"Are you sure about that? You want to risk it? The last present they left for us let the Cleaners selectively jam us and led to us almost getting captured."

Puo shakes his head. "I was generous earlier to make them think our getting captured was their fault. Even if we knew— Even if *you* knew you were jammed. You likely would've gone for it." He talks over me to stop me from arguing. "At any rate, I took care of that in case we're jammed again. The suits now have line-of-sight communications in case they get jammed. You'll lose contact with me, but still be able to talk with each other as long as you're in line-of-sight to each other. *And*, I fixed your helmet—replaced the fuses. Pretty easy actually. Kind of ridiculous you were going to leave it behind."

I wasn't really going to leave it behind, but before I can argue, Winn asks impressed, "You did all that in twelve hours?"

"Yeah." Puo perks up. "I should get a raise."

"Yeah? What was encrypted in Charlie's video then?" I ask him. I'm pretty sure he's forgotten about that.

"The exact same digital package of messages I found on Caesar's yacht that led us to—" He drum rolls his fingers on the wooden table "—Aberdeeeeen, South Dakota!" he draws out like a game show announcer. "I am no longer impressed, by the way. They had those messages ready to go, and when we clearly weren't following the bait in Charlie's video, one of those Cleaners planted it for me to find when they knew I was in Caesar's system. Quick thinking, if not quick fingered."

I stick my tongue at him.

Puo looks past me down to the ice rink and then says before I can argue with him, "White puffer jacket, black leggings."

We all swivel around to locate the honey-colored woman with matching extra-large white earmuffs that look like wolf's ears.

"You went with puffer jacket and not large wolf's ears?" I ask, still smarting from his comment over leaving the helmet.

"Didn't want to get Winn all turned on," Puo says deadpan.

"Aw, c'mon!" Winn looks up to the ceiling, his face turning a deep shade of red.

I burst out laughing and Puo cracks a grin.

Then Puo continues, "We're about to do something incredibly stupid. We need to focus, Winn. We can't have your little brain thinking about furries the whole time."

"Those aren't so bad," I say, suppressing laughter. "I could wear a pair of those—"

Winn looks down at me sharply.

"—if it'll help you get it up next time we have imaginary sex."

Winn switches to banging his head on the wooden high table. "I do not—" He sighs. "What about Chao?"

"What about him?" I ask, teeing Puo up.

"I don't think Mr. Chao has erectile dysfunction," Puo says. "Why? Can you sense that in other men? Like, it takes one to know one?"

"Could be why Lucy's gives off such a frustrated, bitchy vibe," I say. "A girl can only survive on wet noodle for so long."

Winn comes to rest his head against the table and starts rolling it side to side. "He keeps weirdly deferring to Ham."

Yeah, about that. I share a look with Puo. All three of us are picking up on the same things. Four, actually—Ham tried to tell me something before the Caesar job. "We need to work as a team though, right?"

"Yeah, we do," Puo says. "I'm not saying trust them completely. I'm saying—"

I raise my hand up. "I get it." I don't want to hear Puo drone on and on about working as a team anymore. "Which one is hers?" I ask to distract him.

"Hycoa M9," Puo says. "Gray, tinted windows, third row back toward the street."

I glance out the window beyond Puo and locate the four-door hovercar. The M9's are a popular, affordable model—the workhorse of the working class. But, most importantly for our case, they come with a steel reinforced frame, standard emergency protocols, and a closed trunk.

"I'll go make the lift."

# Chapter Twenty-One

I'S A LITTLE after midnight, a few hours after the ice skating rink, and a blue timer floats off in the void to my left, ticking down to when things will get interesting: one minute, thirty seconds.

"That's some powerful gas you got there, Backstabber," I say to Nova, who's braced in the dark next to me in the trunk of the Hycoa M9 hovercar I lifted, zooming toward the Old New York City necropolis. We're both lying on our sides facing each other with our feet resting on the backside of the backseat, our arms braced above us, and wearing backpacks full of goodies.

"We are in air-tight suits, Deserter," Nova snipes back. "You're probably not used to the stench of your own self-righteousness in such a small space."

"Very powerful gas. Ham smelled better." Like hell he did, but she doesn't know that.

"One minute out," Winn says from up front, driving the hovercar with Lucy in the passenger seat. "Christmas Tree in sight."

Nova grumbles over the comm.

Or maybe she does know better. I pitch my voice like a middle-school girl discovering a delightful new secret, "You like Ham, don't you?"

"What!"

"I knew it! You loooove him! You can't stop thinking about him, like alll the time—!"

"I do not—!"

"Thirty seconds out!" Lucy shouts. "Shut up back there! Initiating failing hovercar."

"You really should tell him how you feel," Puo smoothly breaks in over the comm. "By the looks of it, he really likes you too—"

"I do not!" Ham yells in the background over Puo's comm.

"Quiet on the comm!" Lucy growls. "Beginning to lose altitude."

The hovercar engine cuts out and pitches forward.

My stomach flutters at the sudden loss of gravity. The jackknives are there, lurking like wolves in the underbrush—but kept at bay by a fresh round of meds.

"Me thinks they doth protest too much," I say.

"Much too much," Puo agrees.

"Do they always talk this much?" Lucy snaps.

"Yeah," Winn draws the word out. I can hear his smile growing through each drawn out syllable of that word. Although I'm not sure if the smile is from memories of past jobs or the hovercar's freefall. That man always did love freefalls.

Me, too, now that I think about it. But we've never done a freefall while in a hovercar before—or at least, not on purpose. Well, at least not staying *in* the hovercar on purpose.

The hovercar nose dives and Nova and I are now standing on the back of the seat.

"Twenty seconds to emergency drogue," Lucy calls out.

She wrote this bit of code, but Puo looked it over, of course. People pay a whole lot closer attention to their work when it's their ass on the line.

This whole descent is a carefully choreographed farce. Lucy's code should be sending out all the proper signals of a failing hovercar, along with all the bells and whistles indicating the emergency safety measures are failing too—until we need that emergency drogue, that is. We need to hit a very particular spot on the southeast side of 70 Pine Street, after all. Isn't that convenient?

The real question—well, the first question really—is, will the authorities hear the hovercar's automated distress calls and respond? Normally, it'd be no question unless we intentionally suppressed those calls. But the real trick here isn't to fool the authorities, it's to fool the Cleaners nestled in their little underwater clubhouse.

At a minimum, the Cleaners monitor the area to make sure their secret ass-glitter factory stays secret. It was a pretty logical guess from there to suspect they probably scrub anything suspicious from any intercepted comms in the area, and calls to the authorities would be number one on that list. There was no way to prove that ahead of time, but Puo did a cursory search of distress calls from Old New York City and there was a gap of calls around the financial district as opposed to other areas—not that there were a lot of distress calls to begin with. Aliyah then started going on about confirmation bias and Puo told her take it easy with the fancy college words, we're all friends here. Although, I'm not sure about that last part.

"Emergency drogue deploying!" Lucy calls out.

*Ka-chunk, thump!* The hovercar jerks in its descent.

"Ten seconds to impact!" she calls out.

"What's it look like out there?" I ask.

"Dark!" she yells right on top of me.

"Well, that's not very helpful," I say.

"Not very helpful at all," Puo agrees.

"I think this might be the first time she's done this," I say.

"A virgin!" Puo exclaims.

"Will you shut up!" she snaps.

"It's okay if you're a virgin," Winn says. I can still hear his smile in his words. "There's no shame in it."

"Yeah," I say. "Spinster here is saving herself for Ham."

"I am not a virgin!" Lucy snaps at the same time Nova sputters a response.

The hovercar slams upward, shaking as the agitator lasers mix water and air to slow our descent. Something substantial rips off and clatters past. The goodies in my backpack slam against my spine.

"Everything all right up there?" I ask as I brace myself against the trunk.

"Yeah," Winn grunts. "Came in a little hot. Cooling down now."

The hovercar shakes violently, globbing and popping as large bubbles whoosh past.

"You said this would work. Like a stiff hug!" Lucy shrills.

"You know you don't need to shout, right?" I ask.

"Definitely a virgin," Puo says.

"Makes sense," I say, "not familiar with a stiff anything."

Lucy shrieks at us.

"No squiddies in range. Activate sonar," Puo says.

We didn't say this would work, we said this would *probably* work. And that it felt like a stiff hug when we dropped in alone, not in a freaking hovercar. That was the whole point in being picky about what hovercar we lifted—the M9 model is known for having a steel reinforced frame and easily bypassed emergency protocols. We added the agitator lasers and a low-power active sonar system to map the area on the descent, but modifying the agitator lasers for the hovercar's surface size and mass were still best-guess calculations.

"Activating sonar," Winn says. A soft *ping* rings out.

The sounds shift to a deep chugging. The shaking strips away to lighter vibrations. A steady, icy stream splashes down the back of my neck.

Goosebumps flare down my arms. I stifle a gasp. The transition is always the worst part, when the suit doesn't know what's going on. Is it in air? Is it in water? What temperature is it? Either way, the heater stays off.

"We're under," Winn says. "Sixty feet and falling."

"Looks like you came down south-southeast of the target over the eastern rubble edge of 60 Wall Street skyscraper," Puo says.

"Roger," Winn says. "I have my bag. Evacuating the hovercar." To Lucy he says, "Grab your bag and let's go. Make sure to push the mapping to everyone."

A blue pixelated map of the street from the hovercar's active sonar pops into existence in the formless void of my HUD.

"Got it," I say. "Cut the active." There's no upside to keep the active going once we have the layout other than to announce we're here.

Water rapidly fills the trunk now. The hovercar shifts and rotates in the water as it falls.

Nova and I stay put for the roller coaster ride down to the bottom, while Winn and Lucy swim out to try and find the secret, big-ass submarine entrance.

"Computer," I say to Puo, "pipe in the music, and what's the squiddie situation?"

The theme music from Jaws comes on the comm-link.

"Can you pick something else?" Lucy snaps.

"I agree," Nova says.

"Virgin, Spinster, quiet on the comm," I say.

"I am not a Spinster—!" Nova complains at the same time Lucy objects to her new moniker.

"Quiet!" Puo yells over them. "Code names are required on all jobs. It's tradition you don't get to pick your own."

Ham objects in the background to which Puo says, "You don't count."

"Now," Puo says, "back to Harpy's question—"

"Hey!"

"Quiet!" Puo yells again.

Nova snorts and I swear I can hear a smirk from Lucy. *Freaking Puo.*

"The two closest squiddies are … one over by the New York Stock Exchange to the west and another northwest a couple of blocks. Both are headed in your direction."

"Roger," Winn says. "Keep us informed. Approaching south-east corner."

"To the best of our knowledge," Lucy mutters about the direction they're heading.

"Don't trust the sonar?" I ask.

"I'd trust it more if we could use the handheld one we have with us. It's like swimming in a bad VR game except the sharks are real. Can we *please* change this theme music?"

They're probably close to eighty feet down on a cloudy night. Even with nightvision Winn and Lucy wouldn't be able to see anything until they're right on top of it.

"You're not going to want to go active in the water with an approaching squiddie," I say. Puo and I ignore her music request.

The icy water in the trunk is up to my chest, but that's not the reason I measure my breathing. Old New York City is a large, dense area of rubble, and high on the hit list of any underwater reclamation specialist. As a result, authorities expend a lot of resources protecting it, but since it's a large area they have to be smart about how they deploy their assets. It's too large an area to cover with squiddies, instead they rely on a network of ploppers to vector in squiddies as needed.

We're counting on the Cleaners hiding in their secret clubhouse to take care of both for us. If this is the central hub, they're not going to want the semiautonomous assets of the government stumbling on their location. They're going to have a suite of tools available to mitigate that risk.

The fact that there haven't been any alarms from the ploppers bodes well, otherwise more squiddies would be headed our way, and a lot faster. The two squiddies' who've moseyed on over to investigate so far is standard for detecting a large splashdown. The real question is: will the Cleaners turn them away before they make out Winn and Lucy? All bets are off if the squiddie identifies divers in the water. Whatever protocols the Cleaners have in place may not be enough at that point.

The suit heater finally kicks on. *Thank goodness—*

The hovercar slams into something, twisting and tossing Nova and me around like rag dolls. Horrible crumpling and screeching sounds cover Nova's girly screams.

Nova and I scramble to steady ourselves and stop slamming into each other as the hovercar continues to tumble, but, before either of us are successful, the hovercar crashes down and comes to rest as if it were parked on the side of the road.

"Harpy," Winn says, "Are you okay?"

"Yeah," I grumble as I untangle myself from Nova in the trunk's tight confines and straighten my backpack. I'm a little banged up, but nothing serious. "Spinster?" I ask.

"I'm fine," she says.

"Squiddies definitely heard that," Puo says.

*Great.* I go through my HUD's menus to turn on my helmet lights to their lowest level. Nova has pushed herself to the opposite side and searches for the trunk release.

"Well," Puo says, "I'm pretty sure they heard that. They haven't changed speed or trajectory though. If they didn't hear the crash, they definitely heard your courageous, girly screams."

"Don't worry," I say to Nova, "Ham's a coward too."

"Wasn't talking to Spinster," Puo says.

Nova snorts.

Before I can put Puo in his place, Lucy comes on the line panicked, "The squiddies are still coming. One is three hundred feet and closing."

"Consort?" I ask Winn his status. He has a lot more experience in the water and isn't prone to panicking.

"I see it," Winn answers. "It's still closing. But Computer's right, the girly screams were pretty loud—"

Puo snorts.

*Freaking Winn.*

"—but the squiddie hasn't deviated. Also, it hasn't gone active. It's not acting right. I think it may already be under the Cleaners' influence."

"Hurry up and get in the building anyway," I say. It's easier to hide in the clutter. He really doesn't need to be told this, but sometimes it's impossible not to state the obvious.

"Roger." He then saves me from a snarky response from Puo about stating the obvious, by asking, "What's your status?"

"Going to sit tight until the squiddies clear out. What's the status of the squiddie to the north?"

Puo pipes in, "Still closing about a block north at Maiden and Pearl."

My heartbeat thumps against my ears as the seconds peel away. Even with the theme music from *Jaws* it's quiet down here. Actually, maybe that choice of music wasn't such a great idea.

The jackknives are out on the periphery, prowling around outside the firelight of meds waiting for an opening. I always was terrible at waiting—I hate it. But alone in the dark, with predatory music, awaiting the outcome of something I have no control over....

This was a bad idea.

I focus on my diaphragmatic breathing. *In. Out.*

The edge of the panic presses on me, a dam stretched to capacity holding back a roiling sea of adrenaline. The memory of that sensation. Fresh. Real.

Ready to burst.

*In. Out.*

Winn finally breaks in whispering, "We're in the building. Squiddie passing by now—still not going active. Definitely not acting right."

The pressure on the dam lessens but doesn't dissipate. It's still there. It's always there now. How long is it going to be like this? Should I have taken two pills?

Winn continues, "It's passing right by. It's not investigating the entry point or going active."

"The one to the north," Puo says, "is turning up Cedar Street and will pass by on the building's north side. It's ignoring your girly screams entirely—not very chivalrous."

The strain on the dam has pushed all the banter out of my head. "Understood. Wait until both are out of the area and then let's proceed to phase two."

"Roger that," Puo and Winn answer.

# Chapter Twenty-Two

IT TOOK ANOTHER few minutes to verify that the squiddies were out of the area and swimming away before Nova and I were ready to move.

We're now making our way through the rubble of 60 Wall Street tower. We're below street level swimming through what's left of a hotel kitchen.

The water is clear, undisturbed. The space is frozen in time from eighty-six odd years ago when the mega-quake hit. Pots and pans, mixing bowls and kitchen utensils lay scattered on the floor from where they fell and pushed up against the wall from a crush of water. Oven windows are smashed. Plates are scattered around, most broken but not all. Stainless steel prep tables are pushed around and knocked over. Silt drapes over it all.

The *Jaws* soundtrack is now on the fourth or fifth song. This one is softer, but still creepy, with a slow increasing tempo. Why are all the songs from *Jaws* so creepy?

I swim over a central plating area. Nova follows. It's too quiet down here. There's no other sound except the creepy, rising instrumental. No movement. Our helmet lights cut through the space like grave robbers in the night.

"At the end of the kitchen—" Puo interjects in a normal tone of voice.

My heart jumps at the sudden intrusion. *Fuck.* That dam of adrenaline is still there, waiting to burst. It's the memory of it bursting, of being completely overwhelmed that's so terrifying. I nearly tell Puo to cut the *Jaws* crap and whisper from now on, but decide the hassle of explaining why isn't worth it. Puo and Winn would get it, but I don't want to have to explain it to everyone else. This team stuff is bullshit. *Should've gone with my plan.*

Puo continues, completely unaware: "—there should be a hallway at the end of the kitchen on the north side. Take a right and then a left at the first opportunity."

I send our acknowledgments and kick forward through the frozen-in-time kitchen, resisting the sudden urge to sprint, to use that pool of adrenaline about to overflow.

"We're coming around the northeast part of the building now," Winn says. "Getting ready to go active."

"Roger," Puo says. "Squiddies are far away and still opening. You're clear to go active."

Winn and Lucy are trying to find the entrance to the Cleaners' secret lair. Fortunately, it shouldn't be hard—all they need to do is find a submarine-sized hole in the building. That's why we targeted the hovercar crash site near a corner of the building, to give the sonar a chance to map two sides of the building. Turns out, we chose the exact opposite wrong corner.

Nova and I come to the hallway at the end of the kitchen and turn right. There's a chunk of concrete ceiling on the floor the size of a sewer grate and several inches thick. No other debris. No indicator of what caused its collapse.

I tell Puo about it and he *mmms*.

"Have Spinster's unrequited love look into it," I say. There's something weird about that chunk of concrete.

Ham grumbles in the background while Nova sighs heavily and then says, "You do realize I'm swimming behind you with one of these stunners in my bag, right?"

We're lucky the stunners are low tech and easy to make since we lost one of the two we had in Aberdeen. One trip to the hardware store later and now we're all outfitted with one.

I turn left and stop in the entrance into a maintenance tunnel. "Don't take your sexual frustrations out on me."

"Says the woman who couldn't finish."

The quip doesn't have any sting since it was all a farce anyway.

The maintenance tunnel floor has turned into gray concrete with white cinder-blocked walls and wire conduits running along the ceiling.

"We're in the maintenance tunnel," I tell Puo.

"The tunnel should lead under the street to the target building," Puo says.

"Roger, we'll sit tight until—"

"We found the entrance," Winn breaks in. "It's on the building's northwest corner. There's a large, caved-in section. Heading there now."

I kick back over to the chunk of concrete while we wait for Winn and Lucy to get into position. The concrete is rough around the edges except for what I come to realize are regularly spaced drill holes.

"Where are you going?" Nova asks me.

"To have a look around." I swim up toward the hole in the ceiling.

"We're supposed to wait here."

"Then wait there." We have time. Winn and Lucy need to swim down into the entrance and then assess how best to kick off the next part of the plan. Someone drilled out this hole. *Why?*

"We need to stick together—" She then growls in frustration and moves to follow me.

I kill my helmet lights as I pull up directly under the hole.

"Spinster, look up toward the hole. I want to use your helmet lights." She does as I ask and I dial my nightvision in to make maximum use of the secondary light.

Someone drilled out this hole. No one goes through that much effort unless there's a reason, which means I need to be cautious about what could be on the other side.

I peek up slowly into a giant ballroom. There's a whooshing sound in the space with a low mechanical whir mixed in. The hole is along the edge of the ballroom and there are more of these holes regularly spaced around the room. There's a larger hole with a grate over it in the wall above me. One of two chandeliers lies smashed on the floor, the other clings to the ceiling. Specks of ocean crud filter through light cast up by Nova's helmet lights.

A plopper sits square in the middle of the room, a trash-can-sized device used to identify threats and notify the authorities.

"Shit." I duck back down.

"What?" Nova and Puo ask and I quickly outline what I saw.

Puo's quiet for a minute while he chews that over and then he says, "It's probably a water intake room for their cooling unit. They're trying to prevent any detectable currents from the outside"

"Yeah," I agree. "The important bit is the plopper."

"Agreed," Puo says.

"What's a plopper?" Winn asks. I quickly explain that he knew them as full-sized squatters before we renamed them during the British museum heist.

"And what's the important bit?" Lucy asks annoyed. I can perfectly picture her face with poop smeared under her nose.

"The Cleaners aren't going to tolerate a plopper tied to the authorities in their space," I explain. "That plopper is under Cleaners' control."

"And if they have one," Puo says.

"Then they have many," Winn finishes. "Entering the caved-in section now. Turning on active sonar."

Nova and I get back into position.

The rest of us fall silent on the comm. The music is frantic now. It makes me twitchy—like I want to get my stunner out ready for a fight.

The constant building tempo jacks up my adrenaline against an already straining damn. Fuck looking weak and having to explain. "Computer," I say, "switch the music to something less distracting."

Lucy, Nova, and Winn all speak on top of each other.

"Agreed."

"Seconded."

"Thanks."

Puo sighs. "Bunch of ungrateful music snobs." The creepy, stalking, death music switches to some generic piano solo.

Winn starts narrating, "We're coming down through floors of condos."

"The floors look to be deliberately collapsed," Lucy says. "They made this passage."

I find myself nodding—makes sense from what we've seen so far.

Winn continues, "It's angling down into the center of the building. No sign of the Cleaners or any resistance."

"I'm not seeing anything either," Lucy says. "Sonar's not picking anything up."

Which doesn't mean jack shit. If the Cleaners made this passage, they're going to have it under surveillance. They're watching Winn and Lucy.

"The floors are switching to generic office space," Winn continues, "cubicles and whatnot. I estimate we've traveled down about eight floors—"

"Something's coming!" Lucy shrills. "And fast!"

"I see it," Winn rushes. "Take cover in the cubicle there. Computer?"

"I'm tracking it through your sonar, but not seeing it on anything else. Whatever it is, it's not tied in with authorities' normal suite of tools."

"Understood. Taking cover."

Tense seconds beat by, serenaded by a soft, melancholy piano solo. At least it's better than the *Jaws* theme music.

"It's a squiddie," Winn says. "It's making right for us. Virgin, when I tell you, dart out that way and keep swimming. I'll stun it as it passes by."

"You dart out and I'll stun it," Lucy says.

"There isn't time to argue," Winn says. "You've never used one of these before. Dart when I tell you."

Lucy starts to argue when Nova comes on the line, "Virgin, do as you're told."

"Excuse me? Did you just call me Virgin, *Spinster*? I don't take orders—"

"Now!" Winn yells.

"I—"

"Now!" we all yell.

"Aaaargh!" Lucy yells and presumably launches herself out there.

"It sees you!" Winn says. "Keep—! Oh."

"Oh! What do you mean—!" Lucy yells.

"It's circling around. Come back! Come back! Pass by the other direction!"

Lucy's heavy breathing fills the comm.

"Shit!" Winn swears. "It may have seen me."

"May have?" Lucy yells.

"Yeah, it's casing the situation."

That is definitely not normal squiddie behavior.

"It's not going to pass by me!" Winn yells. "Uh, run!"

"Run! Are you serious!"

"Sorry! Swim! Hide!"

Lucy lets out a primal scream of frustration.

Both of their heavy breathing fills the comm for several heart-thundering seconds.

Is this what it feels like to be Puo? Always sitting there hearing this horrible stuff and not able to do anything? This is awful.

Several more seconds slide past.

Eventually I can't take it anymore. "Status?"

"It's avoiding us," Winn says confused.

Definitely not normal squiddie behavior. Normal squiddie protocol would be to grab a swimmer and drag it to the surface like an overzealous bloodhound.

"I think it's trying to scare us," Winn says.

"It wants you to leave," I say, putting it together. The Cleaners want to stay hidden. They want any looky-loos to think the authorities are watching this area. But they don't want any dead bodies, which tends to happen when squiddies get excited. Dead bodies bring more questions and authorities.

"Should we ignore it?" Winn asks.

"No," I say, thinking quickly. If they ignored it, it might get more desperate. It'll also tip our hand that we know it's not dangerous and belongs to the Cleaners. "Take it out." That'll kill two birds with one stone.

"How?" Lucy asks.

"I have an idea," Winn says before I can snap that I can't think of everything. To Lucy he says, "Lead it deeper into the cubicle maze."

"Why?" Lucy asks, the smear-of-poop-under-her-nose look clear in her tone.

"So I can set things up here. I don't think it's seen me after all. When I tell you, start making your way back, getting ready to sprint."

"I am not bait!" she shrills.

"Yes, you are!" both Nova and I, surprisingly, yell at the same time.

"Fine."

There's a minute pause and then Winn says, "It's following you. Setting up now."

"What are you setting up?" I ask.

"A surprise."

That raises my eyebrows. "What are you setting up?"

No response.

"Consort ...."

"Don't worry about it. It'll work."

What wouldn't he want to tell me? I start thinking through the tools he has in his bag and the stupidity he could get up to—*oh.*

"Consort—!"

"It's all set up," he talks right over me. "Virgin, start making your way back. Book it when I tell you."

"Making my way back," Lucy says.

I shake my head, but keep my mouth shut. There's nothing for it at this point. He better not be doing what I think he's doing.

"Book it!" he yells. "Sprint to the cubicle I was in. There's a DPV in front of it. Grab it and get to me! Hurry!"

Motion and panting carry over the comms.

I catch myself holding my breath, leaning forward. The DPVs were supposed to come out later.

More panting and frantic motion.

And more panting and frantic motion.

Humans are just not that fast in water. Walking is faster than most people swimming.

"Got it!" Lucy yells.

The distant DPV's whir comes over the comm.

"Hurry!" Winn shouts. "To me!"

More whirring.

And more whirring.

Apparently, DPVs are not that fast either.

"Now!" Winn shouts, followed by a sharp explosion over the comm.

*That stupid, stupid man—*

The explosion's distant rumble reaches us below street level in the tunnel.

"Keep going!" Winn shouts.

The comm fills with the sounds of careening, crashing, and wrenching of great concrete slabs slamming into each other.

The damn tower is clasping around him.

"Consort! What did you do?" I ask, knowing full well what he did.

"Took care of the squiddie!"

The far-distant rumbling of Winn's stupidity reverberates down the tunnel while the thundering crashes continue on the comm. The crashing continues on for several seconds with no signs of tapering off.

"What's going on over there? Is the whole tunnel collapsing?" I ask.

"Not the whole tunnel," Winn says.

"Just the north side of it," Lucy says.

"What's your status?" I ask with visions of Winn and Lucy being crushed under a mountain of debris.

"Continuing to make our way down the tunnel, sans squiddie." He sounds way too proud of himself, while metal wrenching and concrete slamming down come over the comm.

"The south side of it," Lucy clarifies.

"Well," Puo says, "they know we're here and not friendly."

"Which," Winn says, "was always part of the plan."

That's why he's so pleased with himself. Announcing themselves was part of the plan—blowing up half the building, not so much. "Keep going down the rabbit hole," I say. "Try not to get crushed. And no more going boom without permission."

"Roger that."

# Chapter Twenty-Three

WAITING AROUND sucks.

The rumbling and crashing went on for what felt like hours. In reality, it was probably less than two minutes. But that's what waiting around does to a person, slows down time to an interminable slog.

Nova and I float here the whole time, resting on our knees, at the end of the maintenance tunnel, the silt only now beginning to settle down after our soft landing from investigating the water intake room above. Time is still an interminable slog.

*How long does this tunnel go?*

"Sonar is mapping the bottom," Winn says over his DPV's whir. Once the building settled around them, he got out his own DPV—no need to hide now.

I perk up. Things will finally get interesting once they reach the gingerbread house at the end of the tunnel.

"Another few minutes to the bottom," Winn says.

I can't help groaning.

Ham says something in the background.

"What'd he say?" I ask, ready for a fight to distract me.

"Nuthin' helpful," Puo says at the same time Lucy pipes up with, "That you really should've finished before heading out."

*Finished what?*

"Which," Lucy continues, "he's got a point. Being sexually frustrated is no way to go through life."

Shock pushes all retorts out of my head like an expanding bubble. Then the bubble implodes. "Ham, you sly pig," I say, "you deflowered Virgin! No wonder Spinster is all uptight—"

"I am not into Ham!" Nova snaps, at the same time Lucy says, "I am not a virgin!"

Puo pipes in, stepping over that perfect set up with, "Enough! ... Enough. We need to focus to work together. Ignore the sly pig—"

I stifle a snort.

"Eunuch—" That's the call name for Aliyah. "—beat Ham if he injects any more strife into the team," Puo instructs.

There's some chatter in the background. "That's you," Puo says to Aliyah. Apparently, she didn't know she was Eunuch. More chatter. "It's out of my hands," Puo says. "Now," he says to the rest of us, "Want me to tell you a story?"

"No!" I want to be moving, not deciphering a weird Puo tale.

"Are you sure?"

"Yes!" we all collectively say.

"Well, all right—" Puo starts, which I'm pretty sure was him starting to tell a story anyway.

We're saved the tale by Winn breaking in, "We've reached the bottom of the tunnel. It bottoms out in a parking garage. There's nothing here. It continues upward. It's an elbow."

I'd bang my head on a desk if there was one.

"*NEE-eu! NEE-eu! NEE-eu!*" suddenly screams over the comm-link.

"A plopper," Winn says over the racket. He picks up the new term seamlessly.

"It's there, behind the concrete piling," Lucy says.

"I see it," Winn says. "Do you think it's motion activated or are they still trying to scare us off?"

"Either way," I say, "shut it up." The noise is super annoying.

"Roger," Winn raises his voice over the racket.

The siren rises to an ear-splitting octave, before cutting off with a half-hearted chirp.

"Hunh," Winn says. "The plopper—" He picks up the new term seamlessly. "—looks like it's wired in. Look," he presumably says to Lucy.

"Yeah," she says, "I think you're right. The wires travel up the piling. They couldn't bury them."

"Plug in," Puo says—another key part of the plan, but if the Cleaners are going to offer us an opportunity so early, it'd be rude of us to decline.

"Roger," Winn says. "Getting the dry dock ready. Virgin, get the squeegee ready."

Lucy has Izaak's squeegee for this outing, while I have Caesar's. If we're going to bust into a hidden Cleaner space, we're going to hedge our bets and bring the real McCoys.

"Roger," Lucy stumbles over the word, more of a question than an affirmation of understanding.

Winn mutters instructions to Lucy and puts the dry dock in place. "Water's pumping out now," he tells the rest of us.

Crashing and slamming come over the comm, followed quickly by the distant rumble from down the tunnel.

"Whoaaa," Winn says, at first surprised and then drawing the word out.

"Everything all right?" Puo asks.

"Yeah," Winn says, "I think so. Just things settling down some more."

I shake my head at him freaking collapsing part of the building.

"Well, good, 'cause you have two objects inbound from the other end of the tunnel," Puo says. "I'm picking it up on your sonar."

"Roger," Winn says, but he's distracted. "Getting ready to splice into the cable."

"What—?" Lucy starts to ask about the two objects, panicked.

"Plug in," Winn instructs over her. "I'll deal with the incoming. Get your leads ready."

I resist the urge to tell Winn no more explodey things as a way to deal with his problems, but I don't want to spook Lucy—a little high strung, that one.

"Splicing in now," Winn says. After a beat he says, "Plug in the silver lead first." Then right after, "now the black one."

After several seconds, Winn asks, an edge to his voice, "Are you in?"

"I'm in," Lucy says.

Then nothing for several seconds. Then several more seconds. Silence on the comm.

I tilt forward in a pointless attempt to hear more.

"I think the incoming are squiddies," Winn finally says. "Two of them."

"What's your plan?" I ask.

"Stunner—only option."

*Shit.* I was afraid of that. A stunner may work on one, but not two squiddies. Not in the time frame he needs. Lucy is going to be their target.

I open a private line to Puo—well semi-private since Aliyah and Ham are with him. "Computer, can you take over for Virgin so she can get out of there?"

"Negative. There's not enough bandwidth for me to see all the data the squeegee is dealing with to make decisions on."

*Damn it.* I click back over the public channel. "Virgin, how much time do you need?"

No response.

"Consort, puppy guard the squeegee." They'll have to get past him to get to Lucy and hopefully he can use the parking garage's smaller space to his advantage.

"Roger that." Then to Lucy, he says, "Get your stunner ready."

Again, no response.

"Virgin!" Winn yells.

The low classical music is still playing. Why isn't she responding?

"They're right on top of you," Puo rushes.

"I see them!" Winn yells. "They're coming in!"

Hot sweat breaks out across my body. My heart thunders. Doesn't matter who controls the squiddie—squiddies are bad news in tight confines.

I kneel there, adrenaline crashing through my system, my heart threatening to burst, waiting.

And waiting.

"What the ... ?" Winn asks. His question is followed by the sound of two heavy metal hunks crashing into the pavement nearby.

"I'm in," Virgin says innocently.

"You did this?" Winn asks.

"Did what?" I ask at the same time she says, "Yes."

"Nice," Winn says.

"Thanks," she says in a tone clearly not used to complements.

"Did what?" I ask again. My heart, now that it's kicked over into overdrive, refuses to slow down.

"I'm in their system," Virgin says. "I shut down their defense network."

"Did you get a read on their system?" Puo asks.

"Yes, sending it to you now."

"Did you get into the central hub?" I ask in a rush, more of a demand—a byproduct of too much adrenaline. That'd be perfect, making things way easier than we feared and my and Nova's presence completely unnecessary.

"No—"

*Figures.*

"—I think the hub is on a separate network."

"But she did," Puo says his voice getting more excited, "get a comprehensive read of the defensive network. There's a plopper a hundred feet in front of Harpy and Spinster in that tunnel, deactivated now of course. And, guess what else I've found?"

I know that tone. "The central hub?"

"The central hub!"

"It's not on that network," Virgin says.

"No, it's not," Puo agrees. "But it's not just about what's on the system and where. It's about what's missing and where it's missing from. I found its physical location."

"And you can also see it on their surveillance, right?" I ask.

"That too," he agrees magnanimously. "Harpy, Spinster, you're clear to proceed to the next phase."

About time. I push up from kneeling on the ground and turn my helmet lights back on. "Let's go," I say to Nova.

"Consort, Virgin," Puo says, "you're clear to proceed to the next phase as well. I'm pretty sure they're already focused on you, but make sure to keep it that way."

"How?" Winn asks. "Didn't Virgin shut down their ability to track us?"

"Good point," Puo says. "Virgin, can you turn on some of their cameras and sensors? Make it look like the system is struggling to come up— Hang on. I'll set it up and push it to you. That way we can keep the cameras/sensors off that are most advantageous to keep off."

I leave Puo to that for the moment. Eventually he needs to tell us where to go next when we get to the end of the tunnel.

The tunnel itself is utilitarian in design, bare except for some regularly spaced lighting, with white cinder-block walls and gray slabbed concrete floors, wide enough to drive a car down but low-ceilinged, maybe seven feet high. Thin yellow silt drapes the tunnel floor and clings to the grooves in the walls and the ceiling's light fixtures. I've always wondered why that is. There's no life down in this tunnel. No fish. No plants. No light. But still this silty stuff?

The water is still as we swim forward. It's thin. Cold. Our helmet lights cut through the undisturbed water ahead like afternoon sunlight through a window.

"Coming up on the plopper," I say.

The chest-high trashcan-sized device squats in the middle of the walkway. A gossamer layer of silt covers the top and reveals a thin wire traveling up to the light fixture above. It does not light up and start screaming at us.

"Computer—" I decide Puo's had enough time. "—where we goin' at the end of this tunnel?"

"Onnnneee secccoonnnd," Puo says.

One second turns into minutes as Nova and I approach the end of the tunnel. I'm about to ping Puo again when he says, "Okay. Sending the program. Virgin, upload and activate it."

"Roger," Lucy says, the term becoming more familiar.

"Harpy, Spinster," Puo says, "take a left at the end of the tunnel. There's a stairwell on the left fifty feet down. Wait once you're there while I map out the rest of the route."

"Understood," I reply. There's a stiffer edge to the adrenaline now. Before it was waiting around, useless, but now it's one of anticipation. We're only going to get one shot at this.

"Uploaded," Lucy says.

"Roger," Puo says. "Proceed to the next phase. Now that you've plugged in, I've got a pretty good idea of the layout. The tunnel should come up into the Burrow Theater."

It takes several minutes for Nova and me to reach the stairwell. I notify Puo and he tries to push us off again.

"Computer—" I start to say.

"I'm working on it!" Puo whines. "We need to find a back way into the theater."

Winn pipes in with, "Yeah, it's definitely a theater. We're coming up into the performance hall—whoa. It's an underwater base spreading out from the stage. It's all pressurized."

The pressurization makes sense and what we were counting on. Creating a large enough air pocket down here would be nigh impossible, and the pressure too great for long-time occupation.

Winn continues, "The base extends out from the stage over the seating. That's where the submarine docks into it. I can't see how far back it goes."

"Heading up the stairwell." I ignore Puo's order to wait. We're too far out of position. We need to be closer.

Puo exhales over the comm, but keeps his mouth shut.

I pull myself up the metal railings. The cold metal presses through my gloves as we climb. Silt billows out. We pass a silt-draped sign for "Basement Floor 2."

"Okay," Puo says, "I got it. Get out at the lobby level and then I'll direct you to be below the theater and we'll take it from there."

"Roger." I continue to pull myself up.

"What cameras/sensors are still active?" Winn asks. "And, uh, where are they?"

"Doesn't matter," Puo says. "I left all the ones in the seating area of the theater active—"

Another round of crashing and wrenching comes over the comm. Vibrations travel through the railings.

"Are we going to be able to get out?" I ask.

Winn scoffs, "Don't worry—I have a solution for that."

I reach the door to the lobby level and brace one hand on the frame to push it open. "Pushing out into the lobby level."

"All right," Puo says. "I'm going to direct you to where the central hub is from below. Consort, Virgin, keep their attention on you."

"Roger that," Winn says. "Placing dynamite now."

# Chapter Twenty-Four

NOTHING SAYS, "Pay attention to me!" like placing dynamite around a pressurized, water-tight living area. Particularly, when you've already detonated one explosion, bringing down half the building.

Winn and Lucy are currently doing their best to make sure the Cleaners inside their super-secret base are aware they have sticks of dynamite and are placing them around the base.

I can't help but imagine Winn and Lucy taking the dynamite out in big exaggerated motions and winking and shouting at each other, "Do you know what this? Why, yes, I do know what that is! That is a stick of dynamite!"

This is all to hide my and Nova's approach. Hell, even the way we broke the teams up factored into that—Lucy was paired with Winn specifically to look like me in the water, since the Cleaners have a good idea of how we operate now.

If all goes according to plan, not only should the Cleaners be blind to Nova and I, but they should also be spooked enough to be shifting the central hub processing to a backup unit somewhere else. That last part is key.

The central hub is the Cleaners' clearing house. They're going to have all kinds of monitoring software and security layers in place. If they shift operations over to a backup unit, they won't be paying as close attention to the main unit. It's not the current traffic we care about, it's the archived traffic in memory. And they're not going to shift that large amount of data to a backup unit. At best, their plans are either to pull hard drives before abandoning the site or simply destroy the data if they have to.

Of course, we're not going to know if they shifted operations until after we plug in to the central hub.

So, the more the Cleaners on site are concerned about being blown up, the better.

"Whoa," Winn says, "they just turned on all the lights. It's like a football game under the lights here now."

"Keep each other in sight," I say, "stay close." We want the Cleaners focused on Winn and Lucy, but I would've preferred it if the Cleaners simply sat in their underwater base quivering in fear. Their first layer of defense consisted of trying to hide, the second layer of trying to scare people away. There's no telling what a third layer might be.

"Computer, how much farther?" I ask.

"You're almost there," Puo says.

Puo's instructions have been straightforward: go down this tunnel, turn right, go up the stairs, et cetera. Easy, boring, and a bit creepy. I'm used to being in the sunken cities, in people's homes, rummaging through time to find hidden treasures. There's something unsettling about moving through a space like a hotel lobby designed to hold a constant thrum of people.

Our route first brought us through the building lobby, a grand but ultimately sterile space, and then into a hotel lobby right off it. The contrast is stark. The building lobby was designed to move a large amount of people quickly, where the hotel lobby was designed to be warm and inviting.

It's easy to imagine people in the deteriorated chairs and couches waiting to meet up with friends and family, hear the chatter of all the people. Now layers of silt are draped over everything like plastic thrown over furniture to keep the dust off. Small strands of the eaten-away carpet float up in places. You can't help but think of what happened all those years ago.

As I said: creepy.

The more worrying part is I haven't seen any signs of the Cleaners' surveillance, which means either it's really good or they didn't bother surveilling this route because they knew it was pointless.

Once we're past the hotel, we move through the building's hidden hallways connecting all the various spaces and used for moving deliveries around without inconveniencing the buildings patrons.

"Whoa!" Winn suddenly yells as Lucy screams at the same time. "Gun in the water!" Winn yells.

I go cold. An underwater gun can only mean one thing: a wet team.

"Take cover!" Winn shouts. "I have eyes on one! Fuck!"

Commotion dominates on the comm-link with frantic swimming, breathing, and cursing.

I find myself sprinting through the hallway for no other reason than it's something to do. Even if we were supposed to meet up with them there's nothing we could do, we're too far away.

"Are you okay?" Winn asks Lucy in a rush.

"Yeah—I think so," Lucy says.

"We broke line of sight," Winn says to the rest of the group. "Continuing to open, but it's going to be difficult with all these lights on."

"Are *you* okay?" I ask.

"Yeah," Winn says. "Only saw one of them. Looked like a rifle. Firing flechettes."

"What's your plan?" I ask. Wet teams usually operate with at least two people for the same reason we operate with two—the underwater environment is brutally unforgiving if you get in a tight spot or have an equipment failure.

"I have an idea—" Winn starts, but before he can get too far the building shifts again. A heavy grinding shakes the walls around me, kicking loose flecks of silt.

Puo then pipes in before I can follow up, "Harpy, you're almost there." He gives me the last of the directions and I sprint through the water, Nova following after.

"What are you going to do with that?" Lucy asks.

"Force them to stop shooting at us," Winn says.

"How?"

"By demonstrating the consequences of their continued shooting at us."

Nova and I push into a new hallway.

Lucy says, "No. That's a terrible idea. Harpy said no more explodey things."

Large, black cables with yellow bands regularly spaced down them travel along the floor. They're as thick as my thigh. This is it. There's a water current here and a low hum.

"Consort," I say, "what is she talking about?" I follow the cables down the short hallway to the stage below the stage, the water current getting stronger. It's full of old backdrops and scenery on pulleys, lights and props pushed to the edges, white markings on the floor in places.

No silt—the water current pumping through here is too strong.

There's a large piping system snaking around everywhere down here like a huge radiator, doubling up in places to create waist-high walls scattered around.

The current pushes me along and I have to grab onto things to keep from being pushed too far. The walls opposite me have large sewer-grate–sized holes pumping water through this space.

But the coup de grâce is a large cylindrical tank in the center opening up to the stage above. Bright lights filter down over a server farm submerged in crystal clear water—it makes the seawater look filthy in comparison.

The piping is a huge heat sink, and the whole room uses the ocean water to bleed away heat from the server water. It's a two-stage system.

"It's the only thing that will work," Winn says, splitting my attention.

Cables run all over the floor and this current is not helping matters. I visually follow several cables back to their source and pick one down-current that looks to be going to the central hub complex.

"What is the only thing that will work?" I ask Winn. "Spinster, meet me over by that cable and get the dry dock out." I point to the cable I picked out earlier.

I let the current drag me over to the spot over the cable.

"Dynamite," Winn says. "Make it clear if they keep firing at us, I start blowing them one by one."

Nova bumps into me as she comes to hover over the cable.

I get a laser cutter out. "That's a really stupid idea. You already have them under threat. They're going to—"

"Too late!"

The explosion rocks the whole room and I nearly lose my grip on the cable. Nova grabs onto me.

The explosion wave passes over us. The cylindrical tank shakes. Red lights blink on in the server farm.

"Damn it, Consort!"

"It's fine!" he yells back. "No one was hurt! Just a warning boom. Not even a full stick."

Except the building continues to rumble.

"Get ready," I say to Nova. I slice into the thick cable's outer casing and work free one of the wires in the twisted braid.

Nova slips the dry dock over the wire and activates it, while I get Caesar's squeegee out.

"No more explosions!" I yell at Winn.

"Roger," he says. "It worked. They're leaving us alone—"

Lucy screams. "They're firing at me!"

"Get out of there!" I yell. "Both of you!" Their purpose is fulfilled now. The Cleaners will still be preoccupied with them as they leave. We're almost done here.

The comm-link is full of Winn's and Lucy's adrenaline-filled coordination as the dry dock finishes pumping the water out.

"Get the squeegee ready," I say to Nova. "First the silver lead, then the black lead, when I tell you."

"Roger," she says over Winn's and Lucy's mad dash above and the building continuing to rumble all around us.

I shimmy myself down to use my legs to brace myself against a bend in the metal piping and use the controls on the dry dock to grab the wire and make the cut—that's the easy part. The hard part is stripping the wire for the lead to connect to. It takes me two tries on the first wire, but once I know the gauge, I strip the other half on the first try.

Nova connects the two leads as directed.

"We're in," I say over the growing clamor. "Pinging the system now."

Seconds tick by. Packets received: 0.

"Computer," I say, "it's not working."

"Can you read any data?"

"No. It says zero packets received."

"Is there data moving on the line?" Puo tells me what to type in.

"Yeah," I say, "it looks like data is moving across it." At least that's what the readout indicates.

"I was afraid of this." He has me do another test. All the while, the building's groaning builds and Winn and Lucy are in full-on retreat trying not to get shot.

"Yeah," Puo says. "It's a one-way comm channel. Data can only flow one way. In this case, you found the data flowing *into* the central hub. You can issue commands, but you can't read back any data. You'll have to find an outbound cable to plug into."

"I thought you said it was one-way. If I'm plugged into the outbound, how do we issue the commands to download the pieces we need?"

"You'll have to issue the command on the channel you're on now. Put it on a delay and get over to the outbound channel to receive in time."

"Are you kidding me?"

"No. You better move."

*Oh, we are so having words when I get back.* Rather than argue with Puo right now I cast around to try and find an outbound cable.

They all look the same. They *all* look the freaking *same*.

The adrenaline dam bursts. A great rush of heat grips my face. The torrent of sudden panic wipes away my ability to make decisions. If I choose wrong, we could miss the download. If I don't choose soon, we could miss the download *and* be discovered.

I can't decide. It's not that I won't decide. I can't. I physically can't. I hang there, paralyzed.

*No, no, no. This can't be happening right now.*

"Harpy," Nova urges.

*Oh, fuck. Which cable do I choose? They all look the same.*

"Harpy," Nova prods me again, more insistent.

"What?" I ask, unable to hide the tremor in my voice.

There's a beat where she pauses before saying, "The cable behind us, past two rows of this piping: it's the outbound cable. You can tell by the twist of the yellow banding."

I glance back at the cable.

*Okay.* "Okay," I say, then to myself I say, *I can do this. One thing at a time.*

"Sending the signal now on a two— no, three-minute delay," I say, the hollowness of my voice apparent even to me. "Spinster, pull the leads now."

Nova does as she's told and I quickly fit a shrink tube over one wire, tie the two wire ends together, and activate the shrink tube to seal the wires together. After that, the dry dock removes quickly.

Loud crashing smashes down from above. The lights shining down over the server farm through the cylindrical tank flicker. The heat-sink pipes shake as we run our hands over them while the current pushes us to our next destination.

"What was that?" I ask.

The low thrum and current in the room cut off as we approach the cable.

The large cable with yellow banding is nestled down between two heat-sink pipes doubling up on themselves to waist height to create a little cranny.

"Part of the building is collapsing," Winn huffs.

"Part?" I've lost track of Winn and Lucy. I squeeze down in the space and have to scrunch in my legs to make room for Nova.

Puo breaks in to state the obvious, "Better hurry."

Nothing like an actual death threat to wipe away the paralyzation from a fake, panic-induced death threat.

Except that isn't really true. It's all still there. My heart pounds. My hands shake as I cut into the cable to place the dry dock. My mouth is a parched desert.

If we don't get this, Charlie is going to die. This is it. There are no other leads. No other options.

While terrifying, the thought oddly helps me focus. No options. No decisions to make. Only execution.

I pull the wire out and put the dry dock in place. "Ready?" I ask Nova.

"Silver lead, black lead," she repeats back to me.

The room shifts, shakes. The heat-sink pipes vibrate up against our jammed-in bodies. There's no obvious source for it this time.

We need to get this download.

The dry dock pumps the water out and I make the cut, strip the wires and Nova attaches the leads. Once Nova's done, she pushes out of the tight space to give me more room to work.

"We're in," I say. I look at the system clock—we have twenty seconds to spare. "It sees the command and getting ready to pull the information down. How long is it going to take?"

"No idea," Puo says. "But there's only so much memory on the squeegee. The program is set up to download the most likely places first. So, five, maybe ten minutes."

Now, I'm really ready to kill Winn. Those five to ten minutes be a problem if the building weren't falling apart.

The program connects and the download starts. "Six minutes," I say. Although if this estimated download time is like any others I'm familiar with, the estimated time is essentially meaningless.

The next few minutes pass by in rumbles and groans. The brief pause gives me time to check in with Winn and Lucy. They're not so much as fleeing the crumbling building, but playing a dangerous game of hide and seek.

"Is the damage to building structural?" I ask.

"No," Winn says. "It doesn't appear to be. Loose floors and walls falling down, but not load-bearing pilings. Although, I can't really say for sure. How much longer?"

I shake my head at "loose floors and walls." "Two minutes, forty-one seconds."

The squeegee readout is less than an arm's length away. Once Nova clipped on the leads, she backed out of the space to let me work and now I have a cozy little spot nestled in the heat piping. Depending on how strong these pipes are, if the building collapses I might have a nice protected pocket to slowly suffocate in.

"Any other signs of resistance?" I ask.

"No," Winn answers. "We have one frogman in pursuit."

Time crawls by, taunting me. Charlie's salvation could already be on the squeegee. We won't know until we take it back to Puo and let him comb through it.

Two minutes.

*BOOM! BOOM!* A huge double crash shakes the room. Followed immediately by another, *BOOM!*

Nova yelps, the sound buried amid the thundering in the room and ringing in my ears.

New light shines down from a fresh hole in the stage directly overhead where we spliced into the inbound cable, now crushed under the weight where they cut away the floor.

"Are you okay?" I ask Nova, floating above me.

"Yes—"

*Pfft!*

I flatten myself against the ground. *Fuck!*

Nova scrambles away, water turbulence washing down over me. "Shots fired!" she yells. "Shooter dead ahead from above!"

*Pfft! Pfft! Pfft!*

The shooter is tracking Nova with an underwater handgun firing shots as he descends into the space. I don't think he sees me.

He's not a good shot. Underwater guns are difficult to aim, handguns even worse. He looks unpracticed at both shooting and at being in the water in general. He's a Cleaner, forced out into the water as a last line of defense.

Nova hustles to get the cylindrical tank between her and the shooter.

I squeeze down more in my nook. I can't leave the squeegee.

One minute, forty-five seconds to full download.

As long as Nova distracts him, we can finish the download then get out of here. "Keep him occupied," I whisper.

Nova doesn't bother to respond.

She's a pro—she can handle it.

A deep mechanical chugging kicks on followed by a low whir that matures into the thrum from before. The current in the room picks back up again; dust and debris from the ceiling collapse drifts overhead.

Nova grunts as the current catches her, while the frogmen's shadow passes over me as the current catches him, carrying him closer.

I press myself down, holding my breath.

I'm a sitting duck here. Going for the stunner in my bag would only draw his attention and stunners are only useful in close-quarters combat. Even with an underwater handgun, it would be difficult to miss a motionless target while floating overhead.

The thrum deepens. The current picks up. And picks up.

"Argh!" Nova yells in frustration. "Damn it! I can't—"

The frogman passes overhead. The current carries him as he tries to line up a shot on Nova.

"My foot's stuck!" Nova yells. "The current's too strong!"

*Fuck!* One minute, twenty seconds. Charlie's dead without that download.

*Pfft! Pfft!*

"Fuck!" Nova yells.

We can't lose that download. One minutes, thirteen seconds.

The current drags the frogman closer, around the bend in the cylindrical tank.

Nova tries to free her foot, grunting in panicked effort.

*Damn it. Damn it. Damn it.* I have heard that panic, that desperation, too many times in my life. Paranoid Pete. Hayes's squeeze.

Seen it in my father's eyes.

I push up into the current, glancing at the hole above—it's clear, light shining down from above—then twist to face the frogman and Nova. I can help Nova, then come back for the squeegee.

No time to get the stunner.

Nova's right foot is stuck in the heat-sink piping and the frogman's about to get line of sight.

The current accelerates me as I sprint toward the frogman.

My heart shudders when a shadow passes over the bright light shining down from the hole behind me.

Another frogman.

*Oh, fuck.* I try to stop, to get back to the squeegee, but the current is too strong. It drags me away.

The new frogman lingers in the hole above, watching me.

The thrumming in the room suddenly cuts off. The current lessens and disappears and the building creaks and groans in the silence from Winn's earlier shenanigans.

The new frogman descends into the room. He had been waiting for me to get out of position. The two are working in tandem and must be able to call to a third to control the room's current.

But he's not aiming a gun. He's not even looking at me anymore. He's singularly focused on a spot on the ground—the squeegee.

*No. No. No.* He's going to get there before me.

I wildly cast about for something, anything to slow him down. Nothing. There's nothing.

He drops down in the crook and rises almost immediately, Caesar's squeegee in hand, leads dangling loose behind.

Slow. I'm too slow even without the current.

*Pfft!*

"Fuck!" Nova frantically grunts as she tries to free her foot.

I jerk around. The other frogman has gained line of sight and is trying to position for a better shot.

*Fuck!* I can't leave Charlie to my father's fate. I can reach that squeegee before it escapes. I can get it back.

I have to.

They're not as practiced as I am in the water. If I can get to him, I can get the squeegee back. Charlie's only chance is on that squeegee.

*Pfft!*

"Aaaa!" Nova screams. "I'm hit!"

I have to get that squeegee. It's the squeegee that matters, not Nova. Puo and Winn will understand.

The low mechanical chugging sound kicks back on. The current picks up.

I can still make it.

Puo and Winn will both support the decision to go for the squeegee, but there'll always be something there now between us. They'd always wonder if I would leave them if the mission were on the line.

But I would never leave them.

I turn my back on the escaping squeegee and use the growing current to sprint toward the other frogman.

The chugging rises to a thrum.

The frogman doesn't see me. He's lining up another shot.

*Pfft!*

I smash into him from behind as he gets the shot off. I grab his right arm in the initial clamor, and apply pressure to his elbow in the wrong direction.

He drops the gun and the current carries it away as it falls to the ground.

We're drifting fast toward the sewer-grate sized holes in the wall sucking out the water.

I need to get rid of him without killing him. Underwater combat isn't like normal combat. Water is thicker than air which blunts most blows, but a disabling strike in air will mostly likely kill underwater since the victim will drown. But the upside is, most people don't train for underwater combat—it's what makes the authorities' frogmen so dangerous. They do train, and their equipment lineup is chosen specifically for underwater combat.

This Cleaner, pretending to be a frogman, has not chosen his equipment for underwater hand-to-hand combat.

He's in a dry scuba suit with an insulated hood and goggles instead of a sealed helmet.

I rip his goggles off, and all the fight he had in him goes with them. The shock of cold and sudden blindness is enough to convince him he has bigger problems than Nova and I.

The current keeps pushing us toward those sewer-sized grates. I work my way down and grab onto Nova who reaches up for me. She grunts in pain as she pulls me in.

"Are you okay?" I shimmy down to look at her stuck foot. The strong current makes it difficult.

"I'll be fine," she says through clenched teeth. "I got hit in the leg. Flesh wound."

I see it as she says it. A black metal flechette is embedded in the middle of her thigh. Looks to be more than inch deep.

"Okay," I say. "Let's get you free and get out of here." I glance back toward the light shining down the empty hole. Shadows flicker from the escaping frogman.

I pull myself up to her stuck foot to study it. "I'm going to pull it free from the other side."

She acknowledges and I lift up above the metal piping to get hit in the face with the current. Has it gotten stronger? It pushes hard and I struggle to pull myself to the other side.

I flip around and face Nova, putting my back to the current and bracing my legs and arms against the metal piping like I'm about to do a bear crawl. The maskless frogman several rows beyond Nova hangs on with his legs splayed out behind him.

I grab her boot with both hands and she grunts in pain.

I pull it toward me, using my legs like I'm doing a squat.

Nova howls as I pull it free. I lose my footing and the current pushes me into the metal pipes and pushes Nova into the next row of metal piping.

"Let's go," I say to Nova. "Stay low, use the piping to break up the current. Can you do it?"

JEFFREY A. BALLARD

"Yeah," she labors.

I pull myself over the next set of heat piping.

"Aaaa," Nova screams. She breathes heavily and then says, "No. I can't. I can't fight the current and pull myself over at the same time with this in my leg."

"Okay." Rather than argue or curse the situation, I reverse direction to help her. I brace my legs against the metal piping to pull Nova over. "Give me your arms."

We lock arms and I pull her over, trying to keep her injured leg from hitting the piping. We both breathe heavily after getting her over the first one.

My grip slips on the second one and she scrambles to catch herself. "Oww!" Her injured thigh smashes into the piping.

We can't take the flechette out down here, she'll lose too much blood and let in the near-freezing water. We regroup, and I pull her over the next set of heat-sink piping, struggling as before. Just seven or eight more of these until we reach the door we came in from.

We're both panting hard by the fourth one. The hole looms above us, light filtering down. No more flicker of shadows.

I keep an eye out for the escaping frogman, but he's gone. The other frogman is slowly making his way in the same direction as us, but it's not a chase. It's an escape. He's blind in the water and spends more time feeling his way forward.

Fuck him. The frogmen definitely have comms, based on the coordination of turning the water turbines on and off earlier to pop down and grab the squeegee. Let his friends come get him.

"You should've left me," Nova pants.

I roll myself over the next set of heat-sink piping, my chest muscles burning.

I huff and catch my breath. "I'll remember that next time."

260

Nova gets into position and grabs onto me again. She's silent for a second, and then says, "Thanks."

"No problem," I say, thinking of Puo and his team nonsense.

But it's a big fucking problem.

We lost Caesar's squeegee, and with it, any lead to Charlie that may have been on it.

# Chapter Twenty-Five

THE BLINDED FROGMAN behind us definitely has called back to his nun-pounding friends. The water turbines' high thrum cuts off the second we manage to pull ourselves back into the hallway.

"Can you swim?" I ask. My chest muscles burn from pulling her over the heat-sink piping.

"Yeah, I think so."

I realize in the sudden silence there's no classical music anymore. Jammed.

"Computer, Consort, do you copy?"

No response.

"Spinster, do you hear the music?" The two of us have line-of-sight comms—Puo fixed that after the Aberdeen debacle. If the main channel is jammed, then our comms switches to line-of-sight. We need to add an alert when that happens.

"No."

I try to remember the last time I heard the music and fail.

"Do you remember the way out?" she asks me.

"Yes." That is one thing I'm good at—memorization. I glance back to make sure she's with me before I take the first turn. She's only halfway down the hallway behind me. *Damn*. She may be able to swim, but not well.

"How are you doing?" I ask.

"I'll make it."

"Spinster, time for some real talk. I need to know how you're doing. No brave face, no dissembling. How bad is it?"

She hesitates before answering, "I can't bend my knee and bending at the hip is no picnic. It's deep, but I'm still alive, so it missed the artery. It's barbed—"

I wince. That's going to hurt coming out.

"I can swim, but slowly. I don't think we should try and remove it down here. As long as we don't have to sprint, I should be fine."

"Understood," I say, "and agree about not removing it down here."

I wait for her at the corner. It's going to be slow going but shouldn't be difficult—as long as the building doesn't collapse on us. Hopefully, Puo's program is still blinding parts of their defense network, but even if it isn't, we're not trying to be stealthy anymore. We need to get out of the water to call for our pickup, connect with Winn and Lucy, and then figure out what we can salvage from this total and complete cluster fuck.

Not only did we not get what we came for—I lost Caesar's squeegee.

The jackknives unfurl. *Fuck. Bad thought. Bad thought. Bad thought.*

I glance back the way we came toward the room with the server farm in the cylindrical tank. If I could break that tank .... Ham was adamant they would shift operations away from the central hub as soon as they knew we were up to no good, including shifting this scrubbing code. If I can get my hands on some hard drives, who knows what Puo might be able to find.

"Spinster," I say, "go on ahead." I give her the directions with landmarks along the way. "I'll catch up."

"What are you going to do?"

"Salvage what I can." *And quiet these damn jackknives*, I think. "If you get confused, don't guess. Sit tight."

"This is a bad idea. We won't have any way to know if something goes wrong for either of us."

*Damn.* She's right. As soon as she gets too far away, we'll lose line-of-sight comms. But if I could just get inside that server farm, I could grab some hard drives.

"I'll wait here," she says. "Go. Hurry."

I hesitate. At first, I don't know why. Something's off. Like my body knows it's wrong to go back but the jackknives are forcing me to do it anyway.

The jackknives win and I swim toward the door back to the central hub room. The lights suddenly cut off in the room. Before I can even ask, heavy decompression pops reverberate down from above.

"Time to go!" I say—a horrible realization of what those pops mean dawning on me.

Nova starts moving before asking, "What's going on?"

I catch up quickly, turning on my helmet lights to full—it doesn't matter at this point. "They're abandoning their base. Destroying it so it can't be tied back to them. They're going to bring the building down on top of it once they're clear."

"Shit."

"Yeah. We need to get out of the building. Computer, are you there?" I ask knowing the answer, but hoping anyway.

No response.

"We need to make our way back to the lobby. We can get out from there." It's too risky to deviate and try and find another way out. We could end up trapped and lost without Puo to guide us.

"Roger."

"You're going to have to push it."

"Understood."

"How'd you know which one was the outbound cable?" The last thing I need is her passing out from the extra effort and pain. If I can keep her talking, at least I know if I have a problem.

She subtly shrugs as she tries to swim. "I guessed."

"What?" I ask surprised.

"Sometimes a decision just needs to be made. You'd be surprised at how often that works."

My heartbeat increases at the thought she could've been wrong. Although, in the end, it wouldn't have mattered. The jackknives dance in my failure. *Fuck, that hurts.*

"Tell me how you got started as a mercenary," I say to keep her talking and my mind off of the jackknives.

"I'm not a mercenary," she answers through pain, taking breaths between sentences. "I'm a defense consultant. I protect people."

"Potato, tomato," I say.

"That's not how that saying works."

"Really?" I'll have to ask Puo about it when we reconnect. We're rushing through the hidden hallways the way we came. Well, Nova is rushing. Her injured speed isn't really rushing for me.

"Really. It's potato, pa-ta-tah."

"All right then. Mercenary, defense consultant: potato, pa-ta-tah." I map out the route in my head. This is taking too long. This building is going to come down any second.

"No— It's not— Do you like being called a thief?"

We enter the first of three stairwells. *Can I take this all the way down to the ground floor? Find a way out from there?* Damn it, I really need Puo.

I shrug at Nova's question. "It is what we are."

"I thought your preferred term was Underwater Reclamation Specialist."

I shrug again. "Depends on who you're talking to and the context. I have no illusions on what we are."

The silt is disturbed from where we passed through before. Nova's able to move faster pulling herself along the railings.

"I find that ... surprising."

"We weren't given a choice," I say. "Both Computer and I were born into a crew off-grid. No citizen chips. No public schools. No options but to become thieves."

I glance down the rest of the stairs once we reach the floor we need to exit on. They continue on for quite a ways, but I have no idea where they lead. It's too dangerous. Damned if I do, damned if I don't. At least if we follow the way we came in we stand a chance.

"What about you?" I ask. "How'd you get started?"

"Military brat. Followed in the family footsteps. Had a few detours before ending up in the seventh group—a special forces unit," she explains.

"That's an airborne unit, right?" That's not the unit we got the anti-gravity suits from, but we learned the layout of the U.S. special forces to understand what we were dealing with and to try and verify the information the engineer-with-a-gambling-problem told us.

"Yeah." She sucks in a breath as she pulls herself into the hallway. "How'd you know that?"

Our helmet lights reflect off a silty mess like a dark foggy morning.

"Part of the life of being a thief, a lot of disparate random pieces of information accumulated over a lifetime. So, after you got out, you didn't want to give it up?"

We pass by gray double doors to a fitness center, each with push metal bars and strings of silt hanging down.

"It's a valuable skill set—"

Deep-seated explosions rattle the hallway. The building gives a sickening lurch.

"It's coming down! Through the fitness doors!" I scramble back toward the double doors. The bastards pulled the trigger. First, they destroyed their underwater base, now they're burying it under a collapsed building.

I shoot past Nova to the doors and force their rusted hinges. Panic-fueled adrenaline can work wonders when there's a direction to actually funnel it.

We're in a back storage/break area. "Follow me to the front!"

Fitness centers often have a wall of windows they stack the gerbil machines up against. *Please let them have windows. And please let those windows be broken.*

Nova starts alternating between grunting and low volume screaming as she tries to sprint. It's not enough to cover up the sounds of the building starting to collapse.

I come out in the main workout area, a large open space with machines scattered around, mirrors and dumbbell racks up against the walls, and a row of gerbil machines against the opposite wall of windows.

"Yes!"

"How ... break ... window?" Nova struggles to ask.

*Shit. They're all intact.* "Just get to the window."

The floor lurches downward away from the windows, dumbbells and weights spill out over the floor. A white medical box with a red cross on it flaps open spilling its contents.

I sprint over and grab an external defibrillator the size of a small briefcase by its handle.

"That's ... not ... going ... " Nova is halfway to the window.

The floor's pitch grows, the windows begin to angle toward us.

"Don't worry about it." I catch up to her, still casting about for more parts. There isn't time to explain everything. "Take it to the window. I'll meet you there."

Nova grabs the defibrillator and saves her energy for hobbling toward the windows rather than arguing.

I sprint-swim back over to the closest dumbbell set, half still resting in the rack while the other half are spilled out across the floor. I estimate how much I think I could lift, but quickly realize it doesn't matter. The numbers on the end have rusted off.

I grab one with four of the plates on each side. *Nope.* It falls with a muted thump.

"Harpy," Nova says, I can hear the sweat on her face, "now what?"

"Get the batteries out."

"Roger."

The floor shifts another few degrees. The weights clink and clatter together as they shift toward the back of the room away from the windows.

*Shit, shit, shit.*

I grab a dumbbell with three plates before it rolls away. *Ooof.* I use my buoyancy controls to help and use two hands and kick my way back over.

"Six D batteries," Nova says.

"Take one, put the little nub side against the window. I'm going to hit it with this thing."

"You mean the positive side?"

"I don't know all your fancy-schmancy special-forces jargon!" I snap, my forearms burning. "Pointy end against window."

"It's not—" She shakes her head once to clear it of whatever nonsense was passing through it. "Understood."

I build up as much speed as I can, aiming for Nova holding the battery against the window.

*Boom!* The entire building shifts, the window tilts toward us.

*Bang!* Weights and dumbbells tumble of the racks onto the floor. *Bang! Bang! Bang!* The lighter machines start to slide toward the back.

I swing the dumbbell back and bring it forward screaming in effort.

*Crack!* The window shatters out a hand-sized hole. The rest is an extensive spiderweb of cracks.

"Move your hand!" I swing back and aim for the area around the existent hole with the dumbbell. *Crack! Crack! Crack!*

Another disparate random piece of information—tempered glass isn't hard to break if you know how.

Soon there's a big enough hole to squeeze through. "Go!" I tell Nova.

She doesn't argue and squeezes through the hole.

The window moves with her as the building collapses. As soon as the flechette is past the window, I push on the soles of her feet to hurry her up.

Nova screams in appreciation.

"Get to the surface!" I shout over the deafening cacophony of the building imploding.

The building shakes violently as it tumbles, the fractured glass breaks free, falling around me as I hustle my way out. Weights and machines crash against the back wall.

Once free, I set the buoyancy controls to head to the surface and turn back to look at the collapsing building. It's a mess of cracking façades, broken glass and dust and silt billowing out.

The building falls out of my helmet lights quickly as I rise. Nova's up ahead. "How we doing?" I ask her.

"I've been better. What's the plan?"

"Get to the surface. Coordinate with Computer. Once our helmets are in air, they shouldn't be able jam us anymore. We'll sync up with Consort and Virgin, then find a spot to hole up and wait for Fat Cat."

My heart flutters at the thought of Winn. They should've gotten out. They were already on the run before it all went to hell.

"Fat Cat?" Nova asks.

"Your employer, Virgin's chaperon," I explain. Mr. Chao shouldn't be too far off. The building collapsing actually helps here, the more attention and traffic the collapse brings the easier it will be to slip away. I would make a sizable wager Puo has already leaked it to urban thrill seekers, social media "influencers," and the authorities.

"Kill your helmet lights," I tell her and do the same for mine. A major building just collapsed in Old New York City. All the people Puo leaked to will be descending on this place. The authorities might already be aware from seismic sensors, and are dialing in their satellites to get visuals. The last thing we want them to see is two people popping up from the water.

*Shit.* They can still see us even with our lights off. The helmet lights will only make it easier for the satellites.

"Level off," I say. We're currently at ninety feet and still jammed. "Consort, Virgin, do you read?" They're the ones with the active sonar.

No response.

It's pitch black down here. There's no ambient light from above. It's one in the morning and the moon is completely dark right now. But the building is still collapsing, the noise sounds like it's coming from all around me.

*Fuck.* Disorientation flushes through me, starting in my forehead and rippling to the back of my neck. I close my eyes and take a deep breath.

"Kick on your full heads-up display," I tell Nova and then walk her through how to do that.

Blue readouts and arrows float out in front and I immediately feel better knowing which direction is up and north. I'm pretty sure we came out on the building's southwest side. Normally, I'd have Puo to help tell me where exactly I ended up.

"Turn your helmet lights on to ten percent power. Just enough so we can see each other."

As she does that, I do the same and set an anchor point at our current location and start swimming to the southwest.

"We have to come up in a building," I tell her. "They'll have the area covered by satellites from the building collapse."

"How do you know that?" she asks, still sounding like she's trying not to scream. Or puke.

"It's the standard response to a half-submerged building collapse. First, assess how bad the damage is, and if there's anything nefarious going on. Second, send a rapid response team to get people on site to determine if others are needed."

I work my way through some bowels of menus in my HUD and find the sonar overlays Winn had been pushing me before we got jammed.

"That's very specific." She takes a breath. "How do you know that again?"

I select the overlays and try to push them to the HUD, but keep getting a failure about not having an anchor point to affix them too. The anchor point I set earlier wasn't tied to a latitude/

longitude, it was a free-floating point so we could estimate how far we had been swimming.

*Gah! Damn it, I need Puo!*

To Nova I answer distractedly, "Part of the life of being an underwater reclamation specialist—staying out of jail."

I remember from the maps how far apart the buildings are, but I don't have a good sense of where we came out. That's the problem, I don't have a point of reference. We've already swum about twenty-five feet.

I turn more westerly. It's Old New York City, we'll hit a half-submerged building eventually. The real problem is, will we hit it before the authorities get here? Aside from satellites, they're going to be vectoring squiddies in and, without Puo, by the time we become aware of them we'll be screwed if we're in open water. Whatever fix the Cleaners had in place went down with the building.

The dark is getting to me. Another wave of disorientation rolls through me. It's so dark down here. The only way I know we've moved is from the floating readouts.

I'm blind. I can't see anything. I can't feel anything. Authorities are on the way. Puo and Winn are out of comms.

It happens again, another reverberating blow to the dam of panic being held back. *Fuck.* I didn't even know the dam had reset.

*I lost Caesar's squeegee. I blew the only lead to Charlie.*

A dangerous adrenaline wave spills over the dam to send my heart into overdrive at the thought.

*Bad thought, bad thought, bad thought.* Deal with that later.

My hands tremble as I breast stroke. My legs feel separate from my body.

*Fuck, I don't need this right now.* It's so black down here. Why is it so fucking black?

"Too … too fast," Nova calls after me.

I fight the urge to flee faster and slow down. I can't force myself to completely stop. My arms won't let me.

Nova struggles to catch up. "Are you okay?" The irony of her asking with a flechette in her thigh is not lost on me. "You're breathing heavily."

"Just trying to get out of open water," I lie.

She's quiet for a second before struggling to get out, "This whole team thing … works better when people … are honest with one another."

I'm quiet at first as I think about her words. I suppose we are a team, but that doesn't mean I want to reveal, or even talk about, my fucked-up head right now. Instead, I settle for a half truth, "We've been out of comms for too long and we're in open water with squiddies and worse on the way. I'm getting antsy."

"Can you put a tracker on us so we can see each other?"

That's a good idea. "Yes, but it doesn't matter." A shadowy skyscraper looms in the distance. "We're here."

We swim up to the side of the building but stay on the outside and head to the surface. It's the fastest route to getting back into comms. We'll have enough time to duck into the building and hide out if any squiddies enter the area. The whole side of this building had windows in its heyday, most of which are broken now—it's only my luck that the fitness center still had intact ones.

The ascent proceeds quickly. I don't exactly sprint up, but neither do I feel the need to baby Nova anymore. I kill my helmet lights thirty feet from the surface and instruct Nova to do the same. Blackness engulfs me, but it's not so menacing this time since I know where the building is.

"Computer, do you copy?" I say as soon as I break the surface. I swim through a broken window into the building to break line of sight from any satellites. "Computer?"

"Harpy, is that you?" Winn says, relief breaking over the comm.

*Oh, thank God.* "Yes!" We both start talking over each other asking after the other.

Lucy is accounted for. I'm fine. Nova's been hit with a flechette, but should be fine. *Where?* In the thigh. *How deep?* I don't know. Winn and Lucy got out before the Cleaners blew the building. We barely got out. By the time I get more specifics of what happened, Nova pops her head up. Maybe she can answer all of Lucy's questions about her injury.

I wave Nova over.

"Did you get a hold of Computer?" Nova asks as she struggles to swim over.

"No." The question crashes me back to reality. "Consort, Virgin have you been able to get a hold of Computer?"

"No. Lost contact about seven minutes ago."

Some rapid math puts that around the same time as for us.

"Wait," Nova says, "how are we then talking with Virgin and Consort? Are they in line of sight?"

A quick discussion of where everyone is commences while my stomach drops out from under me. Winn and Lucy are in a separate building northwest of here. They are definitely not in line of sight.

We're not on line-of-sight comms. We're on the normal party line. We're talking on the party line. If we were jammed that line wouldn't be open.

*Oh, God.* I feel like I'm outside my body, watching it all happen to someone else. Sweat breaks out all over. I can't catch my breath. My heart *hurts*.

"Harpy, is that you?" Winn asks panicked. "Are you okay?"

We weren't jammed. I don't know why couldn't we talk to each other in the water, but we weren't jammed. There's just no one on the other end of the line.

Something's happened to Puo.

# Chapter Twenty-Six

T HE NEXT THIRTY minutes are the worst of my life. I can't
stop shaking. I can't calm down.

I can't fucking breathe.

There's nothing I can do. Nothing. Simply wait around for
Mr. Chao to come get us, where every second feels like minutes
and an accomplishment to get through at the same time.

No one disputes my panicked analysis.

I can't stop muttering, "Something's happened. Something's
happened. Something's happened."

Nova is tight, too. If something happened to Puo, something
probably happened to Aliyah. She was left behind precisely to
protect Puo from that rat bastard Ham.

Ham has to be at the center of this. But there was no other
option other than to leave him back at the apartment under su-
pervision and off any systems. Incorporating him anywhere else
in the plan would've been more dangerous.

Mr. Chao picks us up in a reappropriated NYPD speed boat
and Winn ushers me alone down into its bowels. Winn tries to
calm me down, walk me through breathing exercises, but all I
can do is pace.

"Don't tell me to fucking breathe!" My heart slams against my ribcage so hard it hurts.

Winn stands there in his scuba suit, helmet off, looking wretched. "I know," he says. "I know. Try. Just try."

I shakily inhale and pivot again to cross the small space. My arms hurt from where my fingers dig into them. "Have you tried reaching him?"

Winn nods yes, and leaves the result unspoken.

I pivot again. "And we tried reaching him on his tablet?"

Winn nods.

I can't fucking believe it. How stupid am I? I left the snake in the nest with the golden goose. Was it planned this way all along? Did Ham get to Aliyah? They are mercenaries, after all. How high was their price? Did Nova play me?

"What about using the comms on the boat?" I ask.

Winn nods, but says, "Let's go try again."

Once again it yields nothing. Not even the cackle of an empty line. Just silence.

Mr. Chao is grim-faced. Nova is laid out across the padded seats built into the side of the boat, her injured leg elevated. Lucy sits near her, attending to the wound. Both avoid eye contact with me. Winn's chest rises and falls and it's then I realize he's breathing nearly at the same rate I am. He doesn't know what to do either.

None of them do. They all know how bad this is.

The drive to shore is at a turtle's pace, a speedboat puttering along at full speed. We should've arranged for a hovercar, but the speedboat provided the perfect cover—another boat among the several descending and swirling around the site.

I go back to pacing, thinking, scheming, trying to figure out a way to get to Puo faster, or have someone I trust look in on the apartment, or get some kind of eyes out there I can use. I come up empty. Nothing's viable. Nothing's fast enough.

"Go," I croak at Winn, my mouth parched, "go make sure a hovercar is waiting for us."

He hesitates a second, torn, then nods and leaves.

And I pace—back and forth. Back and forth. Back and forth.

\*\*\*

There was no hovercar waiting for us. I knew there wouldn't be when I sent Winn off. Everyone was either on the boat with us or missing. No one was available to prep one—Mr. Chao had caught a rideshare to NYPD's dock. But that wasn't the primary purpose in sending Winn away.

I needed to be alone. I needed to be allowed to spiral. And for once, I didn't need to be the one to figure everything out.

And Winn came through. There wasn't a hovercar waiting for us, but Winn had identified where we could go steal one—hiring a rideshare with Nova's leg would raise too many questions. He and Lucy even identified the best approach route and how to move Nova with her injured leg to it without raising suspicions.

I still had to do the boost and it had to be an older model since I didn't have Puo on the other end to clean up some stuff, but I was still the one doing it. My heart still thumped against my chest. Cold sweat drenched my skin. My body still felt like it belonged to someone else. But boosting a car? That I could do. It was something *to* do.

Hell, it felt good.

Walking into the apartment building does not. It feels surreal. Not just happening to someone else, but like I'm trapped in this other person's body, forced to witness this strained, almost staggering, march down the hallway. Can't run—too much noise will draw attention to us in the middle of the night.

Besides I'm pretty sure a few seconds isn't going to matter at this point. Deep down, a part of me doesn't want to walk through that door. I saw my father murdered only five days ago and I've been fucked up ever since. Granted, I was already trending in that direction. But ever since then my life has been careening between one panic attack and the next.

Who knows what's on the other side of that door? Who knows what it will do to me?

The contemporary dark wood apartment door looms ahead. The silver handle glints like a knife. The punch-code pad menaces the hallway like a ticking bomb.

We traipse down the hallway, our footsteps soft against the lattice-patterned, emerald-colored carpet. I lead the group with Winn and Mr. Chao right behind me, while Lucy lags behind helping Nova hobble down the hallway. We're going to have to get her medical help—yet another problem to solve. I have no contacts in this part of the world and we're being hunted on both sides.

"Do you want me to go first?" Winn asks softly.

I had stopped at the threshold of the door, my hands anchored in my jacket. The overwhelming silence presses down, louder than Nova and Lucy shuffling behind me. I shake my head no, punch in the code, and open the door.

There's no going back. There never was.

Tendrils of coppery violence assault my nostrils as soon as I enter.

My pulse pounds in my ears.

I run down the short entrance hallway to the main living area.

All the lights are on. Everything's still in its place. No signs of a struggle.

Aliyah's dead—shot several times in the body and once more in the head. Thick, congealing, maroon blood spreads out from her.

Ham and Puo are missing.

The sight snaps me back into my body. I run for the other bedrooms to check for Puo. I've finally found my voice again, but I don't dare use it. We're in an apartment with a murdered body in the dead of night. The last thing we need is a concerned neighbor calling the cops.

Winn and Mr. Chao rush past me to Aliyah.

"Don't touch the body," I warn them, running across the room to the bedrooms.

Winn stops and looks at me, understanding dawning. We're going to have to leave the body. We can't have any fingerprints on it for the authorities to track back to us. Mr. Chao's face is pale, his eyes wide. He fights the urge to go to her against my warning. We're going to have to wipe down the whole apartment.

The bedrooms are all empty. *Thank God.* If Puo were here, he wouldn't be alive.

I hurry back out to the main room to study the room, to see if there are any clues indicating whether Puo was hurt. Or what happened. Or where they took him.

They have him. They actually have Puo. The object of all of this. Is Charlie even still alive anymore? The jackknives sink deeper into my stomach and I stumble. *Oh, fuck.*

Lucy, Nova, and Mr. Chao are all distraught, staring at Aliyah. Winn stands in front of them, holding them back, repeating my warning. It's clear she's dead, but the instinct to check on her is overwhelming.

I hurry to Puo's spot at the dining room table. Everything is still in its place. The system is even on. It looks like he got up willingly, or at least wasn't physically forced. I sit down where Puo sat. The wood seat is cold. My pulse quickens—I'm not sure how much faster it can go. He's been gone for a while.

We've always known each other's passwords—a security protocol. I sign in to Puo's account and check the time. He's been gone for a little over an hour. I don't touch a thing, but stare at the screens. Is there a note here? A clue? None of it makes sense. My eyes see the windows open, the bits of code, but my brain can't make sense of any of it.

Why can't I understand this? I know the individual words, but I can't put them together in strings to derive meaning. I don't have time for my brain not to work. I need to understand this. Doesn't it understand what's at stake?

I sit up straight. "Winn," I say, my voice sounding panicked in my own head, "come here and look at this."

Winn rushes over. "What?"

"You need to read this."

Winn stands over me, looking between me and the screen, confused.

I grab his hand and squeeze. It's hot. Real. "I can't make sense of it," I whisper. "My brain, it's not ... it's not working."

Winn nods and sits down in the chair I vacate.

I stand, looking out over the room, a thick band of tension ratcheting around my head in a vise grip. Winn's clickings on the keyboard are like tiny hammers to my frontal lobe.

Lucy starts to kneel down to Aliyah.

"Don't touch her." My voice comes out harsher than I intend due to the ever-tightening tension band around my head.

Lucy snaps her head to me, tears in her eyes, but she obeys.

Before either of us can respond Winn says, "Ham was on Puo's system."

I turn back to Winn, alarm in my eyes, hot needles rippling down my neck.

"It looks like Puo locked down our public comms channel to keep it open. Then someone came in after and tried to shut it down. The best they could do was shut down in-water comms."

That's why we lost the music and comms to each other in the water, but could talk once we were in air. Puo was trying to keep us informed. He was trying to give us a chance.

Mr. Chao helps Lucy over to one of the couches, clearly intending to help her sit down.

"No!" I shout. "Don't touch anything," I rush on, my thoughts leaping lightspeed ahead of my words. "Puo was forced to leave. There has to be a clue here somewhere."

There has to be.

We need to read the room. Understand what happened.

But my brain isn't working. Couldn't make sense of a computer screen. What if I can't read the room?

Puo's gone. The golden goose. They're going to do everything they can to make him talk and once they know his secrets, they're going to kill him. They're going to use Charlie against him.

My vision swims.

I have no idea where he is. I have no idea where Charlie is.

I lost our only lead to Charlie. Now that they have Puo, they have no need to engage with us. Charlie's video led to the trap in Aberdeen. There's nothing left to go on, no need for them to lead us on.

I can't breathe.

There have to be clues in here. Have to be.

Why can't I see straight?

The room is too hot. The blood too thick. The stench too rank.

I have to get out of here.

*Oh, fuck.* The jackknives eviscerate my stomach, shred it to pieces.

I— I can't catch my breath.

I clutch my chest. My hands shake. My ribcage is too small to contain this treacherous heart.

"Isa," Winn says deliberately calm, "come sit down." He's gotten up, approaching me like a wild animal, his arms out ready to catch me.

"Don't touch me!"

He pulls his hands back but keeps them extended, ready. "You need to come sit down."

"He's gone, Winn! He's gone!" Whatever's left of the dam breaks, fully and completely. I sob. "We have to get him back! We have to!"

Winn steps forward and wraps me in a bear hug.

"Let me go!" I shout, tears leaking out. I wriggle and push away.

He holds me tight. "We'll get him back," he whispers.

"How?" I sob. "How?"

I can't keep doing this. I can't keep running for our lives all the time. I can't keep putting Puo's and Winn's lives in danger.

"I don't know," Winn says, and then adds quickly, "but he's Puo. He'll have left us a clue or find a way to reach us."

Left us a clue .... Puo's voice from earlier on the comm destroys me, *Want me to tell you a story?*

Oh, God. What have I done? Why didn't I listen? I can't stop shaking. Why am I shaking so much? "Oh, God Winn— I can't— Why—?"

How am I supposed to find a clue like this? I can't think. I can't even control these fucking panic attacks.

I think I'm going to throw up. I'm hot. So impossibly hot.

"Just let your body work through it," Winn says.

"You better not tell me to fucking breathe," I warn him, my voice shaking. He's too close.

Winn shakes his head no, of course not. "Let it pass." I start to object to this stupidity but he talks over me. "Your body can't keep this up for more than twenty to thirty minutes. Your body is being flooded with adrenaline and hormones. Eventually, it'll run low and stop. It *has* to pass."

"We don't have twenty to thirty minutes!" I push away from him. He holds me tight and I fight harder. "Let go of me!"

I break free and take several haphazard steps away from him. This room is too small. They're all staring at me, watching the spectacle. I can't breathe. I can't fucking breathe.

I need to get out of here. I need to— I need to—

I can't— I can't think straight.

Puo. I need to get to Puo.

"Isa!" Winn grabs me by the arms and looks in my face.

How'd he get so close, so fast?

"You need to breathe! No!" he yells me down from snapping hysterically at him. "You want to get Puo? Then breathe, in through the nose, out through the mouth. Sit down."

*You want to get Puo?* It's that question that breaks through. I sit down on the nearest chair at the kitchen table. My hands can't stop shaking.

Winn produces two of those little brown pills and sets them on the table. "Breathe," he reminds me when I stop to stare at the pills. He walks me through an anchoring exercise while going to get water.

All I can do is stare at the pills. Is this my life now? Is my body not my own anymore? I need chemical help just to function? I've already taken one, not three hours ago, before the op.

Winn comes back with the water. "Take the pills. They'll help get the symptoms under control, slow your central nervous system, stop the rapid firing from stress hormones."

I continue to stare at the pills.

He sits down next to me and takes my shaking hands. "Isa, I love you. I'm trying to help you. If ever there was situation these meds were made for, this is it. But if you don't want to take them, then don't. But we need to help you before we can help Puo. Listen to me. Work on the breathing. Work on the anchoring."

My breath comes in a ragged cadence, my rapid beating heart making it difficult.

Nova, Lucy, and Mr. Chao watch us through tears in their eyes. They're shaken too. Pale faces, fear in their eyes. Uncertainty on what to do next.

Winn's right. To first help Puo, I need to get my shit together. Or at least get back to functional. I scoop up the pills and swallow them with quick swig of water.

"Okay," I say shakily. "Lead me through a grounding exercise."

I can do this. For Puo. He would come for me.

And I am coming for him.

# Chapter Twenty-Seven

THE NEXT TWENTY-FIVE minutes are a shit show of panic. Every breath. Every heartbeat. I feel them all. Adrenaline slows your perception of time, which is helpful in life-threatening situations, but when you're sitting around with nowhere to direct it, it's fucking awful.

Winn walks me through exercise after exercise.

And I do them. I really try, because there's no other choice. Either I anchor myself to the here and now, or get lost in the torrent of panic of what could be and what I can't do.

The pills' effects wash over my mind in an ever-rising tide, calming as it goes. Slowing the panicked thoughts and my heart rate. The danger and panic are still there. They just now occupy a normal place in my brain. A place where I can deal with them. I'm not me, I'm not normal by any means. But I can function again. The pills have rebuilt the dam, and forced the panicked waters to recede.

"Okay," I say to Winn as he finishes the last exercise and tells me to keep up the diaphragmatic breathing. "I'm— I'm better."

He eyes me. "You look better. But don't rush yourself."

"I'm okay." I stand up, surprised my legs aren't shaky. "I'm ready." I take a deep breath through my nose and continue the diaphragmatic breathing as instructed and slowly take in the room around me.

Nova sits on the floor against the edge of the entrance hallway to the main area, her injured leg outstretched. Lucy stands in the kitchen facing toward the main area, working on her system, flipping through windows and typing rapidly.

"Where's Mr. Chao?" I ask.

Lucy looks around her float screen at me. "He went to pick up supplies." She looks over at Nova and it's clear what she means.

"I'll be okay," Nova says when she sees us studying her, but her voice is tight with pain. "I'd be better though if Doc has got any tricks up his sleeve for me?" She looks at Winn.

I smack myself in the forehead—Winn's a surgeon. He can remove the flechette. "Winn can you remove the ... ?" I peter out because they're all smiling at me, except Lucy, she's just shaking her head. "What?"

"I already looked at her on the boat."

"And gave Ken the list of supplies we need," Lucy adds.

Winn continues, "We had to cut away the dry suit to get it off—I'm afraid the suit is a loss. But the placement is lucky. It'll hurt like hell, but shouldn't have any long-term damage."

Nova nods once like she's already preparing herself for the pain. "So, no extra goodies for me?"

"No," Winn says, "sorry. I am not stocked up on pain killers."

"Just—" Lucy starts.

"Just medicine to treat conditions I already know about," Winn cuts her off with a sharp look.

I realize Lucy knows the name of the meds. "How do you know the name of the brown pills?"

She studies me for a half beat and then says, "Takes one to know one. I had them in high school—"

"And you got better?" I ask eagerly. That was what, four years ago?

She shrugs. "Yeah, I got better. But it's always there, in the periphery. Some days it's fuzzier, almost soft, fading into the background. And other days—" She shrugs again. "—some days are harder than others."

"You still deal with it?"

"Yeah. But it's manageable."

My shoulders slump. *Manageable?* I want to get Puo, Charlie, and burn the Cleaners to the ground and then never have to deal with this shit again.

Winn sees my shift and says, "One thing at a time. Everyone's experience is different. Let's work on removing your triggers first before working on long-term solutions."

I nod. *Right.* Read the room. Find the clues to find Puo. He must have left us something.

"What are you looking at?" I ask Lucy, who went back to flicking through her float screen.

"Security footage from around the area. There's nothing," she answers my question before I can ask it. "No one coming. No Ham or Puo leaving. So, whoever came here definitely had a Cleaner with them."

We already knew the Cleaners were involved. Or a Cleaner. "How do you know it wasn't Ham?"

"Where'd he get the gun?" Nova asks. "The wounds look like small caliber entries with no exit. And no one heard the gun shots and called the cops? That means a silencer. They chose their weapon very deliberately. And look at the grouping. No missed shots, no stray bullet holes. Whoever it was, was a pro. Unless Ham has some hidden skills we don't know about, it wasn't him."

I nod, thinking. I didn't really think it was Ham. Whoever took Aliyah out put a bullet square in her forehead after the fact to make sure she was dead. Ham may be a lot of disgusting things, but stone-cold killer isn't one of them. Oh, he's not high-minded like us, he just won't do the dirty work himself.

"Okay," I say. "What else could you tell from the room?"

Nova shakes her head. "Only that the shooter was likely where I'm sitting—it's why I came over here. I think they took—" Nova stumbles over almost saying Aliyah's name and her face flushes. "—took her by surprise."

I study the room to give Nova some privacy. Puo was sitting at his computer. Aliyah was roughly standing where she is now lying, watching the proceedings. Where would Ham be? Aliyah would want to keep both in view. Which would put her back to the door.

"The door was locked when I entered," I think out loud.

"It locks automatically," Lucy says.

"So why didn't Aliyah hear the beep from the punch code?"

"She may not have heard it," Winn says.

Nova's shakes her head. "There's no way she would've missed something like that. Either it was too loud in here or—"

"It was already unlocked," I finish for her. These locks are all smart locks so the building's owners can change combos and lock people out all without having to get up off their ass. "Ham must have hacked in." Something like that is child's play for a Cleaner. I turn to Lucy, "Can you—?"

"I'm on it." She's already typing and swiping. Then she adds, "But I don't expect there to be anything. Those things are stupid easy to get into. Should be illegal honestly—"

My eyebrows rise at that.

She keeps going without noticing, "—and just as easy to get out of without leaving a trace."

I go and sit down in Puo's seat, looking over the screens properly this time. My heart flutters at the memory of not being able to make any sense of them, but I breathe that away when I realize that's not happening this time. There are command windows up, internet browser tabs of maps, one of a story of a missing North Dakota couple found, text files of squiddie call frequencies, and Puo's custom software interface for encrypting our comms.

Winn comes to stand by me.

"Show me where Ham was on the system," I say.

Winn pulls up an audit log for the custom comms software of entered commands and points it out to me. "It starts there. Those don't make sense if it was Puo. Puo wouldn't try and shut down a channel he just forced open and Ham wouldn't have forced the channel open."

I can't really follow the specific commands in detail, but the important bits are the timestamps. "Look between twelve for-ty-five and one a.m.," I tell Lucy. I think back to the disaster in the water. That's when we were in the central hub vortex room— the last time I remember talking with Puo.

"There's nothing here," Lucy says like that's what she ex-pected. "Either in or out. I can see us leaving and coming back, but not— Oh."

"Oh, what?" I ask.

"Ham and Puo leaving and the door relocking should've been logged. But there isn't anything. Whoever did this was definitely in the lock." She thinks and then shrugs. "Which doesn't really tell us anything we didn't already know."

It confirmed one of our suspicions, but I don't correct her. "When is Mr. Chao getting back?" I ask. I want him to sit down and look through Puo's computer. I can read the key-logging files, and command histories, but I've been around Puo long enough to know that's barely scratching the surface.

"He's checking out now," Lucy says, looking at one of her windows—a messenger app by the looks of it. "Ten, fifteen minutes. And his name is Ken. Mr. Chao sounds like my father."

He could be her father, but I let it slide. "Which one of you is better?" I ask and then clarify, "I need someone to look through this system for clues."

Her initial suspicious stare falls into a contemplative one and then she eventually answers, "Better wait for him."

I nod and look back out over the room, trying to reconstruct what happened, find where there might be inadvertent clues.

"Can we put something over her?" Lucy asks, studiously staring at her screen and not at Aliyah. "Or at least close her damn eyes."

I glance over at Nova, hoping she'll be the one to answer: no, we can't. We need to pull whatever information we can from here and then wipe the place down, physically and digitally, and then disappear. We can't even risk calling the authorities once we leave to take care of the body. The bottom line is, the more time between us and the discovery, the better off we're going to be.

Nova declines to answer and I can't catch her eye. She's sitting between the main room and the entrance hallway. Her back rests against the hallway wall with her outstretched injured leg covering almost the whole distance. She stares up at the ceiling, the single hallway light on. The white walls are blank except for a generic piece of art across from her and a row of jackets above her.

Wait a minute.

I get up and walk over toward Nova staring at Puo's moss-colored ski jacket.

"It's Puo's jacket," I say excitedly.

Nova looks up, wincing in pain.

Lucy stares at the jacket as well. "So he didn't bring it with him."

I shake my head, grinning like an idiot.

"What?" Winn asks. "What am I missing?"

"Exactly!" I say. Hope rushes through me, wiping away the panic attack's lingering effects. "What are *you* missing?"

Winn looks at me like I've lost my mind—but in a good way this time.

"Puo's jacket is there," I say, "where is yours?"

Winn's eyes widen in understanding. Winn had left his ski jacket behind since he was in a scuba drysuit for the drop—the same exact ski jacket Puo has, only a slightly different shade of green. "He took it with him."

"He took it with him!" I rush back over to Puo's system. This time, knowing exactly what to do, I start typing.

"I'm missing the significance of this," Lucy says.

"Actually," Winn says, "me too."

"There's a tracker in your coat," I say in triumph. *Puo, you beautiful genius, you're going to lead us right to them.*

"You put a tracker in my coat?" Winn asks, surprised with a definite note of offense.

"You left." I shrug and keep typing, too excited to explain further how Puo and I determined to keep tabs on him until we were sure we could trust him. It's only been three weeks since we reconnected in Vancouver. Either way, we have a ticket out of this mess.

"They're going to scan for a tracker," Nova says.

"Let 'em," I say. I'm one hundred percent confident in Puo's tracker. We've already used it once to fool the Cleaners in Vancouver. "It's low power, short duty cycle, and cycles on and off at irregular intervals."

"Clever," Lucy says.

*Damn right it is.*

I bring up the tracking software and look at the map for the last three hours.

Got him. "He's moving northwest. Once Mr. Chao's back, Winn removes the flechette, bandages her up, then we scrub the place and split."

They all nod.

But I can't sit still right now. Once that dot stops, we can start the real planning. "C'mon," I say to Winn and Lucy, "let's start packing and sanitizing."

# Chapter Twenty-Eight

Y ou need to get some sleep." Winn walks into the one-room cabin, letting in a blast of cold air.

I don't look up from Puo's old-school monitor where I sit alone huddled in a plush maroon blanket. "Puo's dot hasn't moved in the last three hours."

We're in a series of one-room cabins a few miles north of Old Forge, a small town in the Adirondacks of upstate New York. Everyone else is either out gathering supplies or sleeping.

"We already knew that," Winn says.

"No." I shake my head. "Puo's dot hasn't moved within the fort since he arrived. That's where they're holding him. That's where his cell is."

Puo's dot first stopped moving three hours ago, twenty miles northwest of Old Forge. It was the Aberdeen farmhouse all over again—wide open spaces without any civilization nearby to use as cover. We can work around almost any impediment with enough time and incentives to motivate us, but time is the one thing we don't have. And we're without Puo's magical digital fingers to make up for it.

Fortunately, Mr. Chao and Lucy started to pull their digital weight and were able to hack into a tech company's "research" satellite. Research is in quotes there because what a tech company needs high resolution imagery for is anyone's guess—Mr. Chao and Lucy couldn't tell me. All that matters is, we have eyes on the Citadel: a repurposed old revolutionary or civil war fort with modern infrastructure smashed in the center.

Leave it to the Cleaners to smash their modern monstrosity on top of a historical site.

"We can come in from the southwest—" I say.

"You need to get some sleep."

I look up and stare at him properly, making it clear how stupid I think the suggestion is since everyone else is awake.

He walks up to stoke the coals in the stone fireplace behind me. "Everyone's caught a few hours here and there, except you. Mr. Chao and Nova are resting now."

"She's injured—"

"You're obsessing, going in circles—"

A huge yawn escapes me.

Winn stares at me as if that makes his point.

"So, you're here to drug me?"

Winn shakes his head. "I don't think you need it. You've been awake for almost twenty-four hours straight. Forty-eight since a proper night's rest."

I scrunch up my face in thought, trying to remember what happened forty-eight hours ago.

"Before the Caesar job," Winn says, helping me out.

"I slept on the ride back from Aberdeen." That was twenty-fours ago. Have I really been awake that long? I can't sleep anyway, so what's it matter?

"That wasn't sleep. That was exhaustion, scrunched over in a hovercar, and for only a few hours. It's been forty-eight hours since you've gotten real sleep and your body's weathered some intense anxiety attacks in the last twenty-four. You *need* to sleep. Lie down. You'll be asleep in minutes."

Maybe, but for how long? It's not falling asleep that's been a problem, it's staying asleep.

"I'll take it under advisement." I go back to studying the monitor, mapping out a route from the southwest site to Puo's location.

Winn sniffs. A small fire crackles to life behind me.

"We need to get him back," I say softly.

"We will. We have a good plan. There's nothing you can do now but sleep. Nova and Mr. Chao are already resting. Lucy's monitoring the site, and I'm about to head out to meet Durante."

Another causality of no time. Any idea that *might* work gets run with, not slapped on to some pro-and-con chart to be labored over. Oh, impersonating a cop might be helpful? We'll work out exactly how on the way back from stealing their credentials—that's where we're at. So when the idea of calling Durante—my father's second in command—or Colvin came up, we ran with it. We can do more with more bodies, and we *need* more bodies.

Although I would've preferred to work with Colvin. There's a level of trust there with what happened in the Seattle Isles and his sisters that I don't have with Durante. But Durante was physically closer—that whole time thing again.

"Be careful with Durante," I say. "Don't let them stray into the Cleaners' territory."

Winn nods. "I know. Get in, set up, get out. I'll keep on them."

I knew Durante, and likely Colvin, would be eager to strike back at the Cleaners, but Durante is surprisingly supple. I'm worried he has his own agenda—well, I *know* he has his own agenda. I'm worried his agenda will collide with ours and screw everything up.

This is a rescue mission, not retribution. I may have implied I have a way to take out the Cleaners and a full-frontal assault would scuttle that chance, which is a half-truth. I do have an idea, but I don't know if it will work—I need Puo to know for sure. Which is the primary objective: rescue Puo and Charlie. If the opportunity presents itself to stab the Cleaners in the heart, then great. If not, I'm grabbing Puo and Charlie and getting the fudge out of there.

I yawn again. *Twenty-four hours, huh?* The fire's warmth rolls over me. Burning wood cracks and the scent of wood smoke permeates the cabin.

"Okay," I say. "I'll lie down. But if I can't stay asleep, I'm calling to harass you while you're out."

"Naturally. Just try, that's all I'm asking. If you can't sleep, don't worry about it. You've been running on enough adrenaline for ten people."

*Yeah, tell me about it.*

I gather up the blanket around me and stand up. Of course, Winn will be out of comms for this next part—it's the whole point. The Cleaners are going to have the whole wilderness area around their fort under heavy surveillance, sniffing for electronic signals. So Winn is going out to do some prep work for our visit tonight without any electronic signals coming from him.

It has to be tonight: New Year's Eve—it's too good an opportunity to pass up.

Lucy rushes in, letting in another cold blast of air, and stops when she sees me getting into bed. "Oh— Uh, sorry. I, uh—"

"Out with it," I say, "and close the door."

She closes the door and moves closer to the fire.

I wrap the maroon blanket tighter around myself.

"The National Syndicate is there, at the fort," she says. "All of them."

*All of them?* My heart races. "How do you know this?"

"I saw them arrive. The satellite is in geosynchronous orbit over the whole northeast with time history—"

"How do you know it's them?" Winn asks.

Good question. We know their names, and where they operate out of, from Puo decoding the blockchain back in the apartment. We do not know their faces, their races, physical descriptions, or genders.

"Their vehicles," Lucy answers. "I traced every arriving vehicle back to its origin point through the satellites—"

The plural use of satellites catches my attention, but I keep a neutral expression. Aliyah's murder galvanized the three of them. There was no hesitation or debate about getting Puo back or having to permanently deal with the National Syndicate. Our goals are now fully aligned. Parting with Aliyah's body was emotional, but in the end, they left with a lot less fuss than I expected.

Lucy continues, "—All the important ones came from cities with National Syndicate members. It's them."

"Important ones?" I ask. "What does that mean? And how do you know they're the actual members and not underlings?"

"Caesar greeted each one personally when they arrived. Those are what I mean by important ones, he doesn't greet all of the hovercars personally. And—" she adds quickly, "—their appearances are consistent with assumptions about their races and genders. It's them."

There's that edge again, pushing down on my chest. It makes sense and I want to believe her reasoning, but it's thin.

But it is *something*. Now that it's there in front of me, I can almost pull it out of the air and put it all together. Upon reflection, it's not surprising they all gathered together. Puo's been the target this whole time for his ability to manipulate the blockchain. They all know about it. They're not going to want—

My mouth falls when the thought snaps into place. I squeeze my arms tight to my body to keep my hands from shaking under the blanket.

"What?" Winn asks.

"It's Ham. That stupid bastard just gave us everything on a platter."

Both look at me quizzically.

"To save his own ass." I shake my head and start over. "They want what Puo knows, but what they really don't want is for one of them to have it and not share it. If Caesar had Puo without the others knowing, he could extract the info, kill Puo, and refuse to share it. But then how did the others learn Puo had been captured?"

"Ham must've told them," Winn says, putting it together.

"Exactly! Ham couldn't deliver Puo alone to Caesar for that very reason. Caesar would kill Ham to keep it quiet, and Caesar already wanted to kill Ham. Ham used Puo to barter with all of them for his life."

It fits. They're really all there. *Holy shit.*

"You're not going to sleep anymore, are you?" Winn asks.

I shake my head no, lost in thought. They're all there. They're all in one place. We can end this.

The mission just changed.

# Chapter Twenty-Nine

I SLEPT. Six hours actually. Which is pretty good for me right now. It was a deep, solid sleep, the dreamless-dead-to-the-world kind. The kind I needed. Winn was right. I was exhausted. I fell asleep instantly.

But staying asleep continued to be a problem. As soon as I was the least bit aware I was sleeping my body jacked fully awake, my heart pounding. No gradual wakeup, no switching positions and gently falling back under. Bam! Now you're awake and about to die.

I'm grateful for the six hours I got.

Now I'm in a hovercar at eleven fifty at night, zooming toward Caesar's mutant fort at twenty-two thousand feet. Why twenty-two thousand feet? Because it's the highest this particular hovercar we reappropriated can go.

If we had Puo I'm sure we could've found a better hovercar, but this was the best we could find with a speed/altitude combination that might work. Twenty-two thousand feet is a little more than four miles in the air and since radar travels upward at an angle, that corresponds to approximately a one-and-a-half-mile blind spot directly around their mutant fort for the radar we think the Cleaners have, based on the satellite feed surveillance. I even remembered to correct for the elevation above sea level—Puo would be proud. Of course, the Cleaners' property line extends out several miles *past* the one-and-a-half-mile blind spot so they're not likely worried about it. And that's just for the radar; I'm sure they have other upward-looking electronic sensors to scan for exactly what we're about to do.

No matter—that's where Winn and Durante's prep work comes in. As for the Cleaners' other electronic sensors? Well, we're not going to drop *directly* on top of them. That'd just be rude.

Nova's driving the hovercar in a slate-gray winter jacket and a pair of jeans with her leg bandaged. Lucy sits up front, while Winn and I are in the back. The three of us are in anti-gravity suits. Dropping in the suits was the only option where we stood a chance of not being immediately discovered. I'm also pretty sure Nova and company already knew about the suits from decoding the blockchain and everything that happened in Aberdeen. They readily accepted the existence of such suits and what the suits could do. They put up some disbelief and request for demonstration. But they already knew. It takes a con to know a con.

"This suit is huge." Lucy shifts around in Puo's anti-gravity suit in the front seat uncomfortably. "Are you sure it's going to work?"

"Yes." There wasn't time for any tailoring. "It only needs to be a closed system, not a tight fitting one." It'll work. It might give her some rug burns around where it catches, but it'll do the job.

"Then why couldn't Winn take this one, I take yours, and you take his? Seems like then we all would've been slightly off."

Because then we would all be uncomfortable. "Too late now," I say.

"We're two minutes out," Nova announces.

"Helmets on," I order. My nose scrunches up against the inside as I slip my helmet on. I click it into place and with a hiss, the helmet seals to the suit and pressurizes. Heads-up displays spread out before me.

We're exactly twenty-two thousand, one hundred and eleven feet up and traveling one hundred and fifty miles per hour due west-northwest. It's seventy degrees inside the hovercar. No wind. Arrow markers indicate where Winn and Lucy are.

I select Lucy's arrow. "Blink twice with both eyes to give me control so I can set the marker."

I look out over the dark landscape below. It's black out there. No lights of civilization. Too far up to see any campfires. Brief explosions of lights—fireworks—begin to erupt below and ahead of us. Those fireworks are the key.

I pull our location from the hovercar's GPS and set the marker for the southwest drop zone. I push the distant blue bullseye to Lucy and confirm she sees it.

The clock ticks to midnight.

"Here we go!" Nova jerks the car more northward toward the bullseye, straight into the Cleaner's territory, and accelerates to the hovercar's max of two hundred and fifty miles per hour.

Fireworks erupt all around the edges of Caesar's mutant fort's property. The specially designed fireworks erupt at high altitude filled with radar chaff at the proper Doppler frequency. They explode over the edges of Caesar's property, creating holes in their coverage.

I'm betting the Cleaners don't get a lot of fireworks in the area and won't know what to make of it. They won't even notice the fireworks are special high-altitude builds. I mean, how often do you notice the height of a firework? They probably won't even go outside to look at them.

We tried to make it look like a bunch of scattered campers shooting off fireworks for the next five minutes all hootin' and hollering, building to a grand finale. *Happy New Year!*

That'll be enough time for us to get into position, drop, and for Nova to get back out of their territory so when their radar clears up, her little blip is right back where it should be: traveling west-northwest at twenty-two thousand feet and a hundred and fifty miles per hour. Not suspicious at all.

*Yeah, right.*

Of course they'll be on high alert after something like this. They kidnapped Puo. They know we're coming. But here's the thing—they won't know *when* we're coming; they probably think we'll drop directly on their mutant fort; and, they won't know those fireworks aren't normal fireworks. It is New Year's after all. And how often do their radars detect fireworks anyway? I'm betting close to never.

The blue bullseye zooms closer.

"Just breathe," I say to Lucy, but for myself as well. "The suit will take care of the z-direction. All you have to do is maneuver in the x-y plane."

Lucy nods once; her deep breathing travels over the comms.

"One minute," Nova says.

"Get your backpacks on," I order.

All three of us slip on black canvas backpacks loaded up for the job ahead.

A one-minute timer pops up on my lower left.

"Follow the directions to the bullseye," I say to Lucy. "All the computations are done in the helmet. Use your arms like wings to move around. Winn goes first, Lucy second, I'm last. Ready?"

"Ready," Winn and Lucy echo back.

"Cutting comms."

The chaff is blinding their radar screens, but those aren't the only sensors they have. It's hard to imagine they're not scouring their whole area for EM signals. There's no way to know for sure, but we can't risk it. The only signal we'll risk is our LiDAR pointed straight down to know where the ground is—which is pretty important. They're unlikely to be able to detect a laser pointed straight down.

I scooch up behind Winn to prepare to exit out his door.

Winn pushes the door open at the five second mark. Cold wind rushes into the cabin. I double tap him on the back of his helmet. He jumps out into the firework-lit night.

I scoot forward to catch the door and turn to give Lucy the go-ahead but only manage to catch the flapping of Puo's suit rippling downward before her door slams shut.

I leap out into the void.

Cold wind rushes past as I fall headfirst. It's beautiful. Fireworks explode all around below me, like bursts of color on a dark canvas.

I rest in the spectacle for a few seconds before I snap out of it and start paying attention to my readouts of vertical and horizontal velocity, my dropping altitude, and that blue bullseye that oddly fits in with all the exploding fireworks.

Eighteen thousand feet to the ground.

It takes me another second to spot Winn—he's close by and looks to be on track. I can't spot Lucy. No EM signatures. I lost the trackers when I cut off comms.

We need to be able to find each other on the ground.

*Where is she?* I cast around to look for her while maintaining my headfirst dive. We need to get on the ground fast.

Sixteen thousand feet.

*There!* She's tumbling out of control and way off. *Damn it!*

Her descent isn't as fast as it needs to be.

I flatten out to slow down my descent and angle over to her. "I'm going to get her!" I call out to Winn, only to immediately remember we have no comms—old habits die hard.

It's hard to see her against the dark landscape below. If it weren't for the sporadic lights from the fireworks, it'd be impossible. I have to use several rounds of nearby fireworks to position myself above her.

Thirteen thousand feet.

I pitch forward and slam into her backpack midtumble.

She panics and flails as I scramble to her front.

Eleven thousand feet.

She stops fighting when she realizes it's me. I can tell she's yelling based on her head movements, but I can't hear anything.

I flick through the HUD menus to tell the suit I'm adding a hundred and twenty pounds to its load. Lucy's suit should still be reading the altitude and kick on the anti-gravity routine at the same point as mine, but it's easier for me to add the extra weight now, and delete it later if I don't need it, than the other way around. She was tumbling out of control—there's no telling what she might have accidentally done on her HUD.

I direct her arms and legs around me in a bear hug under my backpack, and flip on my stomach to get my bearings. Even if I wasn't concerned about her accidentally shutting off her own anti-gravity routine, I need to physically guide her to the drop zone.

Puo's loose suit slaps up against my sides—on second thought, maybe sticking the smallest person in Puo's suit wasn't the smartest idea.

I angle us back on target.

Nine thousand feet.

I pitch down headfirst to speed up. I still can't hear anything but I imagine Lucy screaming. She sure is gripping me tighter.

I've lost sight of Winn, but I'm not worried about him—he knows what he's doing.

Three thousand feet.

The blooms of fireworks explode above and below me. Hopefully, Durante heeded my warning in clearing out of the area once the fireworks wrap up.

One thousand feet. Five hundred feet.

*Here we go.*

The anti-gravity routine kicks in. It feels like a hook in your gut, but tugs at the armpits and crotch.

*Oof.* I'm slowing too fast.

Lucy's suit slows her down too. She's too light, so I'm not as heavy as the suit thinks I should be. The extra pull nauseates me.

I modify the weight in my anti-gravity routine but keep a hold of Lucy.

Two hundred feet. Almost to the forest canopy.

It's then I realize I'm not in the right position. I'm not going to be able to land on my feet, my knees absorbing any excess energy. Lucy's extra weight is compensated for by her anti-gravity suit, but the irregular drag on the oversized suit is not. It's throwing my brain off.

One hundred feet.

I twist to land on my back.

*Smack!* My back slams into the hard ground. Sticks jam into me in greeting. Lucy knocks the air out of me.

I push her off.

*That was weird.* Strange how the two anti-gravity routines intermixed with each other. I think hers cut out before mine did.

Lucy scrambles to the kneeling position and takes off her helmet.

We're on the side of a rocky, wooded hill. I sit up, taking off my own helmet—it's the only way we're going to be able to communicate.

"What the fuck!" she whisper-shouts at me.

Her tone stiff-arms my initial response. I was about to say, "You're welcome," but all I can come out with is, "What?"

"Why did you grab me?"

I can't see her face well in the dark to know if she's being serious. "You were tumbling out of control—"

"I was getting it *under* control. You gave me this ridiculous suit—"

"You were also off the mark and flying farther off." My voice heats up. The indignation helps get my feet back under me. "If I hadn't grabbed your tumbling ass, you would've missed the mark and—"

"We were at thirteen thousand feet, well above the decision altitude. I had plenty of room left to get the backslide under control."

"Then why did you grab on to me for dear life?"

"There wasn't time to try and explain—"

"Exactly!"

"You're too stubborn, with a warped savior complex, to get anything through to you quickly. If I didn't grab on, God only knows what you would've done next. So I grabbed on and had to trust that you didn't want to die." When I don't say anything, she adds under her breath, "I could've done it."

There's a gap between "could've done it" and "successfully did it" huge enough to fit Puo's and Charlie's bodies into.

Winn steps on a stick behind us, saving me from losing my temper. He waves when we snap our heads in that direction. He's uphill and not wearing his helmet. He walks/slides down to meet us. More sticks break. Rocks tumble.

Good gracious. How'd I miss that? He sounds like a drunken beaver rolling down a hill.

"You do have a weird savior complex," Winn whispers, and then adds quickly, seeing me spin up, "and a too-easily overridden self-preservation system—like yelling in the middle of the woods behind enemy lines."

"I was not yelling," I whisper so low he has to lean forward.

Rather than argue, he comes and sits down next to me. "So now we wait?"

We hit our mark. We're a mile and a half southwest from Caesar's mutant fort, under their radar but still in their backyard.

I nod and pull on my helmet. We still can't risk any EM signals, but the helmet needs to be attached to activate the internal heaters.

Now we wait.

# Chapter Thirty

I NEVER WAS good at waiting, but these past three hours were something else entirely. I'm pretty sure I just experienced a little slice of what my personal hell will be if God is the uptight rule-follower everyone makes Him out to be.

We couldn't communicate over comms, and the suit heaters wouldn't work without the helmets on. Warmth or communication, not both.

The fireworks may have alerted the Cleaners, but you can only maintain constant vigilance for so long before your mind begins to wander, before you start thinking it was just normal New Year's revelry. The human brain has a wonderful capacity to normalize things.

So we waited. Three hours in the dark woods, not moving, not talking. Not anything. The whole point was to remain hidden.

Alone with nothing but my thoughts—and that's not a safe place for me right now.

I went over, and over, and over the plan—over contingencies, over what could wrong, over everything. Eventually though, the quiet settled in.

The jackknives feed in that quiet.

I think I lived three lifetimes in those three hours, each lifetime worse than the previous one.

We can't keep doing this. I'm not sure my body can handle this anymore. But I don't know how to stop, how to get us out.

We need to get Puo. Then the three of us can figure it out together.

The trek to the fort was slow but uneventful once the three hours were up. It was at least quieter than Winn's earlier stomping around, or so I think. The nightvision in our helmets lets us avoid crunching sticks and whatnot in the dark, but we never did get around to being able to pipe in the ambient soundscape into the helmets, so it's hard to say how quiet we really were.

As for navigating, our helmets' compasses work without giving off EM signals, but we still had to use dead reckoning without GPS—which would need to be connected and giving off EM signals. It's why hitting the targeted drop zone was so important. Otherwise, we wouldn't have known where the fort was to a high degree of certainty. Being off only a few degrees over a mile and half trek could have us miss it entirely. But we got to the fort on the first try—I could've been a girl scout in another life. Amazing how the threat of death focuses the mind.

The three of us are inside the tree line a hundred feet from the southwest starred point of the walled bulwark surrounding the fort. Lights from the inner fort glow upward in a mix of yellow and bright halogen. A cold silence drapes over the fort.

"You have the beacons ready?" I whisper to Winn. We took our helmets off to be able to communicate before our approach. The heat of my breath evaporates out into the night.

Winn looks up at me from kneeling over the three hand-sized spherical drones spread out on the ground in front him. "Yeah—wish we had more."

I nod. *Me too.*

It's simply not possible to penetrate the fort undetected, not on this kind of timeline. So, the best we can do is use the beacons to create blind spots and confuse them long enough to get in and get out.

Three beacons are good. Five would've better—one for each point of the star fort. But three is all Winn grabbed from our Seattle home three days ago. Three days—another lifetime ago.

I study the fort in the distance. The wall is old masonry twenty feet high, cut directly into raised earth. The approaching land a hundred feet around it is smooth snow—that's the problem with old forts, they intentionally cleared the surrounding area out to make it easier to shoot people, and Caesar kept up the practice.

"Are we clear on the plan?" I whisper to Winn and Lucy.

Winn nods. "Cut the hole, follow after."

I nod back. We're splitting up initially so he can distract and lead them away.

"Clear," Lucy whispers.

"Can you handle the jump?" I ask her.

"Can you manage to keep your hands off me midair?"

"Juuusst checking," I say, as if to a surly teenager. "We're not going to be able to set the marker on the second jump until we're midjump, near the apex. If you're flopping all around—"

"I'll be fine," she bites off.

She better be. She's carrying Izaak's squeegee and I need that, and her, for this to have a chance of working.

"Ready?" I ask.

They both nod.

I motion for Lucy to give me her helmet.

"What?"

I motion more strongly for her helmet.

"Why?"

I can't see the details of her face in the dark, but the tilt of her head has an annoyed I-don't-want-to-listen quality.

I want to snap, *Why can't you just do what you're told?* But an argument in shouting distance of the fort isn't worth it. "So, I can set your first marker to make sure we land together. You'll have to jump right after me on the second jump and watch where I land to set your second marker. So, we need to jump from the same place."

"Shouldn't I practice setting the marker then?"

"She's got a point," Winn says before I respond.

"Then hand her your helmet," I say.

Winn puts his helmet on in response and looks away from us over to the fort.

I stifle a sigh and say, "Set the marker north of here, let me review it and then you can set mine." She may have a point.

It takes Lucy longer than a jump would've taken setting the marker in her own helmet, but once I review it and give her mine, she sets my marker in seconds and hands it back—quick study.

So, fine, she had a point.

"After the first jump set the initial second marker on the opposite side of the fort. We'll reset it midair."

She nods and I slip my helmet on and the dark night comes alive into blue pixelated detail along with a marker several hundred feet to the northwest.

I give Lucy a thumbs up and ask with gestures if she and Winn ready to go.

They both give me a thumbs up and I pat Winn on his shoulder to tell him to launch the beacons.

Winn kneels and activates the beacons. They rise up with small whirs and fly off to their preprogrammed locations to blank out surveillance in those areas.

After a slow count of ten, Winn runs and jumps up into the sky toward the outer fort wall. He comes down, a black smudge against the white snow and stone wall, and gets to work cutting a hole in the wall to give the Cleaners something to focus on.

I tap Lucy and then launch myself into the air.

It's easier to do this maneuver in water than in air. Water is thick. It makes it easier to steer, change direction, use other equipment for forward motion. The anti-gravity suits help you move in the z-plane, moving in the x-y plane is left to plain old momentum, which means you need a running start.

I keep the jump low, trying to avoid any sensors, and I miss the mark, coming up fifty feet short.

Lucy lands ahead of me, short of the target and ten feet off the line of bearing. We'll both have to do better on this next jump. I run forward to join her.

The fort sits stolid in the distance, the yellow, halogen glow undisturbed for now. No visible clues that they saw our jumps. Winn is now hidden by one of the star points.

Lucy gestures she's ready for the second jump at my prompting.

Here's where it gets interesting. Puo's marker has come to rest in the center of the fort in the mutant building.

I set the marker for where I think the fort's opposite side is and then run and jump. The suit jerks me upward. It's a balancing act. I need to be high enough to see over the wall where to land, but not so high as to stand out.

The fort isn't a perfect star; the entrance side is longer than the others. The outer walls are ten, fifteen feet thick with earth piled up against the inside. It looks like it could take some serious damage.

The inside of the star has been razed of any old buildings, and a modernist building of concrete, glass rectangles, and hard angles sits in the middle. Several hovercars sit parked outside. The grounds look groomed with heated crushed stone walkways and fresh snow everywhere else.

There isn't a living soul out in the night. Our beacon, on the other hand, floats off to the right of the building. I can only spot it since I know where to look. *We really needed more of them.*

I set the marker on the corner of the modernist building closest to me, the one where Puo's marker had come to rest.

I grunt as the suit forces me down more quickly to meet the new marker and then stifle a yelp as it suddenly pulls me upward to break my momentum to land. Delicate landings of old, this is not.

I hit the roof hard, skidding on my butt. *Ow.*

At least that's one good thing about concrete: it absorbs sound.

Lucy comes in hot and too high, flailing.

I jump, grab her leg and we crash down together onto the roof. *Oof.*

I push her off and unsling my backpack to retrieve the laser cutter and an older model microwave scanner Mr. Chao procured in Old Forge, since our original one was thoughtlessly left in Aberdeen—we simply forgot it in all the commotion of being nearly captured and Nova trying to worm her way into our hovercar.

We both keep our helmets on for now.

I turn on the microwave scanner and set it down against the concrete. Without Puo, there wasn't time to figure out how to jack the output directly into our helmets, so Lucy and I huddle over the small LED screen. It's not as powerful as the one we left behind, but it'll at least let us see directly on the other side of the wall.

No red and blue stick figures. It looks like an office of some kind? *Perfect.*

I set the laser cutter for a two-foot depth and start cutting a large hole in the roof below me, making sure it's big enough to get Puo and Charlie out.

Lucy gets out Izaak's squeegee and readies to drop through the hole.

If the fireworks and beacons haven't alerted the Cleaners something's up, a large concrete chunk crashing down onto the floor will certainly do the trick.

The large circular chunk vanishes into the dark below with a loud crash.

Lucy's through the hole and down before I can finish wincing.

Her helmet lights flare on as she moves toward a desk.

I drop in and run toward the room's only door and flip the lock, which feels really anticlimactic, like throwing a glass of water at a charging bull.

I cast around for something to shove in front of the door. The room is an office in the minimalist design—there's not a lot of things to work with.

Lucy hunches over the desk, working Izaak's squeegee.

I run over to a midcentury thigh-high storage table against the wall. It looks solid enough—it'll have to do.

The wooden legs *screech* across the floor as I push it toward the door.

"What are you doing?" Lucy asks over comms.

"Blocking the door," I grunt. I deny her the satisfaction of asking if she's in their system—she wouldn't have reactivated comms otherwise. "If you're done over there, come help."

"The guards are mostly stationed outside the house." She stares at Izaak's squeegee. "I think they're vectoring to Consort." She stops and comes around the desk. "Toss me the laser cutter and scanner," she says instead of coming to help.

I toss her my bag and go back to pushing. "Cut the hole right beneath the other one," I tell her. Then on the general comm I order, "Roll call, who's on the line?"

Nova, Mr. Chao, and Winn all check in.

"Consort, status?"

He's still at the outer fortress wall cutting a red herring hole. "I'm almost through."

I glance up at the hole in the ceiling. He should've been here by now.

"What's taking so long?" I finish pushing the storage table in front of the door and turn to join Lucy.

"It's thick!" Winn huffs at me. "This is the second round. I'm almost through. Do you want them to believe we came this way or not?"

Lucy abandons the microwave scanner and laser cutter on the floor and goes back to the desk with Izaak's squeegee. The microwave scanner's small LED screen shows a suspiciously empty room below us. *Where are they?*

"Are you really almost through?" Lucy asks Winn.

"Yes, why?"

"I think they're already headed your way, but I'm about to remove any ambiguity to send them away from us to you to tumble down the rabbit hole."

"Roger that," he says.

Lucy works for a minute. "They're inbound."

I pick up the laser cutter and start cutting into the floor around the large concrete chunk from the ceiling above, making sure the holes are aligned.

"What'd you do?" I ask Lucy as I concentrate.

"I malfunctioned the beacon covering Consort, made it sputter in and out."

"Why'd you have to jack in for that?"

"Make sure they saw it."

Winn better hurry up.

"They saw it," Mr. Chao says. "Virgin patched me in—I can see what they see. They're amassing on that side of the compound."

Lucy shakes her head, annoyed at her Virgin moniker, but keeps her mouth shut.

"Do you have eyes on Computer or Abuela?" I ask.

"Yes," Mr. Chao answers, "they're right below you in separate but adjacent cells. There are two guards outside the cells, but they don't appear worried. The whole space is a locked-off area with only one way in. My guess is you can't open the space except from the inside."

Good thing we're not planning on coming in that way.

I finish the cut and the chunk crashes down into a lit room below—a living space with couches and a fireplace.

I jump down and immediately start cutting the last hole, cutting around the thick concrete wafers stacking like a birthday cake. Our luck avoiding Cleaners isn't going to last forever.

Lucy lands besides me and keeps an eye out.

The large living space Lucy and I land in opens to other parts of the house. We're open, exposed here.

The microwave scanner shows three stick figures, the one directly below me is strong and looks distinctly like Puo—weird how I know it's him. The other two are weaker, out of the field of view.

"Fuck!" Winn swears.

I jump at his sudden voice.

"They've spotted me."

"Jump back to the woods," I say, keeping my hands as steady as I can on the laser cutter—Winn would've been better at this.

"Lead them away." That's what the hole in the fortress wall was for anyway, a distraction. "We're almost done here." Well, at least as far as Lucy and Mr. Chao know.

"Roger."

I check the microwave scanner. The stick figure cowers at the farthest point of the room from me—definitely Puo. At least he sees the hole I'm cutting.

*Wham!* The concrete pancake stack slams down to the ground.

Puo, still in Winn's coat, stands in the cell's front corner and whips around to look up with wide eyes.

I drop down and pop off my helmet. "Hiya, Puo. Nice coat. Ready to go?"

The fear in his face dominates the foreground, but it's the group of people outside his cell door that arrest my attention.

"Isa Schmidt," Caesar says, "so kind of you to drop right in."

The rest of the National Syndicate is behind him, including a very alarmed-looking Ham. So much for Mr. Chao being able to see what they see.

# Chapter Thirty-One

THEY KNEW WE were coming. I mean, of course they knew we were coming. They probably congregated down here as soon as the beacons went off—why go through the trouble of trying to find us when they knew exactly where we would end up?

Hell, they might have all been here since the fireworks. This is probably why the house has been so empty—they're all down here. I'd place a high wager this cell area has booby traps like the house in Aberdeen. Good thing we didn't plan on coming in the traditional way.

The front of Puo's cell is a glass wall and door. It's why the microwave scanner didn't pick up the larger group beyond the wall—the glass wall attenuated the signals. But now the floor-to-ceiling glass actually works to our advantage—no gaps for bullets.

Caesar looks up at the hole in the ceiling with a smirk. "How exactly are you planning on leaving?"

He clearly doesn't know the full range of what these suits can do. He probably thinks they only help with landing.

Rather than educate the asshole, I wave with my helmet in my hand at the terrified-looking Ham being held in the middle of the pack. "Hiya, Ham! Thanks for the tip!"

Ham blanches and tries to move but is held in place.

I give Puo one of the two extra comm-links I'm carrying. Then I run over to the wall, set my helmet down, and start laser cutting to Charlie.

"What are you doing?" Puo slips in the comm-link.

"Getting Charlie."

"She's on that side." Puo points to the opposite side of the cell.

I scream in frustration and run over to the other side.

"Fat Cat," I say, "they know we're in the system." I explain about Caesar and all his cronies as I cut a hole to Charlie. Then I whisper to Mr. Chao with my head turned away from Caesar, "Keep these cells locked."

Puo picks up the shop talk with Mr. Chao, whispering and heading to the back to work on keeping the door locked.

Lucy drops down.

I turn my head again so Caesar can't see me whisper. "Virgin, get Computer out of here. Meet upstairs where you plugged in." I'm halfway around cutting a waist-size hole to Charlie to duck through.

Lucy moves beneath the hole and Puo comes to join her. He looks like an overgrown teddy bear giving an orphan in over-sized clothes one last hug.

*Almost there.* Only a quarter of the way left to Charlie.

Caesar starts to taunt me, but cuts off when Lucy and Puo vanish upward.

"Open the cell!" Caesar yells.

*Surprise, asshole!*

"Keep those doors locked," I order Mr. Chao. Then in a flash of inspiration, I order, "Virgin, give Computer your squeegee. Computer, keep these doors locked."

"You got it," Puo says over the comm-link.

There are no words to convey how good it feels to hear Puo's voice on the other end while I'm in the thick of it.

Caesar continues to yell and I startle when one of the National Syndicate members tries to kick the door open. They literally tried to kick a *prison cell* door open. Good gracious, they're not very smart, are they? Maybe we've been giving them too much credit this whole time.

Ham tries to edge his way to the back of the group but is held in place.

I complete the hole and kick the concrete. It budges, but doesn't break free. *Shit.* I channel pure panic into kicking the chunk loose.

*Damn it. Damn it. Damn it.*

It's only getting more wedged.

I ready the laser cutter again when I hear, "Move out of the way girlie!"

The concrete chunk jerks forward and I scramble to the side. Two more jerks and it's clear enough for me to pull it clear.

Charlie crawls through. She looks awful. Sweat and dirt streak through her graying afro. Her normally full face is pallid and she hasn't changed clothes since they picked her up. The pep in her movements is from desperation, not normal vitality.

She takes the comm-link I offer her and slips it in. "Took you long enough," she says.

"What are you talking about?" I say. "There's still a whole day left on your timer. We're early. C'mon." I stand up below the hole in the ceiling. "Hold onto me for dear life. Understand?"

She nods, trying to suppress a grimace.

"Can you hang on?" I ask. Falling off midjump would not be good. She nods again. "Stop looking at me like that, it's not that bad."

"Open the damn door!" Caesar yells and pounds on the door.

"You look pretty bad," I say. "At least seventy years old. Maybe eighty. A little frail for all of this, honestly."

She rolls her eyes. "Shut up, girlie. I'm not that old. I'm only in this mess because of you." She steps over to me.

"You're only in this mess because you got old and slow." I grin at her expression as I shove my helmet on.

"Now you listen here girlie—!"

I tap my helmet to indicate I can't hear her, then wrap my arms around her.

She wraps her arms around me. I modify the anti-gravity suit for the extra weight and set it to fall to the home office above.

Caesar's really losing his shit now.

The suit jerks us upward and I almost lose Charlie, but she scrambles to grab on like a drowning cheetah.

My arms strain with the effort. Fortunately, the jump isn't long or difficult and we pop up to the home office in seconds. I shove Charlie off to crumple on the floor, while I shoot upward at the sudden loss of weight.

I come down quickly, my knees able to absorb the small fall.

Lucy has her helmet off and stands by Puo over the squeegee at the desk.

"Are you okay?" I ask Charlie over the comm-link.

She groans on the floor. "I never should've taken you in. Worst decision of my life."

She's fine.

"Are you sure you're okay?" I ask. "That was a nasty fall, and you're like ninety. You didn't break a hip, did you?"

"Shut up." She pushes herself into a sitting position. "Now what?"

Now it's time to end this. "Virgin, strip out of the suit, give it to Computer." I unsling my backpack and start taking my suit off. "You take this one, carry Charlie out of here. Spinster, time to come back around. You have three for pickup."

"Three?" Nova asks. "What about you?"

"Yeah," Puo says, "what about you?"

I stop to look at him. He's pale. His dark eyes are wide. His long dark hair is frazzled in a sloppy ponytail. He's lost a lot of weight since Vancouver three weeks ago. He doesn't look like he's changed clothes or showered since they picked him up. But underneath all of that, I recognize that stubborn look. "They're all here tonight—the National Syndicate," I explain, "in this building. They'll never stop coming for us. I can end this here and now."

"How?" Puo asks.

"A crazy-ass stunt with only a hope and a prayer of succeeding."

"Do you have a way out?"

"Of course. I'm going to stroll right out."

He stares at me.

*Why is he looking at me like that?* Before I can ask, he says, "Virgin, give that suit to Charlie. I'm going with Harpy. Only two for pickup."

"It's Empress," I say distractedly, while I process what he just told me.

Charlie snorts.

"Either way, *Harpy*," Puo says, "you're going to need my help."

*Yeah, I will.* But I wasn't going to order him to stay. He hates being in the field on good days. I can't imagine what's going through his head after being kidnapped.

Panic makes you want to run, to flee, to get anywhere except where you are. Something I'm intimately familiar with. And here he is, wanting to stay. No. *Needing* to stay. It's the only thing that makes sense.

I really look at him then. Study him. He's changed.

"Mind if I get in on that pickup," Winn breaks in before I can comment on Puo's shift. "I'm still leading them away, but I think they've lost interest."

Probably right around the time we dropped down in Puo's cell in front of the entire National Syndicate.

Nova confirms Winn's pickup.

"Pick me up on the way," Winn says.

"No," I say, sliding out of the suit and shoving the in-side-out legs back in to give to Lucy. I know exactly what Winn's thinking.

"No?" Nova asks. "It's on the way and makes sense—"

"Consort, you can't join us. Stay up there, protect Charlie."

"I—" he starts to argue.

"I need you up there. I need you protecting Charlie. You said, 'we're in it together, no matter what happens.' Did you mean it? Because now's the time. You want to be together? You want to be back on the team? Then you take orders. And this is the way it's always going to be. So ... are we in this thing together or not?"

He doesn't hesitate, "I'm in. Protect Charlie, aye."

Puo nods solemnly at me.

I mockingly nod back and pick up my backpack of goodies I set down when I stripped off the anti-gravity suit. "Shouldn't you be reading their system or something?"

"Nothing like the shrill of the harpy to ruin the moment." He goes back over to the desk.

"See if you can keep them locked up in the holding cell area," I tell him and go over to Charlie to help her with the suit. Putting those things on is difficult in the best of times, like squeezing into a wet T-shirt, at least when they fit right.

"What is this thing?" she asks, but doesn't fight it.

"Your ticket out of here." I explain softly about the suit and how it works. I tell Nova to pick up Winn first after all, I want him on hand in case Charlie needs help.

Charlie, like the champ she is, accepts reality and takes everything stoically. It helps that she saw the suits already work to get up here.

"I'll set the marker for you," I say and put the helmet on to do so.

"I'm ready to make my run," Nova says. "Ready on the ground?"

Lucy is fully suited up—my suit fits her much better. "We're ready down here," I answer.

"Ready," Winn says.

"Starting run."

With comms reestablished, it's easy to find the hovercar, set a marker on it, and set the suit to auto jump to it when it's directly overhead.

I take the helmet off and hand it to Charlie. "Put it on. Everything will take care of itself."

"You sure about this?"

"It'll work."

"Not about this." She taps the helmet. She looks at Puo. "About that. You can really end this?"

I nod. "What've you always told us? Never leave tools behind or money on the table. I'm bringing in every tool available for this one."

She raises an eyebrow as she slides the helmet on. "Nice to know you were actually listening."

"I don't look at my ass nearly as much as you think."

A snort escapes from under the helmet before I help her seal it into place.

"I have Consort," Nova announces. "One minute out."

"A countdown should appear for when the suit will rendez-vous with the hovercar." I push her to stand next to the hole in the floor. "Step into the hole right at zero to make sure you don't hit the ceiling on the way out. Understand?"

She nods once and on pure instinct I hug her. "You're going to be okay."

She hugs me back and damn if that doesn't feel good. We should do that hugging thing more often.

"Ten seconds out," Nova says.

"Try not to throw up," I say and move toward Puo at the desk.

Charlie steps into the hole and yanks upward out of sight. Lucy follows next, leaving Puo and me alone in the office.

# Chapter Thirty-Two

THE SILENCE OF the departure settles over us in the office once Nova confirms Lucy and Charlie's pickup.

"So. How am I going to need your help?" I ask Puo. He had something specific in mind when he said that.

"Aside from the fact that you always need my help?"

"Yes, aside from that. What specifically did you have in mind?"

"The scrubbing code Ham told us about is being run from here. One of Caesar's minions let it slip. Once the central hub went down, they transferred everything here. If I can turn off the scrubbing code and then—" He holds up Izaak's squeegee. "—upload this. No more need for a guild to control access to the code."

"No more need for anyone to approach the guild for their services," I finish for him. Sometimes I think Puo and I spend too much time together. That's scary close to half of my plan to take out the Cleaners. The fallout won't be instantaneous, but it'll work. The Bosses will see to that. The guild only exists to control access to the code and centralize power.

"Great, can you do that from here?" I nod at Izaak's squeegee plugged in.

"Nope. I need to be at the servers."

"Where are those?"

"Basement?"

"You telling me or asking me?" My eyebrows rise up.

"Telling you ... I think?"

"Do you know where in the basement?"

"Yes?"

The door to the office shunts inward. We both jump.

The lock holds for now.

*Damn it.* I cast around for options. That door isn't going to hold for long. The thigh-high storage table I dragged in front of it looks comically small and pointless. They don't even need to break down the door—they just need to find a key.

"You want to go on a wild goose hunt," I ask, "deeper into the complex?" I run over to the hole in the floor and immediately pull my head back as bullets thunk into the ceiling above. Well, that route is closed. Apparently, they're not trying to hide and be clever anymore to try and trap us.

"Well, what's your plan?" Puo unhooks Izaak's squeegee and comes around from the desk.

"It's, uh, in flux," I answer, trying to think how to roll in this new information and get us out of here. "All good plans are."

"No they're not!"

"Yeah, well. It'll come together. I promise." I run over to the window and look down.

"No," Puo says.

"You have a better idea?"

The door shunts inward again, harder. *Can't wait for the key?*

"Use the laser cutter to cut into the room next door?" Puo asks.

"Good idea." I run over to an inside wall and place the microwave scanner up against it. Empty. I start cutting a hole in

330

the wall, just small enough to be believable. I point at the window and gesture for him to go out of it.

"But you just said—"

I make a face at him to just do it. He sticks his tongue out, but goes over to the window and opens it.

Voices outside the door in the hallway rise as they argue.

The laser cutting moves fast—the wall between rooms isn't as thick as the floors or the walls between the cells.

Puo is out the window and hangs and drops without any more complaining.

The door slams in its frame. Voices are yelling.

*They're really impatient, aren't they?* "Through the hole," I say toward the door with a raised voice.

The door slams again.

I throw the microwave scanner and laser cutter back in the backpack and hurry to the window and look it over before climbing outside. *Damn it's cold out here without my suit.* I hang on the outside and close the window as much as I can from the bottom of the frame before using the panicked friction of my hand against the glass to close it the rest of the way—hopefully, they won't notice greasy hand smears on the window.

I glance down—Puo's off to the side looking up at me. I drop the ten feet or so to the ground. The frozen earth greets me mercilessly. My thighs burn from the fall.

"Now what?" Puo whispers at me.

"Now we get to the basement."

"We're not inside."

"I know that. Do you know where we need to go?"

"But, we're not—"

I roll my eyes. "Laser cutter, microwave scanner." *Duh.*

"Oh." Understanding dawns on Puo's face and he huddles up against me and the concrete wall behind us, fishing out Izaak's squeegee.

Yes, *oh*. But needling Puo right now isn't going to help so I keep my mouth shut and wait for him to figure it out.

He shows me the small screen of Izaak's squeegee. "Here's where I think the servers are. Where are we?"

"Which way is north on this screen?" I study the layout.

Puo furrows a bit and then says, "That way."

I reorient myself and then point to the opposite side of the building from where we need to be. "We're here."

Puo doesn't even question me—he's well acquainted with my skills. "How we going to get across?"

"Carefully." I rapidly think if there's anything we can do or call in to help. "How much time do you need with the servers?"

Puo shakes his head in thought. "I don't know. But the more time the better."

Yeah, I was afraid of that.

The building's exterior is going to have surveillance and we don't have the anti-gravity suits anymore to cover ground quickly. We're already exposed out here.

I look down at the snowy ground and then at the building behind me, doing some quick spatial calculations from memory of Puo's cell's location.

"C'mon." I hug the building's edge, staying below any windows. We move north about fifty feet, just long enough, I guess-timate, to be past Puo and Charlie's cells.

I brush away the snow. My fingers burn red from the cold.

"You're going under?" Puo whispers at me.

"Well, we can't go over. And it's too risky to go around, or through."

Puo hesitates a second, no doubt trying to think of another way. He bites his tongue to keep from explaining how stupid this is and drops down and helps clear the snow while I fetch the microwave scanner and laser cutter.

The ground is frozen solid. We can't get more than the top snow layer off. Ripping off the dead layer of grass is proving to be a waste of time. The soil attenuates and distorts the micro-wave scanner. It's clear something's down there but not what, or who, as the case may be.

I set the laser cutter to its maximum depth and start cutting a hole in the ground and down into the basement—hopefully. It's slow going. The ground fights me the whole way.

Mr. Chao breaks in, "They're still searching the upper floors."

"You're in their system?" Puo whispers excitedly.

"Yes, when Virgin plugged in earlier."

Puo smacks himself in the forehead and turns to me. "What else haven't you told me?" He whips out Izaak's squeegee and starts play-ing on it and tells Mr. Chao to start forwarding him information.

I ignore Puo and focus on cutting—halfway there. The dead grass cracks and sizzles.

Puo looks up from his squeegee and looks around furtively.

"What?" I ask.

"We should've punched in over there." He points fifteen feet farther along the edge.

"Stay or go?" I ask, continuing to cut. Three quarters the way there.

Puo looks back down at Izaak's squeegee.

"Stay," I make the decision for him. If we should've moved, he wouldn't have hesitated.

Puo nods, still studying the squeegee. "Fat Cat—" He looks to me to verify that's still Mr. Chao's moniker and I nod. "—keep them busy upstairs. Make it look like we're trying to get to a hovercar." He then looks at me sharply to make sure that wasn't part of my still-in-flux plan. It's not. "I'll keep an eye on our route," Puo finishes.

"Roger," Mr. Chao says.

"I thought you didn't know where the servers were?" I whisper. I'm almost done with the laser cutter.

"I don't. Not exactly. But I have a good idea, a better one now that Fat Cat pushed me a direct feed."

"You ready? We're going to have to move quickly."

Puo nods once.

I complete the hole and the whole thing shifts downward but doesn't fall.

"Are you sure—" Puo starts.

I kick it and it vanishes into a lighted tunnel below with a crash.

I drop down into the tunnel. "It's clear," I call back up. Puo worries over the drop a bit before sitting on the edge and dropping down. He hits hard and comes to one knee.

"You okay?" I ask.

"Yeah. But let's not do that again. The window drop was enough."

"Which way?" The tunnel leads under the house, perpendicular to the house edge above.

Puo points under the house. "The other way is a connecting tunnel to the fortifications."

The concrete tunnel walls are a pockmarked dirty gray while the floor and ceiling are the clean gray of the concrete above.

We quickly come to an intersection and slow before approaching it. Puo has Izaak's squeegee out, while I use old-fashioned analog surveillance—my ears and memory. To the right leads to the holding cells. A dull roar of computer fans comes from straight ahead, while the left doesn't have any audible clues.

Puo taps me and points left.

We argue in sign language, but he's insistent, even after acknowledging the dull sound of the fans, so I head left.

He pushes ahead to take the lead and we come to a more open columned space with stairs leading up at one end.

Distant voices and footsteps echo down the hallway behind us the way we came.

Puo rushes to the left, to one of two metal doors flanking the stairs, and jabs a finger at the lock with an insistent look at me.

I take one look at the lock and decide I don't have the time or tools to deal with it properly and instead get out the laser cutter, setting it to a shallow cut depth. I cut a semicircle around the lock and door handle.

The metal door is thin and seconds later we crowd into a small access closet with a bunch of tools. I ease the door shut behind us. Hopefully, no one will look too closely at the door handle.

I tap Puo's shoulder with my face, clearly saying, *Now what? We can't hide in here for long.*

Izaak's squeegee illuminates the small closet and Puo looks between it and the space we're in.

I glance at the squeegee and see the map—a large room, probably the server room, is on the other side of the back closet wall. *So, we weren't randomly hiding in here?* Puo's earlier insistence makes more sense. I give Puo a pat of *attaboy* and point to the back wall with the laser cutter.

He nods and I set to work, checking first with the microwave scanner.

As soon as I get even a little of the way into the cut, the roar of computer fans spills through.

*Yeesh.* I alter my cutting angle to be able to put the chunk we cut out back to try and block the sound. That thin metal door will help, but we really don't want to draw any attention to it and the thin, burnt-out cut around the lock and handle.

The thigh-high cut takes a long two minutes. I feel every heartbeat. Cold sweat clams my skin.

Over the roar of computer fans, I ask Puo, "Back when we were entering the central hub in Old New York, you wanted to tell us a story. Did you know something?"

"I know lots of things."

"No. I mean did you know Ham was up to something."

"Oh. No."

I feel a weight slide off my shoulders. *Whew.* I knew it. If he really knew something he would've told it anyway. "Then why did you want to tell a story?"

"They're fun?"

I shake my head, but keep my hands steady on the laser cutter. "All your stories have little meanings and morals."

Puo snorts like I'm a pretentious twit. "Sometimes a story is just a story."

I grind my teeth but focus instead on finishing the cut. I look back at Puo when I'm done. He holds a hand up to wait and then types on Izaak's squeegee.

He waits for something, and then nods.

Here we go.

# Chapter Thirty-Three

I PUSH THE thigh-high chunk at its base, alternating sides, trying not to tip it over. I wiggle through as soon as there's enough room.

The deafening roar of computer fans greets us. The air is a mix of warm plumes in a background of air conditioned cold.

Puo works his way into the space and prairie dogs his head up to survey the room.

While he sorts that out, I push the concrete chunk back into place, leaving enough of an edge to pull it back out later.

The server racks are lined up parallel to the wall we came through and Puo's moving along the row of servers to the right. He runs his hand along the servers and occasionally points and mouths something. I don't have the foggiest clue what he's looking for.

The wall all the way down to my left is glass, and probably where the entrance is, while the wall all the way to my right is concrete. The entire span is about a hundred feet.

I hurry after Puo, taking more in about the space.

The server racks go from the floor to four-fifths the way to the ceiling. There's a gap at the top where gobs of wires rise up to cable bundles running around the ceiling. The racks are three feet wide and stacked right next to each other. The back of the servers face the wall. Hot air blows off them in a steady thrum. Cold air billows up from regular spaced vents in the floor with ducting directing the cold air under the racks.

Puo stops at an intersection and then disappears around the corner. At the intersection I get a sense of the other dimension of the room—about another hundred feet.

Puo communes with the servers, brushing his fingertips across select ones. Eventually, he finds what he's looking for and turns down a row.

By the time I follow, he has a server pulled out at waist height and a float screen hovering above it. The servers in this row all face forward, flat fronts with blinking blue and green lights.

"Find what you were looking for?" I ask over the fan noise as I walk up.

"About to find out." Puo connects Izaak's squeegee to the server and continues working.

I look around, letting Puo do his thing. I'm used to Puo working on computer stuff, but usually I have other things to do, or can go off and find something to do. We're not normally right next to each other on a job.

I wander toward the glass wall at the front. "Fat Cat, how's it looking up there?" I ask to test both the connection with all the fan noise and to make sure I keep comms open to Puo.

"They're getting wise," Mr. Chao says. "The upstairs isn't that big and they've already searched it all. They released the National Syndicate members in the holding cell area and now they're starting to sweep back to the home office you started in."

"Start messing with the first floor somewhere," Puo says.

"How much time do you need?" I ask Puo.

He's silent for several seconds before answering, "I found the scrubbing app, a few more minutes at least."

I turn around and wave at him getting his attention. When he looks over at me, I say, "How long would it take to add the blockchain-breaking code and push that into the open?"

"Two, three minutes," he says confused. "You want me to do that?"

"Yes." I shake my head no and wave him off to make it clear *not* to do that. I point to my ear to make it clear who this conversation is for. "If it's public information, there's no reason to come after us anymore."

"Roger that," he says. "Destroying the world as we know it."

"Wait," Mr. Chao breaks in. "That's a bad idea. It will crash the entire financial system and undermine government currencies. Overnight, governments won't be able to pay debts, people won't be able to move money around—"

"Not to mention," Nova interjects, "hyperinflation, civil unrest. You can't do that."

"But," I say, "no one will want to kill us anymore. They'll have bigger problems to deal with."

Winn breaks in with, "'Want' is a bit of a strong word there."

"You are good at making friends," Puo says.

"Fine," I say annoyed, "no one will have a reason—a financial incentive," I talk over Winn who was starting to quibble over my word choice again, "to kill us."

"You can't do this," Mr. Chao tries again. "The unintended consequences will be catastrophic. People will die."

"I'm with Fat Cat and Spinster," Lucy says. "You can't do this."

They're right, of course, which is why we're not doing it. I only need them to believe we are. "Computer, you with me?" I ask.

Puo hesitates and then says, "I'm with ya. It'll be fun." He shrugs. "What could go wrong?" Then in an undertone he adds, "I'm buying up gold before the info's loose in the wild though."

"Perfect," I shout over the others on the line trying to talk him out of it. "Put it on a timer."

I approach the end of the row toward the glass wall, ignoring the stream of objections and alarm on the comm-link. I ease up to the edge and peek around the corner.

Nothing.

"How much more time do you need?" I ask Puo.

"Another minute or two. Almost done."

More objections stream over the line from everyone except Winn. I wonder what he thinks. I didn't tell him this little wrinkle in the plan. We were strapped for time, and I couldn't risk the rest of the group learning of it. He would—rightfully—object to this. Yet he hasn't. Does he know we would never really do this? Or is this him being back on the team—not voicing objections in front of the others?

I watch the glass wall. The seconds beat by.

Puo continues to work.

Movement catches my eye. Caesar and the National Syndicate, escorting Ham in the middle of the pack, round the corner heading straight for the server room entrance.

"Computer," I say over fan noise and the continued objections to try and talk Puo out of it, "we got company."

"Roger—" Panic enters his voice. "—I'm done here. Let's go."

"Is it done? Is the blockchain hack out there?" I turn toward him and mime the number fifteen.

"Yeah. It's locked and loaded on the system. The scrubbing code is down. It'll be everywhere in fifteen minutes."

"Can we pull the plug if we need to? Keep it from escaping?"

"Yeah, for another ... fourteen minutes and fifty-four seconds."

"Perfect. I'm counting on you to keep me alive for this next part."

"Uh, what?" He looks at me in alarm.

"Trust me. Stay there and look busy." I step out from the row of servers, wave at Caesar, and head over to meet him at the doors.

*Ohhh, heee looooksss pissssssed.* This is going to be fun, assuming I don't get shot.

He's flanked by nine others, all with the same imperious faces. Ham looks terrified and is clearly being shoved along. They don't trust him any more than I do. I recognize most of the others as the people outside Puo's cell—the National Syndicate. Good.

I come to stand in front of the door and hold my hands where they can at least see them, if not exactly up in the freeze position.

Caesar punches in some codes and pushes the door open.

"Welcome!" I shout with a big smile and open my arms to the servers behind me. "Have I got an offer for you!"

"Where is he?" Caesar snarls at me.

"He's just preparing for your arrival. Now—" I fold my hands in front of me like a flight stewardess about to go over boarding procedures. "—let's go over some ground rules."

Caesar starts to move past me, but I step in his way and smile. "If you'll just bear with me one moment, I'm sure we can all—"

He tries to push past but again I step in front of him with a smile that says—I've been in way more physical confrontations in my life than you, do you really want to press it in front of your friends here?

Oddly, there have been no guns. *Yet.*

I'm pretty sure that means the National Syndicate members don't bother carrying them or, more likely, agreed not be armed when around each other. Either way, I'm sure the goons with guns are on the way.

Before Caesar can start blustering, I say, "I have a mutually beneficial way out for all of us. You, me, and the Bosses."

"I don't have—" He starts to try to move past me again.

"Wait!" a middle-aged Indian woman says. "I want to hear what she has to say." She looks familiar. Her dark hair is braided in a single ponytail.

Caesar's scornful gaze settles on her. "You only want to hear what she has to say because she spared your daughter after her failure."

*That's why she looks familiar!* She's an older version of that snow demon Indian woman Cleaner on the driveway in Aberdeen.

"Careful, Caesar," she says dangerously, "about bringing up failures."

Caesar's gaze turns from scornful to murderous.

"If she has a way out," she continues, "we should hear it. Or have you forgotten the state of your rushed debacle?"

Interesting. They're not united. Some didn't agree with the war or the timing. It only makes more sense they would all gather to keep an eye on each other with Puo in custody. *Can I use this?*

The others look like they want to argue when Ham bursts out with, "Don't trust her." He stares at me to make it clear who not to trust. "This is a trick."

Caesar looks ready to agree and bowl over the others.

I raise my hands for them to stop. "I'm here when I could've escaped. The blockchain hack. That's what all this is about—" They all share looks. "—You'll never stop coming after us. I have a way to salvage this for everyone. One where you come out ahead from where you were before, and the Bosses agree to stop the war." Most look interested in a face-saving option. "And one where, Puo, Winn, and I live."

Caesar again prepares to speak, but the older Indian woman speaks first, "We're listening."

The majority nod and voice their agreement.

Caesar's face turns red. His eyes bulge.

"I'll buy you a new boat," I say out of the side of my mouth to placate Caesar. "Promise. Bigger than the first." To the rest of the group I say, "But first the ground rules. One: no guns, no shooting." I make finger guns at them. "No bang, bang." I move to start checking them over, which they let me with guarded eyes. I show my hands empty before I start and empty afterward. I'm pretty sure they don't have any guns since I would've already seen them at this point, but I'd rather be unnecessarily thorough than get shot. "Second: hear us all the way out to the end. It's a compromise, but a way out for everyone. Last, you're going to have to make up your minds fast."

They all share looks with each other.

"Are you interested?" I ask.

The group, except for Caesar and Ham, collectively nod their assent. Ham shakes his head no.

"Do you agree to the terms?"

"For now," Caesar says in a tone that makes it clear that goons with guns are on their way.

"Very good," I continue my flight attendant spiel and turn on my heel. "If you'll follow me right this way, we can get started."

I lead them straight to Puo, who can't help giving me what-the-fuck glances from whatever he's doing on the server, while I smile serenely. I stop when we're a few feet away and turn back to the National Syndicate members.

"It's the blockchain hack that's so valuable and precipitated all of this," I begin.

"And the fact that you stole my code," Caesar butts in.

"So we did," I admit.

The group shares surprised looks among themselves that I would admit this. Ham gives Caesar a vindicated look but is quickly quelled.

"But it's the blockchain hack that you're after," I continue.

"And you're prepared to share that with us?" the Indian woman from before asks.

"Yes—"

"In exchange for what?" an older white guy with a pointy head asks.

"In exchange for welcoming Puo as one of your own. A new, fully-fledged National Syndicate member."

There's shocked looks and murmurs. Ham is appalled.

"He's practically already one of you anyway," I add. The best of them actually, but there's no need to antagonize them, particularly when this is already going so much better than I thought it would.

"What's to stop us from killing you once we learn the secret?" Caesar asks.

"Yeah," I say, "about that. In the near term, Puo has shut down your scrubbing code and put the blockchain hack on a timer to be released. Thanks, Ham! Wouldn't have known about that scrubbing code without you."

The others look at him in disgust and he tries to defend himself but the older Indian woman cuts him off.

"Ten minutes," Puo breaks in with. "Actually, nine minutes, forty-seven seconds."

"When the timer goes off," I continue, "the code is available for everyone. It's worthless if everyone has it."

Caesar goes to the nearest server and pulls it out with a float screen popping up. He works and then stares at Puo.

Puo smiles back and points at his screen. "Single point of entry. Nice trick, right? The one-way central hub traffic gave me the idea." That smile is pure I'm-three-hundred-pounds-come-and-try-to-move-me.

"In the longer term," I continue, explaining why they shouldn't kill us, "keeping me and Puo alive will help end the war with the Bosses. I can take over my father's territory as Boss and easily spread out into contested territories if you pull back. With Puo in your ranks, and me in the Bosses ranks, we can negotiate a cease fire and a code-sharing agreement with the blockchain hack."

"You want to give the Bosses the blockchain hack?" the Indian woman asks.

None of them like that idea.

"You started a *war*. It's the only thing that might, and I emphasize *might*, bring them to the table to stop."

Caesar shakes his head and the others look dubious.

"Seven minutes, twelve seconds," Puo adds.

"I'll give you a couple of minutes to discuss it." I turn and go to talk to Puo.

In a low voice, but loud enough to be picked up on the comm-link back to the wider group, I say, "They're not going to go for it."

"Agreed," Puo says.

"Will the blockchain really be released?"

"Yes."

I take a heavy breath. "Okay. But you can call it off at the last second if you need to?"

"Yes."

Nova, Mr. Chao, and Lucy all start their pleading again to not do this.

"Quiet on the comm," I order.

But they don't listen and it plays right into my hand.

"Puo," I say—there's no need for code names when the National Syndicate is five feet away staring at us, "remove them from the comm-link since they won't shut up."

"Roger that."

The line goes silent. Now it's only the roar of the fans and the murmurs of the National Syndicate. Ham's insistent voice keeps rising and being cut off.

I take a deep breath. The cards have all been dealt at this point. Now all that remains is to see how they play out.

"Four minutes," Puo calls out.

The Indian woman steps forward and takes the lead. "We do not believe this offer is genuine."

Ham stares intently at me.

Of course it's not, but I feign surprise at the statement. I actually thought I did a pretty halfway decent bit of lying there.

Indian woman continues, "You have not demanded payment or retribution for your father's death."

The statement is a gut-punch. *Holy shit. How did I forget that?* Because I wasn't really negotiating with them. I was stalling for time.

The reminder of my father, of the stakes of this moment, and of our absolute vulnerability, trapped in the server room with the National Syndicate, comes crashing down. The dam of adrenaline that had been so strong for so long crumbles.

I freeze in place, all except for my heart. I'm growing sick of being so painfully aware of every heartbeat, of the lancing pain. Sweat breaks over me in rolling heat waves.

Time slows. I'm aware of all the tiny details around me, of all the individual fans blowing hot air.

All I want to do is run. Disappear. Go to a safe place and hide. Time. But it's time I need.

Puo starts to step forward and it's only then I'm aware of his hand on my shoulder. I reach up and squeeze it, but step in front of him to keep him where he is.

Minutes. I can hang on for a few more minutes.

"You're right," I say, the adrenaline giving my voice a disembodied feel. "We can't simply sweep everything under the rug. But before discussing the finer points, we needed to agree on a framework."

"In ten minutes or less?" the Indian woman asks. "Those are quite a few finer points to work through."

I glance back Puo's screen. One minute, thirty seconds.

I smile and turn back to them. My shoulders relax. Relief floods through me where the adrenaline had once been.

They all regard me with sudden suspicion. It's Caesar that can't take the silence. "What?"

"Where are your friends?" I ask.

"What?" Caesar betrays his tone by glancing back down the row of servers toward the entrance, no doubt realizing his goons with guns should've been here by now.

"What have you done?" the older Indian woman asks alarmed.

The entire group looks like they're about to rush us. Except Ham, who's looking behind him panicked.

"Me?" I ask. "Nothing."

The last word is drowned in a cacophony of glass breaking and several pairs of boots running into the server room. Authorities in black tactical gear shouldering rifles run down the server row yelling "Freeze!" and "Hands up!" at us.

They're loud and aggressive. Their fingers are on their triggers.

The National Syndicate members look around fearfully.

I do as the authorities ask and raise my hands.

Ham starts to make a run for it and is tripped by the older Indian woman who remains standing.

Some of the National Syndicate members also make a run for it and are quickly chased down. More tactical officers dressed in black show up at the opposite end of our server row.

"Step away from the server!" one of them shouts at Puo.

"Step away," I tell Puo. Fifty seconds left on the timer.

Puo does as he's ordered.

The lead tactical officer runs toward the National Syndicate. "Which one of you can reactivate the scrubbing code?"

Caesar shoots his hand up.

"Go!" the lead tactical officer shouts and escorts Caesar to Puo's terminal. He keeps his gun trained on me as they run by.

Other officers take up positions around the National Syndicate. One kneels down on Ham's back and I smile at Ham when he catches my eye.

Caesar works fervently, but shakes his head and sniffs to himself when there're twenty seconds to go. At five seconds he relaxes. "Done. Scrubbing code reactivated." He turns to Puo. "Weak trick."

"It was set up to be easily disabled once you agreed," Puo defends himself with.

Caesar's reply is cut off as the authorities start shouting again and the zip ties come out.

Soon we're all zip-tied and Puo and I are pressed face down on the ground, tactical officers hovering over us with knees in our backs.

Puo looks over at me, his cheek smushed up against the concrete floor. "Is this part of your plan?"

"I told you we were going to stroll right out of here."

"A perp walk is not a stroll," Puo says.

It's hard to shrug with a knee in your back. "Potato, pah-ta-ta."

Puo looks at me quizzically. "I don't think that's how that goes."

"I know, right!"

"Quiet!" the tactical police officer shouts with a knee in my back.

Despite the knee, I smile and relax. This arrest, unlike the last one, went exactly as planned.

# Chapter Thirty-Four

NEVER UNDERESTIMATE the slow crawl of bureaucracy. It was pretty clear within an hour of strolling right out of Caesar's mutant fort in zip ties that I wasn't being officially processed. I was led to an unmarked hovercar and then flown to a faux log-cabin motel on the edge of Old Forge.

The authorities have taken over the whole complex—you can tell by the parking lot. It's filled with generic black SUV hovercars with too-clean tinted windows. Any random parking lot will have a mix of hovercars in various states of cleanliness. A parking lot full of clean cars is either a car dealership, or people following some kind of regulation. And who religiously follows regulations? Authorities.

Either way, official jail or not, they're not processing me. I was led into a motel room with yellow fluorescent lighting and told to sit facing away from the window. I've been here for an hour.

I haven't seen Puo or anyone else.

One middle-aged woman with a narrow face came and tried to question me. But she left when my only response to her questions was, "Puo, Puo, Puo ... Puo," over and over in a cadence of normal speech.

So now I wait.

Puo is probably on site, doing the exact same thing. Winn's probably here too, although I bet he clammed up. Charlie ... I'm not sure what she'll do. She has her own resources and contingencies for these situations. I'd bet she'd clam up as well to first get the lay of the land.

"You played us." Nova Contreras limps in, favoring her injured leg. She's wearing the same clothes as earlier, a slate-gray winter jacket and a pair of jeans, except for a shiny authority's badge hanging around her neck—it's not one I recognize. "When did you know?"

I smile at her. There're many things I could say to that, many things I want to say, but instead I go with, "Puo, Puo, PuoPuo ... Puo."

She rolls her eyes. "And if we bring you two together, you'll start talking?"

They already decided to bring us together. It's one reason we haven't been processed, but instead of pointing that out, I nod. "Puo, Puo—"

She waves at the door.

Mr. Chao, wearing a similar shiny badge, leads Puo into the room, his hands still zip-tied behind his back. His face is light, relaxed, none of the worry of how we're going to get out of this on his face. It's then I confirm they want to recruit us. I can see it on Puo's face. They already made him an offer but he wouldn't negotiate without me.

Mr. Chao retrieves an extra chair from somewhere outside the door and Puo sits down next to me.

"When did you know?" she asks again.

"Winn, Winn, WinnWinn ... Winn," I start.

She scowls and crosses her arms. It looks she's about to object when Puo starts, "Winn, Winn, WinnWinn ... Winn."

She shakes her head in frustration. She nods again at the door like sending out an errant child. "Anyone else?"

Puo and I look at each other. I think back to Nix secretly working with the Mounties and the power that secret had over her. If we're really about to go down the road I think we're about to go down, then I don't want to keep it secret from the people close to me.

"Charlie," Puo and I say at the same time.

"No," she says.

The casual finality of her tone throws me off. Why bring the three of us together but deny Charlie? Is this an I'm-in-control issue? "No?"

"No." She looks like she wants to say more but then smiles at me the same way I smiled at her.

I stare at her, trying to figure out the play. An awkward silence settles over the motel room as we wait for Winn. I can think of several reasons to keep Charlie out of this, but which one is it? Leverage over us? Does Charlie know something they don't want us to know? Do they even have her in custody?

While we wait, Lucy joins us, badge dangling off her belt. She stands next to Mr. Chao off to the side, leaning up against a dresser.

Several minutes later, Winn is escorted into the motel room. His lips are pressed into a thin line. His black curly hair is disheveled. Somewhere along the way, he changed out of the anti-gravity suit and into jeans and a cream-colored long sleeve T-shirt. His eyes light up when he sees us, but he keeps his mouth shut. Another chair is retrieved for him and he's seated next to Puo. The three of us face the three of them.

"So, when did you know?" Nova asks. She walks over and closes the motel room door.

I flick a glance at Mr. Chao standing off to the side with Lucy watching the proceedings. They haven't officially arrested us. They brought us all together. Puo looks calm. I decide the best play is to play ball.

"When did I know? Or when did I suspect?" I ask.

Nova cocks an eyebrow at me.

I start at the beginning. "Getting us over international borders. First to France and then back here to the States. It was way too easy and smooth. It's possible to do, but it was so easy it was suspicious. Especially combined with the speed at which you removed us from British custody. But the real first clue was when Mr. Chao didn't know about the cold storage and deferred to Ham. Cleaners *never* defer to anyone. They're all prima donna dick unicorns snorting their own flatulence."

Mr. Chao exhales and shares a look at Nova.

I continue, "Those all pointed to your not being entirely forthcoming about who you were. The first clue that pointed to your connection to the authorities was the squiddie responding too fast on the Izaak grab and stash. The only way it could've been in position and responded so quickly was if it was tipped."

Nova agitates and crosses her arms. "I told them to stay back."

"Is Izaak in custody?" I ask. I honestly haven't thought about him much, but it makes sense the authorities would go in and grab him after we left.

She nods.

That's one loose thread clipped. He was the only National Syndicate member not in Caesar's compound.

"And the article on Puo's system about the missing couple from North Dakota being found. That's the couple whose house the Cleaners took over, isn't it?"

Mr. Chao nods.

I continue, "No one knew they were missing—partly their age and isolation, and partly Cleaners covering their tracks. Except they were found twenty-four hours after we were there. Another pretty strong indicator."

"Indicator," Nova says. "When did you know?"

I try to hold up my finger to her to let me continue, but my hands are still bound. Instead of answering Nova directly, I say, "There were other clues. You were also fixated on the anti-gravity suits, sniffing around them. Then later you said you used to be special forces and finally, Lucy, who was supposed to be a Cleaner, started using niche skydiving terms like 'decision altitude' and 'backslide' in the heat of the moment." My mouth falls open when I make a sudden connection. "You're the special forces team the anti-gravity suits were made for, aren't you?" I'd guessed they were special forces, but not *that* special forces.

It's the suits, that's what they've been after this whole time. It was why she was so interested in Winn's entry/exit into the Izaak job. Why they bugged the suits with those cheap chips. Comms listening wasn't the goal, *tracking* the anti-gravity suits was.

Nova stares at me.

"Oh, come on!" I throw my head back. "You're going to try and maintain your cover? Now?"

All three of them share a look. Mr. Chao is the one that answers, "We are a special unit organized under SOCOM. And yes, the anti-gravity suits were designed for us."

"I knew it!" I say.

"Whaddaya mean you knew it?" Puo snorts. "You *just* figured it out."

"Still knew it before you did."

Puo sticks his tongue out at me.

"Wait," I say thinking. "If they were made for you, how come I needed to help Lucy hit the mark?"

Lucy's eyes widen and she takes a step forward ready to argue when a motion from Mr. Chao stops her short.

"They were designed for us," Mr. Chao explains, "but they never got them working."

Puo and I burst out laughing. Here we thought the engineer with a gambling problem we bought the plans from had intentionally messed them up to assuage his conscience. We never even considered that the designers didn't have it already working. Hell, we expected the engineer to do something like that and Puo went specifically looking for a missing component—that may be why Puo was able to find and fix the problem in the first place.

I explain all this to them and they have a mix of rueful headshakes and regarding Puo contemplatively.

*They never even got them working.* I'm having trouble wrapping my head around that.

"How'd you find us?" Winn asks.

That is a good question. The three of us turn to Mr. Chao.

Nova explains, "There was nighttime video captured from a cargo vessel out of the North Sea in early October of something falling *up* from the sky—"

Puo scowls. "I knew it!"

"You did not know it!" I argue.

"I knew that whole thing was an immense stupidity."

"One video does not lead them to us. And we got away with it."

"Oh, yes—" Puo struggles with his hands zip tied behind his back. "—we totally got away."

"Still—"

"It gave away our existence!" Puo explodes. "It was reckless—"

"Yes!" I shout over him, my face burning. "It was reckless. I admit that now. I—I wasn't in a good spot. You know that. I wouldn't make the same decision again." The confession surprises me, but it's true. The experiences of the last several weeks haven't dulled my edge. They've changed my risk calculus. Puo starts to say something but I add petulantly, "And not just because of the video. It was reckless regardless of the video."

Puo tilts his head back, studies me, and then slowly starts to nod. "Okay."

I cock an eyebrow at him.

He flicks his gaze to Nova and group and I'm suddenly self-conscious of their presence.

Puo turns to the group. "She's right. One video does not lead you to us."

Mr. Chao picks up the explanation, "We knew you were an underwater crew due to what happened in Amsterdam. At that point, we waited. The British Museum heist was likely you, but we didn't have anything."

Nova breaks in, "Then there was another rather striking video out of Vancouver—"

*Oh, hell.*

"—Of a person leaping impossibly high from one hovercar over to another and free falling with it out of the sky. We were able to get a height and approximate weight and gender. At that point, it wasn't hard to connect you to the tour boat explosion."

"You do know how to lie low," Lucy observes dryly.

"That wasn't our fault," I say.

Puo gives me a sidelong look.

"Not directly anyway," I mutter to Puo. To the other three I say, "Wait a minute, they reported us dead. How—?"

"That was us," Lucy cuts in. "Well—" She waves her hands around. "—we intercepted Nix's request to the Mounties and made it happen."

"It was to our advantage to stop others from wanting to look for you after you escaped from the hospital," Mr. Chao says.

"And what you might have on you when they found you," Nova clarifies.

"That's also how we got an image of both of you," Mr. Chao explains. "We pulled it from the hospital records. At that point, we knew when you reentered Britain—"

I think back to the British customs system being slow when I entered two weeks ago and the cognitive engagement questioning shenanigans. Was that them or the British authorities? The more I think about it, the more it makes sense it was them. The British authorities had no leads on us at that time that I know of. It wasn't until I joined the Amateur Sleuths Birmingham Chapter that the mole Arleen marked us.

Mr. Chao continues, "—we followed you there and had already been prepping to bring you in when you were arrested."

"Your arrest did throw a wrinkle into things, though," Nova says.

"And the Greensboro crew bit?" I ask. They knew who the Guild Master was and that the guild had been wiped out.

"Angela Jimenez was an informant," Mr. Chao says.

"For special forces?" I ask.

"For the FBI," Mr. Chao clarifies. "We just borrowed the intel."

"That's why the National Syndicate moved against her," I think out loud. "She was helping the feds."

Mr. Chao nods. "So we think."

"But you haven't answered my question," Nova says. "When did you know? Not suspect. Enough to *know* to manipulate us into moving. If you were wrong, you would've been dead. So you had to have been sure."

"Aliyah's death," I say soberly.

Puo stiffens next to me. He was there. He probably witnessed it.

The faces of the three grow still. Their gazes fade to unfocused, far off.

"I left the apartment under surveillance," I explain quietly. "The authorities showed up an hour after we left to collect the body."

Nova looks at me sharply.

"You left the body too easily. And it was clear you were all one team from your initial reactions, even if you were playing different roles. That's when I knew. Although the satellites didn't hurt."

"Satellites?" Puo asks, latching onto something to get his mind off of bad memories.

I fill him in on the satellites. Despite Puo's prodigious skills, hacking into satellites isn't something we've done before. There's always been an air gap to overcome that wasn't worth the risk for the gain. So, for Mr. Chao and Lucy to claim hacking into one so easily and pointed right at where we needed it to be pointed was another pretty clear marker they were authorities.

The room had grown somber during my sidebar with Puo. I turn back to the other three. "What was her real name?"

Nova and Lucy look to Ken who says, "Before we get to that, we should talk about what happens next. You didn't put the blockchain hack on the network after all. Thank you for that."

"I needed to make sure you would come—I'm not a monster."

"Indeed. We did find the modifications you made to the scrubbing code though, and your upload," he says to Puo. "You'll be pleased to know it's already gone viral."

Puo grins. Then to me he says, "I set it up so the scrubbing code wouldn't recognize their own Cleaner's code anymore and then uploaded Izaak's squeegee. As soon as they turned the scrubbing code back on: boom! They released their own code into the wild."

I laugh. A great wave of relief washes through me. The Cleaners are done. Their code is out there, and not just any code, National Syndicate level code—a Guild Master's code. And if it's gone viral, then the Bosses already have it. It's over, now we just need to lie low while the Bosses crush any pockets of resistance and the authorities lock up all the National Syndicate members.

"It seems you're at a bit of a crossroads," Mr. Chao says. "We agreed at the start to help you procure new hardware for your CitIDs and help remove your images from the British Government databases. Is that something you're still interested in?"

Before I answer, I ask a question that's been niggling at me. "Why didn't you take the suits and run once you knew we had them if that is what you were after?" It's what we would've done. Instead, they bugged them.

"We recovered a Kevlar bag full interesting tech in Atlanta that gave us pause. Some of which was custom built for the Amsterdam job."

Oh, hell. I was wondering what became of that.

"We needed to know how many suits you had, and what other advanced technology you might have. Then there was this business between the Bosses and Cleaners needed to be contained. And ... it's not often we come across people with your skill sets."

"We didn't all agree on that last one," Nova says.

"And now?" Ken inquires of her.

She shrugs her acquiescence.

"I'll be blunt," he says back toward us. "Puo's skills are nothing short of extraordinary. In the right capacity, directed at the right targets, he could have a real impact on the world—"

Puo's grin widens.

"—But we know he would never leave you behind."

"Darn right I wouldn't," Puo says. Then he turns to me with the biggest smile I've ever seen on his round Samoan face, "Who knew *you* were *my* sidekick this whole time? I'm totally taking over the master suite back home."

"Like hell you are," I say. *Freaking Puo.*

"So, here's our offer," Ken says. "Join our outfit, all three of you. You have real leadership potential," he says this to me. "You're bold, cunning, and fast on your feet."

I stick my tongue out at Puo.

Ken turns to Winn, "And you—"

"Are real pretty," I finish for him, grinning at Winn.

"I was going to say," Mr. Chao says over me, "have medical training and experience in the anti-gravity suits. All three of you would be an asset to the team."

"And we're not impervious to flattery, right?" I ask.

Ken shrugs. "I've been impressed and I want to make it clear this is not charity. If you join, you're joining on your merits and you will be expected to pull your weight."

"So, then what's the actual offer?" I ask.

Ken answers, "Three real CitIDs—not the modified ones—records scrubbed, images erased—both domestically and abroad. A chance to start over. A real chance to make a difference in the world."

I look to Puo and Winn. All three of us study each other. Chances like this never come along. A chance to go legit. Real CitIDs. Such things aren't possible without government intervention. They could just threaten us with jail time or threaten to turn us over to the British authorities if we don't cooperate, but they're offering us a way out. A way to become partners rather than indentured servants.

"And if we don't agree?" I ask.

"We'll honor our original agreement. New hardware for the modified CitIDs, but the image removal in Britain is too risky for the payoff if you're not part of the team." When he sees my obvious disbelief they'd honor the original terms of the agreement, he adds, "Call it payment for figuring out the anti-gravity suits—which we're keeping."

I can tell from Winn and Puo's expressions they're looking to me to make the decision. They don't object on principle, but they know it'd be hardest on me to make this transition to a law-abiding citizen.

It's a good offer. It's only pure, dumb luck at this point we haven't ended up dead or arrested—or at least, convicted. We can't keep this up. Either of those things will eventually find us. People don't normally retire in this business.

We now have the cash never to have to work again. But I can't sit still for long. I know myself. I'd be scouting jobs anyway. Once they're scouted, I'd pull them off to prove I can. At least this way, it'd be government-sanctioned jobs.

I'd have government backing, official resources. I wouldn't have to worry about Puo and Winn being arrested, at least not by this government. We'd have a larger team and resources to mitigate risk.

Real CitIDs. A real topside life. There's only one problem.

"I'm not good at taking orders," I say. I've been calling my own shots since I was a kid, taking the lead from the first moment Puo and I met up. Just as I know I'd be scouting a job eventually, I know I'd chafe at taking orders. Being told when, where, and what we're supposed to be doing. Particularly if I don't agree with it.

Before Mr. Chao can respond, Winn looks at me contemplatively and says, "I think I have a solution for that."

# Chapter Thirty-Five

"HARPY CONSULTING?" Kathy asks with an eyebrow raised looking down at our fancy new business card.

It's a week and a half later, and Kathy and I lean over her large butcher-block center island over cups of tea on a cold sunny Wednesday morning. It's the first opportunity I've had to visit and fill her in on everything that's happened.

I scowl. "Freaking Puo. It was supposed to be Empire Consulting." That's the last time Puo is doing something unsupervised. Ken puffing him up with complements has gone to his head.

"No. It fits." But she can't say it without a grin tugging at her lips.

"Well, thank you for that," I say dryly.

"No problem—" Then she bursts out laughing.

I snatch the card back and stick my tongue out.

"Oh, that's not at all harpy like," she says between giggling fits.

*Freaking Puo.* He's starting to rub off on everyone around here, not just Winn. Winn insisted we get health insurance and "proper treatment." He refused to continue to act as our personal doctor—some "conflict of interest" malarkey.

It's good to hear Kathy laugh and eventually I smile back. "I'm so getting him back."

"I have no doubt that you are. If you need my help, let me know."

That's one reason I've come to love Kathy. In addition to her balanced outlook on life and lived wisdom, she has a mischievous side.

"So," she asks, "you're real security consultants now?"

"Yes. Real, live, legitimate security consultants." This is opposed to a few months ago when Kathy and I met, and our cover story at the time was as security consultants.

"And business is good?"

"Business is great." I nod and smile at her, answering her real question. The worst is over.

All the National Syndicate members have been arrested and are awaiting trial. I'm assured convictions will come. They have an insider—Ham. That oily bastard. They assure me the only thing he can negotiate for is a cushier prison and not to be housed with those that are less than pleased with him—which I assume means solitary confinement.

We'll have to move again since so many people seem to know where we live, but we're not going to go far. I like it here and our permanent headquarters we started setting up months ago is finally finished—or close enough anyway—and not on anyone's radar.

"Wes have one client on retainer," I say to Kathy, "but with what they're paying us, we only need one."

She then cautiously proceeds to give me financial advice about relying on one client, which I do my best to take seriously. Money isn't a problem anymore.

Puo went ahead and patched the blockchain code, to prevent the type of hack he discovered, and inconspicuously released the patch into the world. All without notifying the authorities beforehand. Ken was happy. I had mixed feelings. We made sure to siphon off enough funds that our great-grandchildren will never have to worry about money, but despite how I may feel some days, I really don't want to burn the world down.

Besides, the business isn't about money. It's about autonomy and keeping our skills sharp. Setting it up this way means we're not officially a part of Ken's team, but that suits me perfectly and ultimately didn't affect the deal in any significant way. We all have real CitIDs, our records and images have been expunged—although we had to agree not to set foot in Britain again. But, as consultants, we can refuse jobs or walk away at any time. I'm not sure I'll ever break the habit of always having an escape route.

"I'm sorry about your father," she says quietly.

"Thanks." I study the wooden butcher tabletop. The funeral had been this last Saturday and had been ... strange. I've never been to a proper funeral before, but I imagine even the normal ones feel surreal. One for a Boss—that was something else entirely. We were never close, but it feels strange to have him gone, a security blanket ripped away from a child. I didn't even know I felt that way until the casket was being lowered.

I take a deep breath. "Thank you for the flowers." She had sent a nice bouquet. It was a miracle I even found them in the flower nursery that had sprouted around the funeral. It was all part of the pageantry of the event, one part goodbye to the old Boss, one part hello to the new Boss.

Durante has officially taken over. He offered me an adviser position, and when I turned it down it became clear the offer was perfunctory and an excuse to draw the line between us now that my father was gone. Any favors going forward are over.

I shrugged in response. I'm done with that world. If they aren't going to do me any favors, then they don't expect me to do them any favors. A clean break.

Besides, Durante isn't going to make a good Boss. He's too rigid. He'll coast for a year or two, but when an enterprising underling starts moving for more territory or responsibility, it'll start to come undone.

Kathy reaches out and squeezes my hand. "It's never easy to say goodbye to someone, especially those we have a history with."

I squeeze her hand back and open my mouth to respond when my comm-link buzzes, sending a jolt of adrenaline through me. I freeze, waiting to see if that jolt heralds more to come.

It's been that way ever since the full-blown panic attack when Puo was taken, always waiting with an edge to see what the next day, what the next hour, will bring. I haven't had to take any of those little brown pills since, but I've had more than a few shitty mornings and I still can't sleep through the night.

Winn says it'll pass, that I'm on the road to recovery, but it'll take a long time and it won't be a linear path. My brain chemistry got all jacked up and that's not something a round of antibiotics can take care of in a week. Which is ironic, since my new doc put me on a round of antidepressants. Both she and Winn insist it'll help, but it's only been a week.

The comm-link continues to buzz.

I look at who's calling, hoping it's Ken—which isn't his real name, but he'll always be Ken Chao to me. A job right now would be perfect to distract me from those awful mornings.

It's Colvin.

"Everything okay?" Kathy asks.

"Yeah." I wipe the grimace off my face. "A loose end is all." I wait to get my beating heart under control before answering.

"Go!" I answer, remembering how he likes to answer.

"Ah, Ms. Sanders—" I can hear him exhaling out his nose.

"I've ... missed our little chats, but we need to speak in person. Can you meet me at the park?"

I raise an eyebrow at the question—which sounds genuine. Bosses don't politely request a meeting. They tell a person when and where to be. The fact that he framed it as a question signals quite a bit.

The park is nearby Blaine Field Park, where we met after the Christina Chavez debacle back in August that kick-started this whole shit show into overdrive.

I say yes to the meeting and we work out when to meet—in fifteen minutes, to which I roll my eyes. Colvin may be trying to be more cordial, but he's still a Boss and wants what he wants when he wants it. Which for Bosses is always NOW.

I finish my tea with Kathy and make plans to have her over for dinner with the boys later this week—Winn's a great cook, a hidden attribute I've only recently come to appreciate.

I huddle in my winter coat against the biting wind as I hurry over to the park. It's sunny out in the mid-forties, but the wind makes it ten degrees colder.

The walk is quick and uneventful. I call Puo and Winn to let them know about Colvin and decline any backup. This doesn't feel like a setup or an omen of anything portentous. Still, I scan the area as I approach, but I can't spot any of Colvin's goons lingering anywhere.

Colvin sits on the same wooden bench we talked on last time. He's wearing a charcoal gray wool trench overcoat over a suit, and waits patiently staring off into the distance away from me.

"No goon squad?" I walk up and sit down.

"Not today." He looks over at me, flicks his gaze over my shoulder. "I thought you might appreciate that."

"Why is that?"

He looks properly at me then, holds my gaze with his dark brown eyes. "I heard a rumor you were getting out. Going clean. Seems like the last thing someone going clean would want is a bunch of goons crawling all over their neighborhood park."

"As opposed to a Boss."

He smiles to himself. "We have some unfinished business."

"Your sisters," I observe. Puo and I had set up emergency protocols for his sisters and their families in case they came under threat.

He nods.

"Did they get out okay?" I ask. With everything that went down, our protocols should've been activated.

"Yes. They're back and settled now. The children never even knew something was up. So, thank you for that. I would like to retain you again for the same purpose."

I think about it. I really don't want to get tied back up in that world. But creating escape routes to keep people safe, particularly people that have nothing to do with anything, doesn't feel like I'm going back on my pledge to go legit. Still, I'm wary of letting Colvin get even a single hook into me.

"That would require me to keep tabs on the world I'm leaving behind."

"You may be getting out, but I can't believe you would remain ignorant. You're too cautious for that."

He's right, but I keep my face neutral.

"Besides, I think I can offer you something you'd be interested in to help you in your new endeavors, aside from money."

"And what is that?" I ask.

"Assurances that your old world does not find your new one. An eye on the inside, careful to divert any potential entanglements away from you."

I raise my eyebrows.

"This would, of course, extend to your friend—the master fence in Atlanta," he explains when he sees my confusion.

He pauses then, holding my gaze, using the silence to ask what Charlie is to me, but I stare back in dumb silence. *There's no way in hell I'm explaining it to him.*

"At any rate," he says, "rumor is, she's retiring too."

"Yeah, she is," I say, my anger awakening. *Is he threatening me with this?*

He holds his hands up quickly. "No threat here. Only trying to sweeten the deal. I want my sisters taken care of, and you've proved highly effective before. The two of you are clearly linked—"

I scowl in frustration. Fucking Cleaners, broadcasting Charlie's face everywhere, made her practically famous. Made it impossible for her to go back to being a master fence, even if she wanted to. Which she says she doesn't.

She's staying in Atlanta setting up a foundation to work with abused and orphaned kids—she received a rather sizable public donation, and a second private one all from an anonymous donor with magical, digital fingers. She won't have to worry about money anymore, but a nice, quiet, retired life isn't what she has in mind. She wasn't kidding when she said she "liked to give the universe the finger when it deals an extra shitty hand to orphans." Except this time, she muttered, at least they won't get her kidnapped and almost killed.

Colvin continues, "—anyone trying to get to you could try and get to her first—"

I raise my hand for him stop. He's not wrong, but it's pissing me off anyway and I want to say yes before I get too irritated to think clearly. Having someone on the inside looking out for us would be useful. And there's no one better for that then a Boss at the top. As long as they remain there at least. And I can tell Kathy we have two clients now.

"You can't pull us into anything. No disputes. No wars. No small favors. No *anything*. We are a nonentity."

"Agreed."

We spend the next few minutes working out some logistics and when we're done, we stand, shake hands, and part ways.

I feel good on the walk home. I trust Colvin to keep his word; it's in both our interests he do so. I also have no doubt he'll test that line of not involving us in the future with small requests every so often, but I'll shut him down each time it comes up.

Warm air engulfs me as I enter our Queen Anne home. The space is warm, inviting. Sunlight filters through open windows, rich wood paneling decorates the space, the comforting smell of popcorn permeates the house. *Popcorn?*

Winn and Puo come marching out of the kitchen singing the Green Acres theme song. Winn is in a three-piece suit and carrying a pitchfork, while Puo is in a patchwork plaid jacket and a green hat with an upturned brim. We've been making our way through the collection of classic American television Winn got me for Christmas and are currently on Green Acres.

I can't help but laugh. "Where did you get a pitchfork? And those clothes?"

Puo shrugs with a grin. "We're loaded. What's it matter?"

I'm about to lecture them about frivolous spending when Winn says, "I got you this." He pulls out a princess diamond necklace like the one Eva Gabor's character wore.

*Whoa.* Those are real. My hands tremble as I try to put it on. Winn helps.

"It's not a digi-scrambler, is it?" I ask. This is way too ostentatious to be functional. I miss the single pearl necklace one he gave me all those months ago.

"No." Winn's smiles makes me a little weak. He uses the opportunity to slip something into my pocket, which I pretend not to notice.

"You were saying?" Pu*o smirks at me.

I stick my tongue out at him. The diamond necklace isn't frivolous spending. These diamonds are real. This is diversifying.

Winn starts humming the theme song again and smacks the butt of the pitchfork on the ground to the beat of the song. "Season three! Follow me!" He marches out of the room.

Puo follows and looks back at me, too, with a big grin in perfect imitation of Green Acres' Eb on his round Samoan face. "You comin' Mrs. Douglas? I wouldn't want ya to miss it. Ya ready for the next season?"

I slide my hand in my pocket and find the single pearl necklace digi-scambler Winn slipped there. I smile to myself—I'll slip his caduceus pendant digi-scrambler I picked up recently in his pocket this evening.

I grin back at Puo and run to catch up and thread my arm through Winn's where I then belt out singing the Green Acres song in a Hungarian accent.

Am I ready for the next season? Why, yes. Yes, I am.

The End

*Sign up for my newsletter on jaballard.com to be the first to learn when new books are set to be released. All newsletter recipients receive an exclusive free short story that tells the tale of how Isa and her crew stole their copy of the Cleaners' code, The Skim Job. Your email address will never be shared and you can unsubscribe any time.*

373

Read the story of how Isa and the gang stole Ham's squeegee in *The Skim Job: A Sunken City Capers Short Story*. Exclusive only to newsletter receiptents—read how to sign up on the next page.

Ground Sensors. Chemically-laced air. Molecular-realigning windows.

How hard can hitting a smart house be?

Forced into the company of Ham, the friendly neighborhood Cleaner, Isa must balance her desire to complete the job and her desire to kick the obnoxious ass in the throat. But when things go from bad to worse, both are soon only hoping for escape.

# Author's Note

Word-of-mouth and reviews are vital for any author to suc-ceed. If you enjoyed reading this story, please consider leaving a review wherever you purchased it. Taking a moment to leave a few lines sharing your thoughts would be helpful for other read-ers and very much appreciated. Thank you for reading!

Jeffrey A. Ballard is hard at work a brand new series. If you want to be the first to know when the new series is going to be-come available (and receive free Sunken City content available to newsletter subscribers prior to the public, and occasional other goodies) you can sign up for his mailing list at: http://www.jaballard.com. Your email address will never be shared and you can unsubscribe at any time.

# About the Author

Jeffrey A. Ballard writes and lives in the Texas Hill Country just outside of Austin. From a small child he has always been fascinated with the ocean, leading him to earn a B.S. in Ocean Engineering from FAU and a M.S. in Acoustics from Penn State.

His overactive imagination followed him into academia, where he is currently a researcher at the University of Texas. Eventually, he circled back to a boyhood ambition of writing down all his dreams/daydreams/fantasies, an active playground for that overactive imagination. He writes daily now and has found a wonderful second life for his college textbooks.

Learn more about Jeffrey at jaballard.com.